ELCO PARKS

A Novel

Sandro Laudadio

AOS Publishing, 2025
Copyright © 2025 Sandro Laudadio

All rights reserved under International
and Pan-American copyright conventions

ISBN: 978-1-990496-99-8

Cover Design: Chanelle Poupart

Visit AOS Publishing's website:
www.aospublishing.com

To Merrilee

The interest of the dealers, however, in any particular branch of trade, is always in some respects different from, and even opposite to, that of the public. The proposal of any new law which comes from this order ought always to be listened to with great precaution... with the most suspicious attention. It comes from an order of men...who have generally an interest to deceive and even to oppress the public, and who accordingly have, upon many occasions, both deceived and oppressed it.

Adam Smith, from *The Wealth of Nations,*
Book I, Chapter 11.

Pretend I'm dead and say nice things about me.

Trimalchio, in *The Satyricon*

....1

This time, there were about twenty-five of them. None wore any clothes. They ventured outside the lodge as soon as it stopped raining, walking single file along the narrow dirt pathway between the main lodge and the Stony Grounds, the broad scoured swath that extended from the top of the ridge to the edge of the inlet. All of them, no matter how used to the routine as some of them were, winced as a carpet of stray pebbles poked into the soles of their feet. The steep trail led to a barren rock slope decorated by deep glacial ruts, still wet from recent rain. The sun's heat was barely sensible through the dissipating blanket of clouds.

Everyone knelt and lied down on cue from the woman leading the procession, flat against the rock, and then rolled and rubbed their bodies. Most shut their eyes; a few of them grunted stoically, and others moaned. Some uttered an aggrieved squeak when a sensitive body part rubbed against an unruly knob of rock. Before long, they rose to continue down the footpath towards the creek. It was easy to spot the novices, scraped raw and bloodied due to excessive fervour. The path ended at a roiling pool at the base of a waterfall, just inside a glade of conifers.

The ritual concluded with a frigid bath in the waterfall pool. A few of them, especially those who'd drawn blood, wailed in agony upon contact with the cold water. Once immersed, one by one they swam over to be pummelled by the full force of the cascade. A man of about eighty wearing a coarse cotton gown soon appeared at the pool's edge and handed out beige tunics to each of the adherents without speaking a word. Once dressed, the group followed him in silence down the pathway and returned to the lodge.

Carlo Buonsante found it humbling to run laps in what was left of the Circus Maximus. Once the site of public spectacles for an ancient city of more than a million, it was now simply another sprawling artifact among many others, surrounded by the dignified chaos of modern Rome, and, in a congruity to the past that remains common enough, the namesake of a busy metro station.

He clawed back his longish, light brown hair, damp with sweat, thankful for a cool breeze as he made his way back across the river to his apartment in Trastevere, the last night he would live there. Three years earlier, he'd been a barrister in Toronto; after those days came to an end he settled in Rome, allowing him frequent visits to Sannazzaro, the seaside hamlet on the southeast coast where most of his family lived. It was now time to go, and there was no doubt about why he decided to leave. If anyone asked, he'd tell them that he'd had enough of helping insufferable London solicitors and their counterparts in New York arrange unseemly transactions using Italian banks. That was usually enough to keep them quiet.

So now he was going back to Vancouver, the city of his childhood. People asked: why Vancouver? He wondered about the same thing. Did it not rain enough in Rome? Surely the autumn downpours and soaking spring rains were sufficient to satisfy him. Maybe he preferred to live in a place where water always ran cold out of the tap.

Trastevere was far enough from the Trevi Fountain and other familiar tourist attractions of the city core to remain a characteristically Roman neighbourhood. Its narrow streets were clogged with the customary Saturday evening flow of strolling Romans, many no doubt from distant suburbs, wandering about and engaged in lively chatter. Even so, it was not without a foreign presence. Carlo was vaguely aware of an international university in one of the buildings on Via della Renella, a narrow thoroughfare parallel to the river, and tourists always trickled in. He even heard a few snippets of English on his way home, timid in contrast to more bombastic declarations in Roman dialect.

Just before eight, Carlo was fixing himself a sandwich when his phone rang. It had to have been Mario; everyone else but his father thought he'd already left. Mario Foscolo was his oldest friend. The two of them had grown up together in the same East Vancouver neighbourhood, both children of southern Italian immigrants.

"*Pronto?*" Carlo answered.

Mario unleashed a barrage of expletives, some in English, most in Italian. "At least you finally figured out the time difference," Carlo said after he stopped. "Last time you woke me up, it was three in the fucking morning!"

"No, I did that on purpose. So I guess this is it."

"Yup. I'm out of here tomorrow." Carlo's eyes were drawn to the television; the unmistakable opening music for *Tg1* had just started to play, a spinning silver globe filling the screen.

"Hey, the news! So what's the big story today?"

Carlo read the caption accompanying the lead story. "It looks like yet another instalment of Sex and the Silvio." Carlo gazed around his empty apartment, a few stray copies of *La Repubblica* and *L'Espresso* strewn on the floor. "I don't know." Carlo switched to Italian. "Almost three years in this place, and it already looks like I was never here."

"You said it yourself; it's time to go. Wouldn't want that old bastard to end up *owning* you. And just think, you'll be back on the west coast in a couple of days. Never thought it would happen."

"No, the week after. I'm staying in London with Pop and Linda over Easter."

"In that sketchy neighbourhood full of weirdos. So is Linda still a total babe? I haven't seen her in a while."

Carlo sighed. "Well, she's probably a little, I don't know, more *athletic* than you might remember her. She's taken up exercise classes."

"Hey, it's better than the alternative. Been in touch with her kid sister?"

"Not really." Carlo restrained a passing impulse to bash the handset on the countertop.

"Too bad. She was hot, and you know what? Being a bit more adventurous might not be such a bad thing."

"Save it, Mario."

"Hey, just sayin'...anyway, I'll leave you to your *buon viaggio* party."

"That was last night. No, tonight, just a quiet walk around. It's going to be an early morning."

Total babe. Sketchy neighbourhood. Mario's way of encapsulating things always made them sound squalid. Carlo's father, Vito, would have probably been content to stay in Vancouver had his mother lived, but she died just before his thirteenth birthday. Soon after Carlo finished high school, Vito, an architect, took a six-month contract in London but, as it eventually turned out, never returned. It didn't take him long to meet Linda, much younger (in fact, only a few years older than Carlo), in those days a singer in a blues band.

Quite predictably, the family in Sannazzaro was aghast. Carlo's aunts tried to conscript him as an ally but he gently told them to back off. They ultimately saw what he did. His once morose father was undeniably enlivened by this blonde, English whirlwind, and they eventually grew to like her, even if they rarely understood a word she said. No; no step-brothers or step-sisters, but after a couple of years the two of them bought a renovated flat together, on the top floor of an old building in Soho.

It was well after dark by the time he left his apartment. Carlo crossed the river into the Jewish Quarter and eventually found himself wandering through the disorderly network of narrow streets of the neighbourhood on the rise opposite Piazza Venezia. In a *piazzetta* dominated by a fountain festooned with Americans and Australians, he caught a glimpse of someone he recognized; an older man in a suit, accompanied by a younger woman with blonde hair and uncommonly long legs. Carlo peered at him, even as he tried to avoid being noticed. *That can't be him,* he thought, but there was an undeniable resemblance. The man and his escort disappeared into a restaurant behind the fountain. *I've only met him once. I'm probably mistaken.*

Mere recollection of their meeting two months earlier, arranged in deft style by the older man, still made Carlo cringe with searing shame. When he had received the note, not an e-mail or voicemail message but a note, delivered by courier to his workplace, Carlo was mystified. It was written on the stiff vellum stationery favoured by older European professionals, ornate Italian diction in a plain calligraphic hand.

Gentile Signor Buonsante,

I would be most grateful if you would meet with me, Friday next, at da Timoteo in via Pallacorda. I trust that you are familiar with it. I have reserved a table for 18.30. There is no need to reply.

Sinceramente,
Umberto Tozzi

Da Timoteo. Of course Carlo had heard of it, a venerable wine bar that had been operating in one form or another for more than a century. In recent times, it had developed a certain *cachet,* the place where politicians met to conclude arrangements that were not meant to see daylight. But Umberto Tozzi? Carlo could not think of a single reason why he would want to meet with him. Tozzi, a senior member of the bureaucracy of high rank whose name occasionally appeared in the political and business pages, had a supporting role in the scandals and shadowy manipulations of the past thirty years.

Da Timoteo was crowded almost to capacity when Carlo walked in. In addition to the many couples on their way to the opera or the cinema, there were tables occupied by politicians and their assistants, each seemingly invigorated by the short stroll from Montecitorio, the parliament; all of them were smiling, effervescent, but plainly mindful of who might be listening. Carlo saw Tozzi waving at him from a table near the back. He was a man of the same generation as his father, whose affect and style of dress bespoke his having come of age during the post-war. Although if anything, he looked several years older than his father, Carlo estimated that he must have been of a slightly younger cohort.

"*Il signor Buonsante.*" Tozzi greeted Carlo with a welcoming laugh and rose to shake his hand. "Umberto Tozzi."

"*Piacere.*" Carlo uttered the customary Italian reply.

"*Piacere mio.* It is not too early for an *aperitivo*, in my opinion." Tozzi said. "I have taken the liberty of ordering two glasses of wine. Although in the usual course, if you had the bad manners to order French wine here, they would tie you up and torture you in the old crypt downstairs. But I have certain privileges; I have been coming here since before you were born. So I have ordered two glasses of a *grand cru* Chablis, 1992." He leaned back and regarded Carlo with an indulgent smile. "I suppose that you have no idea why I invited you here today."

His accent, with its familiar southern cadence, put Carlo at ease, even if he remained anxious to find out what Tozzi wanted. "In fact, no; I do not."

Tozzi's smile shrunk to a smirk. "You are, let us say, an acquaintance, of a young lady named Giovanna, is that true?"

Acquaintance? She was his girlfriend of a little more than seven months. In a perverse sort of way, his question actually filled Carlo with a degree of optimism in matters related to Giovanna, something rare in recent weeks. Tozzi might have been an emissary of the archpriest, the censorious uncle she frequently spoke of. Maybe she was telling the truth.

"Yes, that's true."

Tozzi slowly exhaled. "She is my wife." The waiter arrived with two glasses of wine and silently placed them on the table.

The waiter's presence gave Carlo a few seconds to assimilate Tozzi's words. "I had no idea that she was married," Carlo said. Despite mounting shame and a twinge of horror, he was baffled by Tozzi's untroubled levity. It was as if he just told him that he had a coffee stain on his tie. "I am so sorry; I don't know what else..."

Tozzi rumbled with a baritone chortle and raised his hand. "There is no need to apologize. I expected that you were the kind of man I could deal with; *intelligenti pauca*, as the Romans used to say. I have looked into your background. A respected young man, a lawyer, educated in Canada, working in the international transfers department at Banco Tiburtino, father *pugliese* from the province of Bari." He took a sip of his wine and motioned to Carlo's glass. "Please, try it before it warms up too much. Now, I expect that this, this *adventure* will come to an immediate end?"

"Yes. Again, I am very sorry. I had no idea..."

"And I have no doubt that you are telling me the truth. As for Giovanna, she doesn't know it yet, but she and one of my nieces will be renting a seaside villa on Ischia, for three weeks, perhaps more. Have you been there?"

"Yes, once, about a year ago."

"I've found us a place at Ischia Ponte, facing the old castle, what do they call it, the *castello aragonese*? Anyway, it's the only quarter that remains *ours*; the rest of the island has been overrun by Germans." He took another sip of wine and looked toward the window; his smile undiminished. "I trust that you will not attempt to contact her, much less go down there looking for her. But I have to ask you, I will consider it a personal favour. If she tries to call you, do not respond to her message."

"*D'accordo.*" Carlo used the Italian expression rather than the English 'okay', which for years had slipped into popular slang.

"Good." Tozzi finished the last sips of his wine. "Now, if you will excuse me, I must go meet my wife for dinner. We'll have to discuss her upcoming vacation by the sea." His smirk returned. "Everyone has their, their...weaknesses, let's call them, but it is uncivil to display them in public: walking hand in hand along the *lungotevere*, kissing in Piazza Navona." He rose and stood by the table, which Carlo took as his cue to guzzle the remaining wine in his glass.

They walked out of the sitting room in silence and then shook hands outside the front entrance. "I am sure we will meet at some time in the future, under much different circumstances, one hopes. They speak very highly of you at the bank." Tozzi placed his hand on Carlo's shoulder and pulled him closer to speak quietly in his ear. "And just so nobody is mistaken, there is to be absolutely no communication between you and Giovanna, electronic or otherwise. *Capisci?*"

Carlo lowered his head in a gesture of surrender. "Yes. That's the end of it."

"Good." Tozzi released his grasp on Carlo's shoulder and turned away to walk slowly towards the river.

Carlo continued to walk. The chance sighting in the *piazzetta* quelled whatever sense of calm he'd managed to restore in recent weeks. Once treasured memories, images of those rare, sunlit mornings after she stayed the night, her hazelnut-hued body stretching lazily in his bed, now seemed as cloying as some witless romantic comedy that he regretted paying to see soon after the opening credits. And despite the older man's disquieting good cheer, Carlo could not believe that Tozzi wouldn't be out to get him.

Once adrift in the stream of tourists flowing towards the Colosseum, robust even in mid-March, Carlo switched to a different path and crossed the river back into his more familiar Trastevere. He found a bar and sat at an outside table, a luxury he rarely afforded himself.

"*Buona sera.*" The waiter startled him.

He ordered a half-litre of draft beer. "*Leffe bionda, prego.*"

Two girls a few tables away were cheerfully dismembering a stuffed Roman centurion souvenir doll, speaking English with an accent that was neither British nor American (Carlo feared they might be Canadians). "Come on, rip his head off!" The louder one said. "This place is one big Mexico. I'm sure this thing's filled with all kinds of shit!"

After the waiter brought his beer, a strong Belgian concoction, he turned to his newspaper, a *Corriere della Sera* he'd bought somewhere along the way. Berlusconi was bemoaning victimhood at the hands of anyone who took exception to his use of public funds to fly young women to orgies at his villa in Sardegna. Greece was in financial trouble again; Ireland was finally at the brink. And a young Black man - a lawyer, Carlo noted with satisfaction, was now the favourite for winning the Democratic nomination in the American presidential election.

He leaned back and closed his eyes, aware only of disparate ambient sounds. The jarring rasp of a scooter buzzer warning careless strollers. The inviting, high-pitched trill of a feminine voice, admonishing her boyfriend for showing insufficient interest in a purse she spied in a shop window. Two taxi drivers shouting, each accusing the other of blocking the road. It was all so familiar; he would always think of it as home. But there was no doubt why he wanted to leave.

* * *

The following evening, Carlo and his father walked slowly along Charing Cross Road in quiet conversation.

"What's with that enormous *transatlantico* you were dragging around?" Vito asked. "Even *women* travel lighter."

"Well, for one thing, and I went into Bari to say goodbye to Mario's aunt last time I went down to Sannazzaro. She sent me home with *three kilos* of taralli."

Vito was unfazed. "If you think it's too heavy, leave some of them here. Oh, I was talking to Peppino the other day." Peppino, Mario's father, was still in Vancouver. The two men, both prolific gossips, were on the phone with one another all the time. "Did you know that Rosanna is getting married *again*? And he's not happy."

Why would he be? Mario's younger sister, who had yet to reach the age of thirty-two, had already been married twice. "He's not happy?"

"No! Because this time she's marrying a *mallangiùn*."

Carlo cringed at his father's customary reference to Black people, which translated to English as "eggplant". "He's not, Pop. His parents are from India".

"What do I know? Peppino told me he's a *mallangiùn*." They walked in silence for almost a block. "And Mario," Vito asked. "I hear he's still with Letizia?"

"Laeticia. Yes, surprisingly enough, they're doing quite well together. I never thought he would stay with one woman, in an actual relationship, for more than, I don't know; a few days, maybe a couple of weeks."

"Ò, Ò, *relationship!*" Vito waved his hands back and forth in a praying motion. "At one time, people actually got married and stayed that way!" He looked over at Carlo and shook his head. "And what about you? You're getting to be an old man, although I must say, you're well rid of that toothpick. It must have been like sleeping with a mop!" Carlo remained resolutely silent, hoping that his father would abandon this topic of conversation. "What ever happened to, to...*la ragazza chi fosse più...più...corposa?*" He giggled at his father's description, 'the more full-bodied girl', which made her sound like a glass of wine. "She was in Toronto, at Tina's funeral; are you still in touch with her?"

"You mean Laura? No, not recently."

"Now there is a beauty!" He clasped Carlo's shoulder. "I always thought that you two would get married; you two were together for such a long time." They passed a row of street vendors. "She's still in Vancouver, Laura?"

"As far as I know, yes."

"That's good; you should let the past go. Believe me, you could do a lot worse."

Carlo pointed down Shaftesbury Avenue, hoping to change the subject. "That restaurant we're going to, Piccolo Mondo Antico, isn't it back this way?"

"No, no, that's a novel by Fogazzaro, *uagliò*!" He clapped the back of Carlo's head. "The restaurant, it's called Vecchia Romagna. And it's this way."

Carlo heard approaching footsteps behind him and turned to find a familiar woman almost on his heels. "Linda!" He didn't embrace her; he'd figured out years before that the English found it annoying. As odd as it felt to him, this woman, only seven years his senior, stood in the role of his stepmother.

"Welcome back, Carlo." She laughed. "Now where are you two off to? I saw you heading down this way so I rushed to catch up with you." Even now that she was making the transition from performer to booking agent, she maintained the same modish denim and leather edginess, her blonde hair as ungoverned as ever.

"But we're off to the restaurant," Vito said, plainly confused. "To meet you. It's just over here!"

"Well, it's a good thing that you're an architect and not an explorer. I knew that I'd better follow you guys. The restaurant is back there!"

Vecchia Romagna, in an eighteenth-century stone building close to Leicester Square, served reliable central Italian cuisine. Carlo was relieved to find that the trend toward fusion dishes, which several years earlier had descended upon urban Canada like a plague, had made few inroads in northern Europe. Once, at a dinner with some clients at a restaurant in Toronto whose name, Zazù, ought to have excited suspicion in itself, Carlo was compelled to choke down *saltimbocca* that had been slathered with Thai peanut sauce.

After dinner, Carlo's father excused himself before the coffee arrived. "Where are you going, Vito?" Linda asked.

Vito sighed. "Brougham's here; he's at a table by the window. I'd better say 'hello'."

As he walked away, Linda explained. "David Brougham's a big deal with Barclay's; they're financing a project your dad's working on. But Vito hates his wife. Once (when she was quite drunk) she asked him which brothel he'd found me in. Not that I really took offence. Maybe I'd be just as nasty if *I* were married to *him*. Anyway, so back to Canada, I hear. It's not just because of that girl, is it?"

"No, no, of course not."

"Well, then, I can't understand for the life of me why you would return to Canada, especially Vancouver. It's quite literally at the very ends of the earth!" She poured some more wine into his glass. "I really must say that I never thought that you would consider leaving Italy, much less Europe, for good."

"Oh, I have no intention of staying away for good. I need a change; as much as I love Rome, it was starting to drive me insane. And there's no way I'd ever actually *live* in Sannazzaro. There was a position in Paris with BNP Paribas that probably would have been mine if I'd wanted it, but I didn't much relish the thought of working in some glass tower in La Défense. In the end, I decided that I wanted to get back into it, practicing litigation."

"But you could do that here! It wouldn't take a great deal for you to qualify as a barrister..."

"I don't mean to be obnoxious, but London isn't really my kind of place, it's just too..."

"English."

"If you want to put it that way."

Linda laughed. "Your father is worried that once you are back on the other side of the Atlantic, you will never visit. I'm really worried about him. He has been brooding about it ever since you told him of your plans."

"Well, tell him not to worry. *I'll* tell him not to worry; I'll definitely be back for a visit before Christmas."

"Good. And do make sure that you don't find 'that special girl' and settle down. Believe you me, neither Vito nor I want to see you stuck in Canada forever!"

Vito returned to the table, shaking his head. "That miserable bitch is drunk again. What's so funny?"

"I was commenting on your son's marriageability."

"It's a lost cause. Even his Zia Lina gave up."

"Oh, which reminds me!" Linda said. "I told Lizzy that you're in town." Elizabeth, or 'Lizzy' was Linda's sister, eleven years younger. "Look; I know that you two did not part company on the best of terms, but what was it, almost two years ago? And she said that she would love to see you." Linda's mention of her younger sister lifted Vito out of his funk, prompting a smirk that usually came just before an eruption of laughter.

"Sure, what the hell," Carlo said. "But I don't have her mobile number anymore."

"Oh, no need for that. Just contact her on Facebook. I trust you didn't 'unfriend' her."

After everyone else was asleep, Carlo aimlessly surfed the Internet. His father's mention of Laura sparked an unexpected reaction. Before he met Giovanna, it was rare that a day would pass when Laura did not come to mind. First came the inevitable anger, which over time was partially supplanted by pleasant memories, the recollection of experiences he enjoyed when he was very young which he knew that he was most unlikely to ever repeat. That changed the more he became ensnared in his connection with Giovanna. She came to consume all of his waking thoughts, the tangle of unrelated facts, the weighing of bewildering evidence; assertions that at first seemed probable enough, but upon more rigorous scrutiny seemed less probable, even preposterous. Now that his mind was free to entertain different considerations, he thought again of Laura. Even if the anger had not yet entirely passed, it was as if he actually missed her, in spite of all that happened. He felt sure that he would never miss Giovanna.

After a brief bout of indifference, he decided to log into Facebook and send a message to Linda's sister. After all, she was practically family and there was really no bad feeling between them, despite their undeniably bizarre parting. As it turned out, she was on Facebook too; well refreshed with wine, judging by her diction and typing skills. They arranged to meet later in the week at a pub next to Blackfriars Station.

Carlo had not seen her for more than a year. Despite a startling change in her physical form, he recognized her as soon as he entered the pub. The curves she'd accumulated during her middle twenties had vanished, replaced by a lean, angular physique apparently requisite for English professional women.

"Carlo!" She rose to greet him with a peck on the cheek, and then pointed to the young man sitting beside her. "Carlo, this is my fiancé, Nigel." A snide but nonetheless welcome thought entered his mind as he shook Nigel`s hand. *Which mythical creature did you get stuck with?*

"How long are you in London?" Elizabeth asked.

"Until next Tuesday. I'm staying over Easter. Pop ordered some lamb from an organic farm somewhere in Cornwall."

"Ooh, sounds *delish*," she oozed. "I'll have to pry an invitation out of Linda." She turned to Nigel. "Carlo worked in Rome as a solicitor at an Italian bank, which one was it?"

"Well, I worked at Barclay's for a while, but most recently at Banco Tiburtino."

"Where will you be working in Vancouver? At a solicitors' firm?"

"No, no, I'll be working as a barrister. But I don't know yet; I'll start applying at litigation firms as soon as I get back."

Nigel's first words spewed forth in a sudden cascade. "What do you call a thousand lawyers at the bottom of the sea? A good start!" His torso shook as he laughed, a grisly whine.

"Nigel's in management!" Elizabeth said.

"Are you?" Carlo was genuinely surprised.

"Yes," Nigel said. "I manage the take-away delicatessen at Waitrose. The one at Canary Wharf."

"Canary Wharf?" Carlo said. "Isn't that out where you work, Liz?" Linda had mentioned that Liz recently qualified as a chartered accountant and found a position at HSBC.

"Yes!" She put her arms around Nigel. "That's how we met! When I have to work late, I go downstairs to pick up something for dinner. There he was, my knight in shining armour who rescued me from endless cheese sandwiches at Prêt-a-Porter."

"You should come out there some time," Nigel said. "We probably have lots of things that you would like, you know; prosciutto, marinated artichokes."

The waiter finally showed up with his pint. Carlo took a deep draught. "Oh, if I'm ever out that way..."

Elizabeth raised her glass. "Here's to Carlo's safe return to Vancouver!"

The three of them clinked glasses. "Cheers!"

The North Shore Mountains, which only hours before formed an imposing but elegant backdrop to the city, were enshrouded in a dismal fog as rain peppered the Vancouver sidewalk and flooded Thurlow Street. In a more rustic locale, Tofino perhaps, an extended coastal downpour made people inclined to sit back and read a book, gaze upon the waves, or, as the song went, watch the ponds gather rain. In the city, where you were forced to go about your business in attire wholly unsuitable for sustained rainstorms, it merely inspired misery. Laura Thompson, sheltered by a spacious umbrella normally favoured by golfers, walked past people lacking umbrellas and huddled in narrow alcoves. In a majestic demonstration of irony, they would all probably die of thirst if they actually decided to remain in their refuges until the rain stopped.

Laura stopped at an espresso bar just off Robson Street to order a *caffè macchiato*. She was still several blocks from her office, glad for the shelter of a place that had free wireless Internet but still served coffee in ceramic cups. A girl behind the counter who looked like she had yet to leave her teens greeted her.

"Hi!" she said. "Our special today is a latte topped with Burgundy vanilla. Would you like to try it?"

"No, thanks." Laura glanced up at the overhead menu. *Caffè latte* was lame enough; putting vanilla on it was just plain weird. And it seemed that unlikely that any strain of vanilla actually originated from such a cool, soggy locale. "I'll get a *macchiato.* Thanks."

Bending down to take her seat reminded her of the fact that she was dressed in an unusually snug suit, one she bought two years earlier, after common sense temporarily flew from her and she agreed to join in a week-long juice fast with her boyfriend of the day. What did he call himself, Josiah? She never did find out his real name. She usually wore her blonde hair in a flowing style, but for now it was bound in a neat bun. Yvette, her best friend and business partner, told her several years back that leaving her hair unrestrained made her look like a tart. *Yeah, well fuck you,* Laura remembered thinking at the time, but after that she nonetheless usually made herself appear more conservative when she was trying to sell a prospective client on their firm, which engaged in advertising and public relations. After setting up her laptop she rummaged through her purse looking for her cell phone, a new iPhone that she had yet to fully master. She dialled Yvette's direct office line.

"Hey."

"Where are you?" As usual, Yvette sounded tense.

"At Verona's. I just finished the meeting with the Point Atkinson Protection Society. We're hired!" Their new client was a group of waterfront and ocean view property owners in West Vancouver who were ostensibly fighting to protect a beloved stretch of unspoiled coastline, but actually sought to thwart the feared effect a proposed addiction rehabilitation clinic on the slopes above might have on their property values.

"How nice for you. I've spent the afternoon on a conference call with the Freaks."

"Hey, better you than me. But whatever, they're good for at least a half million a year in billings, or at least they were. What's up now? Or, should I say, what are they humming about now?"

"It's all business with you. Those people give me the willies." That much was true: Laura was much more inclined to focus solely on profitability than Yvette, who was of a more creative, artistic bent and given to fits of delusion. They opened their firm almost a decade earlier, and named it DesRosiers & Thompson at Laura's insistence. It was her turn to be the conservative one: traditional use of their surnames was much safer from a business point of view (as far as she was concerned) than Yvette's suggestion. She wanted to name their partnership after a celebrated land-use dispute somewhere up the coast over a river with a consonant-laden, unpronounceable Kwakiutl name. Laura pointed out that they would likely succeed only in pissing off the First Nations and identifying themselves too closely with the environmental movement, which would limit their pool of customers.

"And so?" Laura said.

"Well, you know what, the Freaks are on a roll," Yvette said. "They've got lots for us to do."

"Oh good, more money."

"Yeah, yeah, but just wait. There's good news: at least they aren't dragging us up to, what's that drafty old barn perched on the edge of a bog, Port Ratbag?"

"Rattray. Port Rattray."

"Yeah, well we're not going up there, at least for the time being. We'll have to draft up a series of press releases to buttress Declan," their client's lawyer, "...as he puts together their legal case. Until this afternoon, I didn't know how much sneaky shit the Reformed bunch pulled when they split away."

"Really? Like what?"

"Well, for starters a ton of cash mysteriously walked out the door when they left, and as it turns out, most of their real estate to boot."

"Wow. I hope Declan's up to it."

"Oh, I have faith in him, well, as a *lawyer*, at least. Anyway, I managed to sell them on launching a T.V. and radio advertising campaign for both B.C. and Washington State."

"Ka-ching."

"Oh, you bet. And here's the part I'm *so* looking forward to: we're going to be surrounded by hordes of the lunatics for *three days*! They're having their Convocation: they want to call it the 'Real Striationist Convocation' (we'll have to talk to them about that) at this place in Washington down by Everett, and we have to be there the whole time. They want us to film it; they *loved* your idea about putting together a documentary."

"Even better. But you know how much I enjoy crossing the border.

"Well, you're just going to have to suck it up. And did I tell you when they're holding it? It starts just before Canada Day long weekend!" They'd tentatively planned a wine tour in the Okanagan for that weekend, the first one in July.

"Is nothing sacred? Christ, if those people had any brains, they'd have their Convocation in December or something and rub themselves on their fucking rocks during the summer when it's warm."

"You can stop grumbling. *You* didn't have to deal with them all afternoon, and remember: this year we'll be billing them a lot more than last."

The rain had not relented in the least when Laura started walking down Robson Street toward a taxi stand where she hoped to hail a cab. As she walked quickly past a row of shops that sold nothing but trinkets and souvenirs for tourists, she came upon a group of people, unhappily drenched, who'd found shelter under an awning. They were speaking Italian, a language she hadn't heard in years. *The soothing language*, she remembered; that's what Carlo always called it.

....4

> *The productivity of most modern economies, especially those of Canada and the countries of the European Union, has been hampered by the persistence of underlying religious influences. Even if modern society has turned its back on religion, its moral tenets remain pervasive and difficult to extinguish. The Golden Rule, the most destructive dictum of all, predates almost all of the elements of a modern industrial economy, including the English language. Nevertheless, its underlying influence pollutes almost every transaction. The persistence of such mores defies reason, just like the adherence of Jews and Muslims to preposterous dietary laws devised before the invention of the refrigerator.*
>
> - Gavin Skoff, in *The Amiable Plunderer.*

You never realize what these situations are really like until you live in the midst of one. Gavin rubbed his face with shaving lotion, something French that Tiffany gave him for his birthday, and pondered. No bookstore carried a self-help series that could have prepared him. Unlike the lonely, the unemployed and the morbidly obese, nobody felt the least bit of sympathy for people like him. Everywhere you looked, the movies, television, they made it look, well, commonplace, and so damn easy. Gavin couldn't figure it out. Old celebrities, years, even decades older, fruitfully banged girls young enough to be their granddaughters and emerged sufficiently spruce to pose for photographs for the cover of *Hello!*, yet here he was, a comparatively youthful fifty-three, forever in the depths of fatigue. Each morning his entire being, every cell and corpuscle, collectively begged for another hour of sleep.

Nobody blamed him four years earlier when he jettisoned his wife, Lelani, after she joined the Striationists. When she first converted, she was away from home two, sometimes three days a week for religious retreats at that lodge off in the middle of nowhere, ensconced on a perch above Bute Inlet. Gavin finally decided to take action when she renounced the use of the telephone and then disappeared for several months on some sort of mission to set up a colony of yurts in Alaska. It was worth every penny to pay the process server to charter a floatplane and personally hand her the divorce petition on some muddy islet at the mouth of the Stikine. He wasn't the least surprised to hear that she stayed with the Orthodox faction after the split.

It was Tiffany who turned local public opinion against him. Anyone who gave the matter any thought expected that Gavin, middle-aged but still presentable and richer than the Queen, would find himself a young beauty, but he could have chosen one on the seemly side of twenty-one. His book, *The Amiable Plunderer*, having sold millions of copies in a dozen languages, afforded him such fame that he often found himself in the company of actresses and models whenever he left Parksville, his adopted Vancouver Island home, to make one of his frequent visits to Vancouver. Any of these women would have earned him the approval, even the admiration of his neighbours, but instead he chose Tiffany. They met after a presentation he gave to her high school class; she approached him in the hall, he took her to dinner, and she shared his bed ever since. Even if she was now on the cusp of twenty-two, everyone in Parksville remembered that it was about a year after she moved in before she reached legal drinking age.

"Hey Gav', what time does your open house start?" Tiffany asked as she came out of the bedroom. The sight of her in exercise tights cured his fatigue.

"I don't have to be there until five."

"Cool. We have time for a hike!" She started scanning a row of books on a nearby shelf, where she kept the guide which catalogued every hiking trail on central Vancouver Island.

"A *hike*?" Gavin said, as if trying to divine the meaning of a foreign phrase.

"Yes, a hike. Nothing too drastic, but you'd better be careful or you'll get those love handles back." She flipped through her book, no doubt looking for a trail that would burn off a suitable number of calories. "Oh, here we go. Let's try the Wesley Ridge trail."

Wesley Ridge. Gavin thought it over. At least it wasn't an aboriginal-sounding name, which often implied remoteness, but the word 'ridge' usually connoted a punishing elevation gain. Of course, it was encouraging that there was an actual *trail.* "Sure," he replied with more enthusiasm than he expected to muster. "As long as we're back in Parksville by five."

"Right at five?"

"Yes, that's when I have to be at the Seaview, for that thing with VisualEyes. And TriMar. I can't be late."

"Then you'd best hurry up. I'll meet you out front. And take the Land Rover; the book says that the road in is a bit rough."

Mario sat in silent regret of his decision to stop in at his neighbours' place for a visit. He stirred his disorganized tangle of long black hair in a gesture of annoyance. Their music whirled, whined, screeched and cavorted. Canmore sat erect with his eyes closed, swaying to the lurching tempo. Russell stood next to an obelisk-like speaker, performing an energetic air guitar with his teeth clenched and nostrils flaring. Before busying his fingers, he had almost succeeded in removing the label from his bottle of Budweiser, now empty, beside the speaker.

"I'm not talking about that." Canmore continued a conversation which, until now, Mario had been able to ignore. "This isn't even the same concert. The one you're talking about was in London in 1973. This one is from the 1971 festival on one of the Channel Islands.”

“No fucking way. The BBC version is like, way better.”

“But this is the bootleg!” Canmore said with an authoritative growl. “It’s authentic, just like being there, at the festival.”

That assertion Mario doubted. The recording duplicated not the experience of someone in the audience, but rather that of a condenser microphone hidden in somebody’s crotch. Canmore and Russell seemed to have forgotten he was there until he reached into a nearby bowl of bits and bites and fished out a few salty Cheerios.

“Mario!” Canmore tried to enlist his support. “What do you think? This one or Russell’s boring BBC disc?”

Mario couldn’t even identify the band, much less the song. He strained to listen as the track descended into tuneless droning. Both Canmore and Russell awaited his verdict when he nodded in recognition, after he pieced together the lyrics of a high-pitched stanza.

> *Crying won’t help you;*
> *Praying won’t do you no good*

“When the Levee Breaks”, he finally placed it. “I prefer the version off, whatever, the album with the funny symbols on it.”

“Puppy!” Canmore and Russell derided him together. At least he’d succeeded in temporarily uniting them. Of course, Mario found it incongruous that two grown men, both well past fifty, could spend an entire afternoon debating the relative merits of two Led Zeppelin CDs, one of them of questionable provenance. He did not wonder why they were both divorced. Canmore was poised to argue with him, but the bubbly beeps of his cell phone saved him.

Laeticia didn’t wait for him to say hello. “Where are you?” Mario could hear the din of road noise in the background.

"I'm at Canmore and Russell's place. I finally finished up Pacifica Forestry's website so I popped over for a beer.

"What's going on in there?" Canmore and Russell caterwauled out of tune, both trying to sing along to "Communication Breakdown".

"Oh, nothing, just Canmore and Russell both pretending that they're Robert Plant. Where are *you*?"

"I'm just coming down the other side of the Malahat. I guess we'll have to meet at the open house."

"What open house?" He sensed a moderate eruption of annoyance on the other end of the line.

"The open house for TriMar's presentation, don't you remember?"

"That's tonight? I thought it wasn't until next week."

"Jesus Christ! No, it's tonight, at the Seaview. Meet me there at six, on the dot. Don't be late like you always are. And show up sober."

"I haven't even had a beer, yet."

"Good. And remember, six o'clock."

Russell relinquished his air guitar during a staticky round of cheering between songs. "So, is your wife still working on that project up-Island?"

"Girlfriend." Mario said. "No, she's finished her Ph.D. Now she's a professor at UVic.

She was teaching a class today, down in Victoria."

"I don't think I could stand being with such a smart woman," Canmore said in a philosophical tone. Both Mario and Russell chose not to respond. Then the applause ended and Russell and Canmore started arguing again, this time about the authorship of the lyrics of the song just starting, "Bron-y-Aur Stomp" or something.

"Okay." Mario drained the rest of his beer. "I have to run, boys."

"Well, have a good one, eh."

The Seaview Hotel, a mid-eighties structure overlooking Parksville Bay, greeted visitors with a spare concrete walkway and charmless rectangular façade. Gavin was still buttoning his dress shirt as he walked past the pastel walls and shiny chrome accoutrements in the lobby, to the Mistaken Room, the hotel's largest conference hall, named after a nearby islet.

"Gavin, your face is very red," Irwin Bilbick, the mayor of Parksville, remarked as Gavin closed the double doors behind him. Joanne Trapp, another notable with VisualEyes Vancouver Island (Gavin still wasn't certain what she actually *did*), stood hunched over, mesmerized by her BlackBerry.

"I'm sure it is, Irwin." Gavin straightened his collar. "I've just been for a hike."

Irwin looked down at his shoes.

Joanne acknowledged him with a smirk. "Is that what the kids are calling it now?"

Gavin had known Joanne for more than twenty years, since she worked as a ReMax real estate agent in the lower mainland. Even at fifty-two she had yet to ease into elegance, and had even returned to her style of years before, dressed in an outsized blouse and skirt of earthen colours but discordant design, this time anchored by a bulky green blazer which discouraged the ensemble from undulating in random drafts. Upon sight of her newly curled but short greying hair, he decided that she looked like an upholstered toilet brush. "Is the convention hall set up?" he asked.

"Yes, everything is already in its place," Irwin said. "We had real problems setting up that enormous TV, though." He was the only one in the room who had lived in Parksville for more than a few years, although not even he had actually been born there. It was easy to understand why the town returned him as mayor for seven successive elections. His daily uniform, grey pants, white shirt and a navy-blue sports jacket reminded the hordes of British retirees from Victoria and West Vancouver of their public school days. This did not endear him any less to the locals, who considered him one of their own because he occasionally used double negatives and had been known to piss outside.

Gavin turned to Joanne. "Do you still have that flash drive, for my presentation?"

"No, I gave it to Irwin."

Irwin reached into the lacerated old briefcase that everyone who knew him recognized as his constant companion. "Here it is. I had my grandson check it for viruses."

Joanne looked up from her BlackBerry. "So where's Scranton?"

"He told me that he'd be on the one o'clock ferry," Gavin said. "He should be here by now."

"TriMar sent him over on the *boat*?"

"Maybe he likes the food. That was a *joke*. No, he's trying to make CEO. How would it look if he chartered a seaplane to Parksville? Anyway, let's make sure that the conference room is properly set up, shall we? We only have about half an hour."

The view of the Strait of Georgia usually afforded through the massive panes on the far wall was obscured by bulky transport trucks. Caterers were already busy putting the sandwiches, coffee urns and napkins on collapsible banquet tables. Right after somebody started piping music through the public address system, some Seventies abomination exhorting anyone within earshot to 'knock on wood', a man with blond hair wearing cream-coloured Dockers and a blue sports jacket pushed the door to the boardroom open with his Cordura briefcase.

"Peter!"

"Hi Gavin. Sorry I'm late. The ferry was half an hour behind schedule."

"The *ferry*," Gavin muttered. "Anyway, Peter, meet the mayor of Parksville."

"Irwin Bilbick. Pleased to meet you."

"Peter Scranton." The two men shook hands.

Joanne charged across the room with her hand outstretched, her jacket billowing like a spinnaker. "Peter, how *are* you? I haven't seen you since, well, I guess it was at that Vancouver Real Estate Board meeting last March at The Salmon House." Scranton peered at her, aghast. "Oh, I'm sorry. Joanne Trapp. I'm the treasurer of VisualEyes."

"Yes, yes of course," Scranton mumbled.

Scranton, Gavin and Joanne made passing chatter with the caterers until they saw a chance to gather at the other end of the conference room, standing together near a noisy fan so that nobody could hear them.

"I can't believe that you're going to let on what you have in mind, so soon, at this stage!" Joanne said to Gavin.

"I'm a bit concerned about it myself, Gavin," Scranton said.

"No," Gavin said. "The sooner they get used to the idea, the sooner those who lead public opinion will see it as inevitable."

"Are you crazy?" Joanne made a furtive survey of the room. "Remember what happened to David Wynne when he tried it two years ago? Remember him? Another one of those know-it-all engineers. Even *he* thought the audience was going to lynch him. No, it's better to sneak up on people. Opposition is much less organized when you put them off balance, especially tree-huggers."

Gavin vaguely recalled that the ensuing public clamour prompted Wynne to sell his sprawling waterfront house in some Victoria suburb or another at a loss and move to Seattle. "This approach is the one recommended by any communication expert I am aware of."

"I've had just about enough of your windy theories!" Joanne whispered.

Contrary to habit, Mario arrived early. The rows of metal chairs assembled in the Mistaken Room remained mostly empty. Still, there were people mingling near the coffee urns, most of whom he knew. *Oh, no.* It was him, the one with the brown ponytail tied with sweetgrass; his manner was intense but muddled, like a pedlar who had trouble remembering what he was selling. Once he cornered someone, there was no escape. Mario sidled away unnoticed. What was his name? Beresford or something, a neighbour who lived closer to the mouth of the river. One of the ones that Laeticia referred to as "those people", the Striationists, an astonishingly populous bunch who derived something or another from glacial striations, ungainly ancient gouges. Mario was insufficiently curious to find out exactly what. Someone tapped him on the shoulder.

"Mario!"

He was relieved to see that it was Gavin Skoff, another one of the neighbours. He lived with Tiffany, his much younger girlfriend, in the 1960s beach house enlarged to modern proportions a few lots down from the cabin that he and Laeticia rented. Laeticia made friends with Tiffany soon after they moved into their seaside cabin and the two of them exercised together twice a week.

"Oh hey, Gavin! How's it going?"

"Oh, you know; opening night jitters. Is your wife coming?"

"Girlfriend. Yeah, she's on her way, driving up from Victoria."

"Oh, that's right; she's still doing her Ph.D. or something down there, isn't she?"

"Nope. All finished up. She's Dr. Laeticia now, and she snagged a teaching position at UVic. First year biology."

"Hmm," Gavin said. "Better her than me. But good for her."

"Is Tiffany here?"

"Oh, she might stop by, but she's got some sort of yoga workshop later on in Qualicum. This isn't really her thing, anyway."

Mario glanced at his phone. Laeticia was late; it had now been twenty minutes. A few minutes later, he saw her hurry through the entrance. Now that her twenties were behind her, the Spanish characteristics of her mother's side of the family began to assert themselves, rendering her features more European. When she was younger, she looked a little more African, the genetic gift of her grandfather, a Senegalese. Her attire, jeans, boots (four hundred bucks for the pair, Mario recalled, without despair) and a tight 'Obama 2008' T-shirt, flattered a decorative, rounded physique tempered by frequent yoga. Even so, Mario decided not to let her get away with it this time.

"Remember, six o'clock!" Mario mimicked in a high-pitched voice, tapping on his watch.

"Sorry I'm late," she almost whispered. "I got busted for speeding on that long downhill stretch on the Victoria side of Ladysmith. Dudley fucking Do-Right. A hundred and forty bucks!" Most male Mounties let me go." She fluttered her eyelashes theatrically.

"I think that it's time that we got you a Prius."

"Look, there's Gavin." She pointed to the distant figure pacing near the podium, straightening the suspended screen dominating the front of the hall.

"Yes, we had a brief chat but he seems a bit preoccupied."

"Is Tiffany here?"

"I don't know; haven't seen her."

They found two empty seats near the front of the banquet room, facing the giant plasma screen. Both sipped coffee they'd drained from a tall aluminium urn into styrofoam cups. Mario slapped the front of his head. "Oh, I've got news! From Carlo. He'll be getting in to Vancouver just after Easter."

"Really? I'm shocked! It didn't look like he was going anywhere when we went to visit him last year."

"Oh, it's a surprise; I'm having trouble believing it myself."

"But you know what? I always knew he'd come back here *eventually*. Nobody leaves B.C. for good. And I sure hope this means that he ditched, what was her name? Juliette?"

"Giovanna. Yes, she's definitely out of the picture."

"Good." Laeticia took a sip of coffee. "Fuck, this stuff is vile. I hope he's back in touch with Laura. You said they'd hooked up again on Facebook."

"Who knows? He hasn't said anything about her for months."

"That whole situation is so sad, just so horribly sad." She set her coffee underneath her chair. "So is his dad still living in London?"

"Well, yes. He and Linda own that apartment, it must be worth millions by now, and she would never come here: she seems to think that Canada is still some desolate wilderness wasteland ruled by the Hudson's Bay Company."

"Linda. You know, she's always so sweet, so I'm ashamed to even think this, but she seems like someone who was once sprawled naked on a full page in *News of the World* or something."

"Oh, she was, well, a few years before Carlo's dad met her, but..."

"Don't fucking tell me that you've seen her naked!"

Mario contemplated the coffee grounds in the bottom of his cup. "Well, not like *naked* naked."

"You know, sometimes you can be such a creep. Anyway, I'm just happy that he's finally coming back. Oh, look; it's getting dark in here. Maybe something's happening".

Joanne worked the switches on the console in front of her to close the blinds and dim the overhead lights, extinguishing the lively mumbling which had filled the room. As Gavin rose to the podium, a light blue silhouette of Vancouver Island appeared on the giant screen.

"You have to say it!" Joanne whispered.

He leaned towards her. "Come on; it's such bullshit, and around here, no one cares."

"We've talked about this!" This time her whisper was fierce. "You have to say it, *now!*"

"Oh, all right." Gavin scowled and switched on his microphone. "Good evening, ladies and gentlemen," he said in an atonal drone. "I am honoured to acknowledge that we are assembled here on the unceded territory of the Snaw-na-was First Nation."

The speakers throbbed to life with the opening strains of the theme from *Star Wars,* played with familiar vigour by the London Philharmonic Orchestra.

The music faded. "Throughout history," Gavin announced, "great civilizations have defined themselves by their grandest visions, their accomplishments, their superlative feats of engineering." The silhouette of Vancouver Island slowly transformed itself into an oblique view of an endless series of stone arches seemingly marching across a landscape of rolling hills, with the round, orange central Italian sun setting in the background.

"The Roman Aqueduct."

The aqueduct faded into a montage of a sturdy concrete cloverleaf interchange, an aerial view of a twelve-lane freeway, and a map of Illinois, showing multiple blue lines converging on Chicago.

"The American interstate highway system."

Then a black-hulled freighter on a narrow canal started to supplant the montage, an image that seemed to spring from a distant point in the background, spinning and growing until it filled the entire screen.

"The St. Lawrence Seaway."

The screen slowly transformed into a misty grey. Strains of "Flight of the Valkyries" began to play softly in the background. A mule, a coach and four, followed by a locomotive, and then a 747 jetliner each appeared one after the other as the music grew louder.

Gavin had to shout to be heard above the background music. "But we now have an opportunity to reach beyond ourselves, to abandon our safe but unfulfilling comfort zone!" He raised his arms. "We have the opportunity to become the envy of the world!"

"Flight of the Valkyries" then faded, to be replaced with something more modern, as it blended with the notes of the gentle guitar introduction of "Paradise City", followed by Axl Rose melodically chanting its opening verse.

The Houses of Parliament, with the River Thames in the foreground, followed by the Colosseum, and then the Palace of Versailles each popped up, displayed side by side. As the tempo of the music started to increase, the three pictures started shaking and an intense rumbling replaced the music. An image of the Château Whistler rose from the bottom of the screen and forcibly cast aside the other three. New background music commenced with a tenor's declaration:

Fortunatissimo, per verità!

"Our icons and cultural symbols will soon enthral, inspire and dominate the imagination and consciousness of everyone on the entire planet!" Gavin thundered.

The screen faded as the opening notes to the theme from *Rocky* started to play. A small dot, first appearing in the right-hand corner of the screen, progressively grew into a view of the CN Tower. "Toronto will no longer boast that it has the world's longest free-standing structure!"

Laeticia elbowed Mario in the ribs when he started to wheeze with laughter.

"We will!" Gavin shouted, raising his arms in a 'V', fists clenched.

Sounds of smashing and crunching competed with the music until cracks developed in the image. A few pieces seemed to be falling from the photograph, until the next image, an oblique view of the Strait of Georgia, erupted from the right corner and violently scattered the remaining shards. The theme from *Rocky* played on at rousing volume as a white, serpentine tube materialized like an apparition in the foreground and started to slowly extend toward the horizon, just beneath the waterline.

The music had almost reached its crescendo. "We shall build a bridge to the mainland!" Gavin screamed with evangelical fervour. "It will be a technological marvel which will ensure our prosperity for generations to come!"

Gonna fly now!

The next image was in cross section, showing a wide, white underwater pipe housing a six-lane highway and some sort of rapid transit line beside it. The music abruptly stopped. The screen changed to a blank sky blue.

Gavin started to speak in a quiet, reflective tone. "But in order to do this, we must make some changes."

"We must develop a sense of confidence." The words 'Develop a Sense of Confidence' came on the screen from stage right and were quickly thrust leftward, stopping suddenly at the margin accompanied by a computer-generated sound approximating the squealing of brakes.

"We must be willing to make long-term sacrifices." The words 'Make Long Term Sacrifices' appeared at the bottom right corner, and started to move around the screen in spiralling circles, as if swirling down a drain, eventually coming to rest beneath the first statement.

"And this is the most important one of all. We must put aside selfish, local concerns." The words 'Put Aside Selfish Concerns' seemed to spew forth from the lower right-hand corner, moved diagonally across the screen in a see-saw motion, and took its position beneath the other two phrases.

Now he was shouting. "If we are able to do these three things," Gavin said, and raised his hand, displaying three fingers. "We will build a better..." Before he could finish, the screen display did not perform as he'd programmed it. It was supposed to display his latest declaration, letter by letter, as a huge silver monolith that would dominate the screen. Instead, in his exuberance, Gavin inadvertently clipped the mouse with his wrist, setting in motion an unintended operation.

Please wait while Windows installs updates...
0 of 115 updates installed
Do not turn off your computer

Gavin tried to re-activate the program, but the updating sequence stubbornly refused to terminate. He felt deepening regret for insisting on a screen the length and height of a shipping container as it pitilessly displayed the progress of the clearly overdue procedure.

Joanne hissed something unmistakably insulting and switched off the display. "You know," she said, now standing so close to Gavin that he was overwhelmed by the odour of decomposing cappuccino. "It isn't all about you! Neither I nor Scranton came over here to...to Hell and gone to watch you preen. What about TriMar? And VisualEyes? You didn't say a word about either of them!"

"Look, I'm sorry: the computer packed it in before I got there. But I have to deal with it." Gavin turned to the murmuring crowd. "It seems that we have technical difficulties," Gavin shouted with a nervous giggle. "Perhaps you could go to the display hosted by TriMar and the City of Parksville, located in the Lasqueti Room next door." Lasqueti was the gentle, rustic isle directly across the water, known for its lack of police supervision and abundance of potent weed.

His presentation provoked little response from the audience. It wasn't as if the idea of a bridge to the mainland enjoyed widespread local support; instead, most of the people at the meeting were old enough to have heard similar proposals several times over the course of their lives, and tended to greet them in much the same way as they did feverish predictions foretelling the return of Christ. Mario wasn't surprised when he overheard an older woman remark to her husband, "I always thought that he was just another one of those half-baked crackpots!"

He and Laeticia followed the group into the conference room next door, which had been organized into a series of display tables and booths in the style of a trade fair, to display the projected redevelopment of the town centre. A giant cloth banner was draped from the ceiling, spanning the width of the room.

The New Parksville – Rustic yet Urbane
A little bit of Tuscany by the sea

Mario winced. "Don't worry," Laeticia said. "I'm not going to put you through much more of this. So where is he staying?"

"Where is who staying?"

"You have a mind like a sieve. Carlo! Is he coming to stay with us?"

"No, he's going to Vancouver to look for a job at a litigation firm. He's a fucking *barrister*, he's worked in Toronto, London, *Rome*, even. What would he do in Parksville? Draft wills? Defend drunk drivers and wife-beaters?"

"You haven't answered my question."

"Oh. As far as I know, he's staying in Kits with David and Farida." David Brenner and Farida Hamizadeh; the only couple from their student days to actually get married, now both lawyers and living in a townhouse with their cat in the Kitsilano district of Vancouver. "Well, at least until he gets settled in."

The nearest exhibit displayed the proposed new main route through town, several blocks in length and flanked by two giant, arched gates each giving welcome to those entering the city. Its hostess greeted the approaching mob. "Hello, everyone," she said, "Thank you for coming." Her appearance differed little from most public relations people that Mario had encountered before: a tailored, European-cut suit, fashionably styled red hair.

She pointed to a drawing of the proposed boulevard. "Here is our new main street, the Parksville Gateway! We're having a contest to give the street and the two gates exciting names," she said with a perky squeak. "Just write your name on the back of one of those cards, put your suggestion on the other side, and post it on the corkboard! The winner of each category gets a free head of organic goat's cheese from Cortes Cheeseworks."

It was obvious from the number of cards already affixed to the board that the contest had been open for a while. A consensus appeared to be developing regarding the names of the two gates. The eastern one was almost certain to end up as "the Victoria Gate", probably favoured by some as homage to Queen Victoria, by others to honour the provincial capital; and the one on the west would be "the Edinburgh Gate", no doubt at the behest of the locals, many of whom traced their immediate roots to the Scottish Lowlands. The name of the thoroughfare itself was still a matter of disagreement. Some of the proposed names adopted local geographical features; others, like Saxifrage Lane and Kinnikinnick Row, assumed encyclopaedic knowledge of local flora. Most were of a political bent. "Tommy Douglas Avenue", "Diefenbaker Mews", "Boulevard Pierre-Trudeau", and so on. Mario picked up a pen and started writing on one of the cards. He was going to suggest 'Via Silvio Berlusconi', but changed his mind.

Hunter S. Thompson Memorial Freeway

Mario looked over the busy, computer-generated drawing: tree-lined boulevards, bicycle lanes, a railway and bus station and a pedestrian mall featuring a surging fountain; and the proposed gate to the downtown area, a wrought iron *art-nouveau* sculpture made of black, round steel rods, woven into a bulbous arch reminiscent of the entrance to certain Parisian métro stations, with sculpted metal letters across the gentle arc at the top, fashioned to form the words "WELCOME TO PARKSVILLE".

There were a few more drawings, conceptions of streetscapes that bore a superficial resemblance to busy European boulevards, but instead of sidewalk cafés filled with people sitting at outside tables, sipping coffee or hoisting glasses of beer, listless pedestrians strolled past tables filled with displays of disparate local pottery, vials of ointments and aromatherapy potions, and native-inspired artwork. The sole nod to gastronomy was a counter festooned with orange slabs of smoked salmon.

They were both startled by a burgeoning dispute at the display opposite them, which turned out to be the first showing of a proposed waterfront condominium complex. A group of about thirty onlookers keened as one man pronounced summary judgment in a shrill squawk.

"This is perfectly hideous!"

People around him grumbled in agreement. Mario recognized him as a mechanic for whom he'd once bought a beer at a pub in Qualicum after losing a game of pool. "I mean, just look at this. It looks like a cracker box designed by a vampire!"

An eerily staid computer-generated drawing showed the project from the perspective of someone approaching Parksville from the water, a linear twenty storey monolith standing phallic against the grey silhouette of Mount Arrowsmith. Mario surmised that the developer was attempting to imitate the Marine Building, an art deco structure in downtown Vancouver. But instead of standing as an urban beacon, it merely loomed as a Gothic tower;

imposing and austere, lording over the peasants scattered down below.

"How are people on the other side of that monstrosity supposed to see the ocean?" asked the mechanic's female companion, a slender woman with brown hair and momentarily angry blue eyes.

The host of the exhibit smiled. He was a man in his forties with studiously tousled blonde hair; his voice reminded Mario of the bouncy cadence of music played in mall restrooms. "We have hired a team of consultants from Germany..." he said, as if opening a chest to display gold coins. "To develop view corridors to address that very concern. The people of Parksville have nothing to worry about."

"View corridors?" An older man standing behind Mario spoke up. "What do you mean 'view corridors'? That thing will block the view of everyone west of the Alberni cut-off. There won't be any 'corridors' about it!"

"Well," the host purred, "we're going to have a public observation station at the top of the building, which will be accessible free of charge to all Parksville residents!"

"That's not a *corridor*," the mechanic said. "That's just bullshit! What are we going to do, ride an *elevator*." He spat out the word as if it were a partly chewed insect. "Every time we want to see the Straits?"

"Well," the host effected a gentle bow. "It will be a lovely view."

"Oh, just go home," the mechanic's girlfriend said.

"Wait a second." Laeticia spoke up, to Mario's surprise. "Twenty stories of condos? What are you going to do with all of the sewage? Parksville Bay already has a higher coliform count than False Creek in the middle of Vancouver!"

"Yes, we recognize that as a very serious concern." He turned to Laeticia; his expression funereal. "TriMar is developing a comprehensive Sewage Management Strategy." He pointed to a cardboard pane showing a photograph of an ethnically heterogeneous collection of men and women wearing hard hats, all appearing to be engaged in earnest conversation in a windowless cement room dominated by a lattice of pipes and ducts.

"How is that going to work?" Laeticia said. "Especially now that Bilbick decreed that we don't have enough money to expand the capacity of the sewage treatment plant."

His smile returned with considerable enhancement. "Well, you see, it is our expectation that most of the people buying the units will be retirees, deep into their golden years, who will produce less than the usual amount of sewage."

The mechanic shook his head. "Are you fucking kidding me?"

Laeticia touched Mario's elbow and leaned over to whisper in his ear. "Let's get out of here. I've had enough. And I'm going to have to deal with this bunch again in two weeks, at that Visual-Eyes thingy in Victoria.

"*What?*"

"No, no; don't fuss, you don't have to come with me to that one. But let's go. *Now.* I need a drink."

Mario and Farida met Carlo at the YVR international arrivals gate. Mario was wearing frayed jeans and a T-shirt illustrated with an obscene gesture; Farida was dressed in an aerodynamic charcoal grey suit and costly shoes, her dark hair a little longer than she'd kept it in Toronto. Still, she managed to maintain a certain look of primness, perhaps necessary for a barrister. Mario had changed little in the three years since Carlo left, maybe a couple of strands of grey were starting to appear in his mop of black hair. The sight of them made him chuckle. Farida looked like she was about to represent Mario at his arraignment.

"Ò! Carlò!" Mario embraced him, sparking a boisterous conversation in Italian that attracted the attention of everyone in the broad 'Arrivals' foyer.

"Guys...guys, I'm here!" Farida said "How would you like it if I started yelling at both of you in Persian?"

"Oh, I'm sorry Farida." Carlo said. "We were just..."

Farida gave Carlo a hug and then looked him over. "Well, you look much better than the last time I saw you." No doubt. They hadn't seen each other since she dropped him off at Pearson Airport, an exhausted vision of ruin in the throes of a memorable hangover, with a ticket to London in his pocket. Tina's death was worse than anything he'd ever even imagined. He left Toronto certain that he would never again set foot in Canada.

"I sure hope so!" Carlo laughed. "So where's David?"

"He's at trial; you know, the one he's been talking about for weeks every time you called? It went ahead."

Carlo was no longer surprised by David's absence. Trials encourage lawyers to postpone everything but the most necessary bodily functions. "Poor David. So, how do you like Vancouver so far?"

"So far? We've been out here for two *years*, Carlo. It rains too fucking much, but it's way better than the alternatives. Remember? Going back to Montreal was out of the question, and even Toronto turned out to be much too close."

He'd long known that Farida's family inspired her to fits of rage. Visiting her parents in Montreal, even five or six times a year at the most, required a Zen-like patience she didn't possess. At first, both of her parents were roundly disgusted by her choice of mate, a lanky, lumbering kid of German extraction who, they were convinced, wouldn't know the Koran from *The Great Gatsby.* Three of her uncles grumbled that they wouldn't come to the wedding but showed up anyway, no doubt dragged there by the ear.

As Farida entered her early thirties, her parents' attitude abruptly changed once it occurred to them that David, however substandard, embodied their final hope for the production of grandchildren. Their trips back to Montreal became unbearable.

People in her family did not peddle in subtle hints. Artless coaxing and occasional tirades in mixed Persian and English were bad enough; every sigh or mournful glance conveyed their displeasure at Farida's empty womb. David considered taking up smoking so that he would have an excuse to go outside. Before long, they were never left in peace; not even in Toronto. An incessant parade of aunts, uncles and cousins came to visit, ostensibly to shop for Persian food easily found in Outremont and Italian clothing that was cheaper on Sherbrooke Street, but actually to beseech Farida to get knocked up as soon as practicable. When the two of them relaxed one afternoon at a wine bar in the Annex during a rare weekend of peace, David mused that he wanted to move back to Vancouver because he missed the Coast Mountains. Farida agreed before he had the chance to finish his sentence.

The three of them crossed the parkade, Carlo uneasily pushing a baggage cart. "So what's with that behemoth?" Mario asked. "Bringing back an entire *prosciutto*?"

"No, but I took the train into the city to see your aunt the last time I was in Sannazzaro, and she sent you over some..."

"Here it is! Check it out, Carlo!" Mario said. "A Subaru! How Vancouver can you get? After two short years, they already drive a *Subaru*! It's like..."

"It's like Mario is going to *walk* back home across the Arthur Lang. Just shut up and get in."

Carlo pushed his duffle bag in to the trunk and got into the front seat, his hand luggage at his feet. "Why didn't you put that in the back?" Farida asked. "There's room."

Carlo glanced up at the looming North Shore Mountains, which he hadn't seen in almost eleven years. "Well, as I was saying, I saw your aunt, about ten days ago; she insisted that I bring you some of these. She said that they were your favourite food when you were ten." Carlo held up a spacious, stuffed plastic bag.

"Taralli!" Mario laughed.

"What the fuck are those?" Farida asked. "Pretzels?"

"Ohhh!" Mario and Carlo cooed together in operatic outrage.

"Jesus fucking Christ; you people are worse than Muslims! So what are they?"

"Taralli. Would you like one?" Carlo asked.

The three of them chomped energetically. "These are excellent; way better than the ones you get on East Hastings," Mario said.

"Yes," Farida said, "these aren't half bad. Way better than that vegetable stew you made for us last time you were over."

"What was it?" Carlo asked.

"*Cicoria e fave.*" Mario said.

"*Really?*" It was a peasant's meal made of chicory, broad beans and olive oil, loved by those with origins in the province of Bari but universally despised by everyone else. "You actually fixed them *that?*"

Farida drove through the backstreets of Kitsilano, more crowded than Carlo remembered them. She turned left on to York Street. "Shit, the Reverend's got my usual spot." Farida pulled into an opening near the end of the block.

"The Reverend?" Carlo asked.

"Our pain in-the-ass downstairs neighbour. Just like that neighbour of yours back in Toronto, reedy, priggish and pale; talks with a mid-Atlantic wheeze. He pissed us off the first time when he complained about the noise from one of our parties; well, okay, David *was* playing Nine Inch Nails. Then the prick complained to the strata about my swearing. Asshole! And what difference does it make to him? It's not like I smoke!"

Their townhouse was on the upper row, facing the street. Carlo saw a barrister's black gown and vest, strewn across the back of the chesterfield in the sitting room. "I thought David was at trial."

"Well, as far as I know, he is," Farida said.

"Nope!" David bellowed from the kitchen. "Settled! I harpooned her in cross-examination and she decided to bail." David, a barrister who specialized in insurance defence, often represented policy holders of the province's public automobile insurer in personal injury lawsuits. From what Carlo could gather from David's savage description, the plaintiff was a middle-aged housewife of downcast demeanour from one of the distant suburbs, who claimed that a routine rear-end collision had ruined her life and left her profoundly depressed. "Of course she's a sad sack!" David assured him. "She looks like a beach ball with feet!"

"Well, I'm glad it's over," Farida said as she hung David's gown and vest in the closet. "I've been hearing about her non-stop for the past month."

'So you're back!" David slapped Carlo's shoulder. "Welcome home! It's about time; I thought we'd never see you on this coast again."

"It might be a good idea to get some lunch soon." Mario peered at a photograph on top of a bookcase. "Hey, when was that taken?"

"That's all of us together at that beach on the Toronto Islands; I don't know, 2003, maybe 2004?" David said. "You and Laeticia, me and Farida, Carlo and Tina; the only one of the old crowd missing was Laura."

"What can I say, Carlo?" Farida sighed. "David is still a fucking bull in a china shop, at this point charging toward the Wedgewood."

"It's alright, Farida," Carlo said. "It's been a while. I'm fine."

"Well, still...anyway. Yes, let's go for lunch; what about La Sirena?"

"No, I don't think so," David said. "All that smoked tuna, kale, free range onions. Not only did I leave there with gnawing hunger, but I had diarrhea for a week. Let's go to King's Cross!"

"King's Cross?" Carlo's last encounter with a place of that name was a drab railway station and Underground interchange in central London.

"Yes," David pointed out the front window. "Just out there on Cornwall, by the beach. They have a patio. You probably remember it as Pedro Flannigan's."

The hostess seated them at a table near the street. Two girls, both blonde, both in shorts, walked past them on the sidewalk. David and Mario made approving gestures to bring the pair to Carlo's attention.

Farida didn't even look up as she scanned the menu, "He's single. You two, however, are not. Especially you." She poked David in the ribs.

"Come on, Farida. We were just giving Carlo...giving him *encouragement.*"

"For what? Statutory rape? Oh, and Carlo, if you're tempted to order the *bruschetta*, don't. It tastes like liquorice; I found out the hard way. I should have known better to order it at a place where the waiting staff call it 'brushetta'".

Carlo snorted. "Beverages?"

"Not me." Farida sighed. "I have to get back to the office."

"I'm getting the first of many pints," David said. "Trial's over." He waved at a passing waitress. "So what are you going to do now that you're back in this soggy city, Carlo, hang out? You just got back; you might as well take it easy for a while."

"Nope. I'm going to start looking for work sooner rather than later. I've never been much good at sitting around."

After three days, Carlo was done with leisure. First, the usual legal recruiting websites. Breszver Collingwood was looking for an associate; he'd apply there. As far as he could recall, it had a similar ambience as Winters McTavish, where he'd worked for the first year he lived in Toronto. Oh, look; the firm where he articled had an opening. He wouldn't go back there even if they paid him triple the going rate. Gowlings, a national firm, wanted an insurance litigator, yet another résumé he'd be sending out. Carlo scrolled down the page.

> **Available immediately:** Small Gastown barristers' chambers seeks intermediate associate with at least three years of litigation experience. Firm has a varied civil litigation practice with an international flavour. The successful candidate will have his own file responsibilities but will also work under a senior barrister of almost forty years at the Bar. No family or criminal work. Salary is negotiable. The preferred candidate will be able to start immediately. Please send covering letter and résumé by fax to: Gaskin Barristers, (604) 687-1331.

This one was interesting. Although he would have preferred to work at a larger firm, the idea of working for an outfit that described itself as a "barristers' chambers" appealed to him. He sent applications off to half a dozen law firms over David and Farida's home fax machine and then set out to Granville Island Market to shop for dinner. He was in the midst of choosing tomatoes at one of the greengrocers when his cell phone started to beep.

"Carlo?"

"Yes, this is Carlo Buonsante."

"This is Declan Gaskin; you recently applied for a job at my firm."

Recently indeed. "Yes, that's right. I saw your advertisement on the Canadian Bar Association website."

"Good, good, are you available to meet this afternoon?"

"Sure, of course."

"I have a meeting with a client that should last a couple of hours. I'll call you when I am finished, probably around four. Is that okay with you?"

"Yes. I'll look forward to meeting you."

Without question, it was the strangest job interview Carlo had ever experienced. He assumed that they'd meet at the Gaskin Barristers office. Instead, Gaskin wanted to interview him at a coffee bar in Gastown, a couple of blocks from his building.

Gaskin assessed him from across a hewn wooden table. "You have this schoolboy look about you. It may serve you well with the girls at the bar, but it will not be of any assistance to you in *this* profession!"

His manner came in disquieting contrast to his appearance. Carlo would have been surprised if a lawyer of Gaskin's age didn't exude a bit of pomposity, but his opening volley did not befit a man who maintained the trappings of his psychedelic past: sandals, a loose hemp shirt, shoulder length brown hair, flecked with grey. Carlo took a shallow sip of his *caffè doppio*, which he was in the habit of taking *amaro*, without sugar.

Gaskin stirred honey into some sort of herbal tea concoction. "But you come much more highly recommended than your appearance would suggest. I spoke with your former boss, what's his name, Somers?"

"Winters."

"Yes, Winters. Anyway, it was the most bizarre employment reference I've ever heard. He wanted me to try to convince you to move back to Toronto!" Gaskin stirred his aromatic herbal mixture again. "It seems that you have worked on some very intricate and demanding projects." He smiled for the first time. "You more than meet the requirements of the job. But one issue concerns me. Winters told me that you left Toronto almost three years ago. What have you been doing in the meantime?"

Gaskin must have given his résumé less than even a cursory glance. "I was in Italy."

"Oh? What were you doing there?" Gaskin was still smiling.

"Visiting family at the beginning. After a couple of months, I found a job at a bank in Rome, in the international investments and transfers department, you know, usually dealing with common-law countries."

"Family? Don't tell me you're Italian!"

"Well, yes." Carlo wondered if he was joking.

"Hmm...are you married?"

"No."

"These days, I really shouldn't be so surprised. Not ever?"

"No, not formally, but I was in a long-term relationship before I left Toronto."

"Oh? And just what does 'long term' mean?" Gaskin folded his arms.

"Just over three years."

With difficulty inherent in the physique of a slender man, Gaskin developed jowls. "Not married after three years! This suggests a shocking lack of commitment! So what did you do, just decide to move on to the next one?"

"She died. That's why I left Toronto."

Gaskin sputtered as his jowls disappeared. "Well, I have more work than I can handle. I am prepared to offer you a job as an associate."

And I have to pay the rent. "Thank you. I'd be pleased to work for you."

They shook hands "Welcome aboard! Do you exercise?" Gaskin started to rise from his chair.

"Well, yes. I just took out a membership at a gym over by City Hall, and my plan is to run around the Seawalk three times a week. In Rome I ran four, five days a week; the local gyms were a bit lacking."

"Oh, you really should exercise; it really helps you deal with the stress of this job. I do *tai chi,* religiously."

Gaskin approached a frail man who looked like he was in his early twenties sitting near the door, wearing a "Save East Creek" T-shirt and excavating the contents of one nostril with his thumb, burying it almost to the first knuckle. "You can't dig at your nose with your thumb! What do you think you're doing?" He loomed over him with a disapproving scowl.

The young man, engrossed in an article in *Georgia Straight,* took his thumb out of his nose but otherwise tried to ignore Gaskin.

"Look," Gaskin said, his tone deepening to a purr. "We all have to remove dry detritus from our noses, from time to time. But the proper way is like this, with your index finger." Gasket gave a brief demonstration. "If you insist on using your thumb, you'll have a snout like a pig before you're thirty!"

"Come on, Carlo," Gaskin said once they were out on Water Street. "I'll give you a tour of our offices." They came upon a trio of unshaven men in soiled clothes on their way past the steam clock. One of them was poised to ask Carlo for spare change but all three hastily retreated to the haven of an adjacent doorway upon sight of Gaskin.

Gaskin led at a brisk pace. "Your first day will be on Monday. And I would like you come to an open house at my wife's art gallery tomorrow night, if you're free. You know where Granville Island is? It's called de Bosch Kemper Galleries (it's her maiden name; she's of Dutch background), not too far from the public market."

"I know the area."

"Good. You'll find it. I'll introduce you to the rest of the firm when you're there. And be there by about five."

The offices of Gaskin Barristers took up half of the fourteenth floor of the Harbour Centre, one side facing Burrard Inlet and the mountains north of Vancouver. The fading sunlight of the spring evening filled the office, the blue silhouette of Mount Seymour directly opposite. The layout of the foyer, library and secretarial space was open concept, with the perimeter occupied by enclosed offices.

"This will be your office!" Gaskin said, as if bestowing a lottery cheque. The view to the southeast, with the North Cascades well in the distance, reflected the reddish tinge of the developing sunset. Otherwise, his new office was unusually small, busy with motley décor. It appeared that Gaskin, who maintained a large personal injury practice, used medical models and ceramic skeletons as explanatory aids at trial. Replicas of joints, bones and body parts littered every flat surface except for the blotter at the centre of the desk. A partial skeleton, representing a spine and sacroiliac joint, hung from a rack in the corner. A plastic model eye, round and partially peeled back to show off each layer of tissue, sat on the corner of the desk, gazing toward the doorway, unblinking.

One of a half dozen photographs on the office wall, probably a copy of a magazine advertisement, featured the same skeleton;

its supporting rack perched top of the desk. A young man sitting in the same chair peered through the pelvis.

GASKIN BARRISTERS
Thorough investigation of all your legal problems

"This is my office, over here." Gaskin's office was at the far end, facing northwest toward Stanley Park, its wood panelled walls festooned with photographs and plaques. A few of the pictures showed Gaskin beaming as he embraced accident victims in wheelchairs, or in one example, in a hospital bed, mangled and morose. One or two showed Gaskin pointing at a newspaper, its headline announcing a legal victory. Others depicted him at various stages of his career, either in barrister's robes outside sundry courthouses, or else striking a valiant pose on a yacht or golf course.

The longest of the walls in Gaskin's office was bare, except for what appeared to be a freakish sculpture, a jagged gouge spanning a long, thin tableau of rough rock, mounted lengthwise behind the desk. "I bet you've never seen one of those outside of its natural habitat," Gaskin said. His tight, impish smile served to confirm Carlo's fear that he was gazing upon a statue of a giant vagina.

"It's an actual glacial striation!" Gaskin said.

Carlo stepped back and squinted.

"Don't tell me that you are unaware of Striationism?" Declan said.

"No, I can't say that I've ever heard of it."

"Working here, you will find out more about Striationism than you ever wanted to know. They are a very important client for us; a religion that worships terrestrial energy. To them, the purest form of terrestrial energy was the movement of the glaciers, the great ice sheets that once covered the northern hemisphere.

The glaciers are mostly gone now, but their energy survives in the striations which criss-cross the rocks in our mountain valleys and coastal inlets. And its benefit? Glacial energy creates wisdom, gives energy to its recipient; it can even cure disease."

"Hmm."

"I can see that you're a born sceptic."

"Do you believe it?"

"Well, I have to say that the religion has something important to say, but I am not one of its followers. Besides, my mother would be horrified; ninety-two years old and she goes to Mass three times a week. What would she have to say about a son who worships cracks?"

Farida was setting the table as Carlo carried a heaping bowl of *fettucce all'amatriciana* from the kitchen. "The food around here sure has improved since you came back," she said.

David poured the dregs of his beer into the sink. "Yeah, don't move too far away after you find a job."

Carlo laughed. "Now that you're both here, I might as well tell you. I did find a job today, at a firm run by this oddball; I think he's quite deranged."

"You'll have to be more specific," David said. "This is Vancouver."

"Gaskin Barristers. It's in the Harbour Centre."

"Whoa; I know the firm. That guy Gaskin, what's his name, Seamus or something...no, Declan; he is a total fucking weirdo. I did a mediation with him about two months ago."

"How so?" Carlo asked. "Why do you say he's a fucking weirdo?"

"He thinks he's all that and a side of fries," David said. "His knowledge knows no bounds! He was performing a critique of the mediator's style, and went so far as to tell my client, the insurance adjuster; you know, the one with the money, that she should cut back on sugar; said it was giving her skin eruptions. I mean, who does that? And he even reached into my briefcase to grab my iPod, *and he turned it on,* just to see what music I listened to. Be warned: he has a major hate on for Kurt Cobain, something about being a poor role model. Doesn't seem to know that he's dead." David served himself some pasta. "His legal assistant; have you met her?"

"No. Just him."

"Well, some might consider her hot, I suppose. Long red hair, a bit of a hippie chick, too heavy for my tastes, but she's *very* distracting. Tits the size of watermelons; and we're not talking cantaloupes here, they're..." he laughed, cupping his hands well in front of his chest.

Farida shuddered. "Are you going to open the wine or remain mired in adolescence?"

"Both." David reached for the corkscrew.

"Well, what did *you* think of him?" Farida asked Carlo. "I've met him a couple of times. I volunteer for the Fraser-Coastal Women's Legal Resource Centre; his wife (she's an artist or something) is the associate director. She's an ice queen; he's...well, he's sort of a cross between a hobo and a motivational speaker."

"He strikes me as a bit of an ass, you know, one of those precious old hippies dressing like it's the Summer of Love forty years on," Carlo said. "And his firm represents this crackpot religion, *striationism* or something, I don't know. He even has a glacial striation, pulled off a rock outcropping somewhere, posted on his office wall."

Farida and David both groaned. "*Striationists!* Those people..." David said. "They go up the coast, roll around on the rocks..."

"They don't *all* roll around on the rocks; some of them just talk about it." Farida interrupted. "And then they *all* come back to the city even more pompous and insufferable than they were before they left. Isn't the Premier linked to them?"

"Yup," David said. "He's one of the guys who 'just talks about it'."

"Well, I am likely to meet a few of them tomorrow night." Carlo said. "Declan's wife is having an open house at her gallery on Granville Island."

"Just watch out that his clients don't try to convert you." Farida pointed to her glass. "Wine, David."

....6

Laura walked dragging her wheeled briefcase behind her along Richards Street for a few blocks, following a woman whom she was certain she knew. It wasn't until the figure ahead of her turned to glance into a shop window, displaying herself in profile, that she finally placed her.

"Darla!"

The woman turned to face her, pausing to let her eyes focus. "Laura! It's you! Oh, my God!" The two women embraced. "My little cousin, all grown up. It's been what, eleven, maybe twelve years?" She laughed. "Oh, my God! You still look like the same little teeny-bopper I taught how to put on makeup!"

Her cousin Darla, nine years older. Laura idolized her when she was younger, the raucous beauty always surrounded by boys, with the face and physique of one of the several shrieking girl rockers on MTV, her long, straight black hair always governed, then as now, in the prevailing fashion.

Laura laughed. "Well, I sure hope I've changed, but I'm so glad to see you."

"Well, maybe you've changed a little; you're taller and you never wore fancy suits back then. But you look great! Oh!" She pointed at Laura's giant briefcase. "I met up with Auntie Deanna over in Victoria, I don't know, about three months ago. She said that you're a famous advertising executive or something?"

"No, far from it, actually," Laura laughed. "Auntie Deanna is *so* dramatic. Yvette, remember Yvette? We're running our own public relations agency just down here, on Mainland Street."

"Yvette...Yvette; oh, yes. The tall French girl with red hair. Your old partner in crime. Well that's exciting, public relations! You probably heard that I was down in L.A. Well, I'm back, now; I'm one of the local sales reps for Merck and Ratiopharm, and a couple of other ones that nobody except for doctors has ever heard of. Not married yet?"

"No. You?"

"Nope. And I think I'm better off that way; no, I'm *sure* that I'm better off that way. So, how are your parents?"

"They're doing great, actually. Dad's retired; well, semi-retired. He still runs the construction company but now he's actually hired people to help him. And the two of them work like fiends keeping up their little farm."

"Still the same old place?"

"The very same. I try to get over, once every couple of months. What about you, do you go back to the Island at all?"

"Yes, even when I lived in California I'd try to get back to Black Creek to visit my dad whenever I had time. I just visited him last week. You knew that they were divorced."

"Yes, I heard."

"Well," she sighed. "It was long overdue. My mother, she's living in Nanoose now, waiting tables part-time."

"I didn't know that Auntie Gladys left Comox. At least Nanoose is closer."

"Look, I try my best; I see her whenever I feel up to it. I know I'm not telling you anything that you didn't already know. What can I say? My mother's a cunt, but she's still my mother." A brief but awkward silence. "Well, anyway, we should meet up for lunch or something. My office is over there in the Scotia tower." They exchanged telephone numbers and e-mail addresses, each assiduously typing into their phones.

It had been years since Laura had even thought about that side of the family. Darla was one of the Rafferty bunch, a sprawling clan scattered throughout the central Vancouver Island lowland patchwork of forest and pasture between Black Creek and Cumberland. The five Rafferty brothers, their wives and many progeny came into Laura's life when she was about three, four at the most, after her Auntie Deanna, her father's wild and much younger sister came out to visit them for a few weeks from where she was then living, London, Laura thought, and ended up marrying Frank, the youngest of the brothers.

Auntie Deanna, effervescent and comforting, a vision of flamboyance with her unruly cloud of red hair, stood in stark contrast to the wives of the other four brothers: Laura's aunts Violet, Toni, Gladys and Margaret, an acerbic quartet whom Carlo dubbed 'the Old Skunks' within minutes of having been introduced to them. Auntie Deanna never had any children of her own, but instead acted as the elder confidante and den mother to a populous tribe of nieces and nephews, among whom Laura was the youngest. The Old Skunks were of another stamp. Laura, observing from the periphery, sensed that the boys found their ribald taunts annoying, and probably a little creepy. Their jabs towards the girls were no less sexual but more tactical, finely targeted, caustic barbs aimed at their appearance or attire, often propelling them to run away in tears.

Laura was the youngest by several years. By the time she reached her mid-teens and found herself their target, there was nobody sufficiently close in age to share her agonies, although she doubted that it was just her imagination that they were far nastier to her than they'd ever been to anybody else. And, as it eventually turned out, it was her Auntie Gladys who was the nastiest of the bunch. *Oh, well; ancient history.* After she retrieved four twenties from the bank machine, she made her way back to the office. So much work had piled up that she expected to be there until at least ten.

It was almost eight when Yvette showed up. Laura had set up in the board room, surrounded by computer screens displaying images of tents and hiking boots.

Yvette knocked on the woodwork. "What are you doing here?"

"Trying my best to save Wilderness Co-operative from itself. Reminds me of when I used to build sandcastles as a kid, trying to stop the tide from washing them away. What are you doing here?"

"Oh, I just finished a meeting with an entire committee from Sasamat Casino. It looks like they're going to hire us, but they seemed to really enjoy watching me squirm. Oh, and I just got off the phone with Hamish. We have to meet the Freaks on May long weekend. Just the Elders, Saturday morning, bright and early. In Sechelt."

"*Sechelt?* I guess it could be worse; at least you can *drive* there."

"There's still the ferry. So, Wilderness Co-operative, eh? I don't think that even *you* will be able to pull this one off." Laura gained a reputation as a master of her craft after one of her clients, a once-popular local submarine sandwich chain, faced ruin after the combined effects of a couple of badly chosen temporary foreign workers and a rat infestation culminated in an outbreak of bubonic plague at its New Westminster location. Her efforts allowed her client to stay in business, quite miraculously as far as most people were concerned.

"I know, I know," Laura said, "and they just keep digging themselves in deeper." The co-operative, which started out as a niche supplier of equipment for backpackers and mountain climbers, recently alienated half its customer base, first by changing its logo from a blue, stylized outline of Mount Garibaldi with the word 'Wilderness' beside it to a stark, corporate "WC"; and later by changing the focus of its inventory to fashionable, pastel-coloured outdoor clothing, to emulate a more lucrative outfit based in one of the New England states.

"The new Board of Directors seems to get that people who travel, especially to Europe, might be a wee bit embarrassed to wear clothing with their new logo, but they think it's a big joke. And the new clothing lines? Hikers hate them. The die-hards, and believe me, they're all over Vancouver, have nicknamed the place "the Prada Pit". She turned one of her laptop screens around to face Yvette. "See this? This is the website a bunch of disgruntled hikers have set up. 'Fuck the Prada Pit dot com'. And anyway, it's not like their new outdoor clothing is going to set the fashion world on fire. They wanted me to wear their clothes around in public as part of the salvage efforts, but no fucking way! We'll just say that the way their clothes are cut makes me look like a walking peanut."

"Well, good luck, I guess."

"Thanks." Laura's mood brightened. "Oh, you won't believe who I just ran into on Richards Street on the way here. My cousin Darla, remember her?"

"Darla, Darla; oh yes, I remember her. She's the one who looked like Pat Benatar."

"That's her."

"So, Darla; does she live here now? I seem to remember that she moved down to the States when we were still in university."

"She did. But she's back; she lives in town and has a gig selling pharmaceuticals."

"Just like more than a few of her cousins." Yvette laughed.

"Yeah, but the ones she sells are made in Germany rather than in some basement in Surrey."

"Her mother's your aunt; Aunt Gladys, wasn't it? That one sure was a piece of work."

"Oh, that she is. You should hear what her own daughter has to say about her; called her a 'cunt', no less."

"Hey, it fits." Yvette laughed. "I seem to remember that she created a very ugly scene at your place one night. We were in Grade Twelve, if I'm not mistaken."

"Oh, yeah. No matter how hard I try, I'll never forget it."

It was at a gathering of about thirty people in late March, her father's birthday party, well-attended by the Rafferty bunch, assuring that the night would end in one form of drunken chaos or another. This time Laura dreaded the evening more than usual. The extended clan who hadn't seen her since Christmas were supposed to be there, and she'd grown extravagantly plump in the span of mere months. She blamed her after-school job at Deirdre's Bakery, or maybe it was just some cruel genetic practical joke. Whatever made her blow up, she knew the Old Skunks in particular would relish doling out disparaging digs, accompanied by vile pats and pinches.

She presented herself in leggings and a loose pink blouse, a choice of attire she regretted as soon as she came downstairs. Fiona, at thirty-two the oldest of the Rafferty cousins save for Gladys' daughter Trianna, knelt on the landing, wiping chocolate off the face of her four-year-old. "Well, well, well," she said. "I see that someone's been having a little too much fun."

The Old Skunks were already sitting at the dining room table as Laura set down a breadbasket and a baking dish of roasted onions. The four of them were conversing in stage whisper so exaggerated that Laura could not imagine that they thought she couldn't hear, shamelessly inspecting her midsection as she reached over the table. "Nope, no doubt in my mind. What do you think, Vi? Two months?" her Auntie Toni whispered.

"Oh, Toni! She's already showing. I say three at least, maybe four."

After dinner, Laura and her Aunt Deanna shared a joint in a pleasant grove of fir and maple that had come to be known as the Enchanted Forest, down a short trail that started across the road.

"So where's your young man; final exams, I suppose?"

"Yup. Poor Carlo's buried up to his ears in books this weekend." Laura exhaled a toke. "Right now I'm feeling so guilty. I should really go back in and help. I mean, did you see that mountain of dishes?"

"But I suppose there are people in the kitchen you'd prefer to avoid." Deanna passed back the joint.

"Especially tonight. They seem to all be just sure that I'm pregnant."

"Oh, I know; I've been hearing all about it the entire evening, and Vi in particular can't be told otherwise. But this time, my dear, you brought it on yourself. Sampling too many of Deirdre's pastries has left you looking *quite* domestic around the edges."

"Look, I got a new job; you can stop nagging."

"I know, I'm sorry. I've been a pain in the ass lately, but you're such a pretty girl. Go, go help your mum. I'll be right behind you. I seem to have a calming effect on those four, even when they're three sheets to the wind." Deanna's smile drooped. "You aren't, are you?"

"*No!*"

Laura tried to slink unnoticed toward the kitchen sink. The Old Skunks were all sitting at the kitchen table, sharing a giant bottle of Crown Royal someone had picked up at the duty-free at the border. Only Violet's daughter Fiona was helping with the dishes. "Ha!" Gladys bellowed. "Looks like one young miss larded up in a big hurry!"

"That's enough," Laura's mother said.

"Yup, packin' on the baby weight, that's what happens." Violet said. "They all think that they're too special for it to happen to them. Nope. Get hooked on the 'aah, aah, aah' business and surprise, surprise, before you know it you're gettin' broad across the beam and there's a bun risin' in the oven!"

"How do you change a fox into an elephant?" Toni giggled. "*Knock her up!*"

"She is *not* pregnant. Stop your nonsense." Her mother spoke with a calmness that Laura knew could veer from serenity to inchoate rage in an instant.

Margaret took another gulp of whisky. "Won't be able to hide it for much longer."

Violet finished the dregs from her glass and poured another. "Yeah, Birgitta, you're the Queen of De-Nile! What do you think she does with her skinny little Eye-talian, hold hands? Nope, no doubt about it, four months along." She turned around to swat Laura's rear end with a sharp crack. "And the big fat ass got here right on schedule." Laura closed her eyes.

"It's okay," Fiona said in a soothing tone. Sometimes she played Laura's sympathetic ally, but on occasion she was as mean as any of the Skunks. "I got pregnant too in my senior year. And I see you making the same mistake that I did. You think that you can eat whatever you damn well please." She laughed. "Look at you! You're already getting the cutest little double chin. So you'd better watch out. By my sixth month I was *gross*. Fuck did I get huge, waddling around in a mu-mu. To this day I'm surprised that Pete actually showed up for the wedding!" Laura looked down at her cousin's slender hips and considered her comment with scepticism. She glanced behind her to see Deanna pass the refrigerator.

"Yeah," Violet said, slurring. "You got pretty big there for a couple of years."

"And you're lucky." Fiona took a dish from Laura to dry it. "You'll be able to graduate. I had Tiffany just after Easter; I never finished."

"Yup, looks like you made it just inside the wire. But you're going to need an extra-extra-large graduation gown 'cause by then you'll be a big fat butterball and out to here to boot!" Violet smirked, waving her arms in front of her in an arc motion. The four of them erupted in a chorus of rye-leavened cackling.

"I'm telling you, shut up now, all of you," her mother said, with a timbre that Laura knew signalled a pending eruption.

Gladys slurped from her glass. "No, no; as usual, you girls are all wet. She's not pregnant, just gettin' fat. All that's growing inside her these days are Deirdre Gordon's missing profits, jiggling underneath those tights she's wearing now that she's too fat for jeans."

"Oh, bullshit, Gladys," Violet said. "It's baby time for the little princess!"

"Nope, not yet, but not to worry, girls, she'll be swelling up soon enough." Violet, Toni and Margaret cackled. "I mean, just look at you; you've put on so much weight that you're even more of a Miss Piggy than my Trianna was when *she* got knocked up."

"That's enough, Gladys!" Deanna said.

"But you know what, maybe our not-so-little-any-more princess can put it off for a little longer. Best form of birth control for you? Just ride your little Spic on top," Gladys shrieked, "and you'll snap his pelvis before he comes!" All four Old Skunks erupted in coarse, drunken laughter.

Even if fifteen years had passed, the recollection still made Laura cry. "Oh, stop it!" Yvette laughed. "Although, I guess you could say it was a memorable night. By the time Rosalie and I got there," she said, recalling another one of their high school friends they'd both long since lost contact with. "The place was a fucking zoo; you were gone and everyone was shouting. And your mother and your dad's sister, what's her name?"

"Deanna."

"Yeah, Deanna. Both of them were *screaming* at Gladys, although between your aunt's Scottish accent, and your mother was so furious that there was a lot of Danish mixed in, I had no idea what they were saying. Anyway, when I went to find you in your room, you were a bit of a mess."

"Yes," Laura sighed. "Back in the day, those four had a way of getting under my skin."

"But you know, to be fair, those old lushes weren't the only ones back then who thought you and Carlo had a baby on the way."

Laura looked over the array of electronic equipment surrounding her. "Anyway, ancient history. But what a pathetic pair we are. Eight o'clock on a Friday night and we're here, in the office."

"You've been doing this a lot."

"Yup, it's probably better this way. No boys allowed after Kevin, fuckin' piece of shit."

"Yeah, he was a real winner, but lately, you've had quite a run of them. At least the rest of them didn't *steal* from you."

"We'll just call it an expensive lesson. And it wasn't just the money. Not something that I want to repeat, ever." She started to shut down her assembly of laptops. "But then again, what did I expect, after what I did?"

"Oh, no! That's enough of that. Don't you start up again with *this* bullshit! You're at it again, and this time you're not even drunk."

"It's not bullshit; and you know it. Yes, I've gotten no worse than what I deserved. I wrecked both of our lives, as far as I can tell, anyway. He's had as bad a time as you can imagine, and..."

"Don't be an idiot! And I've said it hundreds of times before. You know very well that you didn't have anything to do with what happened later."

"That really doesn't matter. What I did was inexplicably stupid and cruel. It makes me sick to my stomach whenever I think about what I did, back in the day. And you said it to me yourself: Carlo deserved much better. Karma's a bitch, so I'd better get used to it."

"All right. I'm not getting into this argument with you. Not tonight. Have you eaten?"

"No, not yet."

"Good. Let's go to Pizzeria Vesuvio; it's a new place over on Homer Street. I went there with...with Declan; it was, ah, a working dinner, last week. It's good; just like that place that you and...oh, fuck...well, where you used to go in Toronto, you know, the one on Queen Street."

"Yvette, don't be ridiculous. Pizzeria Spacca Napoli. *Carlo* and I used to go there; it was a good place. So this Vesuvio, it's as good as that?"

"Yes, well, as far as I can remember."

"Sounds good. I could do with a good pizza."

* * *

The de Bosch Kemper Gallery was behind a row of seafood markets in an alley on Granville Island. Carlo got there early; he browsed the gallery before guests started to arrive, a display of paintings and prints, wood and soapstone carvings, statues and metalwork. Most of the works on display were for sale, the creations of local artists represented by Paula's agency. A small alcove contained her own work, delicate ceramic figurines in a classic, northern European style.

Declan found Carlo in front of a glass display cabinet and guided him by the forearm. "Carlo, I'd like you to meet my wife! Paula, meet our new associate, Carlo."

"Hmm...Carlo. Italian?"

"Yes."

"You won't like the wine; Declan chose it."

With pointed reluctance, Paula allowed Carlo to set up a long table and arrange a number of chairs. After he performed his task to her satisfaction, she asked him to open a number of bottles of Chattering Squirrel, a Cabernet from somewhere in the Interior, to allow them to breathe, and then put a few more bottles of "Effervescent Elderberry" into the cooler.

"What is this stuff? I've never heard of it," Carlo said, pointing to one of the green, conic bottles.

Paula looked at him with a puzzled expression. "Oh, that's right; you haven't been here very long. Here in Vancouver, it's *très chic,* and," she said, lowering her voice. "His silly religion owns the factory. It's supposed to be organic and composed of all-natural ingredients, spring water from streams that flow into Bute Inlet; you get the idea. Maybe it is, but if you know what's good for you, you won't drink a sip of it. It tastes like stale almonds and cigarette butts. But some of the people who are coming here tonight would probably drink anything."

The first of the guests seemed to be other artists who had storefronts or second floor *ateliers* on Granville Island. One of early arrivals, Detlef, a German who owned the glass-blowing boutique across from Paula's studio, insisted on speaking to Carlo in Italian once they were introduced.

"Sí, sí, quell' piazza, Campo dei Fiori, mi piace un' sacco." On being told that Carlo recently lived there, Detlef started listing off his favourite landmarks in central Rome, gesticulating with a wine glass which Gaskin refilled on his way past, tilting a bottle of Riesling from a winery in the Okanagan he boasted of owning.

"Mamma mia, you-a guys-a-sure-a-make-alotta-noise-a," Declan said, affecting an accent befitting a canned pasta commercial.

"Declan, you're such a jerk," Paula said.

"Would you like some of this, Carlo?" Gaskin pointed the label towards him. "You better get what you can, before the rest of the guests arrive. Oh, and before I forget; Marika, meet Carlo. Marika will be working as your legal assistant come Monday."

A girl with a long, lush mane of wavy red hair extended her hand. Although she was taller than expected, David's description of her was adequate if uncharitable, and starkly accurate in one unmistakable respect. Carlo strained to avoid staring at her chest.

"You two have much in common," Declan said in a deepening tone. "Marika's Polish too!"

"Latvian, actually." She tilted her head. "I always thought that Carlo was an Italian name."

"It is."

No words. Marika walked over to help Paula, who was placing sausage rolls on a tray. Detlef was soon cornered by a heavily perfumed lady in a luxuriant dress, probably one of his customers. Before Carlo had an opportunity to pour himself another glass of wine, Marika hooked her hand around his arm. "Come on," she said. "Let's go outside while I have a smoke!" Declan peered across the room at them with unconcealed interest as Marika towed Carlo across the gallery.

Once they were out in the courtyard, Marika sat on top of a picnic table and lit up a cigarette. She turned out to be even more substantial than she seemed on first impression, with a daunting silhouette and full, well-shaped legs; someone who would have drawn his abrupt attention if she walked past him, anonymous, on a crowded city sidewalk.

"Declan seems a little confused today," Carlo said after Marika blew out a cloud of smoke. "I've long since given up trying to figure out what he's talking about; half the time he doesn't make any sense. He's like an absent-minded professor." She flicked some ashes into a beer bottle straddling the boards on the seat.

"How long have you worked for him?"

"A little over two years." She took a deep drag from her cigarette. "He's definitely an original. So, anyway, what do you do for fun?"

"I don't know. I haven't been back in Vancouver for long; I was in Italy for three years. I mean, I just got hired yesterday."

"Three *years*? Declan said that you had been away for a while, but three *years*? That's a long communion with your roots. And I asked you what you do for *fun*."

"For fun? I don't know, now that I'm back, other than going out carousing, I'll probably do a lot of hiking, maybe a bit of skiing. Why, what do you do?"

"As you can see, not enough." She patted her hips.

"That doesn't look very likely."

"Thanks, very chivalrous." She shifted on her perch and crossed her legs. "You know, all of the Italians I've known have been lecherous. You haven't tried to grope me yet."

"All of the Latvians I've run into have been clinically depressed. I'm not so much chivalrous as..."

Marika tilted her chin up and laughed. "All right, no more ethnic stereotypes. But we'll have to go out for a drink some time; I'd like to hear all about Italy."

The gallery was filled with fashionably-dressed people once Carlo and Marika went back inside. As Paula predicted, many of the guests avoided wine and beer, both available in abundance, and opted for Effervescent Elderberry instead. Carlo succumbed to curiosity and poured a few drops, maybe a thimbleful of the sparkling grey liquid into his glass. Paula's description proved accurate. He went over to the sink and washed out his glass under a brisk stream of cold water. During his search for a wine bottle, he inadvertently veered into a gap between two large glass display cases and found himself cornered by a woman with an anarchic explosion of hair, rattling with bracelets and necklaces of opaque crystals that anchored an enormous kaftan.

"Your fields of energy!" she shrieked in a manic but musical voice. "And your *aural radiation*! It's so *satisfying*!"

The woman carried on for what seemed like half an hour until Carlo saw Marika appear behind her, his view of her partially eclipsed by tangled tufts of hair. Marika took his hand and pulled him out of the niche he was trapped in. "He's with me, Lydia!"

"I hope you didn't mind," Marika whispered. "You looked like you were being water-boarded!"

"Oh, not at all; and thanks! Who the fuck was that?"

"Oh, that was Lydia Galway. She's rich, I think her father owned a sawmill or something. One of Paula's customers. I don't think she's a member of the religion; she has whacko theories of her own." Marika reached for a wine bottle and filled her glass. "I hate being around her. She just seems like the kind of person who would steal an article of my clothing and burn it in some kind of ritual in her basement." Marika waved at two people approaching, a young Indian woman accompanied by a much older man. "Oh hey, Bal, Thomas, here is our new lawyer Carlo, I'm sorry, I can't pronounce your last name."

"Buonsante."

"Oh, Buonsante. Anyway, meet Baljinder and Thomas. Bal is Declan's secretary (she'll be doing your work, too) and Thomas has been a paralegal there for twenty years."

"Nice of you to date me like that, young lady." Thomas spoke with what Carlo identified as a South London accent. "Buonsante." He pronounced it perfectly. "Italian, are you? My first wife, she was an Italian. I'll try not to hold it against you." Thomas held a dour expression.

"How many wives have you had?"

Thomas punched him on the shoulder. "I suppose you're quick enough on the uptake," he laughed, "to work with us! Thomas Balfour." They shook hands.

Bal theatrically rolled her eyes. "Pleased to meet you, Carlo."

By ten o'clock, the gallery started to empty. Carlo, Bal and Marika cleared wine glasses and fit them into the dishwasher in the small kitchen at the back.

"Does anyone need a ride?" Declan asked in a baying tone, his hands clasped together in front of him. The four of them all accepted the offer. "Hmm, I don't know if you'll all fit. Oh, we'll try, no problem." Declan displayed the effects of many glasses of wine; Carlo hoped that Paula, who'd had little to drink, would be the driver.

"Where do you live, Carlo?" Paula shouted across the gallery.

"Oh, drop me off at Kits Beach, if you could. I'm staying with some friends who live just up the hill a bit on York Street."

"Sure; you're the closest, we'll drop you off first."

Bal, Thomas and Carlo crammed themselves into the back seat of Paula's Lexus, while Declan, reclining in the front passenger seat, started to nod off. Marika opened the back door next to Carlo and placed herself decisively on his lap. Carlo saw Paula glance at them in the rear-view mirror with a smirk. Declan grumbled with a gentle snore.

As Paula manoeuvred the Lexus slowly through the narrow laneways of Granville Island, Carlo glanced out the window and laboured to fill his mind with images of raw sewage and dead rats to discourage the erection threatening to emerge. After Paula dropped him off, Carlo noticed a piece of note paper sticking out of his pocket. He opened it and read it under a street lamp.

Meet me for coffee on Monday am. at around 8:30 at Calista's on Cordova....it's not too far from the office.
M.

7

A group of twelve, five men and seven women, sat assembled in the penthouse of one of the towers on Vancouver's downtown peninsula, facing a blank flat screen. All were dressed in tailored suits of sundry shades of grey. The light of the Toronto Dominion sign atop one of the adjacent Bentall buildings lent the dimly-lit boardroom a greenish cast. Hastings Street stretched beneath them like a sparkling, jewelled ribbon extending as far to the east as they could see. The lights of North Vancouver made the black silhouettes of Grouse Mountain and Mount Seymour seem to vibrate as if alive. While they waited, a girl dressed much like a flight attendant placed drinks on napkins beside each of them.

"What are you drinking?" one of the women asked the man sitting in the chair next to her.

"Eighteen-year-old Laphroaig. You?"

"Nothing so fancy. Gin and tonic: my husband insists that I try to economize."

"Gilbeys?"

"God forbid. Williams Chase. There's no need to get carried away!"

"Ah."

A man with closely cropped black hair with an ample admixture of grey appeared next to the screen. "Good evening, everyone! Welcome to new and old members of the Reformed Striationist Totality," he said in a playful French accent. "We will begin tonight's session. I hope that you are feeling relaxed."

With the lights out, the flat screen abruptly came to life, showing successive images of glacial striations gouged in bare rock bluffs and scoured slopes. The twelve of them sat with their eyes transfixed on images that flashed and faded into new ones every few seconds. Subdued electronic music played from speakers behind them, the opening strains of *Funeral for a Friend.* The music meandered at first to accompany images of peaceful, moss-covered ruts and scratches. But the tempo picked up. Striations alternated with oozing springs, small waterfalls and cataracts, themselves spewing in greater abundance as the music enlivened, until the spirited crescendo, when the screen filled with a stony gap in a rock face that shot out a forceful jet of water, almost like a geyser. The images returned to a subdued, bucolic elegance as the music softened, the screen eventually fading to black. Dim incandescent light illuminated the boardroom.

The man who had been drinking scotch stared ahead, stricken, his eyes agape, unblinking. The woman beside him wept. "That was so inspiring," she whined through a plugged nose.

After someone switched on the overhead lights the dark-haired man rose to face of the group, smiling; one arm outstretched, his fist clenched. "Upward and to the right!" he declared in a deepening voice.

"Upward and to the right!" the crowd chanted in return.

"And that concludes tonight's session. If you were not already aware, you can pre-register on the religion's website for our Convocation at the Bayshore in the fall. And," he said, displaying his teeth in an extravagant grin. "Please remember: you will receive a seven percent discount if we receive payment at least five days before the next session at the end of the month. Thank you for your reverence." He bowed and left the room.

The twelve quietly gathered their briefcases and umbrellas and made their way to the bank of elevators.

8

Artifice is the very basis of contemporary society and the soul of homo oeconomicus. *Modern commerce rests upon outlandish claims and outright deceit. Lies encourage people to improve and excel. Indeed, anyone who fails to employ trickery does not deserve his or her earnings, however paltry. This is not lost on the modern-day consuming public. Most people seem to grasp that expecting the truth is a sign of stupidity. Everyone knows that the only people who still actually believe that insurance companies treat their policy holders with the utmost good faith are either childlike or mentally deranged.*

- Gavin Skoff, in *The Amiable Plunderer.*

They always held the Victoria meetings of 'VisualEyes Vancouver Island!' in a third-floor boardroom overlooking Bastion Square. Laeticia glanced over the ghastly Warhol-inspired poster at the entrance announcing the event, embossed with the VisualEyes logo, a light blue silhouette of Vancouver Island flanked by two pert, feminine eyes. The boardroom teemed with mingling professionals, awaiting the inevitable pep talk and, in the fullness of time, the guest speaker, Dr. Olafsen, a marine biologist from Sweden or somewhere. Those who weren't foisting business cards on one another were leaning against available bulwarks, mesmerized by their mobile phones. Effervescent Elderberry, a local product featuring a salmon leaping over Mount Seymour on its label and containing more alcohol than beer, sponsored the event. Free, uncorked bottles of the acrid potion stood at tables all over the room. Most of the guests ignored them, instead content to pay for Stella Artois and garnet-hued Malbec. The room was suffused with the scent of Aveda products.

Laeticia spotted Gavin Skoff at the other end of the room, first pacing with a brisk gait and now circling a trio of white-haired men like a raptor. Two women sat at the greeter's table at the entrance, coated with pamphlets and rows of name-tags, arranged in alphabetical order. One of them, Patricia Wilson, the reigning Minister of the Environment, rose from her chair and gave Laeticia a fond, sisterly embrace.

"Laeticia, how nice to see you!" Patricia, a slender woman of indeterminate age and shoulder-length brown hair, usually found herself assigned the task of organizing VisualEyes public functions. She pointed toward the tables, set up in a 'T' shape. "I've seated you well away from the remnants of the Canadian Airborne Regiment." She tilted her head toward a group of men of various ages who chirped with unmistakably lascivious chatter, probably members of the same rugby team. Their attentions had been consumed by the conventionally-distracting tall tanned blonde just walking in, but swiftly turned to Laeticia as soon as one of them caught sight of her.

"Thank you." Laeticia said.

"Can I offer you anything to drink; Elderberry, perhaps?"

"I'll have a Stella."

"Good choice. Nobody with any taste actually likes that crap. And I hope you had a decent breakfast. Lunch is going to be a bit sparse. Oh, by the way, VisualEyes screwed up on your place card; by the time I found out, it was too late to do anything about it. Sorry."

Laeticia saw a dishevelled older man, standing by himself and looking out the window toward the Inner Harbour. He must have been Dr. Olafsen. His sports jacket was corduroy and of a style that was at least thirty years out of date. Everybody else in the room seemed elegant by comparison; the politicians and lawyers dressed in dark wool suits and the array of real estate promoters and public relations people dressed in the sleek and costly informal wear unavoidable at wine bars or *après-ski*. One of them was easily recognized: Garth Willingdon, the premier of British Columbia, a tall, imposing man with lucent teeth and a carefully arranged brown *bouffant* that resembled roast beef piled on toast. His short, desperate Minister of Economic Development, Lawrence Roswell Gollander, stood beside him, a man with the twitchy bearing of somebody who anticipated imminent arrest.

Patricia handed Laeticia a glass of Stella. "Come with me, Laeticia, I'll make some introductions. Garth!" She tapped the premier's shoulder. "Garth Willingdon, I'd like to introduce Laeticia Bradbury. She's a junior faculty member in the Biology Department at UVic who's doing some consulting work for us on the Georgia Basin group."

Willingdon, much taller than Laeticia, looked down at her with a benign smile. "Laeticia...hmm, you don't look *that* Black...or African American...or Canadian...or whatever." His voice trailed off.

Patricia sighed. "I'm introducing her, Garth."

"I am very pleased to meet you, Laeticia," the premier murmured.

Patricia turned to the shorter man standing next to him. "I'd also like you to meet Lawrence Gollander. Lawrence, Laeticia Bradbury."

"Lawrence *Roswell* Gollander," He was so ill at ease that Laeticia could actually feel him vibrate when she shook his hand. "Consultant, eh? I hope that it's coming out of *your* ministry budget."

"Of course it is, Lawrence." Patricia sighed. They left the two men standing by themselves. "He really is a very nice man, just a little odd." Laeticia couldn't tell if she was talking about the premier or Gollander. They approached a bulky man whom Laeticia recognized as the Minister of Finance. "Laeticia Bradbury, Terrence Goyter."

"Pleased to make your acquaintance," he uttered as Laeticia shook his hand. He was yet another of at least a dozen middle-aged men whom she'd met in recent months who could speak without opening their mouths.

"Oh," Patricia groaned. "Fabién," she said quietly as a tall, younger man with a cowl of lustrous dark hair bore down on them. Laeticia didn't know his name, but she recognized him as the Minister of Transportation, *de facto* leader of the youth wing of the Liberal Party and a man worshipped by the libertarian faction on campus.

"Well, hello!" He grinned, extending his hand toward Laeticia.

"Yes, Fabién. Fabién Lerche, meet Laeticia Bradbury." Patricia introduced him without even a hint of enthusiasm. "Laeticia is on faculty at UVic; she's been doing some consulting work with VisualEyes."

"I'm *very* pleased to meet you." Fabién's voice deepened as they shook hands.

An unusually short man in late middle age who brought to mind a Toby jug entered the room, followed by a detail of four assistants, all of them younger than twenty-five and three of them female. Laeticia recognized him as Roland Egbert, the chairman of the development permit committee in her Regional District, the principal municipal authority on rural Vancouver Island. Lerche took the man's right hand and clasped it in both of his. "Roland, Roland, how have you been keeping?"

"Not bad, but I'll be much better off once I get a drink!" His lone male assistant scurried toward the bar as if discharged from a slingshot. After a barely perceptible interval of time, he returned to hand Roland what looked like a whisky and soda.

Gavin, still pacing, circled closer to them but was so engrossed in his BlackBerry that he almost bumped into Patricia. "Oh, I'm sorry, Patricia, I...oh, hello, Laeticia. I didn't know *you* were going to be at this function."

"Oh, I'm doing some consulting for VisualEyes through my appointment at UVic; even more now that I have a spot on the Strait of Georgia Basin Research Initiative."

"How did you get mixed up with that bunch of Communists?"

"I see that Gavin, is, well, still Gavin. How are you?" Patricia said. "I didn't know you two knew each other."

"We're neighbours, up in Parksville," Gavin said. "We always seem to meet up at the mailbox."

"Oh. I didn't know that. Anyway, after this is finished, we'll be having a brief meeting in Fabién's office. It's across the way at the Laurel Point Inn."

"Sure, sure. I'd better run," Gavin said, glancing again at his BlackBerry. "The professor's seaplane for Seattle leaves in less than two hours. We'd better get this underway." Gavin walked over to the head of the long table and asked everyone to take their seats. Laeticia had little trouble finding her place card.

Laeticia Bradbury

Graduate Student

She swore under her breath and sat down.

Gavin bounded up to the podium to a growling sequence of guitar strains, the beginning of a song that Laeticia remembered as an old Deep Purple standard, soon joined by a driving, piston-like rhythm. The music faded as the screen behind him illuminated with a photograph of a sunset over the Strait of Georgia, the SeaMent logo gradually appearing as a ghostly presence over the horizon.

"We have…", Gavin started.

Patricia theatrically cleared her throat.

"Oh, yes," Gavin said. "I have the honour of speaking to you on the unceded territory of the Songhees First Nation."

"And today, we have the honour of the presence of Dr. Hans Olafsen, of the Trident Institute in Hamburg." Gavin announced. "For those of you who do not know of Dr. Olafsen, he has been involved in research spanning more than a decade concerning the creation of ceramics from sea water."

"His work has resulted in a patent for SeaMent, an innovative and inexpensive building material in which VisualEyes and a number of manufacturing and construction businesses have become very interested." Olafsen nodded politely. "For those of you who are unfamiliar with his research, Dr. Olafsen has developed an innovative electrolysis technique to blend and bond elements and minerals in ocean water, creating a very resilient ceramic. He has agreed to assist VisualEyes in the role of a consultant, to give us technical guidance in all of our commercial ventures, and in particular, the Vancouver Island Submarine Tunnel project."

Laeticia saw Olafsen cringe.

Everyone in the room clapped in muted applause. "Well, you don't need to hear any more from me. Ladies and gentlemen, Dr. Hans Olafsen, professor emeritus of physics!"

Dr. Olafsen rose slowly from his chair and took the podium. "Thank you, ladies and gentlemen." He spoke with an austere Scandinavian accent. "This is the first time I have ever been to Canada. I must say that Victoria is truly an idyllic part of the world."

Nobody reacted. Laeticia expected that most people in the audience had heard so many complimentary words about their city that they actually found them annoying. "The VisualEyes organization, and the SeaMent project is a wonderful opportunity, with endless future potential. I am honoured to be of assistance to you here in British Columbia."

"The SeaMent construction material initiative is viable, and will eventually allow us to manufacture sturdy, light and inexpensive construction materials, which will reduce the pressure on the planet's forests." Several members of the audience frowned. "But I wish that Mr. Skoff had mentioned that he was interested in a project of such magnitude. The submarine tunnel concept is beyond our current scientific capabilities. Even if we were able to achieve it, the process would be *most* harmful environmentally, and prohibitively costly." As he spoke, a team of serving staff dressed in white and navy blue distributed small plates, each bearing a red, gelatinous dome.

A man with a deep tan and a thatch of white hair leaned forward. "We don't need any more foreigners lecturing us about the environment!"

"That's right," a woman not much older than Laeticia said in a bored, cynical tone. "We have enough of our own resident eco-freaks."

"I am not lecturing you; I am warning you," Dr. Olafsen said. "The necessary technology does not exist. Any attempt to perform the prescribed electrolysis in open water will be very hazardous to, oh, what do you say in English, public health."

"Haaahzahdous!" A prominent local real estate agent mocked Dr. Olafsen's accent.

Dr. Olafsen winced. "I am not saying that you shouldn't do this; you should rather do that, in a purely normative sense. It is much more drastic than that. I am saying that you simply cannot do what Mr. Skoff seems to be proposing. If you embark upon this project, people will die."

"Normative!" A woman in a grey business suit beside Laeticia shouted. "Another damned academic. Tell me, can you give us any information we can actually use?" The two women sitting next to her nodded and murmured in agreement. Olafsen appeared puzzled and turned to speak to Gavin, who shook his head in response.

"I can say this..." Dr. Olafsen started.

An older man in a blue, brass-buttoned blazer interrupted him. "But professor," he started in a deep, melodious voice. "Is

Mr. Skoff's proposal possible? Now, that is a question that can be explored from a number of angles, but I am simply asking, will it work?"

"Now, today, the answer is no. Can it work? Perhaps; but it will take years in the laboratory to determine whether it is technically feasible, before testing it in an open, marine environment. Even if it can be done and it does not present a threat to life and limb, it will not be cost effective."

The woman sitting next to Laeticia spoke up again. "How about it if you leave that question to those who are trained to deal with it; you stick to the science, leave the business case to us!"

"Oh, may I keep the science?" Dr Olafsen remarked with a faint smile. "You're the one who just made fun of academics."

A younger man with red hair leaned back in his chair. "Why don't you just keep quiet? If Europeans actually knew what they were talking about, they wouldn't be broke and overrun by Arabs!" Gavin stared at his napkin.

Olafsen clenched his hands on the rim of the podium but kept his voice even. "I...am...merely warning you...of some very real...peril."

"But Dr. Olafsen," an older woman, seated behind Patricia said in a nasal tone. "Surely you must agree that people in your field have a habit of overstating risks."

"You got that right! What about all this global warming bullshit?" somebody shouted.

"Or second-hand smoke!"

Olafsen looked up at the ceiling and returned his attention to the audience. "If ignorance is bliss, this room must be paradise!"

The man with red hair emptied his dish of aspic into his hand and threw it at Olafsen, who displayed unexpectedly quick reflexes and promptly ducked. The red gel, reinforced with sprigs of arugula, hit the wall behind him and slid toward the floor, finally nudging Gavin from his seemingly anaesthetized state.

"Now people, Dr. Olafsen was kind enough to accept our invitation and fly here all the way from Hamburg!"

But the audience ignored him. A flurry of aspic followed, accompanied by shouting from the crowd; coarse expletives punctuating their opinions of Olafsen and his Scandinavian brethren, all summarily declared licentious and vile. Laeticia doubted that their actual sentiment toward Olafsen actually matched the extravagance of their insulting words, but for the time being, he represented every professor who assigned one of them a failing grade, every community activist who thwarted a questionable development and every loathed environmentalist who protested the injudicious release of effluent. As agitated as this gathering of lawyers, resort owners and real estate agents might have been, their rage would seem placid compared to the surrounding populace, most of whom would have cheerfully dismembered them if they found out that they were conspiring to build a bridge to the mainland.

While she ducked to avoid flying lumps of aspic launched by the people behind her, Laeticia saw a welcome chance to flee and followed a trio of real estate agents through the fire door across from them. She called Mario as soon as she emerged outside in Bastion Square; voicemail, this time. "Hey, it's me. Don't ask. Just reserve at the usual place. I'll be there by seven."

Olafsen left the room quickly without even exchanging a glance with Gavin. Willingdon, his face drained of colour, sat deflated in his seat next to Goyter by the podium. "Come on, Gavin." Goyter spoke with a phlegmatic drawl. "Let's get together at Fabién's office. I'll get a couple of cars to meet us downstairs."

Gavin took a ride with Gollander and Patricia from Bastion Square to Lerche's private office in the Laurel Point Inn, a hotel on the Inner Harbour. He stayed as close to the door as he could without seeming cowardly. The five politicians positioned themselves around the room but avoided eye contact with one another. Lerche stood perusing the Oxford dictionary, splayed open on a lectern.

Goyter cleared his throat. "Are we going to wait for Perry?"

"He's in Terrace," Willingdon said.

"What the hell?"

"Yes," Patricia said. "Public Affairs scheduled him at a Chamber of Commerce luncheon. Then he's doing a ribbon cutting ceremony for the new composting facility in Vanderhoof. Those kinds of events are too tedious to attract serious journalists."

"Poor Perry." Goyter said.

"Poor Perry my ass." Patricia said. "I don't have a great deal of sympathy for him."

Gavin had known Perry for several years. Perry Chatham, the Minister of Health. He'd placed second for the leadership of the Liberal Party, only fifteen delegates behind Willingdon on the third ballot. A Londoner by birth, Oxford educated, he came to British Columbia about eight years earlier with his wife, a cellist lured from Europe to play in the Vancouver Symphony.

Perry's luck changed after his calamitous attempt at health care reform. Even Gavin thought that he should have known better. Any well-publicized attempt to supplant the existing Canadian medical system with a capitalist-infused model would inevitably end in political humiliation, but this one turned out to be, well, a poetic failure. The saga began when Chatham identified an opportunity in a Fundamentalist Mormon enclave in the West Kootenays. "Abundance", an expanse of meadow and timber bigger than many national parks, was home to eight men (the "elders"), their one hundred and four wives, and more than six hundred children. After one of the elders was jailed for crimes ranging from tax evasion to child molesting, the remaining seven scattered like mites, leaving the women and children to fend for themselves.

So there it was: an isolated population in a remote location most people in Vancouver had never heard of. The perfect beta test site, an ideal laboratory. His concept was simple enough: a group of investors would charge a percentage of Abundance's quarterly sales of produce, mainly vegetables that were sufficiently misshapen to titillate aficionados of organic produce, and serve as a management committee, approving or rejecting treatments recommended by a select team of doctors for their captive patients. Chatham even devised a name for it, 'ComuniCare', even if he had no intention of making it public until it achieved token success that he could trumpet to the Vancouver press.

It didn't take Chatham long to assemble a few investors, all of whom could scarcely believe their luck: being paid, even bestowed a handsome start-up subsidy, to provide health care to a community composed of the young and healthy. So they stealthily pocketed the annual vaccination grant, and as long as the quarterly remittance came in as expected, the investors simply ignored Abundance. Rumours abounded in nearby Kaslo and Nelson for two years, and the following spring a few curious high school students went in to see for themselves. Aghast at what they'd seen, they posted photos on Instagram, sparking the attention of *Médecins sans frontières*, the revered Doctors without Borders.

The young doctors dispatched to the district, all hardened by volunteer work in Africa, were nonetheless horrified to find such a scene in Canada; children howling with whooping cough and aflame with measles, pre-teens hobbling around with rickets. Some of the young women bled from their gums, their biological reserves already depleted by serial childbirth. Scurvy.

It was the first real scandal of Willingdon's young government. Chatham offered his resignation from Cabinet, but the premier refused to accept it. After all, Chatham had neither lied nor stolen, and most of the party was in complete philosophical agreement with him. As long as public outrage on the subject persisted, however, Chatham was banished to his townhouse in West Vancouver, a safe enough distance from Victoria.

"Well," Goyter said, "Perry or no Perry, it looks like we have a problem. The professor who invented the process is not on board."

"We have taken a controlling interest in his research company. It's not as if he can *stop* us from using it for whatever we want," Lerche said.

Gavin remained in his alcove near the entrance, as if protecting himself from attack. "I'm sorry. I told him that his technology could have some application to the fixed link project but he didn't have such a reaction..."

Patricia and Goyter were both trying to salvage a bottle of wine after its cork disintegrated when Goyter tried to open it. "You apparently did not make yourself understood," Patricia cut him off. "Look, I'm not the only one who thinks that this is a stupid idea. It's going to stir up no end of protest! We could run the ferries for a century on what this boondoggle is going to cost us."

Goyter released a light belch. "At least there were no members of the press to witness that display. We might have to threaten..."

"Thank you, Gavin," Patricia interrupted. "We'll have to discuss this amongst ourselves, think of it as an impromptu cabinet meeting."

"Of course!" Gavin said, relieved to finally escape. "I will be in touch."

Willingdon rose to pour himself a glass of wine. "Patricia is quite correct on one count. Things will get much worse if the proposal for the McKee McWatney lands development ever becomes public."

Goyter jumped as if poked by a pin. "Let's worry about one public relations quagmire at a time, shall we? We have to get the bridge business over with first."

"It's a fixed link," Willingdon corrected him.

Lerche, now at his desk, cupped his chin in his hands. "These fucking tree huggers are at it again. And those god-damned Striationists; if this keeps up, they'll derail the whole thing."

"Let's not be picking fights with the Orthodox offshoot," Willingdon said. "We're their spiritual heirs, even with the unfortunate event of the schism."

"Garth, have you forgotten who you're talking to?" Gollander said. We joined that bunch of swindlers because we had to, not because either one of us actually believes in it. And as for you, I know very well that your wife drags you by the ear off to St. George's to take Communion every Sunday." It was true. After almost a year of persistent nagging, Willingdon finally relented, as long as they went to a church in a locale unknown to anyone of the political class. He decided on St. George's because it was in an unfashionable district of Victoria that had only recently acquired a Starbucks.

Willingdon chuckled. "*Please* don't pass that little tidbit around."

"Whatever. The Striationists are bad enough, but the environmentalists are worse." Lerche said.

But you're a Striationist too, aren't you?" Patricia said with a mischievous smirk.

"This isn't just going to be the environmentalists, Fabién." Goyter said.

"They're ninety percent of it," Lerche said. "And there is far too much at stake. We have to find some way to neutralize them. The local press is easy to deal with; just take them out for a hockey game and a piss-up and they're our pals. But it's the U.S. and the European outlets, remember that fucking Bolshevik from the *Guardian*?"

Goyter swallowed. "Well, we *were* trying to feed him a lot of horseshit."

The premier pulled his Blackberry out of his pocket in response to a persistent buzzing sound. "It's Smollitt," he said, referring to his communications director. "It seems that word of the little dustup in Bastion Square has spread across the Straits. The CBC has requested a comment." He used his thumbs to type a response.

Lerche pondered framed two posters hanging above his desk, one, a late-Seventies still of the rock group Rush, the other an enlargement of the cover of *Atlas Shrugged*. "We can't let that happen again. No one in Europe bought so much as a two by four from us for almost a year after the Klanawa Rainforest debacle."

"We could hire those spin doctors again, who was it last time; Bundon Larouche?" Willingdon said.

"No," Lerche said. "Too expensive. And we don't need a public relations firm; we need Darth Vader."

Goyter smiled. "Yes, a little violence might be just what we need to get this bunch of college kids and the rest of the CBC crowd to stay home. But it can't be linked to us."

"There are *people* we can hire who do that sort of thing," Lerche said.

Gollander jerked and danced about as if dodging bullets. "This is the sort of respect I get! This is what you think of me! That's what I said fifteen years ago! Remember, when everybody under the age of thirty flocked to Tofino? 'The Rain Forest! The Rain Forest!' they all chanted, as if the rest of Vancouver Island was some kind of desert. Clayoquot River bridge, remember? Kennedies...that bald Australian, Danish princes...they all came, embarrassed us. I said break their legs; that'll get these hairballs to go home. Sure, we were in Opposition back then, but you, you all treated me like a thug, a common pickpocket! And *you*!" He pointed at Lerche. "The only reason that *you* avoided a criminal record was because *you* didn't grow up at Hastings and Nanaimo."

"As for *you*!" Gollander screamed, pointing at Willingdon. "You laughed at me, with your fancy-ass education from Oxford, your stint in the Peace Corps. At least I got an education...I knew how to deal with punks who threatened the financial well-being of our donors. And the rest of you, Point Grey pansies....you...you all behaved as if I was some character in...*West Side Story!*" He started banging his head on the wooden mantle over the gas fireplace, rattling a figurine perched on its edge.

"I went to Cambridge, actually," Willingdon said.

Patricia went over to the fireplace to console Gollander, who wept prolifically into her Hermès blouse. She turned to face the other three, her arms folded. "I suppose you agree with him now!"

"That's the best way to get this to go away." Willingdon mumbled, his voice slowly trailing off. Goyter grunted something about 'business'.

Patricia's eyes narrowed. "Men and their fucking *cosa nostra* fantasies! I have never heard anything so bone-crushingly stupid! Who are you going to bat for? The Striationists? The 'Orthodox' ones are barking mad. The 'Reformed' ones," she shouted, glaring at Lerche and Willingdon, "make Donald Trump look like Saint Augustine. And as for that fucking Frenchman, what's his name, 'Bastard' or something? He makes my skin crawl! So *now* you propose to rough up a bunch of environmentalists who are solidly backed by public opinion. What are you going to do? Garrotte David Suzuki while he's eating his lunch? You guys do realize that *The Godfather* wasn`t a documentary, don`t you?"

Willingdon blushed and looked down at his shoes.

Lerche placed a hand on one hip and posed, facing the other three, leaning against a window sill. "But *you* must recognize," he started in a hushed tone. "A harsh response is exactly what we need. I have always said to you that it is our role as the party of free enterprise to protect those who produce, those with the royal jelly, from the common parasites and pirates who threaten them. Environmentalists are even worse; genetically inferior druids and drug-addled pagans who seek to prevent those who are more innovative and intelligent from making use of the resources that justice and nature demand to be made readily available to them. Violence against them *is* the answer; it is always justified!"

Patricia rubbed her ears. Lerche was speaking loudly enough to address a modest-sized auditorium.

"But it has become obvious to me," he said, his arm sweeping in a broad arc. "Here, in British Columbia, on Vancouver Island, *we,* here in this room, we are the ones who produce, the ones who have the capacity to create, and have a duty, not a moral one but one with its foundation in natural law, to incapacitate those who place themselves in our way. Not a right, not in the manner that Neetchee said, but a duty. Throughout history wherever the productive have neglected their duty, disaster has followed. Look at Finland! We cannot afford to lightly shirk what has been left by fate and the forces of history for us to do."

Lerche ambled from one rhetorical odyssey into another, heedless of the reactions of anyone else. Goyter guzzled his wine and then opened a bottle of Courvoisier that he found on Lerche's liquor tray, poured himself a generous glass and consumed it with rapid sips. Patricia stood erect with the aggrieved wince of someone enduring a cold shower.

"And so here we have arrived." Lerche's voice rose to a reedy whine. "Ours is a spiritual system, based on energy, the energy that comes for our use from the striations left by the glaciers of the last ice age, the terrestrial energy that gives people the drive, zest and vigour to produce! Energy is even more essential than gold! It's..."

"Please stop." Patricia interrupted him, massaging her temples.

"What?" Lerche gasped in the manner of an outraged monarch. "I was merely trying to reconcile our current conundrum with our religion."

Punitive experience taught Patricia not to treat Lerche's observations in a way that he might interpret as dismissive. She was seized by an uncontrollable fit of giggles the first time she had heard him speak, and declared between hoots of high-pitched laughter that such pomposity did not befit a man so young. Her indiscretion ignited a caucus uproar that threatened to split the party. As penance, she was compelled to attend a Friday reading group with the core members of Lerche's adherents, precipitating her finishing off an entire bottle of Chenin Blanc in less than an hour. The resulting headache lasted three days. She was, after all, sixty.

"Yes, it is a conundrum, one that we'd make much worse with such rash behaviour." Patricia sighed. "Just listen to you guys, all of you. Each of you has endorsed a course of action that (if we were actually foolish enough to carry it out) could quite easily see us all facing jail! And all of this precarious, based on a pipe dream that strikes me as being a little bit *too* similar to those 'get gold out of seawater' scams that you used to see advertised in the back of comic books. And now, that poor scientist that we just dragged here all the way from Germany, just to pelt him with aspic; he's a guy who spent years studying the process, and even *he* thinks that using it for the fixed link is lunacy."

"Well, he didn't say *lunacy*, Patricia," Willingdon said.

"He said 'I am warning you of some very real peril'. That's what he said, Garth, and..."

"Maybe you're right, Patricia," Goyter interrupted. "We should probably wait and see if this...this SeaMent deal actually works before we start dealing with the environmentalists."

Laeticia and Mario's "usual place" was a seaside restaurant beneath a bed and breakfast in Cowichan Bay, about an hour to the north. Before Laeticia had a chance to tell Mario about the VisualEyes luncheon or even take a sip from a welcome glass of wine, she heard a beep from her work Blackberry; the arrival of a text message. It was from Fabién Lerche.

Hi! It was a pleasure meeting you Laeticia! Call me some time:

> *778-714-8788!*
> *F.*

"Anything important?" Mario asked.

"It's just spam," Laeticia said as she deleted it.

....9

A gathering of about six shuffled and flinched on the sidewalk outside Calista's as Carlo waited for Marika, his morning habit for almost a month. They were tourists, that much was certain. After years of observing them in the four cities where he'd spent most of his life, he had no trouble picking out the unmistakable indicia of people unfamiliar with their surroundings. When they wandered inside, Carlo commenced his usual self-challenge: yes, they're tourists, but where are they from? At first he thought they might be from somewhere else in Canada, but he noticed that they regarded one another with intense gazes as they bantered back and forth. Scandinavians, Carlo came to a preliminary conclusion, and then he heard a few snippets of their conversation. Danes.

His resumed existence in Vancouver unfolded with unfamiliar efficiency. Within scant weeks of finding a job in Declan's office, he found an apartment, secured a telephone number and bought a used car, an aging Jeep that seemed to work well enough. He'd achieved less in Rome after as many months. His new apartment, a compact rectangle with a loft, was in a concrete seventies structure on False Creek, a short walk from Granville Island, with a view of the glass spires of the downtown peninsula. It took him longer than he expected to find a bed, but at least he could arrange phones, a car and Internet without any need for bureaucratic assent.

Marika showed up in a yellow summer dress that she'd started wearing on dry days, now that the weather was starting to warm up, a distracting display of robust sexual allure that Giovanna, modish and spare, never had. "Hey, Carlo." She was uncharacteristically subdued. "Another espresso?"

"Sure, thanks."

She came back with two biscotti and devoured them both before the barista brought their coffees to the table. "I *really* need coffee this morning. Lots of it. I went out with Petra for martinis last night." Carlo had heard the name before, one of her former roommates. "Sure, they were chick martinis, pear cider and vodka, but fuck, I had eight of them. I'm such an idiot. Don't you ever put sugar in that stuff?"

Carlo sipped his espresso. "Nope."

She's getting too close to the new associate, Gaskin watched with ill-restrained annoyance when Marika came in with Carlo, something he saw almost every morning. More often than not, when he passed the window of the Italian coffee shop down the block, he saw them sitting together, usually laughing. *And all those long cookies. No wonder she's getting so hefty.* He started pacing around the open hardwood floor in an agitated fugue, soon convincing himself that he would have to confront the issue eventually, one which (in addition to everything else) was of central importance to office aesthetics.

Carlo had just logged on when Declan walked into his office and closed the door. "I like to run a tight ship." He stared down at Carlo with a disapproving glower.

Carlo glanced up from the screen. "I'm sorry?"

"I like to run a tight ship. Even though this is a small firm, I (as the guy in charge) have to be alert to contact between co-workers. Accusations of sexual harassment often follow. Wouldn't you agree?"

"I guess."

"You guess! Come on. It's obvious to me that you and Marika are dating."

"No, we're not, we're just..."

"Look, don't insult my intelligence. These provocative costumes she's started wearing, I suppose they're meant to encourage whatever after-hours attention you've been paying to her! And who knows? Maybe you two are at it *during* work hours."

"Look, it's just none of...okay; we are *not* sleeping together. I don't even think we've ever even met for a drink."

"Whatever. I'm not here to conduct an investigation. But if you ever become romantically involved with any member of the staff while you work here, I will expect you to let me know immediately."

"Fine." Carlo shrugged.

"Good." Gaskin spoke in the low, rumbling tone of rippling thunder at the end of a passing storm. "As long as we understand each other."

Carlo did not see Gaskin again until shortly after lunch. He was surprised to once again glance up to see him, this time posing in a jovial stance above his computer monitor with his arms folded, his face breaking out into a broad smile, as if a comforting thought had just occurred to him. "I meant to ask you before; what are you doing for the long weekend, this coming weekend?"

"I was planning to go down to this place I know in Washington State to do some backpacking. Why?"

Gaskin grinned. "How serendipitous! I need you to go down to Seattle for a meeting. I have no doubt that the file involved will be the biggest case you've ever worked on; at least five hundred million dollars will be at issue. A joint project with Sadich."

"Who?"

"Buster Sadich. He's a Seattle attorney I met at an American Trial Lawyers function a few years back. Geunther & Sadich, his firm, is right in the middle of downtown Seattle, just off Pine Street. Introduced him to Striationism. I was shocked that he bought into it for whatever reason (I guess he *was* going through a divorce at the time). He says that changed his life." Gaskin looked over the clutter on Carlo's desk and sighed.

"Anyway, I've already told you about one of our long-standing clients, the Striationist Totality. Well, it has just gone through a schism. We represent the originalist, or, if you will, the old-school remnant, which now calls itself the Orthodox Striationist Totality. The offshoot, known as the Reformed Striationist Community, is, well, a bit more Vancouver, west side. And the split has led to, well, just like any other divorce, financial dislocation. Assets have disappeared; it affects the religion on both sides of the border. Our firm and Sadich's will be commencing parallel legal proceedings, his in U.S. Federal District Court, ours in the B.C. Supreme Court."

"Sounds very interesting."

"Oh, it will be. As I said, it will be by far and away the biggest case that you've ever worked on, I can guarantee you that. Anyway, I told Buster that I would be down on Friday morning, but I've got to, ah, plans with Paula. It's important: something *you'll* find out once you're married."

"Ah. So Friday morning?"

"Yes, if you could go down and meet with them in my stead; I was going to have you draft the pleadings anyway. And keep Canada Day weekend open. The Striationists are holding their annual, I don't know; let's call it a festival, at this new resort in the States. It's called Petunia or something."

Calista's, in mid-afternoon, lacked the usual agglomeration of tourists, leaving a small collection of students and their assortment of electronic devices of varied vintages, who were taking full advantage of the free wireless Internet.

"So he's sending you down to Seattle?" Marika asked.

"Yes." Carlo sipped his espresso. "He said that he wanted us to go down together but something came up, I don't know, with his wife, so I get to meet with Sadich on my own.

"Sadich." Marika hissed. "That perv..."

"Well, Declan mentioned that he *is* divorced."

"That's no excuse. And it's strange. That's the first I've heard of anything going on with the Striatio-loonies in Seattle. Or his wife. Who knows what the fuck is going on; he never tells us anything! And now he's screwing up your long weekend."

"Oh, it really doesn't make any difference. Well, maybe fifty extra dollars in gas. I was going down there anyway, to do some hiking in this place I haven't visited for years. I'll live."

"Sadich is an annoying windbag. And don't expect a penny in reimbursement."

"For what?"

"The gas. We'd better get back upstairs."

Carlo was startled to see Farida walk into Calista's as he and Marika were leaving. "Farida! I've never seen *you* down here." Her office was near the courthouse, a world away from Gastown, a tourist area wedged between the financial district and the bleak Downtown Eastside.

"Yup. Today I'm slumming it. I had a discovery over there at Cordova Reporting." She pointed to a refurbished brick heritage building across the street.

"Cordova? I've never heard of them." Carlo was aware of at least a dozen other small court reporter services in downtown Vancouver where lawyers conducted pre-trial examinations.

"Well, they have a certain classical appeal, what can I say?" Farida laughed. "And they have the best jelly beans in Vancouver." Farida and Marika regarded one another in very different ways. Farida seemed poised to laugh; Marika held her in a contemptuous stare.

"Marika," Carlo said. "This is Farida. She and her husband David are two good friends of mine from back in Toronto. Marika is a paralegal at Declan's shop."

"Oh, hello." Marika relaxed, prompting Farida's smirk to sharpen.

"Pleased to meet you, Marika." Farida walked toward a table and dropped her litigation bags. "Well." She grinned. "You two crazy kids have fun!"

Declan's two secretaries, Samantha and Terri, stopped talking in mid-sentence when Carlo and Marika came back into the office. Samantha, a South African with ruddy skin and straight black hair cackled and then started shouting in Bal's direction. "So you were saying? You and your husband got reservations at Bad Medicine for dinner?"

"Yup." Bal said. "At seven sharp." Bad Medicine was an Asian bistro in Yaletown whose popularity spiked after a Hell's Angels chieftain was assassinated there in his chair two months earlier.

"Oooh, lucky you," Samantha laughed. "Did you two just win the lottery?"

Terri, somewhat younger (Carlo had been told she was nineteen) and notably slighter than Samantha, issued a throaty giggle that reminded Carlo of someone grinding coffee by hand.

Marika grabbed her purse and ran toward the door. "Fuck, I'm late," she yelled in a panic. "I've got to be in Yaletown in five minutes. Meet me tomorrow morning at Calista's, K?" Samantha flashed an indulgent grin at Carlo, as if they were sharing a private joke.

After the rest of the staff left for the day, Carlo looked up to find Thomas looming over his desk. "So, is the Belkin brief completed?" he asked.

"Yes," Carlo said. "We're asking for six hundred and fifty thousand dollars. Declan had recommended that we keep our demand under a half million (he's worried that a larger figure might piss off the adjuster), but she insisted, she was very...forceful in her manner let's say. For someone who claims to be on her deathbed, she's..."

"She's as twisted as Dick's old hatband, she is." Thomas sat down. "I worked with Declan on the file for three years. If she gets fifty thousand, she'll have been grandly overcompensated."

"But Dr. Butters thinks that her depression is so severe that she has symptoms of cognitive impairment." Gaskin sent Mrs.

Belkin to Dr. Butters for a psychiatric assessment. His report, expert evidence furnished at a cost of some six thousand dollars, predicted that a number of psychiatric afflictions, all plucked from the DSM-IV, would plague her for the rest of her days and would most likely lead to premature senescence.

"That old hack would find schizophrenia in the Queen if we paid him enough. Oh, I'm not joking," Thomas said. "I apologize. One tends to become a bit jaded after almost two decades in this business." His usual grimace bloomed into a salacious grin. "Oh, and one thing I've noticed recently, and I can say that I'm not alone in this assessment: it would appear that you have an admirer."

"A what?" Carlo was signing a batch of covering letters accompanying the brief, directed to various defence counsel.

"An admirer."

"You mean Marika?" Thomas nodded, his eyes bright with excitement. "No, no; I gave up women for Lent."

"Lent's over, young man. Someone has to keep that young lady out of trouble. And you could do much, much worse." Thomas laughed, holding Carlo in his gaze. "Oh, I meant to ask you. I heard you conversing in Italian on the phone the other day; it seems to me that your accent is Roman. Am I right?"

"Oh yes, that's right, you mentioned at the art gallery that your first wife was an Italian."

"Yes, and we lived in Florence for twelve years; my former life as an art historian. Can't pay for groceries with that occupation in this country, I'm afraid. So, was I right?"

"Yes; I'm impressed. My accent was probably more southern before but I spent three years right in Rome. My father is *pugliese*."

"Oh, I see," Thomas mumbled in a tone plainly meant to conceal his curiosity. "Does he live in, oh, I suppose, Bari?

"No, he's from around Barletta, but he lives in London."

"Oh?" Thomas said. "That's my old home town. I was born and raised in Croydon."

"Pop lives right in the thick of it, in Soho."

"I see. That can be a good situation or a bad one. Have you been to visit?"

"Many times. I was just there.

"Hmm." Thomas looked at his watch. "I wonder if you would like to join me for a pint. I was going to stop in at the pub on the way home."

"Sure, why not?"

"Good. We'll go to the Duke of York, it's just over, there, in Richards Street. They have some good Yorkshire Bitter on tap, and they have the good sense enough not to chill all the flavour out of it."

10

Gavin searched for the Greystone Building, an eight-storey structure built during the 1950s, now lost in the high-density warren sprouting between Melville Street and the waterfront. He felt distinctly underdressed in Timberland loafers and no tie. Whenever he visited Victoria, the provincial capital, he was always the most dapper man on the street, amongst the rumpled civil servants in their Dockers, most often sporting beards in need of a proper trim. In Vancouver, he always worried that he looked like a hick. He straightened his brown tweed sports jacket in reflexive response to a passing lawyer wearing an Italian-cut wool suit.

He could not help but notice the Greystone's retrograde feel, ancient in comparison to the surrounding sparkle of new construction. The elevator was painted a faint aquamarine, and fitted with chrome rails. Its door squeaked as soon as he pressed the floor button and then slammed shut. Once on the sixth floor, the ambiance abruptly changed. The mid-century colour scheme and quaint decoration were replaced with ochre hardwood flooring, pastel walls of an understated grey, where, at tasteful, modest intervals, Impressionist paintings hung at eye level. Silver letters were affixed to the wall opposite the reception desk.

CHANCERY INVESTMENTS

"May I help you, sir?" The receptionist smiled, a young Asian girl wearing an outsize pair of glasses.

"Yes, I'm here to meet with Mr. Crawley and Mr. Bilbick."

"I'll let them know that you're here. Please have a seat." He sat across from a table in the waiting area supplied with fresh editions of the Wall Street Journal and the Financial Times. Gavin started reading a front-page article about the sepulchral failure of a joint French-Chinese mining venture in the Central African Republic, an event which, much to his amusement, seemed to come as a total surprise to the author.

A short man with hair an unnatural shade of red tapped his shoulder. "Gavin, glad that you could make it. We were just waiting for you in the boardroom."

"Well, hello Aloysius." Gavin had made the mistake of calling Aloysius Crawley 'Al' once, a few years before, provoking a reaction so petulant that Crawley refused to identify the market venture fund he was recommending for investment until he got an apology. "Sorry, but the seaplane was a little late. It's actually raining on the other side."

"Oh, no problem. Come this way." Both Irwin Bilbick and Roland Egbert were both sitting at the long boardroom table, both doing their utmost to ignore one another. Egbert picked his nose while Bilbick used a matchbook cover to clean the grime from under his nails.

"Well, we all know each other." Crawley bellowed. Gavin took a seat opposite the other three. "Mr. Skoff has been working on the underwater tunnel proposal."

"Yes." Egbert maintained a steady gaze on Gavin. "I have a few concerns that I would like to discuss later."

"Would you like to talk about them now?" Crawley asked.

"No, no, it can wait until later, once you have completed your agenda." Egbert had an ecclesiastic way of expressing himself that grated on Gavin's nerves.

"Okay. Irwin; I hear that you're looking for accelerated funding for the enhancement of the new Parksville Gateway."

"Gollander has been ignoring me," Bilbick grumbled. "And now it looks like we're going to have to get it done sooner rather than later. The McKee McWatney lands have been sold."

"They have?" Egbert asked. It was also a surprise to Gavin.

"Oh, yes," Crawley nodded quickly, speaking in a hushed tone that implied he was well-informed. "It's been sold." Gavin started to perspire. How could he have missed it? It was practically in his own backyard. Until now, he was proud of the fact that he was aware of every secret transaction, each unseemly scheme and subterfuge on central Vancouver Island. But this? It was bigger than everything that had taken place over the course of the last ten years combined. He wondered what he was doing at the meeting. Why would they invite such a shut-in, an incompetent?

"Well, then who bought it?" Egbert leaned forward in his seat.

"Oh, it was Midlands Shropshire," Crawley said.

"Midlands Shropshire," Gavin repeated in a whisper, ashamed of his ignorance. He'd never even heard of the outfit.

Crawley rested back in his chair and cracked his knuckles. "Yes, I suppose its name's a bit on the pompous side, but don't forget; it's owned by a foreigner, a 'Mr. Babar', or some such thing."

"So time is running shorter than I expected." Irwin said. "We'll have to get the Parksville Gateway started soon. So far, we haven't even turned the first sod!"

Crawley formed his palms to a point and brought them to his chin. "Calm down, Irwin, calm down. The world is not coming to an end (at least, not yet). "I'll talk to Gollander, he should have distributed the funds from Community Development to you by now."

"Thank you." Bilbick said. Crawley's assurance seemed to calm him.

"How does Midlands Shropshire intend to develop the property?" Gavin asked, trying to conceal the caution in his voice. "I haven't heard that anyone has applied to change the zoning on five thousand hectares. That land is still zoned for silviculture."

"Convertible deed trust units." Crawley grinned. "Don't ask me what that means; I leave that sort of thing to the shysters. Right, Irwin?" To Gavin's recurrent astonishment, Bilbick practiced criminal law before he retired.

"I don't understand it, either." Egbert said. "People have been telling me about rumours that the McKee McWatney lands have been sold to this Midlands outfit. Of course, McKee McWatney is still on title and nothing indicating that the property has been sold has been registered, but I suppose that's nothing new with developers. There is probably some complicated escrow and indemnity arrangement; as you say." He looked directly at Crawley. "Leave it to the shysters. But to my knowledge, there is no such thing as a 'convertible deed trust unit'. It just sounds sexy."

"Come on, Roland," Crawley said. "These guys on Wall Street and the City come up with funky new instruments every day. I doubt that any single person could name them all."

Or properly explain any of them, Gavin thought.

"Look, I don't care about any of this." Egbert shrugged. "Either they want to develop the land or they do not. If the answer is yes, no matter how fancy the paperwork, they will still need a development permit before they break ground." His voice became louder until he was almost shouting. "And, Gavin, I still haven't seen even a hint of an application from you for this underwater tunnel testing project, or prototype, as you call it. I expect that it's not going ahead after what transpired in Bastion Square last month."

"Yes; we hit a bit of bump in the road in Victoria, but nothing that we shouldn't be able to overcome."

"A bump? I was there, Gavin. Olafsen told you to pound sand! How are you going to get around that? He's the patent holder."

"No, his company owns the pending patent, and we own the two-thirds of company. As long as the provincial government continues to fund it, we'll be able to complete the prototype by the end of next year."

"Gavin, Gavin. The good professor not only says that it won't work, but that it might very well turn into a latter-day Chernobyl."

For the first time in years, Gavin let Egbert's imperious manner irritate him. "For love of Christ, what do you know about it? I've just spoken with Christian Davidson; he's the professor at the University of British Columbia in charge of the SeaMent project in North America. We're still planning a public test and demonstration later this year, probably between the Nanaimo seaside promenade and Newcastle Island."

"I can tell you that it's not going to be Newcastle Island. Not even the most remote possibility. I am not going to do it. Don't expect me to issue a permit for such a public, easily accessible location." Egbert said.

"I expect that you will do exactly as I ask. If you won't allow it, someone in Cabinet will."

"Good luck with that," Egbert smirked. "It is an enormously unpopular concept on the Island, the fixed link. Nobody is going to give you political cover to rub Islanders' noses in it. I don't want any publicity; no embarrassing media debates about 'our fragile Island lifestyle' or 'a bridge too far'."

"You listen to me!"

"No, no, Gavin, please," Crawley interrupted. "I know that you have a great deal invested emotionally in this, but you have to listen to reason. It is a very unpopular idea. Surely you must know that."

"Yes, but that sort of thing never stopped me before." Gavin instantly regretted his petulant tone.

Egbert leaned back in his seat. "You made a big mistake with that presentation at the Seaview."

"It was a complete fiasco," Bilbick said. "And in Sam Downes column in *The Salish Sea* a few weeks back - scathing! His coverage of that meeting made you a laughing stock down in Victoria."

"I never read that Marxist rag," Gavin grumbled.

"Gavin," Crawley pleaded. "We understand that the tunnel is important and, in many ways, key to the viability of the McKee

McWatney development. But it's not beneficial to be so public about it. And it's not just the left-wing, alternative press, Gavin. People that I deal with daily in Toronto, Bay Street types. They've gently inquired if you've lost your mind."

"Don't misunderstand me." Egbert said. "I agree that a fixed link would be of benefit, but none of us want to wear it politically. You will have to find a less public (preferably remote) test site. I will approve that, bearing in mind your need for a power source. Find a less conspicuous location; submit your proposal to me in strict confidence. I'll repeat myself: you can't even pitch a tent on any proposed work site without a permit issued by my people."

Gavin had grown used to handling rustic emperors, a skill that he had no choice but to acquire if he wanted to conduct business after moving to Parksville. He knew that he had to surrender. "I'll see what I can do."

"Grand." Egbert nodded and pursed his lips.

After the meeting concluded, Irwin, Egbert and Gavin gathered up their notes and filed them away in their briefcases. "Gavin." Crawley said. "Please stay behind for a few minutes. I want to review an unrelated matter with you." He waited until after the elevator door closed behind Irwin and Egbert. "I have an investment opportunity that might interest you. It has to do with the development of the McKee McWatney lands."

"Oh, yes. It's all happening so fast. What's it all about?"

"Ultimately, it will be a series of small urban enclaves, separated by golf courses, gardens and nature parks, stretching from here to Cumberland." He drew a freehand sketch of the coastline of eastern Vancouver Island. "About fifty-thousand units; the nodes will each have a European motif."

"I see."

"And the investment units are all in the form of shares, each unit at one hundred thousand dollars, representing the fixed percentage of a hundredth of one percent ownership. It's probably the biggest real estate opportunity on the west coast of North

America in history thus far. The returns promise to be enormous, as I'm sure you can see."

"Yes, yes," Gavin said in a distracted tone, confused by both the offer, and the fact that it was the first he'd heard about such a huge project, not even a rumour.

"Are you interested?"

"Oh, in all likelihood. I'll get back to you about it."

"Good." Crawley rested his chin at the apex of his joined hands, almost as if praying. "But don't wait too long; this is going to be an extremely popular opportunity."

Gavin's return seaplane to Nanaimo left at four o'clock, leaving him two vacant hours. He bought a Wall Street Journal from the vendor at Waterfront Station, and decided to read it over a couple of pints of Guinness at the Seymour Club, a place overlooking the water where he still maintained an expensive membership. A familiar face loomed behind him on his way up the front steps. *My God. It's Perry Chatham.* It was a rare sighting, in public and during daylight hours.

"Perry!"

"Oh, hullo, Gavin." Chatham greeted Gavin cautiously, looking behind him as he reached to shake his hand. "What brings you over to the metropolis?"

"I had a meeting with the VisualEyes group at Crawley's office. My seaplane doesn't leave until four, so I decided to stop in for a pint or two."

"I would like to join you, if you don't mind; I mean, if you don't mind being seen with such a social pariah."

"The pleasure's all mine, Perry." They went into the club's small, dark wood panelled pub that overlooked Coal Harbour.

Chatham raised his hand to summon the waitress. He turned to Gavin. "Smithwick's?"

"Sure," Gavin sighed. "Smithwick's."

Perry shut off his cell phone. "It's been what, about a year?"

"No, much less than that. It was at the Vancouver Board of Trade function in January; remember, at The Salmon House?"

"Oh yes, quite right; I must say that my memory has taken a hit. That was less than two weeks before the whole Abundance fiasco became public and they hid me away like an incontinent aunt. My own ideological zeal and native stupidity got the better of me, I'm afraid."

"I heard about your misfortune, not that I disagreed with..."

"No; please, Gavin, that's very kind of you to say, but it's my own fault. It wasn't like privatizing a fish cannery that should never have been under public control in the first place. What I did was as politically unpopular as you can get, and into the bargain I resurrected diseases that had long since left the public consciousness: measles, pellagra, whooping cough! Who under the age of sixty had heard of any of them?" Chatham took a sip from his beer. "And some of those poor people were *so* badly off: a few of the children were veritable fountains of diarrhea. Hell, even some of the adults were running about scratching themselves like flea-bitten cats. Scabies, I'm afraid."

"Still," Gavin said.

"No, Gavin; let's talk about something else. So you were conferring with Aloysius, were you?"

"Yes, I've got several projects on the go over on the Island. Because I'm the chair of VisualEyes, I have to come over to see Crawley every so often."

"Oh, yes. VisualEyes Vancouver Island." Chatham laughed. "I hear that you're still on about that silly bridge. It's a fool's errand, Gavin. Nobody on the Island wants it and people on the mainland would have an aneurism if they ever found out how much it was going to cost."

"It'll be a challenge, that's true; but it wouldn't be the first time that I manipulated my way past public uproar to get approval for an unpopular project."

"Come on, Gavin. This isn't about a row house development in some miserable little bog in Saanich. And you have some very unsavoury allies. The Reformed Striationist bunch is in it past their ears: their protagonist (*agent-provocateur* would be a more accurate description) seems to be a rather unctuous Frenchman, a Bassaba or something, who is always nosing around. And I even hear rumblings that they're mixed up with some scheme to develop much of south-eastern Vancouver Island."

"Yes, I've heard the same rumblings. Do you know what it's all about?"

"No, I certainly haven't heard any details. I have heard a few puffs which may or may not be part of an actual proposal. For all I know, it may all be simply just a heap of rubbish. But what I've heard simply does not make any sense."

"I tend to agree."

"Then you will understand me when I say that you should be extremely wary of these people. You know, ever since I landed on these...these untamed shores I've noticed that the commercial élite is totally good for nothing; they produce nothing of any use except for paper, and most of that is handled by foreigners. They perform no valuable service except to drive real estate prices to the outer layers of the stratosphere. And what do they do to earn their baronial keep? They create a feeling!" he mimicked with a melodic whine. "And a feeling to do what, exactly? Well, to impel, as if by magic, other people, never themselves, to actually get off their behinds and do something useful. VisualEyes Vancouver Island! You should reconsider your involvement with these people; you're far better than they are. They're a bunch of hucksters and mountebanks who contribute nothing to society!"

"You're ranting, Perry."

"And so I should. You know very well that most of those brigands are intertwined with the supposed Reformed crowd, especially. The other ones, the Orthodox ones..."

"I have more than passing familiarity with them."

"Oh, I haven't forgotten about Lelani. But the old school ones, they're sort of cute in their own way, let's say, like ungainly Americans who genuflect to Jesus in their peculiar style, take a good whack on the forehead from 'the preacher' or whoever and fall backwards into a pond. But the Reformed ones, including my brethren in Cabinet, they give an entirely different impression." Chatham sipped from his pint. "And you're well rid of Lelani. Irina (who usually gives everyone the benefit of the doubt, it seems) concluded that she was a gushing imbecile after spending an evening with her. And you've found Tiffany, a much more level-headed girl. It's been what, three, four years? It's time that you made an honest woman of her."

Gavin laughed. "I'm doing my best, but she is against the idea; she comes from a family wracked by divorce. So how is Irina doing?" Irina, Chatham's wife, was at forty-seven, twenty years his junior and (at least to Gavin's knowledge) the world's only celebrity cellist. For her entire career, starting in her native Gdansk, later in various cities in Western Europe and most recently in North America, her image appeared periodically in the tabloids, her long blond hair arranged in her trademark cornrows.

"She's had more than enough of this city. She wants to abandon it as soon as possible." Chatham laughed. "In Europe, people consider it quite preposterous that anyone would describe her as 'old'". Gavin had to agree; although she was perhaps a little less lithe than Tiffany, Irina remained a classic Eastern European beauty who wouldn't have been out of place on the cover of one of those English men's magazines he bought when Tiffany wasn't paying attention.

"But that's not the way people around here look at things," Chatham said. "When we lived in Paris (and this wasn't that long ago), she made an estimable sum doing celebrity promotions. She still has a few endorsement contracts, but the good ones are starting to dwindle now that we've been out here on the frontier for so long." Chatham drew a deep sigh and gazed towards the

North Shore. "And the worst of it is what they offer her over here. In France and Italy, she did adverts in Vogue and Paris-Match for Armani and Vuitton; you know, for sunglasses, even bathing costumes. Here, all she can get is the odd stint touting orthopaedic sandals and absorbent undergarments."

"So I suppose that you're leaving soon?" Gavin asked after his laughter subsided.

"As soon as practicable, my good friend. The problem is mine. I tendered my resignation from Cabinet after the Abundance scandal blew up, but Willingdon wouldn't accept it."

"Well, I guess it's encouraging that they have given you at least *that* gesture of support."

"Ooh, it is meant as punishment, Gavin, not support! Now they have me traversing the hinterlands consecrating public restrooms and homes for the feeble-minded. Willingdon wouldn't have let me off that easily. That would have meant that I was mistaken in pursuing a policy that he whole-heartedly supported. And Willingdon is never wrong."

"Why don't you just tell him to bugger off?"

"I'm poised to do just that. Irina just secured a position teaching composition at King's College. I will be happy to return to London."

"So, back into the financial world of Ludgate Circus?"

"Oh, good God no. I'm not trading one bunch of crooks for another; I'm returning to the pleasantly annoying world of academia. An old classmate of mine is a department head at LSE; she offered me a position as a lecturer."

"Well, congratulations, I suppose. I'll be sorry to see you go."

"Oh, nonsense, Gavin. I'm sure you and Tiffany can tear yourselves away from your tropical paradise long enough to visit us in London.

"Of course we will."

Chatham rose from his chair. "Well, my friend, I have my own seaplane to catch. Off to Powell River to cut the ribbon on the new emergency room. Oh, the irony. So I'll leave you to your newspaper." They shook hands.

"Good luck, Perry."

"Thank you, Gavin." He pointed at the folded newspaper. "It's all lies, you know. The world is going to hell. And when the time comes, remember: you heard it from me first."

11

One misty afternoon, a half-dozen people, all wearing grey gum boots, wool pants and yellow rain slickers, trudged up a mossy track at the edge of a scoured basalt slope. Fog rendered the lake dominating the long valley below dreamlike and indistinct. The group descended into a salal-choked draw, momentarily pausing to wait for the one with the resplendent red beard to steady himself after he lost his footing on the damp underbrush. After a short bushwack, they arrived at an ample creek that thundered down the grey rock face before them in three elegant cascades. The one with the beard re-arranged the hood of his slicker, turned to face the waterfall, and gazed conspicuously upward.

The six of them re-assembled to stand facing one another in a circle, arched their backs, and hummed.

....12

It was the Friday of the treasured May long weekend, when most people fled the city to enjoy the first dry weather in months. Laura left Vancouver early that morning for the short ferry ride and drive up to Sechelt, a coastal town on the liver-shaped peninsula of the same name, for the Striationist Elders meeting. Yvette had made her way up there the previous afternoon, citing something about a lavender farm that failed to capture Laura's interest.

They both preferred to meet clients in their boardroom, a bright space in the upper floor of their offices on Mainland Street, fastidiously decorated by Yvette to her taste over the span of about eight years; a piece of *la belle époque* in early twenty-first century Yaletown. Until the past year the Striationist Council of Elders, the religion's guiding body, did not object to the twice annual trek to the city, but instead seemed to quite enjoy it, ceasing their complaints about the *terrible traffic* only when it was necessary to draw a breath. But there had been a recent change of heart. A few Elders decided that the Fraser delta's dearth of glacial striations meant that travel to Vancouver was against their religion.

By the time Laura arrived at the newly-favoured venue, the Hale Kai Resort on the beachfront strip of motels just south of town, the small parking lot was already filled with a collection of Volkswagen microbuses, two Citroëns and a dented Vauxhall. Yvette's car, a new Audi sports utility vehicle that was one of the few chattels she owned that was not made in France, was parked under an overhang, far from the shade trees infested with feces-laden crows.

She set down the coffee she'd bought at the Starbucks in Gibsons after she drove off the ferry, and straightened the skirt of her customary coat of armour, a business suit – the safest choice. The Striationist Elders did not appear to demand formality, but then again, you never knew what might set these people off.

No one was at the front desk. The Hale Kai appeared to have been most recently renovated during the disco era and bore a faint odour of mosquito repellent. A small blackboard rested in an easel in the lobby.

<h1 style="text-align:center">Meeting of the Striationist Elders
Elphinstone Room
9:00 – 12:00</h1>

Laura pushed open the heavy double doors of the upper floor conference room to see Yvette by herself on one side of the table and the Striationist elders assembled *en banc* opposite her. She had also decided to wear a suit; but Laura, whose suit was grey wool, streamlined and tailored, looked askance at Yvette's paisley suit with its abundant frills.

"I trust you had no difficulty finding the place, Miss Thompson." It was Ruairi Davidson, his accent a gentle, resonant Scottish burr. He always called her "Miss".

"Oh, no, not at all. Hmm...isn't Declan supposed to be here?" Laura asked. She took the seat next to Yvette.

"I don't know what's up with him," Yvette said. "He told me that he was going to be here, but..."

Hamish McPhee answered, an elfin man with a theatrical red beard; the Honoured Elder, Laura remembered, a revolving presidency of sorts. He too spoke with a Scottish accent of sorts, a remnant not unusual among those who lived on the rural B.C. coast. "Declan had to go to Boston. One of those American trial lawyers things." The other six elders gazed towards Laura and Yvette without expression. At most other occasions, they gave the impression of an oddly-dressed humanities faculty. Here, they looked more like a politburo.

"Yes," Ruairi said. "I spoke with him before he left. Apparently he hired a new associate to help him out with our file. That's good to hear."

"Really? Declan has finally found a new associate?" Laura said. This was a surprise. Declan's reputation as a skinflint was legendary in Vancouver legal circles, repelling most applicants.

"Yes," Yvette rolled her eyes. "He told me about him. He says that he's a Brazilian, he came here by way of Berlin or something. He used to translate mortgages for a living."

"Something like that, yes, I think it was Berlin, or Vienna, or Venice, or something." Hamish said. "All right, let's get down to it."

Each of the Elders in turn gave their reports about the events of the previous six months in their Domains, the largest of the Striationist ecclesiastical divisions: tedious recitations of the discovery of sundry outcroppings and waterfalls tucked away amidst remote thickets. Laura and Yvette scribbled notes as they spoke just to stay awake, rather than for future reference.

Hamish turned to Laura after Margaret Davidson, Ruairi's wife, and the Elder who governed the Princess Louisa Domain further up the coast, had finished her report. "I expect that the final transfer of the Sakinaw lands has been completed."

Laura noted with alarm that some of the elders started humming. "Yes," she said. "Declan's office has registered the Princess Louisa Domain as legal owner. The purchase is a done deal."

"Good," Hamish sighed. "I'm very glad to hear it."

It all happened before the schism, about a year earlier. The so-called 'Sakinaw lands' became the focal point of a rustic skirmish after a man who, according to local rumour, made his fortune selling weapons to Al-Qaeda, and had purchased about a hundred acres of land on a hillside above long, azure Sakinaw Lake. He applied for a permit to build a ten-thousand square foot house on a rocky plateau, which would have occasioned extensive blasting near a cluster of hallowed glacial striations. Worse, he wanted to harness the stream next to them for hydroelectric power, destroying a three-tiered cascade that was revered even more.

The Striationists begged the new owner, a German who spoke with a cartoonish accent that made Laura recall after-school reruns of *Hogan's Heroes,* to build his house somewhere else, but he refused to alter his plans and even seemed amused by the exploding dispute. It would have remained a local matter, largely ignored in Vancouver, until the Mistress of the Skookumchuk Gathering, the equivalent of a parish, made pointed reference to the owner's nationality during an interview on CBC Radio One and then compared the threatened striations to Jews. The eruption of public ridicule soon prompted the Striationists to put an end to the spectacle by buying the property for about two million more than it was worth. Hamish conscripted Laura to appear as temporary Striationist spokesperson during a spate of requests for radio and television interviews on the usual Vancouver news programs.

"Yes," Laura said. "The deal was agreed before the split but it didn't close until afterwards. The Reformed bunch didn't get their hands on it."

"Good. A job well done," Hamish said. "Now, that brings me to my next point. The Convocation is in little more than a month. How are you two holding up? Is everything on track?"

"Yes," Yvette said. "We've rented some additional equipment; we expect that we'll have an intern help out with post-production, someone from BCIT."

"Well, what time frame are we talking about here?"

"For the radio and television advertisements, we should have them ready for your review within five weeks. And the documentary?" Hamish asked.

Yvette looked at Laura. "The documentary will take a little more time," Laura said. "The intern will be mainly for my assistance. I expect that we will need two months, four at the most."

"Ooh, two months," said a woman that Laura knew as "Giselle" or something, who always carried on as if everything exhilarated her. "You ladies are miracle workers. Is there anything you need from us?"

"No," Laura said. "But at the Convocation on Canada Day weekend, maybe you could give us access to the conference rooms the night before, so that we can set up the remote microphones."

"Wonderful." Hamish said. "It sounds like we are on track for the beginning of July. Now, does anybody else have anything to ask these ladies?"

"Yes," Ruairi said. "We were wondering, with our ongoing battle with the...that offshoot bunch. We have about twenty boxes stuffed with documents that we're storing up in Port Rattray. What are we to do with them?"

"No, no, Ruairi." Hamish said. "That sort of thing is totally within Declan's bailiwick. I'll talk to him after he gets back. Now, would you two ladies like to join us for tea at Salal Joe's?" Laura remembered it as a herbal tea and organic bread bar in downtown Sechelt, in a new plaza overlooking the sea.

"We'd be happy to!" Laura said.

The Striationist elders rose together from their seats and walked out of the Elphinstone Room slowly, in single file. Laura and Yvette remained behind, packing their briefcases.

"You know," Yvette said, peering out the door to make sure that they were all out of earshot. "They're like ducks."

"Yup, ducks that pay their bill regularly."

"How about if we go into town together my car?" Yvette said.

"Sure."

"Good. Now, let's go drink some dirt."

13

Thomas spread a sheaf of legal-sized sheets out on the desk in front of him, a land title search for a property on Vancouver Island that was first staked out in 1860. "Marika, do you have my stapler again?"

"Yes, sorry. I'll bring it over. Oh, just a second." She reached into her purse for her cell phone, its ring tone the binary wail of a French ambulance. "Look, why are you calling me here?" Marika whispered into her phone. Thomas slid his glasses further down his nose.

"I've already told you." Marika turned to face the door. "I'm not exactly impressed by the way this all went down. What? *No!* And anyway, I said that I'm coming with you this weekend; that ought to be good enough!" She threw her phone back into her purse.

"Is everything all right?" Thomas asked. Marika nodded amidst an exasperated sigh. He returned to his jumble of documents, careful to make sure that he hadn't missed a covenant.

The approach to the border crossing in Blaine was as verdant as a cemetery, dominated by the Peace Arch, a peaked white rectangle straddling the frontier, displaying an interesting inscription:

CHILDREN OF A COMMON MOTHER

Do they mean England, Carlo wondered? If so, the children have proven to be something of a disappointment: the English consider Canadians tedious and Americans insane. Carlo slowly approached a short line of vehicles waiting to speak with a customs agent at an open wicket.

Carlo had stuffed the back of his Jeep with backpacking equipment, all acquired during a visit to the Wilderness Co-operative that exhausted most of a Saturday and almost a thousand dollars. He hoped the fact he dressed in a suit wouldn't incite too much curiosity in the customs agent. Once it was his turn, Carlo braced himself for what he hoped would be a brief interrogation.

"Citizenship?" The guard, with a face and physique suggestive of a bloated horse, spoke with forced good humour. Carlo had dealt with officialdom all over Europe, but this fellow was of another stamp. True, he seemed friendly enough, but he had the eyes of an automaton. Carlo sensed that he was the kind of person who would glumly electrocute him if asked by someone above him on the organizational chart.

"Canadian." Carlo presented his Canadian passport.

The guard looked it over. "Purpose of your visit?"

This was the part that Carlo had been dreading. What was he going to think of a guy in a suit with a Jeep full of camping equipment? "Well, first I am going to meet up with some friends in Seattle, then I want to go backpacking on the Olympic Peninsula."

To Carlo's relief, the agent snorted and handed back his passport. "Okay, thanks."

The boardroom at Geunther & Sadich had an impressive view, its western exposure affording a glance at Alaskan Way and a fog-obscured panorama of the Olympic Mountains. Buster Sadich dressed quite differently than Gaskin's bucolic style: a pastel green button-down shirt, relaxed-fit Ralph Lauren jeans. Carlo felt overdressed in his usual three-button suit and silk tie. Sadich spoke first, without introducing Carlo to the Asian girl who was seated across the table from him.

"The offshoot Striationist group; well let's call them a cult... they have somehow accumulated a great deal of wealth. Far more than would be accounted for from what they've taken from us, but we'll see."

"But Mr. Sadich, from my reading of the file, it would suggest asset-stripping," Carlo said.

"Ah. I don't mean any disrespect, but Declan really should be here, too. I've had Catriona researching it. Catriona with a 'C'." Sadich pointed at her. "Catriona comes from Peking, don't you?"

She sighed. "No, not Beijing; I was born in Hong Kong."

Sadich swatted at his chin. "It's hard to keep track. Anyway, Catriona, tell us what you have been able to find out."

Catriona stood up and approached an easel. Carlo instantly recognized her as a fellow member of the tribe; someone whose dedication to exercise bordered on addiction. She was slim but muscular, dressed in a grey suit tailored to her form, her long black hair upswept. For the first time in months, Carlo briefly stopped lamenting his own singlehood.

"Two of the people who are likely to know about the Reformed group's affairs are on this side of the border. One lives in Quilcene, on the Olympic Peninsula. The other one is Canadian but lives on his sailboat, usually moored in Anacortes." She flipped over the first leaf of paper on the easel and then continued. "It is difficult to trace what the cult is up to due to its tax-free status in the United States. But the information Mr. Gaskin sent me from Canada gives us some idea." She pointed to a schematic diagram depicting a flow of funds. "The fellow on the boat, Jaroslav Kaczynski". She pronounced Jaroslav commencing with a 'y' sound and Kaczinski with a 'ch' in the middle. "He signs most of the deposits and drafts as a 'high director' of the Reformed Striationists despite the fact that our investigator has seen him attending Mass every Sunday."

"The one in Quilcene, Jason Stildt, is both a lawyer (a member of the Idaho state bar), and a CPA. Although he professes to be a humble oyster gatherer, he has assets in the neighbourhood of fifteen million dollars. His post office box in Quilcene is the religion's registered address in this country."

"It's not a religion, it's a cult!" Sadich yelped.

Catriona sighed again. "Anyway, what appears to be happening is that Stildt receives cheques drawn on Citibank payable to him, endorses them, and then turns them over to Kaczinski. The funds come from two sources: a brokerage in Toronto, Canada and an investment bank on Wall Street. Kaczynski in turn deposits them at a branch of the Kitsap Bank in Port Townsend. Although it is unclear how much money is involved, Kaczynski periodically transfers funds from Port Townsend to a branch of the Royal Bank in a town in Canada called Parksville, which I believe is on Vancouver Island." Carlo nodded as Catriona looked to him for confirmation.

"Some of the funds may be going in the opposite direction: from the Royal Bank to Port Townsend and then off to either Toronto or New York. But each of the transactions have the name of one individual in common: each of them has at least one document bearing the signature of one Émile Basaraba." She slid a page across the table. "Because of his French first name, we assume he's based in Montreal, but we haven't been able to verify it, yet."

"All of the declarations filed by the, ah, cult's organization in both countries state that the source of the funds is interest from simple term deposits, but that can't possibly be true unless Stildt has term deposits totalling in the billions. And we have no idea what happens to the money after it arrives in Canada. Although the account is in the relig...ah, cult's name, we have no information as to who has signing authority over it, although it appears that Basaraba may be one of them." Catriona smiled at Carlo as she sat down.

Sadich broke the silence with an inelegant gargling sound. "We'd best get the actions commenced on both sides of the border if we want to find out what's going on. So you two draft the pleadings for both jurisdictions. And remember that our action has to be in Federal Court in this country; this matter has an obvious international component." He turned to Catriona. "The goal here is *discovery*. We don't have to succeed against everyone we sue. When you guys are naming the parties and drafting the allegations, do it with document production, depositions and motions *in limine* in mind."

Carlo had no idea what a motion *in limine* was but he assumed that Catriona could tell him. He followed her to a small boardroom at a remote corner of the office, the table cluttered with disparate folders and binders from the Striationist file and surrounded by bookcases filled with volumes of the *Pacific Reporter* dating back to the 1930s.

"You haven't been briefed, have you?" Catriona asked.

"Sorry?"

"I could tell by the way you were looking at us. This is all new to you, isn't it?"

"Yes. Two days ago I didn't even know that this file existed. I tried to read it over yesterday, but it's more than a metre thick, and it is in, let's just say, random order." Carlo gesticulated to conjure the image of a chaotic heap. "I tried to figure out what was going on, what property might have disappeared, who might have been behind it, but our file is just a tangled mass of paper."

"I thought as much. I didn't know that *you* existed until ten minutes before you showed up this morning; I don't think that even Sadich had much more notice than that. We all thought that Mr. Gaskin would be coming down."

"He said that something came up, something to do with his wife."

"And he still never briefed you about the file?"

"No, he didn't."

"These guys!" Catriona pushed a stack of binders out of the way to clear space on the table. "Shoot me now before I'm one of those old warhorses. Anyway, do you want the condensed version?"

"Please."

"I guess you know all about the fucking Striationists," Catriona said.

"Very little, actually. I hear that they worship cracks that the glaciers gouged into rocks?"

"Basically. They roll themselves naked around on them until they bleed. It's more of a New Age morass than a cult, but it's not really a religion, either. Anyway, the first notice that we had that there was a problem was when the Wellspring (think of it as idiot tax) suddenly disappeared soon after they collected it, by sheer coincidence around the time they split into two."

"How much money is involved?"

"Well, they have about a million members, mainly in British Columbia, Washington and Alaska but also in Oregon and northern California, and they're each taxed (oh, sorry), Wellspringed about a thousand each year, depending on the Domain (it's what the mentally-balanced might call a diocese), so you do the math."

Carlo squinted in surprise. "What do they use all *that* money for?"

"Buying God-forsaken acreages in the middle of nowhere, with exquisitely gouged and therefore *sacred* rock faces. Anyway, they had some large pieces of land, some on the B.C. coast; some in the Cascades, the San Juan Islands, the Olympic Peninsula and then in Canada again, in the Kootenanneys."

"Kootenays. They're called the Kootenays."

"Whatever. And some of these properties had nice, resort style lodges where the faithful would go to heal their wounds after they mutilated themselves on the rocks. There was one on Savary Island, up in Canada (I've been there, actually a beautiful spot); it's worth millions. It was one of the ones that was snatched out from underneath our clients just before the split. And we still don't know for sure how that was arranged, much less what happened to the money."

"I see."

"I hope so. I mean, our clients, they might be totally fucked, but we're ethically bound to help them clean up their mess. So! You don't know our court forms and precedents; I don't know yours. How about if we figure out what we want to say and who we want to sue and then we'll translate it into the appropriate gibberish?"

After about fourteen drafts of the template and a lively debate about those who were to be named as parties, Carlo and Catriona sat behind their laptops to draft documents sufficiently fatuous and unintelligible to conform to the rules of pleading. It was already nine by the time they finished.

"Where's your hotel?" Catriona asked.

"It's one of those executive suite places about a block from Pike Street Market."

"Great. I know a great Irish pub about half way. I'm buying: it was my boss who got us into this."

Everyone at Finnegan's Wake seemed to know Catriona, from the bar staff to most of the customers, sparse late on a Thursday night. The waitresses, themselves all barely of legal drinking age, wore short plaid skirts fastened with giant iron safety pins. Before long, Carlo was sipping on a Harp; Catriona ordered an Irish cider. They agreed to share a plate of nachos (no jalapeños).

"So," Catriona asked, "how long have you been working for Gaskin?"

"About two months"

"What's that like? I'm just wondering...these old hippies with their silly 'religion'."

"Well, you would think that Declan was one of them, looking at the bizarre décor in his office, but he isn't really one of *the faithful.* But he is…a bit odd, we'll say. He has this irritating habit of talking to me in a silly Italian accent. It makes my teeth hurt."

"Really. I'm surprised he isn't one of them. Juvenile bigotry seems to be part of their liturgy. Sadich refers to me as 'the Yellow Peril'.

"*To your face?*"

"No, but these things have a way of getting back to me." She winked.

They stayed for another drink. Catriona curled her lip when the waitress casually brushed her hand across Carlo's shoulder as she placed his Harp on the mat.

"Are you going to the Strationists' meeting in July?" Carlo asked. "It's on Canada Day weekend."

"Canada Day?"

"The first of July. It's like Independence Day down here only people don't get quite as drunk."

"No, I hadn't heard about it."

Carlo related what Gaskin had told him before he left Vancouver. "He said that it was going to be held on your side of the border, at some resort called "Petunia" or something."

"*Petunia?* What the fuck? No, by the time July rolls around I'll be here, probably at that point still putting together the materials for a motion to subpoena the hard disks, e-mails and complete banking records of both Stildt and Kaczynski," she groaned.

"You can *do* that here?"

"Not that I know of, at least not yet. My task is to find a way. Believe me, I'd rather hang out with the lunatics."

Carlo walked with Catriona toward her apartment on a small side street up the hill from the entrance to Pike Street Market; little more than an alley. Much to his surprise, Catriona smoked.

"I'd invite you up for a drink, but it's late," she exhaled a few wisps of smoke. "I'm going to have a full day tomorrow. I'll give you the proper tour next time you're in Seattle." Catriona fell silent for a moment. "No, no, it's a school night. Back at 'er tomorrow!" It started to rain as Carlo walked back to his hotel.

The next morning, Carlo took a ferry to the other side of Puget Sound and made his way across the Olympic Peninsula to a distant river in the mountains. After a three-hour drive, he parked at an uneven expanse of gravel at the end of a dirt road. No one else was there. He hauled his backpack out of the back of his Jeep and started along a shaded trail that descended towards the river.

He hiked for three hours through a forest of tall red cedar and Sitka spruce, which to him was as magnificent as any cathedral. Walking alone through a forest in silence always invited random thoughts, sometimes the fleeting reminder of past embarrassments, the same ones that made him cringe when lying awake in the middle of the night. What he dreaded the most was the intrusion of long suspended recollections, past events that evoked uncontrollable emotions. Elsewhere, maybe behind the wheel, on the subway or the tram, even walking down a city street, they could be easily banished by the flood of urban detail. Here, without much distraction from his own thoughts, they were almost impossible to suppress. So once again, he found himself drawn into a dreaded void, revisiting a past when he was a much happier person.

It was a lifetime ago, back fifteen years. In contrast to his own fogbound celebration two years before in Vancouver, the afternoon of Laura's high school graduation in Comox was blessed with abundant sunshine. After the ceremony, Yvette borrowed her father's BMW, Laura in the front, Carlo and Yvette's boyfriend Damion in the back. They'd gone up to a viewpoint up the Strathcona Parkway to drink champagne and then started back to Laura's place, where some of the parents had organized a gathering before the after-grad party later that night.

"Hey!" Laura looked back at Carlo. "Wall-yo! Any of the champagne left?"

"Lots; there's still half of this one." He handed her a bottle of Moët & Chandon.

"So Laura," Yvette said. "We're meeting up with Deanna and some other people after the party out at Ship's Point to watch the sunrise. You guys in?"

"Nope. We're sneaking off by ten. There's a room with an ocean view at Kingfisher with our name on it."

"You two! Anyway, Damion! Are you taking out squatter's rights out on that joint?"

"Oh, sorry. Smoked it."

"Fuck! Laura, please tell me you've got another one."

"Yes," she sighed. "I do. But when we get inside the gate at my place, keep it out of sight. If the Rafferty's see that we've got weed, that bunch of deadbeats will hit me up for a joint, and they'll fucking try to make me roll it for them, too."

Yvette and Damion were the first to get out of the car, improbably resembling a bride and groom; Damion in a formal black jacket, Yvette in a light beige gown with frills and embellishments. Laura, perceptibly slimmed by her new job detailing cars, wore a brief light blue dress which bared her arms and much of her back. Carlo emerged from the car in a grey three-button suit.

Laura's parents and her Auntie Deanna crossed the lawn, Deanna leading with a full glass of wine. "Look at this beautiful young lady!" Carlo found her Scottish accent difficult to follow unless he'd had a good night's sleep. "I must say, what a good-looking pair. Laura, you look positively elegant!"

"Elegant? She's just a few threads shy of naked." Laura's mother held both Laura and Carlo in a steady gaze. The family resemblance was unmistakable, long blonde hair worn in a style similar to Laura, her face altered little by age. She looked more like Laura's youthful but humourless aunt. "Well, young man, let me get a good look at you," she said in a Danish accent that Carlo mistook for a German one only once. "Just because you are studious doesn't mean that you're not permitted to eat."

"Hello, Mrs. Thompson."

Laura's father reached over to hug his daughter. "You make me feel so old; all grown up, and your young man already even looks like a lawyer."

"Don't talk like that, Jacob. He's only just finished his second year of university. Not a time to slack off, so much more work ahead!"

"Oh, for God's sake, Birgitta!" Deanna laughed. "You're the woman the English had in mind when they came up with the term 'wet blanket'."

Carlo pointed to the bottle of *prosecco* he was carrying. "Mr. Thompson, is there a place I can keep this cold?"

"For the five-hundredth time, my name is Jack!" he laughed. "There's a big cooler full of ice up by the old fire pit. But you'll have to pass by your favourite four ladies on the way."

A Siamese cat brushed his calf, still a kitten, with a deep, mournful meow of a volume unexpected from such a diminutive creature. "Hey, Bruiser, there's a nice little cat," Carlo said as he stooped to scratch its ears.

The Old Skunks were sitting drinking rye at one of the long tables, well back from most of the other guests, peering and pointing at Laura, bantering among themselves. They didn't acknowledge Carlo as he passed them, not even by lowering their voices.

"Well, good on her," Toni said. "She's lost a lot of weight since the last time I saw her."

"Good on her, nothing." Violet said. "The little princess got an abortion. Just like these rest of these girls who decide they want to go to college. Slutty enough to invite the boys inside to play but too special to pump one out."

"Just listen to you three," Gladys said. "Look, she sure got fat for a while there, but pregnant? Forget it! I mean, did you see *that* just now? As if that little Spic managed to knock her up. Men who like cats are all faggots."

The clouds had finally parted enough to allow sunlight to permeate the forest, imparting a golden glow to the beards of dangling moss. Carlo was surprised to find himself laughing; even a few months earlier this recollection inspired tears. As it turned out, Yvette joined the group at Ship's Point by herself after Damion broke up with her in an incendiary exchange later that afternoon. Carlo wondered how many more of the well-dressed couples smiling for photographs that afternoon in the school atrium had since parted company. He was sure of one thing: he never would have imagined that he and Laura would be among them.

Just as he started to worry that either his memory was failing him or that time had so altered the passing foliage that its subtle hints would no longer guide him, he saw the mossy maple glade that formed the sylvan turnoff, the portal to his campsite, a peaceful gravel bar along the river, ten minutes off the trail.

Carlo set his pack down on the sand and retrieved his cup. The immediate foreshore was too shallow to allow him a deep enough draught, so he waded out and stooped to scoop a cup of water out of the river, a broad flume that flowed through a silent rain forest, absolutely clear, without the glacial till that adulterates the water of other rivers on this coast. He took a long gulp of water and marvelled as he looked around the gravel bar, the river flowing quietly as it formed a broad pool, the surrounding forest of maples, cedars, alders and especially Sitka spruce, massive columns looming over the gravel bar like nosy chaperones. *Christ, it hasn't changed in eleven years. Thank God something hasn't.*

14

The corridors of the Sedgwick Building, a two-storey annex at the periphery of the University of British Columbia campus, radiated an odour of stale disinfectant and flooring wax characteristic of public institutions built during the Fifties. Gavin led Lawrence Gollander towards the SeaMent laboratories, all at the far end of the building, with an increasing sense of unease. Gollander's eyes shifted quickly back and forth as he pranced down the hall, as if in fear that a wild animal might suddenly leap out of one of the seminar rooms.

"It's down at the end," Gavin said. They were walking much more slowly than was Gavin's habit, due to his companion's odd, comic gait. "Oh, there he is."

Christian Davidson, the senior scientific advisor to SeaMent, emerged from an intersecting corridor. "Gavin, Gavin, there you are. I was expecting you about half an hour ago." He spoke with a North Country English accent that Gavin sometimes found incomprehensible. Gollander was genuinely short and Gavin was six feet, but Davidson, nine inches taller than that, towered over both of them.

"Yes, Christian, I'm sorry." Gavin laughed. "Vancouver traffic; every bridge and intersection seems to have its own cluster of rear-end collisions. Oh, and Christian, meet Lawrence Roswell Gollander, Minister of Economic Development."

"I am honoured," Davidson said.

"Pleased to meet you, Professor." Gollander turned to look behind him as he shook Davidson's hand.

"Did you catch the ferry over this morning?" Davidson asked.

"No, I have the big shot with me." Gavin placed his hand on Gollander's shoulder, who reacted with a sudden leap. "We came over on the Helijet yesterday and stayed at the Wedgewood." He named a modish five-star hotel downtown. "I left Tiffany to the tender mercies of Vancouver shops."

"My condolences." Davidson laughed.

It really wasn't all that bad. Where most men Gavin knew had wives or girlfriends (or, in a few notable examples, wives *and* girlfriends) who would have been sure to frequent the boutiques and shoe stores of Alberni Street and Pacific Centre, spending hundreds, and probably thousands, Tiffany rarely ventured beyond Lululemon and The Sweat Factory, where she replenished her supply of yoga pants and exercise wear, all delightfully snug. At one time, it used to embarrass him to venture in public with Tiffany, who dressed in spandex attire so tight that she looked like she was nude, perhaps with an odd skin tone, but (as they say) he got over it.

"Well," Davidson slapped Gollander on the back with such force that he gasped a sequence of sputtering wheezes. "I suppose that I ought to bring you gents up to date!" Gollander peered at him as if trying to divine the meaning of a foreign phrase. "Come with me." He led them into a large room the size of a school auditorium, taken up almost entirely by what appeared to be a raised swimming pool with transparent vertical siding. It was traversed lengthwise by a long, ivory coloured tube about half a metre in diameter. "So look at this! We're making progress."

"Glad to hear it." Gavin peered at the tube. "That's the SeaMent? It's kind of, I don't know, *thin*, isn't it?" Gavin asked.

"I know, believe me, I know; it looks like gossamer now, but as it accumulates, it forms an incredibly strong and elastic ceramic-like material. I trust that Dr. Olafsen showed you some of the blocks and panels he produced.

"He did, before he ran off."

"Ah. Well, anyway, we were..."

Gollander interrupted him. "I'm sorry; maybe I'm missing something, but isn't this just like plugging in an electrical appliance and then tossing it in a bathtub?" Gavin had been wondering the same thing for months but he didn't dare ask the question for fear of being taken for an idiot.

"Well, you see, Professor Olafsen designed a process that creates a semi-permeable membrane that surrounds the electrode assembly," Davidson said, as if trying to calm an overly-eager pupil. "It allows entry of the dissolved minerals but does not allow the electrical current to escape." He turned to Gavin. "And Olafsen has patents pending for the membrane in both the U.S. and the European Union. He's a smart guy, some call him a genius; it's too bad that..." Gavin coughed; Davidson stopped talking. For a moment the three men shuffled in silence, each examining the floor.

"Anyway, as I was saying before," Davidson continued, "We were having some trouble with the rate of particulate accumulation. Olafsen's electrolysis method appeared to effectively bind new particulate to what had already accumulated, but the pace of accumulation! It would have taken a year just to get a shaft of even thirty metres. But with our refinement?" He motioned toward the pool. "The rate has picked up exponentially!"

Gollander peered at Davidson as if his every word was an unwelcome surprise. "All of this comes at a price," Davidson said. "The electrodes require an alloy with a richer mix of platinum."

Gavin shrugged. "Not a big deal."

"And I'm telling you, Gavin. The amperage required to power the entire experiment; well, let's just say that you will require turbines in addition to the ones that are already *in situ.*"

"Don't worry about that; there are at least a dozen bankrupt mining operations between Idaho and the Yukon that will be happy to unload suitable turbines for a pittance."

"Good. But there is something, well, that is starting to concern me."

"What's that?" Gavin remained convinced that Gollander understood little of what Davidson was saying.

"Well, I will just say this. The test is just what, three or four months away? It's one thing to perform an experiment here, in a controlled environment, but out there, that five or so hundred metres from Civic Park to Newcastle Island, I just can't say for sure."

"I thought you told me that this water was the same as the sea water in the test area." Gavin said.

"Well, it is!"

"Then what are you talking about?"

"In the ambient location, with a variety of stimuli and factors that we cannot account for here, well, there are a number of things that could transpire."

"Look, Christian, if you have something to tell me, you'd better spit it out. What's the worst that could happen here?"

Davidson stepped back. "It's not going to be some sort of cataclysm, is it? But don't expect it to go off without a hitch, either, Gavin."

"Please, Christian, it's not as if I'm some twenty-five-year-old. I know that."

Gollander interrupted again. "So I suppose if the experiment (we should call it that, I think) is a success, then we could expect that the value of the McKee McWatney lands north of Nanaimo would rise substantially, that would be fair to say, wouldn't it?" Gavin was surprised that Gollander had assimilated enough of the conversation to make a coherent contribution.

"I suppose," Davidson said in a distracted tone. "It would depend on a variety of factors..." He fell silent with the approach of someone else in a lab coat.

"Professor Davidson, it's almost time." By her age and demeanour, she appeared to be a graduate student whose brilliance did not prevent her from presenting like an adolescent Goth.

"Yes. Thank you, Jessica. Gentlemen. I have to attend to, well, matters academic. Gavin, I trust that you will call me so that we can talk about the turbines I'll need."

"Yes, of course."

Gavin and Gollander saw themselves out of the facility. "That was very difficult," Gollander said as they crossed the parking lot.

"Oh, why is that?"

"It was like being in Whistler, dealing with pub staff, or the people who take your lift tickets. I find it almost impossible to understand Australians."

This guy skis, Gavin thought. *Who knew?*

....15

Declan watched as Marika walked out of his office, dressed in a sweater and tight jeans and elevated in a pair of dress boots. She went back to her desk and busied herself rearranging a set of binders and checking her e-mail. It was already almost seven, past the hour when he usually left the office. He had yet to regain his composure. Marika turned to look at him, waiting.

Well, that was certainly interesting, but, under the circumstances, perhaps not so unexpected. He played with an old 1967 centennial keychain ornament as he pondered. Triangles. Experience had taught him long ago that you cannot actually control the actions of other people, but he had no intention of allowing this new situation, this nuisance, to actually develop to its often inevitable conclusion. That would end in certain disaster and, in all probability, financial ruin. He turned to gaze at the darkening silhouette of Mount Seymour as he fell deeper into thought, forming the rudiments of a plan.

16

"I'm glad you had a few minutes to meet up." Patricia set her glasses on the table and took a sip of her wine. "It's the first time we've had a chance for a glass of wine since that...that meeting in Bastion Square. What a fucking disaster! I warned Gavin that showing his hand *now* was a profoundly stupid idea, but he didn't listen. I don't know what's wrong with that man! His book is called *The Amiable Plunderer*, not '*The Honest Plunderer*'. What was he thinking? Bringing it up, the fixed link I mean, on the Island, of all places. I'm sorry," she laughed. "I'm ranting. At least he had enough sense to shoot his mouth off in front of a bunch of *Smuglets*." Patricia used her pet word for the Victoria and Vancouver real estate and financial élite. "Obviously no sense of irony in any of them. 'Visualize Vancouver Island' indeed! And for the most part, they're so gullible and narcissistic that they consider their involvement in whole debacle as proof of their own prestige."

Laeticia took in the panorama from Pinot Grigio's, the wine bar on the Inner Harbour where she and Patricia customarily met once or twice a month. She could see Bastion Square from where they were sitting, across the harbour in Victoria's elegant historic core. She and Patricia became acquainted about a year earlier, at an academic conference in Vancouver on oil spill containment. At first, Laeticia found Patricia's generous attentions mildly disconcerting, but she soon figured out that Patricia, who herself held a doctorate in marine biology, merely sought to befriend someone whom she regarded, in many ways, as a younger version of herself.

"Well," Laeticia said. "It wasn't the first time that he's brought it up in public, on the Island. He made quite a grandiose display of it, complete with Luciano Pavarotti, at the Seaview in Parksville back in April. I almost fell over laughing when his computer packed it in. And then some pretty boy from TriMar peddling a skyscraper tried to tell me not to worry about a sewage problem in Parksville Bay because old people don't shit."

"Seriously? Yuck, those people...oh, yes, all right; the computer malfunction. I seem to remember hearing about this one. And I must admit: Gavin is an original. It's probably a good thing, the world can't really tolerate more than one. But he's really a very decent fellow, once you get to know him. And I've known him for quite a while."

"Really? Were you two an item, back in the day?"

Patricia whooped with high-pitched laughter. "Oh, my God, no! For one thing, he's *much* younger than I am! Oh, yes, believe me, he is; and as recent developments have demonstrated, I'm *decades* too old for him. If you're his neighbour, no doubt you've met the Child Bride."

Laeticia giggled at the way she described Tiffany. "Oh, yeah; we exercise together. Two or three times per week."

"Oh? I suppose I shouldn't be surprised. Anyway, I like Tiffany; to me she's of another generation, but she's a very nice girl, and (I'm shocked to hear myself saying this) she's been good for him. It's no surprise he's done with Lelani (she's his ex), I can assure you of that! My ex-husband and I used to socialize with them a few years back, before Gavin became 'The Amiable' anything."

"In Parksville?"

"No, they lived in West Van back then. My ex and I went over there for dinner this one time, just before Gavin's book came out. You know, that woman served us the most bizarre repast I've ever heard of. Rose petal and honeysuckle salad, and something else that looked like chopped and sautéed earthworms and crickets."

Laeticia convulsed in disgust.

"I'm still not sure what they were, but Gavin assured me that they were vegetable in origin. Whatever it was, it took almost five weeks for my digestive system to return to normal. So, how are you doing? Are you still working on the salmon population project?"

"Yes, we're focusing on the Baynes Sound area right now. And Mario's being such a sweetheart about it. He's going to stay with me in the little cabin they've assigned me. He says that we'll treat it as a romantic getaway, even if I'll be chin deep in mud and seaweed most days. He'll even do the cooking. Oh yes," she sighed. "I almost forgot. Getting back to that Bastion Square thing: I meant to call you about it. Is there anything you can do about that Lerche guy? He texts me daily, asking me out for dinner, drinks; even skiing, Jesus fucking Christ! He won't give up even though I've told him that I'm married, which is only a slight exaggeration."

Patricia sighed. "Well, he won't listen to me! Two years ago, he was, what's the politically correct expression, paying *unwanted sexual attention* to one of my staffers. When I told him to cool it, you know what the little prick said? 'Stay out of it; you're not my mother!' He's younger than he looks, but he's not *that* young. Anyway, he got his. The young lady eventually had to threaten him with a restraining order." A look of concern passed over her face. "These sorts of anecdotes have to stay between us."

"Of course. Which reminds me," Laeticia said. "The next Georgia Basin committee meeting, it's in two weeks, isn't it?" The Georgia Basin Environmental Studies Steering Committee, a supervisory body for research involving the body of water that separated Vancouver Island from the mainland, included a number of academics, including Laeticia, in the earth sciences, economics and geography, as well as elected figures and representatives of local environmental groups. As Minister of the Environment, the role of the committee's *ex officio* chair fell to Patricia.

"Yes. And at least Sandvik," a committee member who taught biology at UBC, "promised me that he's going to refrain from droning on about his fucking reindeer for an hour and a half this time," Patricia said.

"They're elk."

"Whatever. He stinks. Are you going to be able to make it?"

"Oh, for sure; I'll already be down in Victoria."

"Good. And by the way," Patricia said. "The next meeting of the VisualEyes is the week after. It's up on the north Island, in Port Hardy; the rural contingent complained that we always hold the meetings in Victoria or Nanaimo. I hope you'll be there."

Port Hardy, on the very north-eastern edge of Vancouver Island, was a drive of almost eight hours. "I think so. But it's so far away."

"It is. And it's one of the rainiest places on Earth. But look on the bright side: if your young man is prepared to treat a trip to your muddy cabin as a romantic getaway, this would be like a weekend in Paris. Another glass?"

"Sure, twist my rubber arm."

17

Marika was already waiting for him at Calista's. "You're late!"

"No I'm not," Carlo said.

"No, look at the clock. Two minutes, buddy!" No one would have ever described her as subdued, but in recent days she'd become effusive, dressed as flamboyantly as she behaved. Today she was wearing a tight, shiny purple shirt with a hood, and coloured leggings. One leg red, the other blue.

Carlo contemplated the surface tension of the coffee in his cup when she started rapidly recounting the *bargains* she'd found during a recent trip to Costco. It wasn't until she changed the subject that he paid attention to her. "Oh, I should warn you," she said. "It came in yesterday's mail, his new *Verdict.*" It was an American legal magazine that Declan seemed to worship as an infallible font of wisdom. "He was on about some article that he saw in it all afternoon yesterday, when you were off at that discovery in New Westminster, something about how it would help you salvage your career."

Marika's warning proved correct. It came while Carlo was engrossed in the online edition of *L'Espresso,* taking a short respite after he'd spent most of the morning on the phone with an insurance adjuster, arguing about the merits of a rehabilitation program an orthopaedist recommended for one of his clients.

Declan startled him by slapping a shimmering *Verdict* on his blotter, open about half-way. "You should read this piece! It has people like you in mind."

In praise of 'Blending In': Leave failure in the dust by embracing your inner WASP

"It's only common sense." Declan said. "Just think of what it would do for you in the long run if you simply changed your name."

Carlo reset his browser to Google. "I'm sorry, I didn't quite hear you."

"I think that it would put your career on a much better footing if you changed your name."

"Really? What difference would it make?"

"Come on, Carlo! I'm sure that many people seeing your name in the Legal Directory have a very understandable fear that you can't speak English." He slipped into a tone now familiar to Carlo, an elocutionary style best compared to waffle syrup that Declan took on when he was being fatuous. "And clients, well, they like to pay lawyers who they see as one of their own."

Carlo feigned a thoughtful expression. "Indeed. I was just thinking last week: maybe I should change my last name to 'Ng'."

This seemed to take Declan by surprise. "Oh! Do you really think that you could convince anyone that you're Chinese?"

"Doesn't matter; I could just say that I was adopted, and anyway, by the time it becomes an issue, they'd already be in the office, waiting for my advice."

Declan developed jowls and cleared his throat. "Anyway, I came in to talk to you for another reason. It's the Striationists: the whole Savary Island and Wellspring things are really heating up. I was going to go up to Port Rattray myself to interview several members of the Directorate; there are also a few boxes of documents up there that we need to go through and copy. But, ah, I have this American Trial Lawyers conference in Boston coming up (I will be giving a paper), so I won't be able to go there myself. But we have to get this done soon. You go in my stead; Marika will be coming up with you. It's a big job; you're going to need all the help you can get."

"Sure." Carlo shrugged. "When will this be?"

"Tomorrow morning. You guys will be flying out by floatplane from Coal Harbour at nine. You'll need at least three, maybe even four days up there. I've already made the arrangements. You might want to take some notes."

"Oh, okay. What's up?" Carlo slid a note tablet from under a stack of files.

"All right." Declan leaned against the bookcase. "You will be meeting first with Ruairi and Margaret Davidson. They are both Elders, and they're the caretakers of the old lodge at Port Rattray. They also own the fishing resort where you'll be staying. These days, it's one of the few places that has enough dry space to store all of the religion's old records. We need to go through *all* of them, in detail, page by page. Bill them at a slightly lower hourly rate, maybe around, let's say, two seventy-five?

"So anyway," Declan continued. "It's not just the money that disappeared. Fourteen properties were disposed of, in our view, improperly. They were worth a fortune. No one still connected to the religion saw a penny of the proceeds of sale."

"Yes, Sadich got into this a bit down in Seattle, before we drafted the pleadings."

"Ah. I'd forgotten about that. Oh, and also, most of the other Elders will also be there for one of their, I don't know, *synods?* So I want you to interview all of them. If you gather any information which you think is germane, take it as evidence in affidavit form. And I want you and Marika to go through and list *all* of their documents, including their business records."

Declan went over to rearrange the books on Carlo's bookshelf, most of which actually belonged to him, so that the cover of *Unsafe at Any Speed* faced outward, conspicuous among frayed textbooks. "And we've got to talk about July long weekend, the Orthodox Striationist Convocation Festival at that resort; oh, I think it's called Chrysanthemum or something. Anyway, when we're there, I want you to do a workshop on document preservation. That's one of the reasons I want you up at Port

Rattray right away: too many documents are being destroyed whenever some of the faithful take it into their heads that they hurt us. No big rush, but I'd like to see your draft speaking notes before we go down."

"Sure. I'll get started on it after we get back."

About an hour later, Marika came into his office carrying three accordion files, each stuffed to capacity, and a thick binder.

"What the...?"

"Oh," Marika groaned. "It's time that you took a good look at this mess! *Dhaliwal v. Komich.* Nobody has worked on it since Steven was here; that's more than a year ago, and trial's coming up just after Christmas."

"Just sit it over there on my credenza, next to the other train wrecks. Oh, did you know that Declan is sending us up to Port Rattray tomorrow?"

"Port *who*? Where the fuck is that?"

"It's this place up the coast, north of Powell River. We have to interview some of Declan's freaks and take their affidavits, and there are some documents to sort through. He can't do it himself because he's got some Trial Lawyer's thing in Boston."

"Seriously? First I've heard of it. Are we driving there, or..."

"No, you can't get there by car. We have to go by seaplane."

"So I guess I'll have to set up travel arrangements?"

"No need. Declan already made them himself. We're flying out of Coal Harbour first thing in the morning."

"Cool! I've never been on a floatplane before."

Carlo came in an hour early the next morning. While he was busy sliding their laptops, a scanner and the portable printer into Cordura cases, Marika came through the entrance towing a suitcase, dressed in a light grey wool suit that was barely adequate to contain her figure.

"Hey." Marika bore the harassed look of some who had yet to fully awaken. "Need some help?" Declan was lurking next to the reception desk, staring at her.

"Oh, hey," Carlo said. "Yes, please grab some basic office stuff and throw it in that litigation bag over there. You never know what they'll have on hand out in the sticks."

Declan walked over sporting an indulgent smile, invariably the harbinger of unsolicited advice. To Carlo's surprise, Declan was abrupt.

"Well, good luck! I'm sure that you will both enjoy Port Rattray. It's a lovely spot!" Declan clasped his palms together. "And make sure that you bring back *all* of the documents. I'm a bit antsy that they're still up there, unsupervised."

"No problem." Carlo finished zipping the printer into its case. "We're going to scan them all and then pack them all up."

"Good. See you two next week!"

"Bye." Marika whispered.

"Have a good time in Boston!" Carlo said with more verve than he thought he could muster.

"You bet."

The seaplane descended as it skirted the lower slopes of Mount Dunedin, meeting the water on Melbourne Inlet across from Port Rattray, an agglomeration of wooden buildings of varied size, seemingly guarded by three tall, white waterfront fuel tanks. A long wooden sign with 'PORT RATTRAY RESORT' painted in black letters hung above the fuel dock. It was midday; a flotilla of Boston Whalers taxied past, guides taking their clients to the salmon fishing grounds off Cortes Island.

"*Both! Both!* De Plane!"

Phil, the superintendent of maintenance, shouted from his desk next to a window in the resort's second floor administrative office, as he did every time the Malaspina Air flight landed, usually four times per week. Gert, his assistant, still found it amusing after almost three years. Susan, the head of housekeeping, years younger than both of them and wearing her hair in a fashionable style uncharacteristic of the locale, merely groaned. She'd put up with it for less than five months.

Phil picked up a pair of binoculars and watched as Carlo piled bags into a wheelbarrow on the landing. "There's our lawyer guy, in a suit." Marika followed, stepping on to the pier, unsure of her footing in high heels, twisting as if constrained by her snug suit. "Oh my fucking Christ! What a *babe*! Check her out!" He handed the binoculars to Gert.

"No shit, you're not fuckin' kidding! And just look at those *tits*!"

"Give me that thing!" Susan grabbed the binoculars from Gert. "You guys! Your taste is all up your ass. She's a cow!" She watched Marika walk uneasily along the pier and twice place a hand on Carlo's shoulder to maintain her balance, uneasily perched on overpriced shoes. "Look, did you see that? She's getting so fat she can barely walk."

"She's beautiful," Phil whined. Gert made a lascivious moan in agreement.

"Whatever." She adjusted the focus to get a better look at Carlo, the first man she'd seen in a suit since she left Vancouver. Marika used him to steady herself again as he pushed their luggage up the gangway in a wheelbarrow.

"That lawyer, what is he, Greek or something? Lucky guy, eh?" Phil said to no one in particular.

"Oh, is he a fuckin' Greek, like Vasilios?" Gert asked, pronouncing the name of the local diesel merchant by elongating each syllable.

Susan forced out a theatrical sigh, reserved by women to show their contempt for men who are their obvious intellectual inferiors. "He's not Greek, for Christ's sake. 'Buonsante'; are you guys illiterate or something? That's an Italian name."

Phil looked at Gert. "A wop, eh? So what do you want to bet that he's fuckin' her?"

I wonder, Susan thought as she put down the binoculars.

Carlo parked the wheelbarrow beside the office entrance and held the door for Marika. "Someone was supposed to meet us at the seaplane dock. I guess we'll wait in here." A woman came out to the counter, slender, with shoulder length brown hair and the mottled complexion he often noted among unsuccessful vegetarians.

"Good afternoon, you two!" She spoke with a British Isles accent he found impossible to place. "The gods must be with you; the weather is unusually balmy." She extended her hand first to Marika. "Margaret Davidson".

"Marika Balodis".

"Carlo Buonsante. I understand that a group of Striationist Elders will be coming in this afternoon?"

"Yes, at three, for our monthly meeting. But before that, we should get you two set up in your rooms. We saved you a cabin with a view of the beach and one of the upper floor housekeeping rooms in Ballard Hall." She pointed across the courtyard garden at the large, log-framed structure opposite.

"I'll take the room," Carlo said. "Marika can have the cabin, but we'll need some sort of office, with a bit of privacy."

"There's lots of space in the cabin. No one will bother you there. Oh, and we'll make our way over to meet with the Council in Rattray Lodge — it's just there on the other side of the bay — in about an hour. Is that all right?"

"Yes, thanks. Now, Declan mentioned something about a couple of boxes of documents that he wanted us to go through. Where would they be?" Carlo asked.

"Down in the dungeon." Margaret laughed. "And there are about twelve of them, maybe a few more."

"The dungeon?"

"Yes, Declan insisted that we use it. It's a sealed basement under Ballard Hall. They built it back in the Twenties to hide liquor."

Carlo took his luggage up to his room, a suite overlooking the entrance to the pub. A bottle of Effervescent Elderberry awaited him on the kitchen counter, with a note attached.

Welcome to the Port Rattray Resort! We hope you enjoy your stay. We also hope you enjoy this complimentary organic beverage, made from wholesome and natural ingredients from the wilderness of the Coast Mountains!

Cheers,
Susan Wiltshire
Housekeeping Director.

He tossed it in the garbage and pulled a few bottles of Leffe Blonde from his suitcase to put them in the refrigerator. A young woman with straight dark brown hair stood at the sink watching him; he must have left the door to the room open. 'Susan' was on her resort name tag.

"Hi!" She squeaked with vigour that went beyond standard commercial perkiness. "I'm Sue!" She extended her hand. Carlo shook it warily. Giovanna had given him ample reason to be suspicious of pretty, unusually slender women. "I'm the housekeeping director. I just wanted to make sure that your stay is off to a pleasant start!"

"Oh, yes, thanks. So I guess that card..." Carlo stopped himself.

"That beer you're putting in the fridge; is it German?"

"No, no, it's Belgian." Carlo began to regret his suspicion. She seemed pleasant enough.

"Hmm...Belgian. My uncle, (well, an uncle by marriage) he's Belgian; but he speaks French, not like the other kind, what do you call them?"

"Flemish."

"Oh, yes, that's it, Flemish. So you're from Vancouver. What part of town?"

"Just down by Granville Island, on False Creek."

"Oooh!" She squealed. "We were practically neighbours! I used to live at 10th and Alma."

Carlo opted to overlook the fact that the two districts were separated by several kilometres. "Oh! Nice area. So did you work at one of the hotels in Vancouver?"

"Nah, believe it or not, I was a journalist. I used to cover the Striationist convocations in Lund and here in Port Rattray when I worked for the Salish Sea Chronicle." Carlo recognised it as a local magazine popular with academics, known in Vancouver as 'the Sea' and both reviled and revered for its environmental bent. "I've interviewed your boss a couple of times. But when I heard about this job from Ruairi (he's on the Council), I decided to go for it. More money than working for the Sea, and I was ready for a break from Vancouver. You know." She shrugged. "Boyfriend troubles."

"Well, it looks like a nice place to work."

"Yes; I suppose it is. Well, if you need anything, just call me through the front desk. And if you're around, I'm usually in the pub for a bit after eight, if you want to join me for a drink."

"Thanks. We'll see; it depends on how busy the Striationists keep me." He patted his brief case.

"Oh, believe me, I know. They can be quite demanding,"

Rattray Lodge was of another age. Constructed of river stones but framed with metre-thick Douglas fir timbers, it would still be standing long after the glass condominium towers of north False Creek had been felled by a high wind. Carlo read in the

Striationists' Wikipedia entry that the lodge had been built during Prohibition by someone in the Rockefeller family. Electrical service was something of an afterthought; modern light switches looked elfin, embedded in the giant beams. A few embers smouldered in the grotto-like stone fireplace in its central Great Hall.

Margaret and Ruairi led a group of six Striationists, four men and two women, across the Great Hall to a long table next to the fireplace, all of them dressed in thick trousers, grey gum boots and woollen sweaters, even if the temperature outside was at least twenty degrees. Carlo and Marika, busy setting up their laptops and a printer, both paused to look up at the passing entourage.

Everyone in the group took their places at the long banquet table. "Right now, we'll just find out what they have to say," Carlo said quietly to Marika. "Type out anything that sounds important as I question them, and then we'll fashion it all into affidavits. If anything turns up in the documents over the next couple of days, we might have to come back."

"All right, everyone." Ruairi said. "We'll let our legal team get started. Carlo and Marika, and I'm not going to tackle *either* of your last names! Both of them come highly recommended by Declan. I'm told that Carlo used to be a tax lawyer in Berlin."

Carlo coughed and tried to smile. "Declan has briefed me about this, but there are a few things I'd like to ask you about."

"Okay," Margaret said. "What do you need to know?"

"First off," Carlo said, "I'd like to get a better idea of what happened to the Savary Island properties. There were what, four separate parcels, all waterfront, and one with a twenty-suite lodge?"

"That's right," Ruairi said.

"And the Reformed offshoot managed to somehow get possession of it and sell it after the schism in the religion."

Each of the Striationists sat erect and hummed.

"No, no," Margaret eventually spoke in a soothing voice. "Just like all of the rest of them, it was sold before the religion split. We still can't figure out what happened. That's why you're here."

"Well then, perhaps you could explain this to me." Carlo pulled four land title search certificates out of his briefcase and placed them on the table. "They are all basically the same. It says here that a numbered company, 851453 B.C. Limited, bought the Savary property about three weeks after the formal parting of the ways. Are you saying that this is incorrect?"

"It most certainly is!" A man with a theatrical red beard brandished a document of some sort.

Ruairi cleared his throat. "Hamish McPhee. Of the Malaspina Domain. He has a copy of the sales agreement."

Carlo took the stapled pages from Hamish and looked them over with Marika. It was a standard Agreement of Purchase and Sale used by most real estate agents in B.C., documenting the sale of all four properties to a 'Duckabush Investments Limited' for five million each, about a week before the date of the schism.

"Okay," Carlo said. "Duckabush Investments, an outfit that is apparently based in Quilcene, Washington, is listed here as the purchaser."

One of the women interrupted him. "The Duckabush River," she said, as if in a dream. "Just by Jupiter Ridge. It has the most powerful striations on this coast." Everyone at the table rumbled with a gentle purr, except for Carlo and Marika.

"The title search," Carlo continued. "It says that Duckabush Investments is the most recent owner of the property, after it bought it back from a numbered company based in Montreal. But in total, in the ten months since the split, the properties were sold nine times, each time as a block to the same purchaser."

"The point is, why would Duckabush buy the property, supposedly sell it, buy it back less than a year later and then resell it within a month, only to then buy it back again? And tell me, what was the assessed value of the properties, I mean, in total?"

"In the last tax year? Well, let's see." Ruairi shuffled through a pile of documents and handed some papers to Carlo. "About twenty-two million dollars and change."

"And who approved the sale?" Carlo pointed to the signature line.

All of the Striationists abruptly turned away from the agreement and hummed.

Ruairi eventually spoke. "We're not sure. We think that it was our principal secretary and, for a short time, the Master of the Treasure, Ian McHarg. He's my cousin, he came out here about three years ago from Aberdeen."

"Scotland, I'm assuming, rather than Washington?"

"Yes, of course."

"And your cousin, he had authority to dispose of....," Carlo corrected himself. "To sell Striationist property?" The Council members nodded and hummed. "Where is he now?"

"I have no idea." Ruairi said. "Last I saw of him was at a retreat in Nakusp about eight, ten months ago, just after the split. We were supposed to meet up in London earlier this year at a family wedding; he never showed up."

"And the entire content of three of your accounts with the Royal Bank, just disappeared?" Carlo asked, moving to the next item on his list. "How much was in them, all together?"

"It was a week after we collected the Wellspring, something like a tithe, from all of our members. There was at least eight hundred million."

"Well," Carlo leaned back. "Money in a bank account doesn't just disappear. There must be a paper trail."

"Oh, there is!" An older man with a shaved head spoke up. "It was all sent by wire transfer to a brokerage house in Toronto, we'd never heard of it. And I bet there's a good reason for that: it probably doesn't exist."

"Someone must have authorized it." Carlo looked over at the laptop screen as Marika typed.

"Nobody at the bank seems to have any idea who gave the okay; they searched records, computer and telephone logs, everything." Ruairi said. "All they will admit is that the account manager received instructions over the phone from someone on the Council. And the Council was larger then."

Great. Carlo was stricken by a feeling of dread. *We're going to have to sue the bank.* An onslaught of pointless but time-consuming pre-trial litigation would fill his foreseeable future.

Everyone else in the Council turned to look at Ruairi, arched their backs and hummed again. Ruairi cleared his throat. "There is one thing that is becoming of great importance to us; something that we would like you two and Declan to investigate."

"We'll certainly do our best. What's the issue?"

Margaret answered instead of her husband. "It's the Parksville lands. McKee McWatney; oh, I'm sorry, maybe you don't know who they are."

"I've heard of them," Carlo said. He knew it as a logging company that owned much of eastern Vancouver Island.

"Anyway, it looks like somebody's bought up a huge swath from Parksville north, and whoever it is supposedly plan to develop the whole area. But we think it's the so-called 'Reformed' offshoot just trying to block our access to the Beaufort Striations!" The rest of the Council sat erect, still humming.

"Sure, we'll make inquiries."

Marika and Carlo spent the rest of the afternoon putting together affidavits for each of the Council members, most of them simply verifying that they did not authorize any of the transactions. Carlo soon discovered to his amusement that having Elders sign the documents under oath had its own pitfalls.

He placed the first affidavit in front of the man with the shaved head. "Do you solemnly swear that the contents are true, so help you God?" Upon Carlo's saying the word 'God', the man closed his eyes and hummed.

"Oh, I'm sorry. Do you solemnly affirm that the contents are true?"

"Yes," he said with a pout and signed the affidavit.

Carlo had just finished putting the last of the affidavits through his scanner when his cell phone jingled. It was a text message; he was surprised to get service so far north of Powell River.

Wr done! Come 2 my cabin 4 rfrshmts & u rmbr the w9 K.

Carlo carried his briefcase through the sliding glass doors from the deck to the muted opening howls of "Black Hole Sun" playing over the radio, tuned to a Vancouver rock station available thanks to the satellite dish atop a hill behind the resort.

Marika was standing at the open refrigerator, now dressed in her more characteristic attire of tight white leggings and a purple t-shirt. "Oh, hey Carlo; would you like some iced tea? And what's with their fucking humming?" She pulled a pitcher containing an opaque, rust-coloured liquid out of the refrigerator.

"You're asking me?" Carlo laughed. "Anyway, now that the *faithful* have all gone away, I'm having a beer, not tea." After he returned from the kitchen, Marika was already lounging on the sofa. He sat at the opposite end, resting his beer on the arm.

She stretched out, giving full display to her extravagant physique, and closed her eyes. "We've become close friends these past three months, haven't we?"

"Well, yes."

"Confidantes, in fact."

"Um hmm..." Carlo wondered where she was taking this conversation.

"My mother always told me that I'll look like a beached whale by the time I'm thirty. Now it's starting to look like I'll get there before I'm twenty-six."

If she's trying to seduce me, she's going about it all wrong. "What are you talking about?"

Marika sat upright. "Okay, I've got something I want to tell you, and you must promise to act surprised once it is all out in the open."

"Sure; of course."

"I'm ten days late."

"Oh. I didn't know you were seeing anyone."

Marika shook her head. "No, no. Look; this is *bad.* I'm almost certain that I'm pregnant." She fixed her eyes on his. "And if I am, it's Declan's."

Carlo did his best to avoid looking horrified. He took a long draught of his beer. "Well, you can buy those little test thingies just about..."

"Oh, believe me, I know the drill. Four of them so far, and I 'failed' every last one. So I've got an appointment with my doctor next week, on the Tuesday after we get back. Look, I didn't want to involve you in any of this; I'm beginning to think that I've lost my fucking mind. I just wanted to talk, and you and Petra are the only people in this city that I would *ever* tell." Marika stretched her hair through her fingers. "And there's no way I'm going to call my mother to tell her unless I have to. Some of the things that have gone on; I don't even know how I'd go about explaining it (well, not delicately anyway) in Latvian."

"Where does she live?"

"She's still in Montreal."

She'd mentioned, once or twice, that she grew up in one of the inner suburbs, not very far from the neighbourhood where Farida's parents lived. "So Declan, eh? Was it, I don't know, just a fling?"

"No, I'm ashamed to say that it wasn't. We'd been seeing each other for two years, since just after I started. I know, I know; he's married, but it was the usual thing, 'my wife and I don't get along...it's just convenience and real estate, blah, blah, blah'. Then when Paula opened her gallery on Granville Island, I helped her with the arrangements for the open house, I got to know her, and I decided that this was just wrong." She sighed. "I should have left it at that. But it's no lie, they really don't get along."

"So I've noticed."

"Fuck, they don't even *like* each other. So let's just say that I feel for him. She's a complete bitch, always bossing him about, and I suppose that's how we got together. He'd come to me when he needed a bit of...of comforting, I guess."

'Recreation' is more likely. "Well, you obviously...got back together."

"Yes, I was getting to that. Just before the May long weekend, he told me that he was going to leave Paula; he'd had it with her nastiness. He didn't care how much it was going to cost him."

"Hmm."

"Just listen. So we went to Tofino for the long weekend. He'd gone all out and booked a suite at Wickaninnish Lodge and..."

"Excuse me?" Carlo said a little louder than he'd intended. "He took you to *Tofino* that weekend? He told me that he was sending me to Seattle because he had plans with his wife."

"Well, he did, but they went sideways. After you left on the Thursday, he said he'd had a *huge* fight with Paula (they do that all the time) and then she fucked off to visit her aunt in Kelowna. Anyway, he told me they'd booked a suite for the weekend at the Wickaninnish, and now that she'd ditched him, it was the last straw, he wanted to give us another go. No pressure, he said. Yeah, right."

"So for the whole weekend, he behaved like a horny sixteen-year-old, obviously at the wrong time of the month, and he's never been one to use condoms. So guess what, I wasn't very diligent about taking my pills after I tried to end it with him. It's not like I had too many offers in the meantime." To Carlo's surprise, she glared at him. "So here I am, knocked up."

"Well, maybe you're not. And have you..."

"Yes, I told him last week, after I failed the second of those drug store tests. He acted as if I was telling him that it was raining outside; said that it was probably a "false positive". Maybe it is, but I doubt it. And I made it clear that there will be no abortion this time. I've already had one on his account."

Carlo guzzled the beer left in the bottle. Mounting anger toward Declan had rendered his ears warm to the touch, a lifelong symptom of disquiet.

"So I know what it feels like to be knocked up. This is it. And you know what? It's time that he treated me as something more than an escort, a bedwarmer." She glared at Carlo again. "All right. I want to know. What's the deal?"

"Deal? What's what deal?"

"Look, I've just poured my heart out to you. I told you a secret that nobody else but Declan knows about. So I'm asking: what's up with you? Oh, by the way, didn't you say that you were going to bring some wine? I'm sure the little bugger wouldn't mind if I had a glass or two."

"Oh, right." Carlo rummaged through his briefcase to retrieve a bottle of Aglianico.

Marika watched him fumble for a corkscrew in one of the kitchen drawers. "Good man, I knew I could count on you. But *come on*, what's up? Why weren't you immediately smitten by witty, beautiful, loveable me?" She stood up, stretched out her arms, and shimmied from side to side. "I mean," she said, sitting back down on the sofa, "I know that you don't have a girlfriend; and I know that you're not gay. And I didn't make any secret of my interest. I practically sat in your lap!"

"No, you *did* sit in my lap."

"Oh yeah, I forgot about that. There you go. So what's the deal?"

Carlo came back with another beer, wishing that he had brought a bottle of Jack Daniel's with him instead. "Look, I don't..."

"No! What was it? I don't know; you're more athletic than I am (I guess *that's* not very difficult). Maybe you're not into girls with a bit of meat on them?"

Carlo laughed. True enough; she was conspicuously larger than Tina and made Giovanna look scrawny, but Laura was hardly a waif, and if anything, during the time they were together, Liz was even more robust than Marika, as was definitely true of that crazy American who ended up stalking him in her car a few times when he was out for a run through the grounds of Terme di Caracalla.

"Well, I'm waiting. Look, it's not like anything is going to happen between us now. Now that I have a baby on the way, I'm *really* going to try to make it work with Declan." Her wine glass was almost empty. "But I *am*, let's just say, more than a little curious."

She wasn't going to give up. "All right," Carlo said. "Let's just say that for the past few years, my love life has been a bit of a train wreck."

"Oh, yeah?" Her smile was caustic. "Do tell!"

"Well, look," Carlo said without trying to conceal his annoyance, "I've had a bad run in the past two, well, let's say three years. I decided a while back to temporarily give up women."

"Oh, bullshit!"

"No, no. Listen; I'm quite serious. I haven't even been on a date since I got back to Vancouver."

"All right, I believe you: millions wouldn't. So what was it that turned you off females?"

"Temporarily."

She rolled her eyes. "All right. *Temporarily.*"

Carlo gazed out the window towards the sunset glow on Mount Dunedin. "Well, you can start with the last one, Giovanna. We saw each other almost every other day for a few months. She insisted that we maintain separate flats because she told me that one of her aunts and a flock of various cousins regularly travelled through Rome and stayed with her. She was always complaining about the messy habits of her aunt *this* or her cousin *that*. Her family was supposedly very provincial and *very* traditional; an uncle who was an archpriest, or some such bullshit."

"So she insisted that her family would do worse than disown her if they ever found out that she was involved with a man (well, one she wasn't married to) in the big city. Fucking twenty-eight years old! I never actually saw where she lived, even after almost six months. Then, one afternoon, someone delivered a note to my office." He told her about Tozzi and the meeting he'd arranged at *da Timoteo*.

"What does that mean?" She poured herself another glass.

"Timothy's Place. It's a wine bar."

"It sounds so *musical* in Italian."

"Anyway, when I got there that afternoon, I was greeted by a very powerful, elder member of the bureaucratic class."

"Her father?"

"Her husband." Carlo slammed his beer down with such force that foam rose from out of the neck.

Marika tilted her head back. "Yeah, that *is* pretty bad".

"The two before that were (by comparison, anyway) the comic relief. There was Liz, Elizabeth". He mimicked her name in a defective attempt at an English accent. "My stepmother's kid sister. We had a brief relationship that started to fall apart when she insisted that I wear costumes whenever we had sex. It was bizarre! I could deal with the Colin Firth-style frock coats, whatever." Marika giggled melodically. "But Batman! Do you have any idea how much you sweat having sex wearing a vinyl Batman suit? I drew the line when she wanted me to wear an animal costume."

"What kind of animal?"

"A unicorn."

Now she was giggling again. "Tell me that you didn't dress up as a unicorn."

"Please, it's not *that* funny. No, no, that was pretty much the end of it. After that, there was an American, this blonde from Minnesota, Krista. She worked at the American Express at Piazza di Spagna; we met when I stopped a pair of street kids from stealing her purse. She bought me a phone after we had been seeing each other for about a month. I thought it was *nice* of her, but something that expensive after just a month? More than just a *little* odd. I didn't use it very much: I don't know if you've noticed, but I hate gadgetry, even if she insisted on phoning me all the time. Anyway, I broke up with her after I found out why she bought it for me. She'd installed a GPS app, which allowed her to track my every move."

"No shit?" Marika's face pinched into a frown. "I'm not saying that you're ancient or anything like that, but you *are* older than I am. You must have had more than three relationships."

He'd hoped that he'd already satisfied her curiosity. "Yes," he said, speaking more softly. "I was in two very long relationships, both of which ended badly. One lasted almost ten years, then she took up with one of the other lawyers at the firm where I was working at the time, another Italian, this narcissistic asshole named "Lattanzio". And then there was Tina, we were happy; I lived with her for three years."

"Why aren't you still with her, then?"

Carlo rubbed his face and brushed away stray tears. "She was murdered. She was killed one night, just a couple of blocks from where we lived, in Toronto."

Marika gasped. "I'm so, so sorry. I shouldn't have brought it up."

"Oh, don't...you didn't know. It happened and there's nothing I can do about it." Carlo went over to the glass doors to the deck and looked out over the darkening inlet. "You've got a big problem. What are you going to do?"

"I don't know." She sat in a limp, slouching pose. "As I said, I haven't told anyone else, except for Declan, for all the good it did me." Marika closed her eyes. "I have no idea what I'm going to do; knocked up (again) by a guy who's almost retirement age, and all he has done so far is ignore the situation and hope it goes away. But like I said, I'm going to try to make it work. Maybe this will be it, the thing, the *catalyst* that will finally push him to leave his wife. It will be messy."

"I *really* find that hard to believe."

"That's what he said. He always says that he's had enough of her nastiness, life is too short, whatever. But this time, when he convinced me to get back with him, he said that he would be leaving her within the next month or two."

"A *month* or two?"

"Yup. And then he started going on about how compatible we were, how much happier I made him than Paula ever did. The way he was talking (and yes, he actually *said* this), he as good as promised me that once he split with Paula, he wanted to get together with me, like, *permanently.*"

"He actually said that?"

"Yes. He's never said things like that before. I believe he meant it."

That didn't strike Carlo as very likely, especially if it turned out that she was pregnant. Carlo found it incredible that Gaskin would ever think of leaving Paula in the first place. He knew that Declan owned several million in commercial real estate on Vancouver Island and would be less than delighted by the prospect of parting with half of it in a divorce settlement. But the sheer improbability of it was based on more than just money. Paula may have lacked Marika's youthful, buxom allure, but her superiority as a public spouse wouldn't be lost on Gaskin. He'd be shunned if any of this ever came to light, especially by every woman he knew - judges, other lawyers — they would all be roundly disgusted with him. Even if most of his male colleagues, equally aging and lecherous, at first might envy his conquest of this enticing, peach-like redhead, it would soon change to derision once she started to inflate and Gaskin ultimately found himself conspicuously poorer and saddled with a howling infant.

Marika got up from the sofa and joined him at the glass doors. "You know, I've decided that float planes are something that I could happily do without."

"Why's that?"

"They don't inspire any confidence in me whatsoever; up, thousands of feet in the air in something that looks like a Pringle's container with wings. And our pilot: he was old enough to be one of the Wright Brothers. I thought that he was going to fly us into the side of that mountain!"

Carlo laughed. "Yes, and he's probably the pilot who's flying us back."

Marika, so tense minutes before, seemed elated when the opening riffs of "Volcano Girls" started playing on the radio. "All right! I haven't heard this song for *ages!*"

She started dancing, jumping and twisting to Veruca Salt's jarring alternative rock beat. Carlo, now feeling numb, concluded that the music reminded her of a time in her life when wearing eye shadow was a novelty and boys were more of a mystery than a nuisance.

It was already past ten when Carlo left Marika's cabin. The night was dark in a manner unfamiliar to most city dwellers, devoid of any light source except for the moon. In the distance, further obscured by a light fog, Carlo saw two human silhouettes, one of which stumbled and fell, the other appearing to give assistance but ultimately collapsing on top of its companion. As Carlo got closer to them, the two silhouettes rose, swayed and flailed. "Eh! Lawyer!" one of them shouted toward him.

"Hello?"

"We saw you f-f-fly in today. I'm Phil!" He strained to utter slurred words, struggling to maintain his balance.

"Oh; hi, Phil. Carlo."

"This is my buddy G-G-Gert." Gert stumbled backward as he extended his hand.

"Good to meet you, too, Gert." Carlo shook his hand, pulling him upright.

"All we have to s-s-shay is good on you!"

"Yeah, buddy!" Phil struggled with his tongue. "Fuckin' howlin', man." He tried to give Carlo the high-five but missed, almost falling forward into a puddle.

Carlo had no idea what they were talking about. Before going back to his room, he stopped in at the pub, his anger toward Declan by then festering into incandescent rage. *Vile piece of shit.* He didn't believe the 'fight with his wife' story for a second. It was bad enough that he sent him to Seattle with scant hours to even look at the sprawling Striationist file; it could have turned into yet another humiliation he didn't need if Catriona hadn't been there to save him. *The imperious fuck probably thought he'd be exempt from biology.* But she knew *she* wasn't, an obvious truth that made Carlo look away before he followed it to its logical conclusion.

A mist over the water had started to clear; despite his mood, he admired the effect of the crescent moon over the inlet. He sipped fitfully on his beer, a pint of something or other from a local microbrewery. The bartender knew who he was. "You're that lawyer representing the cult, aren't you?"

"Yes." Carlo lacked both the energy and the inclination to debate whether Striationism was a religion rather than a cult.

"You're disappointing me!" the bartender said. "I was one of the ones who would've wagered a hundred that you and that beautiful redhead are an item. I'd hoped that you'd be spending the evening making babies!"

Carlo stifled a mirthless laugh. "Oh, we're not a couple."

"If I were you, I wouldn't be very happy about that state of affairs. Girls built like her, you don't see them every day, even in the city (unless it's changed a lot in the past ten years)."

Carlo decided to tell the bartender what he needed to hear so he could enjoy his beer in peace. "Hey, dude, I'm working on it," he said with what he hoped would be interpreted as a lecherous grin.

"Good man!" The bartender returned to loading the dishwasher.

18

The contemporary fondness for charity, kindness and equity that casts a pall over Western society, and its bastard sibling, the distaste for masculine values such as acquisitiveness and aggression, has resulted in a catastrophic loss of productivity and trillions in foregone capital formation. There are many sources of this economic blight, but it stems principally from the works of Charles Dickens. His preposterous demonization of the parsimonious in A Christmas Carol *and his lampooning of a suitably dysfunctional civil justice system in* Bleak House *has doubtlessly cost the industrialized world dearly. "God bless us, everyone" has incidentally served for generations as a balm for the witless and the effeminate.*

- Gavin Skoff, in *The Amiable Plunderer*

The sky was cloudless; a comfortably warm sea breeze wafted ashore. It was an afternoon that reminded everyone why they moved to Parksville in the first place. Irwin and Gavin walked past work crews assembling Princess Diana Boulevard, the envisioned grand entrance to the town centre and ultimately, all of central Vancouver Island.

"So, Gavin: have you found an alternative location for that SeaMent field test?" Irwin asked. "You and Roland looked like you were about to challenge one another to a duel when we met in Vancouver last time."

"Yes," Gavin laughed. "I think I have. I used a numbered company to buy a twelve-acre chunk of waterfront on Gabriola Island, on the side that faces both the mainland and Valdez Island. It's pretty quiet around there. All I have to do to maintain privacy is keep the kayakers away. So that should keep Egbert from having a stroke.”

“Gabriola, Gavin? Really? All of those islands are infested with busybodies. How are you going to get the hydro access put in place? Once they see equipment, pain in the ass community activists are going to sprout like mushrooms.”

“I’m counting on it, Irwin.” Gavin slapped him on the back. “Counting on it.”

“I see.” Irwin let the matter drop.

“Looking at all of this, I guess we’ve almost used up the first instalment that you got from Victoria.”

“Oh, yeah, but Gollander has sent us the second twenty million. We’re going to finish the Boulevard by early in the New Year.” He pointed toward an intricate assembly of scaffolding. “And the north and south entrance arches should be completed by then, too. All that will be left will be the lindens.”

“*Lindens?*”

“Yup. Linden trees to line the Boulevard. We’re importing them from this place in Quebec.” Irwin furtively scanned the area to see who was nearby. “Don’t pass that around. So many people around here loathe the French.”

“Have you heard anything more about the McKee-McWatney project, I mean, does it even have a name, yet?”

Irwin shrugged. “I don’t know what to tell you, Gavin. A guy from Midland Shropshire, do you know him? A Mr. Backstab or something? Funny little guy, a Frenchman; from France, I gather, rather than Quebec.”

“I think I know who you mean.”

“Anyway, he was here to see me last week, but let’s just say he played his cards close to his chest. He seemed *very* interested in getting office space in City Hall. Sure, what the hell. I gave him the room that we used to store the water cooler refills in before we figured out that we get cleaner water from the river. It’s a windowless cell but he still went away rejoicing. Oh, good afternoon, Feather." Irwin stooped to pet an orange cat that was sitting at the edge of the sidewalk. "And there's something else that he said, which I found deeply, well, ominous. He told me that the first phase of his 'project' is over two-thirds subscribed."

"*Really?*"

"I'm just telling you what he told me. And I don't even know exactly how many units, how many inhabitants are included in the 'first phase', or even how many 'phases' there are going to be. We're supposed to provide services for all these people, and I haven't even been told when the units will be ready for occupancy!"

"Two-thirds, eh?" Gavin rubbed his chin.

"That's what he said."

They walked as far as the Rod and Gun, a venerable pub in the centre of town. "Shall we?" Irwin asked.

"Sure. I'll meet you inside in a few minutes." As soon as Irwin was out of earshot, Gavin scrolled through his cell phone display to find Crawley's number. "Hi, Aloysius!"

"Who is this?"

"Oh, sorry. Gavin Skoff here. Remember that, uh, investment opportunity we were discussing after the meeting? Is it still available?"

19

Marika had been unusually taciturn all day. They'd spent most it in the basement of Ballard Hall, sorting through a jumble of documents stuffed into bankers' boxes. It took the span of almost three days to process the contents of what turned out to be twenty-three boxes, repeating the stultifying process of identifying and listing each document, and then feeding every page into Carlo's portable scanner. "Thank Jesus Christ!" Carlo yelled, startling Marika out of a listless trance. "That was *the last fucking document*! We're finished!"

"I can't believe that we're finally done," Marika mumbled, mesmerized by the screen of her laptop.

"It's already six. Dinner at the pub again?"

"Nope!" Marika shook her head with such vigour that her mane rustled. "No way. Everything's either nachos, burgers or breaded and fried, and I'm about to get quite fat enough as it is. The restaurant, we'll go there. Declan can spring for it whether he likes it or not."

The Redonda Bistro, named after a pair of nearby islands, was on the top floor of Ballard Hall and afforded a view of the estuary at far end of the inlet. The main foyer was empty, except for a long table filled with Americans dressed in Cabela's attire. A woman who bore the same diseased complexion as Margaret showed them to a table overlooking the water.

Carlo surveyed the room. "This is nice."

"You sound surprised. You know, that was just *way* too many fucking documents. I can barely focus my eyes on the menu." Marika squinted at the parchment sheet in front of her.

"Yes, way too many. There's no way we can take them all back like Declan wants. Twenty plus boxes? We'll take back five boxes of originals at the most. Otherwise, we'll crash the plane!"

"I guess." Marika glowered at him. "That's not why this happened, you know."

"That's not why *what* happened?"

"That's not why I'm pregnant," she whispered, looking down at her menu. "I'm not some conniving bitch, who got knocked up just to trap him. *I* was the one who broke up with *him* before, remember?"

"I never thought that you were," Carlo said, careful to avoid betraying his opinion that Declan had no intention of actually leaving his wife.

"I'm sorry; I'm just paranoid. When this all becomes public, and it won't be long before people notice, that's what everyone is going to think." She smiled at Carlo for the first time in a couple of days. "Sorry, look, I just know that I'm going to have a very rough time ahead, especially a few months from now. I guess people will think what they want. But thanks for listening. So, I expect that you will be having the pasta?"

"Are you fucking kidding me? Here, they probably boil it for an hour and a half. I think I'll get the sablefish."

"I was thinking I'd have the grilled halibut. What's 'sablefish'?"

"It's a white fish, too. They used to call it 'black cod'."

"Then why don't they just say 'black cod'?"

"I don't know; marketing, I guess."

The two of them walked back to Marika's cabin along a wooden walkway without exchanging a word until after they were back in the small kitchen, both of them leaning against the counter, facing one another.

"Would you like a glass of wine?" Carlo said after an unsettling silence. "There's some in the fridge."

"No. I don't think so."

"Maybe I should just go."

"Yeah, maybe you should."

The hostility in her tone annoyed him "Okay." Carlo turned to walk toward the deck. "I'll see you tomorrow before we fly out."

"No. Wait."

Marika gently touched his waist. When he replayed the event in his mind later that night, it surprised him how precisely he was able to recall how it unfolded. For a time they were kissing in the kitchen as he held her, her body fuller and fleshier than he'd imagined. She peeled off her leggings and reached her hands under his shirt to unzip his jeans and slide them down his hips. Carlo started to take off her t-shirt; she obliged by raising her arms above her head as he pulled it up. As soon he'd uncovered her breasts, she tilted her head toward the open door of her bedroom.

Carlo took her hand and eagerly led her inside. Her curves were as superlative uncovered as they'd hinted fully clothed. But once they were well intertwined on her bed, she dug a fingernail into his back.

"No! Carlo, please. Stop. We can't do this. *I* can't do this."

Carlo rolled off and rested next to her on his front, his hand still resting on the expanse of her midriff.

"I'm so sorry," Marika said. "But we just *can't.*"

"You're right. We can't. It's just...awkward."

Marika rolled over and buried her face in her pillow, shaking with violent giggles.

"What's so funny?"

"*Awkward?* What the fuck is that? You talk like a lawyer even when you're butt naked!"

"Then what would you call it?"

"It's *yucky.*"

Carlo gave her behind a playful backhanded swat. "Did you just say 'yucky'? Seriously?"

"Hey, stop that! Yes, yucky. I mean, I'm not saying that *you're* yucky, or..."

"Good to know!"

"No, just listen to me. It's yucky just 'cause it is. Look, for a long time I thought that we

would both be much happier people if we'd just gone back to my place and fucked each other's brains out after that show at Paula's gallery, but you know what, the more that I think about it now, the more I realize that it wouldn't have made the least bit of difference."

"Really? Why not?"

"What can I tell you? I'm in love with an old man, and now I'm hatching out his kid. Does that make me insane?"

Carlo grinned, hinting a ready reply.

"No, don't answer that!" Marika laughed. "Anyway, shoo! Shoo! Get out of here and let me get dressed."

"What do you mean, *shoo*? What does it matter? We've just seen each other naked."

"It matters. If we're going to go back to being just buds again, we've got to bring some boundaries back. So shoo...shoo!"

Carlo collected his clothes and got dressed in the sitting room. With a lack of acerbity that surprised him, Carlo considered that it was the second time in less than a year that he found himself entangled in a *situation*, one could call it, with a girl who was otherwise attached to a much older and wealthier man.

Marika emerged in a short but capacious nightshirt, which still managed to cling to her ample contours.

"Did you want me to go?" Carlo asked.

"Of course not! Please, stay for a while. Grab some wine for yourself if you want, but it's iced tea for me."

Carlo came over to the couch with two glasses. Marika sat down cross-legged next to him. "I really don't know what to say, Carlo." She reached over and took a deep swig of his wine. "My bad? What the fuck was I thinking? We can't. Not now. But it wasn't an impulse, an urge, whatever you want to call it. I've thought about it lots, especially now that I'm about to get all huge and gross and responsible."

" *Your* bad? It's not like I was some innocent bystander."

"Okay." Marika adopted an unfamiliar, clinical tone. "Now! If you don't mind, there's something I've been meaning to ask you. I've been thinking about what you told me a couple of nights back. Your ex, the one who hurt you so much."

"Giovanna?"

"No, no, not the Italian girl. That one from before, the one who ran off with someone you worked with."

"Oh. That would be Laura."

"Are they still together?"

"Oh, Christ no. They split up after a few months. A very long time ago."

Marika leaned back. "Hmm. That's what I thought; no surprise there. Those sorts of unions are always short lived, I mean, whenever people abandon someone to be with someone else, the new relationships usually don't last very long."

Carlo peered at Marika in unalloyed amazement. "No, I suppose you're right. They don't."

It was past midnight before Carlo walked down to the pebble beach in a cove next to the resort, brought his iPod to life and nestled in a cedar log which the sea had eroded into the shape of a giant sled. It was like recalling an unusually vivid dream, her petulance unexpectedly giving way to a welcome invitation; the feral allure of her naked body. It embarrassed him to admit that he'd rather still be there next to her, ideally in the midst of one of many couplings, but Marika was right. It was 'yucky', but at least she stopped it in time. One Giovanna in the span of a year was too many.

He stayed in Marika's cabin much longer than he'd wanted, conscripted as silent audience to her manic monologue. For almost three hours, she squirmed and twisted on the sofa, her body forming provocative poses as she talked about the imagined attributes of the child growing inside her, the new, stable domesticity that surely awaited; all of it underlain by her cheerful expectation that Declan, already past sixty, would embrace new fatherhood, and the implicit irrelevance of the incumbent spouse.

Carlo opened his eyes and turned up the volume on his iPod. He scanned the sparkling expanse above him, unleavened by either moonlight or even a wisp of clouds, to find *Gran Carro*, the Big Wagon, or Dipper, depending on how you looked at it; a habit he maintained wherever in the world he found himself under a clear sky. It was right over the inlet. The chattering congas, sussuring bass line and the gentle guitar notes of "Promise of a Fisherman" made the many stars seem to dance in the sky.

Marika's attention was consumed by a pair of playful harbour seals when Carlo caught up with her in the morning, on the pier next to the plane.

"Hey. Where did you get that coffee?" He pointed to the styrofoam cup in her hand.

"Oh, hey." She formed a crooked, tentative smile. "Up there, at the lounge. But don't do it. I'd suggest you wait 'till we change planes in Powell River. This tastes like somebody put some water from a bog in a microwave. And it's decaf."

Susan looked out over the seaplane dock from her desk. Carlo caught her attention first as he heaved boxes into the plane. *Asshole!* He'd ignored her for the past three days. She thought that it went well between them, that time they'd talked up in his room, but no; he'd preferred to stay in the orbit of that fat cow. *Would it have killed him to just give a little hint that he was boning the blimp?* She turned her gaze to Marika, regarding her with casual disgust; her abundant flesh was testing the seams of her yellow summer dress. *Jessica Rabbit after a Baskin-Robbins opened next door. Fuckin' bitch. And it would serve the little prick right.* This was a fine example of why it would be best to avoid even aspiring to romantic entanglements. When she finally found her way back to Vancouver, she wanted to be fully intact.

They didn't get back to Vancouver until after sunset. A taxi whisked them from Coal Harbour seaplane dock, past the Colosseum-inspired public library. Carlo fell asleep after they dropped off Marika, awakening when the taxi stopped at his front door. Once in his apartment, he poured himself a glass of wine and placed a generous square of frozen *pasta al forno* into a dish, turning on the television to CBC to watch opening headlines of *The National.* He briefly considered calling Mario, but it was already ten o'clock.

No! Carlo panicked; it was eight minutes past ten on a Monday night, one of those times he was supposed to call his father. Six o'clock, Tuesday morning, London time, when his dad was usually just about ready to leave for the office. His call would be late; even two or three minutes of tardiness would incite irritation, even panic in his father, whose unusual preoccupation with time was well-known. Everyone, siblings, cousins, friends, anyone he grew up with in Sannazzaro called him '*il tedesco*', the German. He dialled the multi-digit code.

"Are all of the clocks in your house broken?" his father grumbled.

"No, no, I'm sorry; I just got back in from a work trip to this little place up the coast, not a bad spot at all, just a little damp."

"Damp? You want to hear about 'damp'?" It had apparently done nothing but rain in southern England for five days without respite. "And if it weren't for Linda, I'd leave this soggy, God-forsaken...Oh, yes!" He abandoned his sombre tone. "I was talking to Peppino; yesterday or the day before. He says that he's seen you a few times downtown, walking along Hastings Street with a beautiful girl with red hair and a *very* generous shape. He told me he's jealous. So, what? A new girlfriend, *uagliò?*"

"Oh; that would be Marika, we work together."

"That I could have guessed on my own, and so what do you have to tell me: is she the bombshell that Peppino says she is? And you haven't answered my question."

"Oh, she's definitely pretty hot, the kind of looks that are a distraction to men driving past."

"And so?"

"No, no." Carlo tried to laugh.

"Why not? *Madonna santa!* You shouldn't be hanging back, not these days. The way Peppino described her, my God, she's just what you need." He let out a roguish chortle. "A few nights with a girl like that, if she looks anything like what Peppino said, that, *uagliò*, that might lift the gloom that has surrounded you since you parted with that toothpick."

Carlo walked over to turn on the oven, which responded with three high pitched squeaks.

"What's that beeping all about?" Vito asked.

"The oven. I'm heating up some *pasta al forno* for dinner."

"You haven't eaten yet? Do you have any idea what time it is?"

"I told you; I just got in from up the coast. What did you expect me to do, eat a Teen Burger at the A&W in Powell River?"

His father grunted in grudging acceptance. "So, *pasta al forno*, good! Did you make it with *reggiano*?"

"No, it's too expensive around here. I used *grana padano*."

"Ó," he sighed. "It always tastes so much better when you make it with *reggiano*. Behave yourself this week, and anyway, call me on Thursday."

Carlo leaned on the rail of his balcony, pausing to enjoy the view of False Creek at sunset, with its array of sailboats parked in formation at floating docks. The reddish glow of the western sky faded to darkness; a few late joggers made their way towards Granville Island amidst couples strolling along the Seawalk. *So the old bastard knocked her up.* His oven emitted another annoying electronic squeak. Fahrenheit redux. He took another sip of his wine.

You shouldn't be hanging back. Well, once again, his father was right.

20

Before the Georgia Basin Environmental Studies Steering Committee meeting started, Laeticia sat alone in a seminar room in the Cornett Building, a beguiling tan-coloured brick and stucco maze that was among the original structures on the University of Victoria campus. Arriving a half-hour early afforded her a brief respite to mark first-year biology exams. She predicted a superlative failure rate. One of her students, whom she remembered as a short girl so punctuated by metal rings, studs, piercings, and black ink that she looked like a lawnmower engine, concluded a rambling answer to a question about asexual reproduction with a bewildering conclusion.

And that is why so many froggs are dying in so many places in the world: globil warming is overheating all of the swamps and boggs.

The first committee member to arrive was Professor Sandvisk, an ungulate zoologist from Simon Fraser University who had built his career analysing Roosevelt elk herds on Vancouver Island and the Olympic Peninsula. He'd come to resemble the animals he studied; droopy, a dazed and placid demeanour, occasionally bobbing his head as if dodging imaginary black flies.

"Good afternoon, Laeticia."

"Oh, hi, Dr. Sandvisk. How was the ferry trip over?"

"Please, call me Thor. 'Dr. Sandvisk' makes me sound like a mad scientist. No, no ferry today; I've been on the Island for six weeks. Strathcona Park, following the Tlools Creek herd around. I think they're getting sick of me. What are you working on?"

"Well, hiding from my students, marking first-year midterms." She shuddered.

"Ah, yes, the scourge of the young academic. In a year or two it will be replaced be the constant need to publish."

Over the next few minutes, the remaining members of the committee took their chairs around the long table. Patricia was the last to arrive. "Hello, everyone. I'm sorry that I'm late. I found myself on the wrong side of the Point Ellice Bridge. A stalled delivery truck was blocking it."

The section heads gave their interim reports. First came Sandvisk, something about a project some of his graduate students were working on, tracing an elk migration route on the Tsable River, then a biologist from Sechelt recounted every detail about the restoration of the coho population in a creek on the Sunshine Coast. A man in a suit whom Laeticia recognized as a federal bureaucrat boasted about adding oak meadows and a few more of the smaller Gulf Islands to the expanding national park reserve.

Laeticia was the next one to give her report. "As many of you know, I have been working on two projects; one for the Department of Fisheries and Oceans studying sockeye, spring and coho salmon populations in the Qualicum River-Horne Lake system and another about brine shrimp and krill levels in the Island coastline between Parksville Bay and Cape Lazo. Right now, the coho population in the Horne system looks surprisingly strong but the levels of the other two species have gone into a precipitous decline. That is where I'm focusing most of my efforts. The second project, which is the subject of an article that just got accepted for publication in the *Journal of Fisheries Sciences*." She paused as a few of the people around the table murmured words of encouragement. "It has been recently bogged down (excuse the pun) in a consideration of the role of sea grasses in estuaries and the intertidal zone. Currently, my team is focusing their efforts on Baynes Sound. My problem is a complete lack of baseline data."

"Thank you, Laeticia." Patricia said. "Now, as most of you are aware, the Ministry of Highways is upgrading a section of Highway 19 and replacing a number of bridges and culverts. I will send you the specifications by e-mail. I want each of you to go back to your groups, review the project and give me your comments on possible damaging effects and proposals for mitigation."

Everyone around the table scribbled a note of her request. Laeticia saw Sandvisk erupt with odd gesticulations. *What is he doing, crossing himself?*

"Is there something else, Professor Sandvisk?" Patricia said.

"Minister Wilson," Sandvisk said. "We've been hearing rumblings about a massive development project on the central Island that would affect thousands of hectares of elk habitat in the Pentlatch valley, and even in the Tsable watershed, one of the areas where my team is concentrating its research. Is there any truth to these rumours?"

"Professor," Patricia said quietly. "There are always rumours. I can tell you that no applications have yet crossed my desk, and many would in fact be *mandatory* for the kind of project you're describing. And as far as I know, the land remains in the hands of McKee McWatney and they have shown no signs of entering the real estate development business."

"Thank you, Minister," Sandvisk said, visibly relieved.

"Oh," Patricia said. "Laeticia, I might have some of the baseline data you're looking for. Some of the original foreshore surveys of eastern Vancouver Island, some still in pencil, just showed up in a forgotten corner of my ministry's archives. They might help you out."

"Oh, awesome," Laeticia said. "I'm sure that they would."

After the meeting, Laeticia hauled the stack of exam papers across campus back to the office she was shared with four other instructors. Her cell phone whistled with a text message from Patricia.

Pinot's in an hour?

She typed her response.

You bet.

* * *

In the weeks since the trip to Port Rattray, Carlo had acquired something of a fascination for the Striationists, to him as alien as an Amazonian tribe. The Internet proved to be a rich source of information. Still, Carlo couldn't figure out why the religion split into its "reformed" and "orthodox" branches. Both sides maintained a strong online presence, but each behaved as if the other didn't exist. Declan made vague allusions about a difference of opinion over the need to actually have bodily contact with striations. When he'd asked people in Port Rattray to explain, they either started humming or told him silly riddles.

He already knew that the Orthodox Striationists worshipped glacial striations left in bare rock as the big ice sheets retreated at the end of the last Ice Age, but as he was finding out, it was more outlandish than that. As much as they revered the glaciers themselves, they believed that it was the actual striations that radiated sacred energy. After often painful communion with jagged basalt, many of the faithful believed themselves cured of diseases as disparate as herpes and hypertension. One of them, a real estate agent from Qualicum Beach, insisted that a weekend at the Bute Inlet retreat quelled his addiction to nicotine. And it wasn't as if one striation was as good as another. Furrows exposed on avalanche paths on coastal inlets were far more powerful than, for example, shallow ruts on some rocky outcropping in Victoria.

The religion did not seem to stir up strong emotions one way or the other; hardly anyone had anything bad to say about either faction. Carlo was reading an article, an unusual but strident anti-Striationist screed posted on *The Tyee*, when Declan walked into his office.

Crack-Scratch Fever

Why I left the Striationists for good

"*Bonjour monsieur!*" The acute curve of Gaskin's smile portended some sort of announcement. "There's a matter I have to discuss with you." His smile faded into an exaggerated countenance of wisdom as he held a stray envelope up to his forehead. "The Amazing Gaskin sees a trip to Vancouver Island in your future!"

"Sure, why not? So are you sending Marika and me over to gather some more documents?"

"No, no. This is more in the nature of simply interviewing people; most of them are in Qualicum, Comox and Campbell River. There might be a few documents over there for you to sort through. But this time?" He retracted his chin to create jowls. "I think we'll send you on your own. And you have friends over there you can stay with, don't you?"

"I do."

"But not until after their Convocation next month. I have to talk to some more of the elders, get their instructions. The smoke is just starting to clear since the split. So don't forget." Declan turned to leave. "Canada Day weekend. We have to go down to the States on the Thursday."

"It's in my calendar." It surprised Carlo that Gaskin actually remembered that he knew people on the Island, but he was not pleased that he might have to go to Comox, a place he would have preferred to avoid.

Marika knocked on the glass to get his attention after Declan left. "Coffee? I could use a cup."

"So, I'm curious," she said as Carlo held open the door to Calista's.

"You're supposed to say 'thank you' when someone opens the door for you."

"Thank you. Don't you want to know what I'm curious about?"

"Nope."

"Come on; are you going to stay single forever? I mean, be that guy, the old bachelor at home with a shawl wrapped around his knees, watching re-runs of 90210?"

Carlo stopped and turned to face her. "If 90210 is still on re-runs by then, I won't be sitting at home, I'll be jumping off the Lion's Gate." Carlo sighed. "Why are we having this conversation?"

"Come on, I'm just trying to help. That girl at the breakfast burrito truck across the street, over there, she seems to think you're pretty hot. You could do worse."

"She's anaemic."

"Oh, Jesus fucking Christ! What are you on about now?"

"She's anaemic. Just look at her! She's so unhealthy, she looks like she wouldn't survive ten seconds in a blizzard."

"What a fuss-ass."

"Look." He gesticulated with both hands in a classic Italian gesture of exasperation. "She'd be a great fixer-upper for a young doctor, but I'm a lawyer. What can I do? Get a mandatory injunction forcing her to eat meat?"

Marika shook her head. "I'll get a seat. Order me a low-fat *latte*. And a croissant. Please."

"Anything else?"

"Look, I don't mean to be a bitch. Today's the day."

"No, I'm sorry. I know."

Marika worked in silence at her desk for the rest of the morning. She did not even come out for lunch with Carlo, Thomas and Bal, a daily ritual. And Carlo did not see Marika and Declan exchange even a word with one another. It was early afternoon when she left the office for her appointment. As soon as she was gone, Declan announced that he had to visit a new personal injury client that afternoon at a hospital in Chilliwack, two hours distant.

Carlo was waiting for Marika when she came back to work. She first looked over at Declan's darkened, empty office. Without any discernible emotion or change in her gait, she walked into Carlo's office and shut the door. She sat down in a chair facing him and let out a lengthy sigh.

"Yup."

21

As usual, the air at the Gelding Beach Golf and Tennis Club Resort, a seaside spot equidistant from Myrtle Beach and the Georgia state line, was unbearably humid in the hour just after lunch. Padraig Flannery had spent most of the past six months in places just like it, hosting investment displays in ballrooms and golf clubhouses attached to retirement communities, reliable sources of people who had access to a bit of money, but were also likely to nurse a strong aversion to conducting business over the Internet, an attribute Basaraba insisted on.

This afternoon was slower than most; he had seen fewer than a half-dozen people curious enough to approach his tables since he set up the display early that morning. Most days, he would have to field questions from what seemed like hundreds of these people passing in a long procession, their features indistinguishable from one another.

That was probably the most bewildering aspect as far as Flannery was concerned. Back in the village in western Ireland where he'd lived until his early twenties, the old were as varied as the young, sporting starkly differing attire and even appearance, despite their common genetic font. Some were loquacious, some mischievous, others sullen and reclusive. Around here, they all seemed the same, especially the men; each displaying a thatch of white hair of varying abundance, a comfortable paunch and the ruddy skin that befalls people of northern European background who spend too much time in the sun. They all dressed the same, too. Light-coloured slacks, permanent press, and white golf shirts with some sort of designer's logo on them. White shoes. And when they went to dinner, their wives made them don blue blazers with ridiculous maritime insignias. Their manner varied little between individuals: stolid, silent, except for the occasional grunt, regarding both him and his displays with dull, expressionless eyes.

Two such specimens shuffled toward his kiosk. He scanned them for Blackberries, incipient smartphones, or any indication of computer literacy sufficient to allow summary online investigation, the mere hint of which would have prompted him to quickly scare them off. Nothing.

The two older men examined his display, spread across two long banquet tables with bulletin boards behind them. After they rummaged through Padraig's arrangement of binders, pamphlets and photographs, one of them finally spoke. "So this is in England, is it?"

"No, British Columbia. It's in Canada. On the west coast, just north of Seattle." Padraig spoke with a generic southwestern American accent. He had been an actor in his youth, a master of dialects and accents, especially those of the southern United States. He wanted them to think that he was an American; people of their sort tended to mistrust foreigners. Even so, he did not want to imitate the local accent. That itself might have raised a degree of suspicion. "It is already the largest real estate venture in western North America."

"So what's with all this fancy shit?" the other one said, pointing to some of the photographs.

"Germans and Chinamen like it."

This seemed to satisfy his curiosity. His companion, who was poring over another binder, looked confused. "So, are you selling lots? Condos?"

"Nope." Padraig smiled. "Partnership units: you can invest in those, trade in them, or convert them into actual real estate."

"So you can actually trade in these, like bonds or warrants?"

"Yeah." Padraig lapsed into a tone he once used when he played an insurance broker in a State Farm commercial. "But not on a standard stock exchange. There are filing requirements, tax issues that arise with those sorts of things. But they are readily tradable, without brokerage fees, through a federally-certified clearinghouse in Toronto." He was relieved when he saw them both perceptibly nod, implying that they were both aware of Toronto's existence. Of course, calling the clearinghouse "federally-certified" could charitably be characterized as misrepresentation, or more properly, a lie.

The first one stirred from his stupor. "How much are these, these; what did you call them?"

"Partnership units."

Padraig sized them up; Basaraba permitted him a degree of discretion in the price he quoted for each unit. The maturing real estate bubble probably afforded both of these men the status of millionaires. Although they were not truly wealthy, their clothing, which bore the logos of mid-level boutiques rather than Wal-Mart, suggested a degree of financial means.

"Well," he said, preparing a twang-laden sales pitch. "There will be only five hundred thousand partnership units issued. As the modules of the project are completed, the value of its assets can be evaluated by market forces." He continued, secure in his assumption that these two were of an ilk that derived spiritual nourishment from the sound of the word 'market'. "The value of your ownership share will be determined by the value of the project as a whole at any given time. And as I said, at any time the units can either be sold at the clearinghouse or used to buy actual residential or commercial units in the project itself."

"You haven't given us a price," the larger one grunted.

"Oh, I'm sorry," A perfect Texas drawl. "Twenty thousand dollars per unit."

"Do you have a prospectus, or anything?"

"Of course." Padraig handed them two thick, bound booklets replete with colour photographs.

"We'll be back." And indeed they were: both of them returned later that afternoon, surrounded by the odour of bourbon. They purchased two units each. And now he owed Basaraba a call.

Émile Basaraba gazed through the open shutters of his balcony windows at the early evening descending over Rue Didouche Murad. He was old enough to remember when it was still Rue Michelet, before independence and the more recent cascade of Arabic and Islamicist zeal. Although he was of mixed French and Ukrainian blood, Algiers, the city of his birth, was the only place where he felt truly at home. The anarchic din and the cacophony of horns made cities on the northern shore of the Mediterranean, Barcelona, Marseille, even Naples, seem peacefully Celtic.

One of his half dozen cell phones started to ring. It was the one with the London area code; the caller was probably one of his sales agents working in the south-eastern United States. "Allô?"

"Good evening, Émile." It was Padraig, as he suspected.

Basaraba closed the shutters so that he could hear him over the rumble of traffic. He found Padraig's Irish lilt difficult to follow at the best of times.

"I'm in yet another one of these funny little coastal towns (in South Carolina, this time)," Padraig said. "But I've sold almost eight thousand units in the past three weeks; I'll be making a very impressive deposit in Citibank when I get to Atlanta."

"I am very pleased, Patrick. There will be an equally impressive bonus awaiting you in the NatWest when you return to London."

"Well, as happy as I am to hear that, believe me, there may be a limit to the effectiveness of this business model."

"I'm sorry?"

"We had, well, let's call it a sales meeting, last week in Norfolk. Between the six of us, we've sold almost a hundred thousand units in the time that we've been down here."

"Excellent! I didn't realize that it had been so many."

"But we're experiencing diminishing returns, Émile. The market is starting to get saturated. The people in our target demographic have a bit of money they can spare for this sort of investment, but it's not limitless."

"Yes, yes; you're quite right." True enough. And the better known they become in a district, the more likely that some pain-in-the-ass person will start to ask questions, maybe take it upon himself to act as an amateur investigator. "Where are you going next?"

"It's a place in Georgia, a newer one from what I've heard; 'the Kildare Point Country Club and Estates."

"Good. But I think we'll take a change in direction after that. Meet me in Montreal on, I don't know." He consulted the calendar on his laptop. "Let's say the seventh?"

"Sure. Kildare Point. A bunch of rubbish. I'm sure it won't bear the slightest resemblance to the *real* County Kildare."

"You never know, Padraig. There are many Irishmen in the United States."

Émile realised that his parting remark didn't really make much sense. Now he was wary: it was always important to avoid getting too greedy, especially in this sort of endeavour. His recent cursory accounting of the project as a whole suggested that he would ultimately amass the equivalent of at least six hundred million euros for himself, perhaps a little more if he artfully negotiated the terms of the electrical service and the ancillary small hydroelectric project. The people he was dealing with called it 'run of river'.

He shut down and packed up his laptop and two of his cell phones. It was almost eight. The driver he'd hired to take him to the airport would soon be waiting outside. Within a few hours, he would be in his apartment in Paris, in Montreal the week after that, and in the fullness of time, Vancouver, where he would make yet another presentation to that business group, 'Reformed Striationists' they called themselves; the supposed cult he'd been involved with for almost a year. They were mystifying, those people. They did not lack competence, and avarice consumed them as completely as it did other people of the élite class wherever else he'd encountered them. Still, they were an odd bunch. Their peculiar and probably studied habit of irrepressible optimism seemed to have rendered them immune to native suspicion. Nothing he told them seemed to generate much scepticism, and they rarely bothered to subject anything he said to even rudimentary scrutiny. Good for them.

22

The Tulalip Resort rose from the vastness of the lowlands east of Puget Sound, an imposing silver rectangle. Interstate 5, the wide ribbon of tarmac that links British Columbia and Baja California, ensured a constant supply of visitors, often Canadians, who streamed in to abandon their money at the casino that anchors the resort. Carlo's room was on the seventh floor facing the freeway; he'd paid two hundred dollars out of his own pocket to avoid sharing a room with Gaskin. He awoke early, to give him enough time for a morning run before the Striationist Convocation started.

Once exercised and showered, he joined the line at the coffee bar in the lobby. A dozen people were ahead of him, all pouting or sputtering with rage. Two teen-aged girls at the front of the line had ordered intricate coffee drinks with a bewildering wealth of ingredients, keeping the barista busy with the espresso machine, a blender and something that looked like a centrifuge. "*Faccia d'ù cazz'*", Carlo mumbled. He felt a tap on his shoulder.

It was Gaskin. "You'll never get coffee in this line, at least not before lunch. I think they have a few urns in the conference room. How did you sleep?" He didn't wait for an answer. "I'm *so* refreshed! The aromatherapy in this place is fascinating; I find that the teaberry essence gives me an additional burst of energy!"

Carlo equated aromatherapy with voodoo and doubted that tea actually produced berries. "So where's the conference room?" They walked past the pool, already full of splashing, fractious children.

"Over there, the Orca Ballroom, just through those doors. You should find some coffee near the service entrance at the back. Most of the presenters will have tea, but be careful what you drink. The Texada Island Domain people serve Labrador Tea. They pick it themselves in bogs; it will give you a nasty headache."

"Thanks for the warning. Labrador Tea. One of my high school buddies tried to smoke it and ended up in the hospital."

They were just passing the Teanaway Moraine kiosk, staffed by some of the American faithful who believed they'd located one of the coveted portals to the Source of Creation, when Gaskin was accosted by a short white-haired lady who spoke with an English accent. "You're the lawyer, aren't you? I have something that I simply *must* discuss with you immediately...."

Carlo escaped before Gaskin felt obligated to introduce him. He sped past a row of kiosks, each tended by people wearing either fleece or Gore-Tex jackets of Vancouver issue, or oversize, garish garments reputed to come from somewhere in Central America. Arranged chairs many rows deep faced a makeshift stage, probably for a plenary session of some sort. Gaskin hadn't really given him any idea what kind of ceremony this "Convocation" would turn out to be.

There was indeed a coffee urn at the back of the ballroom, next to a kiosk which was notably less rustic than the others. Two women, both dressed in well-tailored urban business suits stood beside it. The one with her back to him, a formidably constructed blonde, commanded his immediate attention, but he was soon distracted by her companion, taller and thinner with long, dark red hair. When he'd almost reached them, he recognized her.

"Yvette?" He hadn't seen her for almost nine years; the sharp contours of her face had hardened.

"Carlo?"

Carlo felt his face veiled by long blond hair as somebody embraced him and pecked him on the cheek. Maybe it was her hair, maybe it was something more subtle. Carlo knew who she was before he saw her face. "Laura."

"Don't sound so excited!" she laughed. "Where have you been? Don't tell me that you're *one of these*!" Her voice trailed off to a whisper.

"Are you living down here now?" Yvette asked.

Now under feminine interrogation, Carlo swiftly reached over to the spigot and poured himself a cup of coffee. If Yvette had noticeably changed, the intervening years had no corrosive effect on Laura. The features of her face might have become a little softer; maybe she was a touch heavier than she'd been when they were together, but she was much slighter than he remembered her just before she left Toronto for good.

"No, I'm living in Vancouver now...and no, absolutely not, I am not one of..." He whispered. "...*These people.* Wait a minute: why are *you* here?*"

Laura looked at Carlo with an anxious expression as Yvette answered him. "Our firm does all of the publicity and media relations for the Orthodox bunch. We're here to get some video footage and some stills for TV commercials and a brochure. Oh, and of course, their website."

"Your firm?"

Yes...DesRosiers & Thompson. None of which explains your presence."

"Yes." Laura said. "Let me guess: are you here to replenish the strength of your inner pathways? Explore your need to nourish your spirit by harnessing the cosmic energy of the earth's magma core?"

"God forbid," he whispered. "I work for Gaskin Barristers. From what I've been told, he does all of their litigation."

Upon mention of Gaskin's name both women shrieked with laughter, startling a group of shrivelled, pale people sitting cross-legged around the next kiosk, all draped in dismal grey ponchos.

"So I guess you've heard of the firm," Carlo said. Declan never mentioned any public relations people.

"Oh, we know Declan!" Laura said.

"He said that he'd hired a new associate a few weeks back," Yvette said. "But for some reason, he thinks you're Brazilian. I never would have thought for a second that he was talking about you."

"Brazilian?"

"Yes." Laura said. "And Yvette heard that he's telling people that you'd just come here from Berlin, where you'd been translating mortgages. Were you in Berlin, translating mortgages?"

"No, I was in Rome, helping the Banco Tiburtino spread corruption to the furthest recesses of the planet."

After her laughter died down, Laura patted Carlo's shoulder. "We'll have to meet up for some drinks before the end of the conference. We have some catching up to do. Come on, we do."

"Well, I'm booked for lunch. Declan and I have to go eat with the Directorate, to catch them when half of them aren't off somewhere writhing on the rocks. Who knows what they eat? Anyway, let's just say, after dealing with these people all day, I'll need at least four IPAs."

"These days, wine's my chill-out drug. We'll meet up later."

Carlo went back to where he'd left Declan, only to find him still talking to the English lady, by then joined by three more women, each wearing a pair of grey gum boots.

She was scolding Declan as if he were a waiter who'd just served her rancid custard. "Do you *not* understand? *They* took all those items with them. *They* didn't account for anything. Most of the missing items were *stripped* from the rectory at Dundalk Creek. It would behove *you* to ask the people who operate the Lodge at Port Rattray to testify."

Declan was not displaying the serenity he customarily exuded when dealing with clients. "Yes, I...I...already told you, we have their affidavits. That will help us immensely." Carlo could tell that Declan had must have already repeated himself at least three times.

"I *still* don't understand what use an affidavit is." Her friends nodded and hummed.

"But..." It was the first time that Carlo had ever seen Declan give up. "Oh, I'd like to introduce you to my associate, Carlo Buonsante. He will be leading the document preservation workshop tomorrow. Carlo, meet Ms. Fox and her two friends, Catherine and Gail."

"*Mrs.* Fox", she said. "Have you ever been to Gorizia, Carlo?" Mrs. Fox pronounced it with an exaggerated, extended rolling of the 'r'.

"No, I have never been to northeastern Italy."

"You should! It has the most powerful striations in the Mediterranean."

Carlo stammered a polite reply as Declan ushered him away. "That woman is going to drive me insane!" he said as soon as they were out of earshot. "I told her again and again, you won't need witnesses at some hearing in Victoria she was on about. But she insisted, that's not the way they do it in the Courts of Queen's Bench in London, and then she started spouting off about something called 'sergeanty'. And the rest of them, that gaggle of old ladies, God save me! Anyway, I think I've already told you: I need to see your briefing notes for tomorrow's presentation. It's not that I think that your legal advice will be lacking, but these people are...a bit *temperamental.*"

They walked past a man with long hair dyed black, wearing a monastic cowl and picking away tunelessly at a lute. He shot a prolonged, purposeful stare at Carlo as he sang.

> *He toils daily for his filthy lucre;*
> *His urine the colour of mud.*

"I can see that."

"Drop off your notes by my room sometime after we're done this afternoon, Oh, yes." Declan said. A patronizing smile. "I saw you chatting with the blonde from the public relations outfit. You're a man of predictable tastes, I must say; a pleasing, generous figure, just like, well...she *does* have bigger breasts than Marika!"

Carlo couldn't decide which he found more disconcerting: Gaskin's exaggeration or the fact that he uttered the observation at all. "Yeah, well, I'll have my speaking notes ready for you after dinner."

The opening plenary started with an abrupt dimming of the lights. Declan and Carlo, treated as dignitaries due to their status as legal counsel for the religion, sat at the front. Yvette and Laura both circulated around the ballroom, armed with the lenses and wands of digital recording equipment. A large screen suspended over the dais at the front of the ballroom abruptly lit up.

The *Real* Striationists
Tulalip, 2008

The public address system filled the room with a din that sounded like the sustained buzzing of thousands of bees. As the buzzing grew louder, a picture of a large gash in a bare granite hillside appeared on the screen. A travelling spotlight paused and brightened to illuminate a young girl standing on the dais in a simple white cotton gown. Carlo expected her to give a speech, but instead the buzzing continued for slightly more than an hour before someone switched the lights back on.

The Directorate luncheon was worse than Carlo predicted. The available fare, steamed tadpoles on a bed of miner's lettuce, was vile and probably dangerous. Neither Carlo nor Declan touched a single morsel, each citing their large breakfast. Behind them, a tall, greying gentleman who spoke with an Australian accent confidently lectured a small gathering about the differing energy fields emitted by striations of varying depths.

Declan was sitting on a tall three-legged stool, talking to Hamish McPhee, who was standing beside him. His beard had been given a vigorous trim since Carlo met him in Port Rattray. "I don't know what to tell you, Declan." Hamish said. "They just up and sold it out from underneath us."

"I know. It's too bad; the Savary Island place was your headquarters."

"Well, at least we still have the Melbourne Inlet lodge, you know, Port Rattray, but the Savary Island place was worth a lot of money. And while you're poking around, maybe you could find out about this land just north of Parksville that I keep hearing about."

"Yes, Carlo mentioned something about it."

"The Reformed bunch seems to think that it's a big secret, but people on that part of the Island are always chattering about it; it keeps popping up everywhere. Maybe that's what they did with the money from the Savary place."

After the Elders' luncheon, Declan and Carlo spoke in the middle of the hotel lobby, dozens of people around them dragging rolling suitcases this way and that.

"They're quite understandably obsessed with the initial — well, let's call it what it is — theft, but I've been reading over your file notes," Declan said. "It's much more than that, all this trading and fiddling around with these old Striationist properties. It's too mysterious; something big is going on that whoever is behind this doesn't want anyone to know about."

"Well, as far as I can tell, it's like I told Ruairi at Port Rattray: they're using a complicated series of trust arrangements and escrow contracts to conceal whatever it is they're up to. But the only way we're going to find out what's really going on is through documentary discovery in the two actions, and even then..."

Declan rubbed his chin but seemed to agree. "And this 'Parksville lands' thing. I've been hearing about it everywhere. At first I thought that it was just the tinfoil hat contingent, but now? As I've been saying, you have a field trip to the Island in your future." Declan placed a hand on Carlo's shoulder as the four

English ladies bore down on them. "You'd best be making your escape."

Before Carlo reached the bank of elevators, Laura appeared in front of him. It seemed to him that she'd been lying in wait behind a pillar.

"Carlo!"

"Oh, hi, Laura, I was just..."

"Yvette and I are meeting at the fancy restaurant for dinner. Want to join us?"

"Really? The Tulalip Bay?" He had seen the menu in the thick, leather-bound resort directory in his room. The average price of an appetizer roughly equalled that of a muffler.

"Why not? We're not paying for it! That's why God invented accountants."

"Sure; as you said, why not?"

"Great! What's your cell number? I'll call you around seven."

They met at the circular bar at the centre of the casino. Both of them remained in business suits, attracting glances from the people around them, most of whom were wearing shorts or loose cotton gym wear. "Well." Carlo said. "It's been what, a bit over three years?" It was true, they had communicated by way of a few stray e-mails and one drunken trans-Atlantic chat on Facebook, but the last time they had actually met, face to face, was at Tina's funeral.

"Yes, I was surprised to see you," Laura said. I never expected that you would have come back here, except maybe for a quick visit. And you haven't changed; I mean really, you still look pretty much the same as the boy I picked up on the party bus. How old were you, seventeen?"

"And you don't look all that much different than the speed metal chick who drank all my wine."

"Well," Laura laughed. "A few pounds heavier."

"I don't know..."

"So, married? I don't see a ring."

"No. You?"

"God forbid. Kids?"

"No. What about you?"

"Don't be silly." Laura took a generous sip of her wine, and then waved her glass at the bartender. "It's scary; so much time has passed. Back in the day, I always thought that *we* would get married." To Carlo's surprise, Laura wiped away a tear. "Look at me, I'm *such* a girl. No, that's it; we're not going to talk about the past any more tonight."

"And here we are," Carlo laughed, "all grown up and in a foreign land, working for the same bunch of lunatics."

"All grown up? Speak for yourself!" Laura lit up a cigarette. "And lunatics they are, but you really have to wonder, who thought it all up?" She looked around the bar. "Shit, there might be some of them around."

"Don't worry; they're all too spiritual to drink."

"Spiritual? The word you're looking for is 'pompous'. Even if you can get past the fact that they're all mentally deranged, it is almost incomprehensible that the religion is only about thirty years old and there has already been a *schism*."

"Yes, 'Orthodox' and 'Reformed'. What's *that* all about?"

"Oh, I don't know." Laura swept her arm in a dismissive arc. "A doctrinal debate, if you can believe it; I haven't taken the time to get my head around it. Life is just too fucking short; something about whether you have to make physical contact with a striation in order to enjoy its power. *Whatever*. But the Orthodox ones tend to be hicks (oh, my God; I can't believe I just said that) from outside Victoria and Vancouver. The Reformed people tend to be rich, urban and...Liberal, well, not real Liberals, but the B.C. kind."

Laura drained her second glass of wine. "Fucking twenty minutes late! Where is that dizzy chick? Anyway, let's go: she knows where to find us. It's supposed to be a fancy place, and I'd like to still be able to taste the food."

"Thanks, by the way, for inviting me."

"Hey; don't thank me. Thank the Freaks!"

After dinner, they each bought a drink and started exploring the casino, a novelty for both of them. Rows of slot machines whistled, chimed and squeaked at a deafening pitch. The mood of the crowds gathered around game tables oscillated between mournful moans and shrieks of jubilation. Neither of them parted with a dime, until Laura encountered a blackjack table.

"Blackjack? That's 'twenty-one', isn't it? I used to play that with my dad. I always won!" She joined a table where two elderly Asian ladies were already playing, probably fellow Canadians. Carlo felt compelled to cheer as Laura won four successive hands.

"Fuck, I'm out of DuMauriers!" Laura said as she shook an empty cigarette package. "And I'm not smoking the camel shit they sell in *this* country." she whispered in Carlo's ear. The dealer gave her an ace to match her queen, which she flipped over triumphantly. She consolidated her collection of chips after the dealer pushed new additions in her direction. "That's a big two hundred dollars, Buonsante." He yawned and nodded politely.

Laura pulled her room card out of her purse. "I've got a great way to help you wake up. Go up to my room and get me another package of cigarettes. The carton I got at the border is sitting on my dresser. Room 714."

Carlo looked at her as if she were presenting him with a bicycle pump.

"Come on; I'm on a roll. Get me my smokes and I'll meet you in the lounge out front in twenty minutes. I'll even buy you a beer. What do you drink?"

"You're not very observant."

"Okay, smart ass, what do *I* drink?"

"Merlot, mostly, and Cabernet when they've run out of that."

"Just fuck off and tell me what you drink," she laughed.

Carlo put the card in his pocket. "Longhammer; any IPA."

"Thanks, Carlo. If Yvette's upstairs, tell her to get her ass down here!"

The first stop was his own room, to print off a hard copy of his notes for the next morning's presentation that Declan asked for. There was no point in sending them by e-mail; Declan loathed computers and did not even own a laptop. After fetching Laura's cigarettes, Carlo went up to Declan's floor to drop off his notes.

Once off the elevator, he saw a tall, very slim woman with long hair the colour of polished copper, barefoot, dressed only in what appeared to be a man's white dress shirt and carrying an ice bucket, come out of a room on the opposite side of the corridor. Carlo ducked back into the elevator alcove as she walked down to the ice machine at the far end of the hall, poking his head out in time to see that it was indeed Yvette walking back, and then as she fiddled around with the card key to open the door. As soon as he was certain that she was safely in the room, Carlo went to confirm what he already knew. Yes, indeed; 1116, Declan's room. It seemed he had a weakness for redheads, irrespective of their girth.

Carlo found a table down in the lounge, a flat cross-section of a sprawling maple burl and set down her cigarettes. A display of masks flanked by carved canoe paddles filled the wall behind it. Opposite him, a reclining collection of about a dozen drunken, thirtyish men filled the benches facing the gas fire. They were all singing, in the midst of collectively warbling "Self Esteem". Before they started the next verse, Laura crossed the lounge carrying a pint of beer and a glass of red wine.

"Sorry." she said. "I didn't expect to be so long; like I said, I was on a roll. Hey, what the fuck?" Someone was whistling at her, one of the men by the gas fire, a guy with a crew cut whose innate truculence had been enhanced by whisky.

"Hey Blondie!" he howled. "Get those slutty lips of yours over here! My cock isn't going to suck itself!" His entourage exploded in uneven, drunken laughter.

"You know, five years ago I would have gone over and strangled anyone who talked to me that way." Laura whispered. "But now, I really can't be bothered. Even with this guy...."

"Chop, chop, Blondie!" the guy with the crew cut taunted. "My dick's getting cold!"

Carlo cocked his head towards the group at the gas fire. "No!" Laura whispered, slapping at his wrist. Don't you *dare* say *anything* to them! These people are always *armed*. Come on; let's just move."

"I don't think so. Wait here."

Carlo walked over to a security guard sitting at the concierge's desk across the lobby. "Excuse me." Carlo said. "That guy over there is bothering us. He has demanded twice that my wife suck on his penis."

"Which one? The little fat guy with a crew cut who looks like Glenn Beck?" He spoke with a slight Mexican accent.

Carlo had little more than a vague idea who the security guard was talking about, but the description otherwise seemed to fit. "That's him."

The security guard muttered something into the microphone strapped to his shoulder. In less than a minute, a trio of reinforcements joined him, all looming over the table of drunks. Carlo heard the guy with the crew cut explain that he was getting married the next day. "Just having a bit of fun with my buddies," he said, his diction indistinct. Carlo and Laura tried to ignore them, but the chatter at the table across from them rapidly heated up.

The guy with the crew cut stood up, facing the Mexican security guard. "*I would like it if you would le-eave!*" he repeated in a mock accent. "Fuckin' beaner!" he bellowed before he lunged at the guard.

With admirable speed, the other guards ejected the other guys at the table, as the Mexican competently subdued the groom, leaving him in a heap in front of the fire with his nose oozing a stream of blood.

The guard took Carlo aside and spoke with him behind a nearby pillar. "Look, if you two are you guests in the hotel, then you and your wife must get back to your room. That guy will need medical attention."

"But we were just sitting here; we didn't do anything."

The security guard smiled. "You're Canadians, right?"

"Yes, we are."

He nodded with a hint of self-congratulation. "Trust me, you don't want to deal with the local police. There *was* some sort of altercation, and you've both had a bit to drink, so they might give you a rough time of it. They're on their way."

Carlo went back to the table. "Come on. He wants us to finish our drinks upstairs."

Laura, unsteady on her feet, looked at the security guard with an expression of disgust and started walking toward the bank of elevators. "Fine. We'll drink in the room. And if we wake up Yvette, too fuckin' bad."

As Carlo expected, the room was dark and Yvette wasn't there. "Where the fuck is she?" Laura said. "I haven't seen her since lunch and she stood us up for dinner." Carlo pondered her use of the word 'us'. They sat on a divan by the window and sipped on their drinks.

Laura seemed to be having trouble keeping her eyes open. "Off to piss?" she asked, pulling on Carlo's tie as he rose.

"Why not?"

"Good; there's more wine on the bathroom counter, red." Laura pointed in the general direction of the bathroom. "Bring it with you on your way back."

When he came back Laura was lying on the bed, with her face buried in her pillow, snoring. Carlo took off her shoes and covered her with a blanket.

The Document Preservation workshop started right after breakfast in the Orca Ballroom. The Directorate had wanted a smaller event with only willing participants, but Declan, appalled by what he'd been told, insisted that they make it mandatory. Each of the Domains, but especially the populous ones on the South Coast, spent the last months diligently burning and shredding their papers to banish any hint of virtue in the Reformed bunch. But Declan knew that judges would soon be called upon to act as referees in the interlocutory squabbles that would inevitably follow, much to the cost of the Orthodox faction once they figured out what was going on.

Carlo sat on a chair up on the portable stage, waiting to be introduced by the gowned elder who spoke in hushed, dramatic tones, as if warning of a deadly epidemic. *I tried to give him a chance to review my notes; if I say something he doesn't like...tough!* But Carlo did not see Declan in the audience. Laura waved at him from the back of the ballroom as she fiddled with a digital camera perched on a tripod next to her. When she took her seat, she rested a console on the empty chair beside her, no doubt the one reserved for Yvette. After a surprisingly accurate rendition of his name, Carlo rose to speak.

"Most of you probably have no idea who I am. I am an associate lawyer at Gaskin Barristers, with whom I'm sure you are all familiar." He heard some murmuring in the background. "I'm here to give you a brief overview of the need to properly preserve and store documents. This is all the more important now that your organization is engaged in a protracted legal action with the Reformed Striationists, one which could continue for several more years."

Yvette peeked through the door and tiptoed toward Laura, emoting like a mime.

"If you remember nothing else that I say, please keep in mind that the requirement to produce documents to one's opponent is based on very technical legal principles, which are regularly subject to revision and scrutiny by the courts. Save everything; the need to review documents to determine if we will produce them is one of the reasons why you've got *us*." His spirit sagged as it occurred to him that the people assembled in front of him behaved much like a group of indigents sitting glumly through a Salvation Army sermon, their compliance assured by the promise of hot coffee.

"Nothing enrages judges more than people who destroy documents, especially because in recent years this sort of behaviour has become more common. In *Balustrade Engineering v. Fossick,* Madam Justice Southwark was particularly pithy in her views on the subject." Carlo read the concluding line of her judgment.

Unfortunately, for a growing number of people, stupidity has become a sacrament rather than a sin.

No one laughed. "Of course, that isn't really very helpful. It's a good thing that the Supreme Court of Canada has considered the issue.*"* He embarked on a brief description of an otherwise unremarkable procedural skirmish in a legendary lawsuit over the ownership of a mountain retreat in the West Kootenays. "In *Ryland v. Schleswig,* the Chief Justice of Canada set out three basic requirements for the preservation and disclosure of documents." An impressive snore erupted from someone sitting to his left.

Before long, Laura was conspicuously battling slumber. The contest was soon over; her eyes shut and she slowly started to slump forward in her chair. Carlo decided to make use of an unsophisticated courtroom tactic which reliably awakened dozing judges. "The FIRST one…" He shouted before smacking his palm smartly against the podium. Laura's eyes opened, her expression startled and, like most of the audience, she lurched forward and sat suddenly upright. The people at the front covered their ears and started to hum.

Carlo ended the seminar by setting out the consequences of getting caught in the act of evading full disclosure. "At minimum, you will be forced to produce the documents you were trying to hide, with a healthy award of costs against you. Worse yet, your action could actually be dismissed!" However dire this fate might seem to most members of the legal profession, it didn't seem to faze anyone in the audience. One older gentleman in a cloak, of a ruddy, Celtic countenance, actually yawned.

That's it. "Thank you, ladies and gentlemen, for your attention." The audience clapped politely.

The gowned elder rose from his chair and rubbed his eyes. "Thank you, Mr. Buonsante. That concludes the morning session."

Carlo found Laura outside the banquet room next to a battery of coffee urns and teapots. She remained in a slight daze, vigorously stirring a small cup. "Hi."

"Hey." He couldn't conceal his admiration. She must have been enduring the intermediate stages of a damnable hangover, but she stood fresh and eager in a pressed suit, her face glistening with sundry cosmetics.

"I don't know, Carlo. That almost finished me off. How can you stand it? I had to poke myself with a pencil, just to stay awake."

"'Look, I warned Declan…"

"I know; he never listens. What do you have next?"

"Something upstairs on 'religious history', no indication about which religion. I'm not done until six, some silly thing upstairs about water quality."

"Water quality? What do they care about water quality?"

"I don't know. I guess they *still* have to wash themselves off after they roll around in the dirt."

"Did you drive here?"

"No. I must have lost my mind. I came down with Declan. Endless NPR; the only consolation was Thelonious Monk interludes and on occasion, Dave Brubeck."

"Well, I can save you from all of that. When you're done, at what is it, the Water Whatever, if you want, you can get a ride home with me; what do you think?

"Thanks." Carlo smiled. "Much better than the alternative. See you here at six."

"Things haven't changed; you're braver than Yvette. She still refuses to get in the car if I'm behind the wheel."

The Water Clarity Workshop took up a mercifully brief half hour. As it turned out, the word 'clarity' took on a different meaning in Striationist circles, heedless of turbidity but instead defined by the depth and "spiritual dynamics" of the glacial striations it flowed through. As he made his way back to the lobby, Carlo spotted Gaskin admiring a native mask displayed opposite the front desk.

"Oh, there you are," Gaskin said. "Yes...sorry I missed your presentation. I was called unexpectedly to a...a meeting."

Some meeting. Carlo didn't press him for details.

"Well, right. I suppose that you need a ride back. After I finish this coffee, I'm going to get my luggage from the concierge. Once you're ready to go, I guess we'll make tracks for Vancouver!" Declan finished on an eerie note of cheer.

"No, no, I'll be staying here for a couple more hours. I'm going to the outlet mall over there to shop for some ties, and then I'm getting a ride back home with..." Carlo paused. "A friend of mine. I imagine that...."

"Oh!" Declan seemed relieved. "Anyway, see you back at the office on Tuesday."

....23

Even with its twelve-dollar drop-in fee, Laeticia preferred to exercise at Hogan's Gym whenever she was down in Victoria, a better smelling facility than some of the other places frequented by outsized men who leered, grunted and spat. True, it was blandly modish. The designer light fixtures and granite surfaces in the change rooms attracted a tribe of young professionals, most of whom joined only to take advantage of the dating network that spontaneously blossomed, but Laeticia mostly ignored them. One afternoon after an hour-long stint with free weights that left her feeling boneless, she saw Fabién loitering in shorts near the front desk, holding a squash racquet.

"Well, hello, Laeticia," Fabién grinned. "Fancy meeting you here."

"Hello, Fabién," she sighed.

"This is indeed a fortunate circumstance." He placed his hand on her shoulder. "Do you have time for a coffee later?"

She stepped back and shrugged off his hand. "No, no, Fabién, I do not, not now; not ever. So you can stop texting me and sending me flowers." She lowered her voice as a couple came up to the front desk. "Please! It's embarrassing. Keep it up and I'll tell my boyfriend about you."

"Oh!" A condescending smile. "And what's he going to do to me? Beat me up?"

"Not likely; he's more subtle than that. He's Italian, Fabién. Piss *him* off and maybe he'll come over to your house one night and dump a horse's head in your bed."

"Hey, the offer's always open."

Laeticia's phone whistled with a new text message before she got back to her car.

Nice seeing you again. À la prochaine!

It started raining just after they left. Laura enjoyed driving her car, an aerodynamic and slinky Acura, at well above even American speed limits. Despite her rapt attention to the road, it was obvious to Carlo that she had something she wanted to say to him. His inner wisdom implored him to let the matter be, but after several minutes of watching Laura sigh and tighten her jaw, Carlo succumbed to curiosity.

"What?"

"*What* what? Why are you asking me 'what'?"

Carlo glanced over at her. "Seriously?"

"Okay. Look," she said, "I don't know if I want to ask you about this; I'm sure that you don't want to talk about it."

"Go ahead. Ask away." Carlo decided that whatever it was, he might as well get it over with. It started to rain harder, vigorously pelting the car. Interstate 5 was soon covered with water.

"I never heard exactly what happened to Tina." Laura said quietly. "No one ever told me. They tried to make it seem sensational in the news for a while, but out here none of it made any sense at the time. And (of course), I never asked you about it at her funeral."

"I had a lot to deal with, believe me; and it was a long, painful process. The police were investigating for what seemed like months. It didn't make any sense. We had just moved into a place by Neville Park."

"Just by where we used to live."

"Yes, just a couple of blocks away. One night, even though it was early November it was still quite warm; we were supposed to meet for dinner at *Da Fieramosca*, that place over in Yorkville. She called me on my cell, said that she didn't feel well, she was going home. I was on my way to a settlement meeting at one of the monster firms, BLG that time, so we decided we'd just meet up at home instead, after it ended. When I got home after ten, she wasn't there. I called the police, searched the neighbourhood. Some kids found her in that ravine off Glenmanor Drive on their way to school the next morning."

"Did they ever find out who did it? The Vancouver stations dropped it after a few days."

"Oh, they did. You could tell that the cops would have given anything to be able to blame me; you know, privileged young Bay Street lawyer kills girlfriend, with all the media frenzy that entails, but they were stuck with the fact that I was at a meeting with forty other people in Scotia Plaza. No, it turned out that it was this guy, a shut-in, really, who lived in an apartment above the laundromat across from the pub."

"I'm so sorry."

"It's something that I think about every day. It was just so...senseless. I was a very bitter, angry guy for quite a while, the cruelty of it all, those fucking police; and then the way the press tried to portray Tina as some sort of slut (so she wore short skirts, big fucking deal). And..." Carlo stopped himself. "But it seems like such a long time ago."

They sat in silence. Carlo saw tears falling down Laura's face, streaking her makeup. "Carlo, I'm sorry, I'm just sorry."

"It has been a miserable three years; for about six months I could barely function."

"I wasn't talking about that. I was talking about...*Lattanzio.*" She whispered his name.

"That was a very long time ago; eight, well, nine years. There's no need to be...I don't..."

"Look, I've got to say it. You know the old saying, 'act in haste, repent at leisure'? Well, that's me, that's the story of my life. There's Kleenex in the glove box." Carlo retrieved a handful and passed it to her. "I was going to say something to you at Tina's funeral," Laura said after blowing her nose. "But that was neither the time nor the place."

"I've tried my best to forget about those days."

"Well, I can't. It happens all the time when I can't sleep, I lie awake thinking about what I did, sometimes for hours. I can't believe that I left you after I fell for such a piece of shit! And it's not like I was just some kid; I was already twenty-three."

"Twenty-three *is* still a 'kid'."

"And I got so fat!" Well, that was true enough. A few months after the breakup, Carlo was surprised to feel more stunned than triumphant when he caught a glimpse of her by chance, ambling past in one of the underground concourses downtown.

"Look, I don't know what to say," Laura said. "I made a stupid, selfish mistake which probably screwed up both of our lives. I hope you don't hate me."

Carlo turned to look at her. "Of course I don't hate you. I *missed* you. I'm just glad that we met up."

"Yes. I missed you too." There was so much more that she wanted to say to him, but she remembered something her mother said years earlier, warning her of getting too inquisitive about a past family scandal. *If you insist on picking at old scabs, don't be too surprised if you open a vein.* "So, how is your dad? How's Linda?"

"He's doing great, he and Linda are still in Soho. He's still plugging away in with his architectural practice, she's still in music, but now more as an agent. Goes to exercise classes now, if you can believe it."

"Her and me both." She reached over to slap him on the shoulder. "Asshole!" Laura laughed. "Don't look so shocked."

"Hey, hey: ten and two."

Laura seemed briefly lost in thought; her lips curved in a gentle smile. "And a random person came to mind a while back," she said with a laugh. "Dunstan." He was one of Carlo's law school classmates. "Are you still in touch with him?"

"We talk on the phone once every few months."

"Remember when I put him out to walk that time on the way home from Whistler?"

"I do." It was an event that Carlo laughed about whenever he remembered it. Dunstan, who should have known better than to provoke Laura when she was in the midst of a punishing hangover, calmly observed that her upbringing on rural Vancouver Island rendered her small-minded and mean. "It's not like he didn't deserve it."

"I bet he's still out banging secretaries. Am I right?"

"Could be, only now, he's married."

"*Married?* What the fuck?"

"Yup. And Mario's another one. Not married, but he and Laeticia have lived together for what, eight years? It must be that long. They're back in B.C. now. Parksville."

"Wow. Mario and Laeticia. That would have been the last match that I would have predicted, back in the day."

After they crossed a long bridge, the rain became more violent. Some of the cars ahead of them started to lose control in the deepening coating of water on the freeway. "This is way too dangerous," Laura tightened her grip on the steering wheel. "If we try to make Vancouver tonight, we're going to get into an accident." She shifted down and signalled to turn towards the exit ramp. "It says that there's lodging down here; let's see what they've got."

They drove for a few minutes along a corrugated rural road, past an Arco station and an expanse of forest. At a three-way intersection they found the apparent lodging, the Horseshoe Lake Cabins and Resort, across from the similarly-named Horseshoe Lake General Store. Perhaps because a fog had descended, Carlo was unable to locate a lake.

"Let's check it out." Laura slowed her car and pulled in next to a building marked "Resort Office". A collection of about twelve plywood cabins were scattered throughout the wooded grounds. Once in the office, Carlo and Laura had to wait while an older couple filled out a registration form. The woman behind the desk was clearly in her fifties, with an outpouring of big, blonde hair of a style that had been fashionable about twenty years earlier.

"More refugees from the storm! You really shouldn't have been caught by surprise, you know. They've been forecasting this for days."

After the people ahead of them left, they decided to take the cabin close across from the restaurant.

"You need some plastic?" Laura asked.

"No, no; I got it." Carlo gave the desk clerk his Visa.

"Bonsaint." She squeaked as she squinted at Carlo's credit card. "That's a strange name for a white man!"

"So we're in cabin 8?" Carlo asked.

"Yeah, that's the one!" She pointed behind her with her thumb. "And if you want dinner, just remember, the restaurant closes in an hour!"

The cabin was not only spacious beyond expectation, but for only eighty dollars, its fixtures were surprisingly up-to-date. Carlo had expected a dank seventies period piece that reeked of Pine-Sol. "I'll take the hide-a-bed." He tossed his suitcase on the couch.

"Believe it, Buonsante, there's no need to be chivalrous with me," Laura laughed. "Hurry up, we'd better get to the restaurant before it closes."

They were the only customers in the restaurant, served by a relentlessly talkative woman who insisted that they call her 'Rachel' every time they spoke to her. By the time the two of them finished dinner, they'd heard too much detail about her most recent divorce, and the fact that her son had a marked preference, lamentable in her opinion, to date Asian girls.

"So!" Laura said after Rachel finally left them in peace. "You were telling me about Dunstan. Married; I'm almost speechless."

"It's not that surprising. She's perfect for him: bouncy, giggly blonde. Could have been an extra in *Clueless*. And for Dunstan, there was the clincher. Remember that Australian comedian back in the day, that song of his that Mario used to sing all the time? Something about girls fucking on first dates and having a dad who owns a brewery? Well, her dad owns three breweries, as well as a hotel chain and a small investment bank based in the Caymans.

"Well, there's a big surprise. Kids?"

"Not that I've heard. But he's still on Bay Street, working his way up the letterhead at Binton Winstanley. She's got a gig on The Weather Network. And she's a bigger tree-hugger than I am; makes him take the streetcar to work. He bought a Jaguar about a year ago but she won't let him drive it during the week."

"There is a God!"

Rachel returned with two menus. "How about dessert?" she shouted. "How about I leave y'all with the dessert menu!"

Laura waited for the bus boy to clear away their dishes. Once he was gone, Laura leaned toward Carlo.

"This is the first time in longer than I'd like to admit that I've stayed overnight with a man at a secluded resort." she said in a clipped, clinical tone. "What about you? There must have been, oh, I don't know, some dark-eyed Roman hottie."

Dark-eyed Roman hottie. *Her eyes are as blue as yours.* "No, it's been a while for me, too. Berlusconi kept them all busy."

"So I've heard, disgusting old letch." She scanned the dessert menu. "But you, a young, and hey, I'd be the first to say it, good-looking guy, a lawyer to boot. You must have gotten *some* action, more than you're willing to tell me about, anyway." A mischievous grin.

"Truck loads," he laughed as he finished his last sip of wine. "No; all joking aside, the past three years aren't really worth talking about. 'Action' is about all that I got. Lately I've missed *you.* I've missed *us.*"

Laura didn't take her eyes from the menu. "You know what? I probably don't need any desert. Even a few mouthfuls of any of this shit would have me bursting out of every suit I own.

Let's go wait for the next deluge in the cabin." The same mischievous grin. "Do you suppose that the little store across the street sells wine?"

"In this country? I'm sure that it does."

"Let's take a wander over and find out."

On the way back from the store, the rain had let up enough so that they didn't need to share an umbrella. Laura took Carlo's arm. "I hope this wine is drinkable. The last wine I had that was made in Washington State tasted like cranberry juice."

"It's got to be better than that crap David used to bring to our parties."

Once they were back in the cabin, Laura poured both of them a glass of wine and walked over to join Carlo on the couch. She curled up next to him and sipped her wine. "This stuff isn't half-bad. So, anyway, how long has Dunstan been married?"

"Seven, maybe eight years. Last I heard, they bought a place in the Annex."

"Really? I never figured him as one for the white picket fence. But then again, back in the day, there were people so unimaginative that they assumed that we were on track for the white picket fence." She laughed. "We sure proved them wrong, and in grand style, didn't we?"

"That we did," Carlo said as they clinked glasses. After Laura had drained her glass, she leaned against him and emitted a gentle snore.

Laura shook herself awake. "Shit! You know, on the way back from the store, I was looking forward to a *much* more energetic evening. I'm so sorry, but I'm just spent: I feel bloated and exhausted and hung over. I had way too much to drink last night."

"Maybe just a little." He rested his hand on an exposed expanse of her thigh.

"*Don't* roll your eyes!" Laura sat back against him and sighed. "Look, I'm sorry, Carlo," she said, her voice high pitched and contrite. "I think that all I'm good for right now is a bath and a long sleep. But please sleep in the bed with me," she smiled. "As long as you behave yourself. If you slept on the couch, I'd feel bad."

Can't have that, Carlo thought as he quelled a monumental erection. After a few more sips of wine, Laura got up from the sofa to start her bath. "Good night. She gave him a peck on the cheek. "I'm sure I'll be livelier tomorrow."

Tomorrow? What did *that* mean? Carlo found the television remote and started scanning the channels. After rapidly flipping past twenty or thirty screens, he settled briefly on a fishing show, his attention captured by a narrow lake surrounded by steep, wooded hillsides. Two chubby men swaddled in camouflage gear pulled giant trout out of the lake one after the other, each wriggling vigorously on the line. Then he scanned a few frantic *telenovelas,* and with a sigh of resignation, landed on CNN.

It was the commercials in America that startled him the most. Canadian commercials were characteristically wry; Italian ones most often appealed to an uneasy mix of an imagined bucolic past and sensuous sexuality. Shapely female rear ends were used to market everything from *ricotta* to floor wax. Here, they initially seemed almost comically earnest, but eventually demonstrated their inevitable underlying guile. Advertisements for prescription medications at first touted their miraculous benefits, soon to be replaced by a hushed, male monotone in the background that enumerated dire afflictions that would befall people foolish enough to put the product into their mouths. And what kind of idiot would buy insurance from a talking lizard who speaks with a Cockney accent?

Carlo decided to call it a night after he finished his second glass of wine. Laura was still in the bath. He fell asleep almost upon touching the pillow, but was soon jarred awake by the crack of the bedroom door. "Carlo!" Laura said in a fierce, gleeful whisper. "I've got my second wind." She'd come to bed naked, fresh from her bath; his annoyance at having been suddenly awakened was soon supplanted by the rapid return of his erection. "Come on, wake up!" she giggled, as she slid in beside him.

His throat was arid when he awoke; daylight already brightened the sitting room. He rose to fetch a glass of cold water. When he came back to bed Laura was uncovered, snoring with abandon, a lush vision of robust curves and ivory-coloured skin.   With reluctance, he had to admit it: Declan was right. Laura's form was about as full as Marika's, but with one obvious difference. Laura, rounded but sinewy, radiated vigorous well-being. Perhaps that was the answer, the reason why he was at first repelled by Marika. She was no less attractive, and almost a decade younger, but Marika's hefty body bespoke languor and indulgence; someone who sought a steward rather than a companion and would no doubt grow increasingly bulky and helpless as time passed.

Carlo curled up next to her, expecting the same groan and sleepy rebuke that it often earned him on mornings when they lived together. Instead, she enlivened with startling speed and pulled him closer. Before long, he was inside her again, where he had spent most of the past few hours.

"It's twenty to eleven!" A glance at the bedside clock jolted Carlo from his post-coital stupor. "We've got to be out of here in twenty minutes." He rushed to load the car. Laura emerged from the cabin with fresh makeup, in black leggings and a crisp white blouse, her suit draped over one arm. Carlo, unshaven, in jeans and an untucked shirt, looked like a beggar. A young man loading a car in front of the cabin opposite grinned at Carlo and made a thumbs-up gesture with both hands.

"What was that all about?" Laura asked.

"I guess we made a bit of noise last night."

"I need coffee, now."

Rachel wasn't working that morning. Instead, they ordered coffee to go from the woman with the big, blonde hair who'd been on the front desk when they checked in. She poured the coffee with irritating good cheer as she hummed a tune that sounded like "Oops, I Did it Again." "You people are from Canada, aren't you?"

"Um...yes," Carlo said.

"Well, I distribute a product here that they don't sell in Canada. Yennaflex." She winked at Laura. "It's the perfect shampoo for girls like us who rely on the miracles of modern chemistry to keep their hair blonde."

"No, no," Laura stammered, "this is my natural colour; I don't..."

"Oh, come on, honey. I can see your dark roots as plain as the warts on a witch's chin! So forget this nonsense, maybe you'll consider buying a bottle?"

"No, I don't really need it." Laura flashed a phony, acerbic smile. "In Canada, we have the best shampoo in the world. It comes from Montréal." She used the French pronunciation. "You know, in the *French* part of the country."

The desk clerk returned Laura's smile in kind. "I see. Well, you two have yourselves a real good trip back to the border!"

Once out of the restaurant, Laura walked to the car, with a tight, determined expression. Carlo shut the passenger door as gently as he could. They drove in silence back to the entrance ramp to the freeway. Once they'd merged into traffic, she finally spoke. "What's with these fucking people? '*Get those slutty lips over here!*' I mean *really*? *Slutty*? Dark roots (I mean, is she on *crack*?), and Yennaflex, whatever *that* might be made of!" She turned to Carlo, who remained studiously quiet. "Did I ever tell you how much I fucking *hate* crossing the border?"

Roland Egbert's office was a continent removed from Nanaimo, a vision of what one might expect of an Oxford don's accommodations; walls of dark wood decorated with Vanity Fair prints, bookcases filled with yellowed, sequential volumes of the *English Reports*, all radiating the scent of pipe tobacco and furniture polish. Egbert received Gavin dressed in his habitual morning pants and tweed jacket; Gavin wore an expression bespeaking the utmost patience.

"You don't seem to understand, Gavin," Egbert pronounced, his hands formed into a steeple, the apex nestled underneath the cleft in his chin. "That's not the way things are done, not the way people behave, here on Vancouver Island. And you conveniently ignore that this all requires *my* assent, and with a project of such dubious merit ..."

"Oh, for the love of Christ, Egbert!" Gavin sighed. "Have you forgotten? I *live* on Vancouver Island. I've been here for twelve years."

"Not impressive. Three of my grandparents were born here."

"And you're in *Canada*. You're *Canadian*. You're not some poohbah in a sultanate somewhere. All I'm asking to do is allow some of my researchers to use the narrow channel between Gabriola and Valdez Island to gather data for an ongoing research project. Nothing exotic. This may be an island; but it's not Sicily. What do you expect me to do, kiss your ring?"

"That was uncalled for!" Egbert gasped. "Look, everyone knows exactly what you're up to." He tilted his head at an imperious angle. "Do you not recall? We were discussing this in Vancouver some months ago. You haven't made a secret of it; you were blabbering about it in Parksville a few months back and a couple of weeks later, you very nearly started a riot when you presented that professor, what was he, German or something, at that do in Bastion Square. And if I whispered in the ear of any of the locals in the mall across the way and told them that I have you right here in my office, they'd be delighted to drag you on to the next ferry out of Departure Bay and keelhaul you."

"Look, I don't deny that I'm trying to develop the technological capacity for a fixed link." Gavin took a breath, mindful of his composure. "Let's just say that I accept, however reluctantly, that regardless of the amount of guile, deceit and trickery that is brought to bear, there is no way that a bridge, tunnel, fixed link, call it whatever you want, will ever be approved. The technology could be used for a variety of purposes: construction materials, repair of underwater structures. Don't you think that we should at least complete the research? It could result in a multi-billion-dollar industry."

"Please don't exaggerate so. It makes you sound like an American. I don't know, Gavin, it's against my better judgment. Your overarching goal is still something that's profoundly unpopular." Egbert fell silent, his chin again resting on its digital apex, as if meditating.

"All right, Gavin. For reasons that I suspect go beyond mere luck, your project has yet to attract much in the way of environmental protest. The last thing I want to see is boatloads of Greenpeacers, or, worse yet, Rainbow People." He spat out the name of a detested group of latter-day hippies. "Infesting the Island once again like they did fifteen years ago. If you can give me a guarantee that streets of Nanaimo won't reek of patchouli oil, you've got your permit, but only for, what did you say you needed?"

"Three days."

"Good. Three days. And it better be carried out safely."

"You worry too much, Egbert."

On his way back up to Parksville, Gavin stopped in at the Woodgrove Mall, a sprawling relic of the 1980s on the northern edge of the city, to find a CD that Tiffany had asked him to pick up by somebody named 'Pink' or something; he'd never heard of her. After he left HMV and made his way back to his car, he encountered Mario loitering outside a shoe store.

"What are you doing here?" He slapped Mario on the shoulder. "Checking out the chicks?"

"Need you ask?" He pointed to Laeticia, who was seated on a bench trying on shoes, with a stack of boxes next to her and a young clerk bringing out armloads of additional boxes to augment the pile.

"Ah, yes; the everlasting male cross to bear. My turn isn't far behind, I'm sure." Gavin remembered that he'd wanted to ask Mario something. "Yes, I meant to call you. I hadn't seen you at the mail boxes lately. We're having our annual end of summer party at my place in Whistler. It's going to be in September, on the sixth. The weekend after Labour Day."

"Oh, yeah," Mario mumbled.

"Now, now. Look, I get it. I know that the one last year was a bit of a gong show. It's not going to be just the real estate and financial crowd. I'm inviting all of my friends from UBC, some of them are academics; some are IT people, like you."

"Hmm."

"And Tiffany is inviting everyone from her yoga classes in Nanaimo and Victoria."

"Sure," Mario shrugged. "Your parties are always, well, almost always, a good time. The sixth?"

"Of September. And feel free to invite some of your friends. I like a good shaker," he laughed. "But just once a year." Gavin peered into the shoe store and then waved at Laeticia before he resumed his walk down the corridor. "Hey, better you than me, my friend!"

Mario sighed as he glumly watched the pile of boxes next to Laeticia grow ever larger.

* * *

Laura decided to get up and make coffee. Yes, it would have been more comfortable if they'd spent the night at her place, but she was anxious to satisfy her curiosity: how did Carlo live after being single for three years? She picked her way through his kitchen. He'd strayed little in the way he organized it since their domestic arrangement years earlier: the coffee in a plastic container in the freezer; coffee filters above the stove. But she had to search for the Melita. All that she could find on the stovetop was one of those Italian contraptions that makes a couple of tiny little cups. The expected Canadian Tire plates, yard sale cookware, even a set of wine glasses. Kevin had three dented aluminium pots from an old camping mess kit and an empty pizza box. As the kettle started to boil, she heard the melodic jingling of keys outside the front door. She peeked into the hallway and saw a familiar face, perhaps a bit more unshaven and hairier than she remembered him.

"David?" she shrieked.

"Laura? That *is* you." He started laughing. "Don't look so horrified. You'd think that I was a Jehovah's Witness or something. What are you doing here?"

Laura was paralyzed. Although she was dressed in a short t-shirt that covered her chest and a bit of her midriff (she was thankful for her ultimate decision to wear panties), she still considered herself naked. Then she remembered that David preferred a darker, narrower type of woman. She took comfort in her assumption that he didn't really enjoy the view.

"I'm here with...with Carlo." Laura went back into the kitchen, aware that David was scanning her.

"I sort of gathered that. But I haven't seen you in what, three years?"

"I know. Carlo and I met up again."

"I gathered that, too"

"At Tulalip."

"Tulalip? That's lame. It should have at least been Vegas!"

"Oh, just fuck off!" She laughed. "Why are you here?"

"Carlo's chicory, oh, and his tomato plant. Out on the balcony. He asked me to water them while he was down in the States."

Laura went up to the bedroom to wake Carlo, only to find him dressing and stirring his hair with his fingers. "He's here? At this hour?"

"I gave him the key," Carlo said. "The plants on the balcony would have otherwise died of thirst. I didn't tell him when to show up."

Carlo went down to the kitchen, in time to find David draining the last of the coffee pot into his cup. "So, Tulalip, eh? Just back from Italia; I guess you don't know any better."

"It was for Gaskin and his fucking Striationists. Wait a minute; you just took all of the coffee!"

"Make another pot."

Laura came down from the bedroom, wearing a snug pair of Carlo's jogging pants. Her concern that they probably hadn't been washed in more than a week was well outweighed by her unwillingness to continue displaying her thighs to David.

David slapped his forehead. "Hey! What are you guys doing tonight, I mean, for dinner?"

Carlo looked over at Laura, at first with a certain caution, but he shrugged after she nodded. "Nothing, as far as I can remember."

"Good, great, we'd love to have you over. So that boat at the fisherman's dock is still selling fresh spring salmon from the Skeena," David said. "Don't worry; I'll cover half. You can pick that up, can't you? And that pasta you made a couple of times when you were staying at our place, 'tricky' or something?"

Carlo laughed. "Amatriciana?"

"Yeah, yeah, I think that's the stuff. Can you make it again?"

"Sure, why not?"

"So, sevenish?" David said. "We've got wine. And thanks for the coffee, buddy."

"You know," Laura said as soon as David shut the door behind him, "I just don't get that guy. I haven't seen him in three years. He hasn't seen us *together* in almost nine, and he spent more time inspecting my legs than he did asking why...well, look; we were obviously sleeping together. It's as if he sees us every day!" She poured herself more coffee. "And then he invites us over for dinner and then demands that you cook it?"

"David is David."

"He must drive Farida, he's still with Farida, isn't he? He must drive her insane!"

"She keeps him in line, and I doubt she's a joy to live with. Anyway, what did you want to do for the rest of the day? Anything planned?"

"Nah, I'll have to stop by home at some point, and I was going to go into work later on. But screw it. What time is it now?"

Carlo peered at the digital display on the stove. "It's 9:36."

"It's early yet. Let's go back to bed for an hour or two."

"Sounds like a good idea to me."

"And he offers to go halfers *just* for the salmon," Laura said as they walked upstairs to the loft. "Does he think that pasta is free? And did you notice? He didn't even water your fucking chicory."

Laura laughed as they passed the Emily Carr Pub just off the Seawalk, on their way to the fish boat wharves next to Granville Island. "Listen! Don't you recognize the music?" She punched him in the shoulder. "It's...it's *our song*! Come on!" Laura said "We have to go in." The opening verse of "Nightrain" grew louder as the host led them to a table overlooking the water, Laura attracting nervous glances as she danced in front of Carlo on the way, lip-synching as Axl Rose shrieked the chorus.

The two of them met eighteen years earlier on a party bus, back then a well-known insurrection on wheels, as it wound its way toward a ski resort along a narrow mountain road on

Vancouver Island. Later on, emboldened by the alcohol that flowed in abundance during a party at the lodge where they all spent the night, the two of them dared one another to perform a karaoke duet of a Guns 'N Roses tune that had been ephemerally popular at the time.

"I'd tried my best to forget about that." Carlo said. "Thank Christ that there was no such thing as YouTube back then. And I've never had so much as a drop of Tequila since!"

"Neither have I. But we had worse than YouTube. We had Yvette, and she didn't have nearly as much to drink. She remembers it vividly, and she isn't shy about reminding me about it. She says that we were quite the spectacle."

"I'm sure we were. I'd forgotten that Yvette was still around when we were up on the stage."

"Oh, yes; she was. Did you know that she got together with Mario that night?"

"*What?*"

"Yup. She's said it a few times since then: he's the shortest man that she's ever, well, *almost* slept with. But I find that difficult to believe. Mario's not unusually short, and her standards aren't always all that exacting."

No shit. "If I remember correctly," Carlo said. "*We* managed to sleep together that night, but we were too hammered to get naked."

"We were probably better off. Hey, what are you getting? More of that penitent's brew you were drinking at the casino?"

"Nope. A Cuervo, in honour of Axl. But just one."

"What the hell; a Cuervo. But how far is David and Farida's place from here?"

"About twenty minutes."

"Your twenty minutes means that it will take us about an hour. I'm in heels."

After they left the pub, Carlo bought a chunk of a thick filet of spring salmon from a guy on a fishing boat, and then the two of them made their way to the brick and polished cedar warren where David and Farida lived, just up from Kits Beach. "Nice place." Laura appraised the condominium complex, arranged in a cluster of three-level townhouses. Carlo buzzed in and opened the gate.

David came to the front door and thrust an open bottle of Kokanee in Carlo's free hand. "You're late!" David laughed. "And I think I know which one of you is to blame. Wine, Laura?"

"Just this once."

Farida appeared behind him. Carlo saw the two women both scowl upon sight of one another. Both were wearing the same abbreviated summer dress, each bearing a distinctive white and light blue design light arranged in vertical waves. One of the boutiques on West Fourth Avenue must have been having a sale.

"Hi, Farida," Laura said.

"Oh, hello, Laura," Farida said, her tone lacking a hint of emotion. "It's been a while, hasn't it?"

"It has."

"I'll go get you that wine David offered you. I could use a bit myself."

Carlo was in the midst of dicing some *pancetta* when Farida came back into the kitchen. Laura was on the deck smoking a cigarette; Carlo could see David talking with much animation, gesticulating in the direction of the barbeque, a shiny metal contraption that looked like a jet engine.

"It's new." Farida smiled. "He bought it on Thursday."

He looked up at her as he pried loose two cloves of garlic. "So, when did he tell you that Laura would be coming for dinner?"

"About five minutes before you guys got here." She slapped him on the back of his head. "What is wrong with you, getting mixed up with her again?"

"It *has* been nine years, Jesus Christ! People change."

"People never change; they only get worse."

Carlo laughed. "Yes, they do change. You might recall that David had a, let's just say, *disreputable* record (come on, he was such a dog) before you two hooked up."

"Yes, but here's the difference: he never cheated on *me*!"

"Look, Farida, when I think about what has happened in the recent past, it couldn't get much worse. And let's face it." He grinned at her. "She's as hot as she always was."

"Fuck, Carlo!" She looked around and lowered her voice. The sliding glass door to the deck was open a crack. "Have you forgotten what she did? And with Lattanzio, that piece of shit New Age lounge lizard." Carlo chuckled at her characterization of Lattanzio. "Did you I tell you? I saw him on Alberni Street, on vacation I hope, about six weeks ago. His hair's gone almost completely grey; he had this beautiful brown girl (she looked Indian, about thirty, if that) wrapped around him. I ducked into the Helly Hansen outlet store to avoid him. You know how much I love Gore-Tex."

"It's not actually Gore-Tex, it's..."

"Fuck off." Farida laughed. `You know what else pisses me off? She shows up for dinner here, in the same dress that I'm wearing. Don't you think that it's a bit rude?"

It surprised him that Farida took refuge in such tenuous logic. "Well, I guess that's one way of looking at it; here is another: you greeted her at the front door, wearing the same dress *she* is. Of course, she hasn't complained yet."

"And if you wanted *hot*, why didn't you take that paralegal, what's her name, Mattie or something? Why didn't you take *her* for a tumble? When I saw you that time at Calista's, she looked like she wanted to fuck your brains out."

Carlo turned the sauce down to let it simmer. "No." He smiled and shook his head.

"You know what? It's like I've told you many times before. You're too quick to give people the benefit of the doubt. In this situation?" Farida poked her finger into his back. "She cheated on *you*, I don't care how long ago it was. And you know that I favour swift, medieval forms of punishment for infidelity. It wasn't for nothing that *your* homeboy Dante reserved the lowest circles of Hell for adulterers! And you're trying to put your life back together, and doing a great job of it. A good way to fuck it up is to welcome that sleazy, untrustworthy slut back in your life!"

He stopped cutting the salmon in mid-slice and paused to deliver what he hoped was a poisonous glance at Farida. "That's enough! Fuck off and just give it a rest. It's time you shut your fucking mouth."

"You know, you're almost thirty-six and you still don't have any brains."

"Don't you speak English? I said that's enough!"

David and Laura came back into the house. "Carlo!" David shouted. "Okay, the grill is hot. Are you ready to put the salmon on?"

"Is there anything I can do?" Laura leaned forward into the kitchen, careful to keep her feet in the sitting room. Nothing had changed. Whenever she approached a kitchen, she always behaved as if she were walking into a Shinto shrine.

"Yes, please; could you stir the sauce here?" He handed her the spoon. "So!" He turned to David. "Fancy new barbeque?"

"Yup. It kicks ass! It's on the gas connection, stainless steel, ceramic grills. Cost us thirty-five hundred dollars." Carlo saw Farida roll her eyes.

"Thirty-five hundred dollars! Ò! For a barbeque? Are you insane?"

"Hey, don't knock it, you'll see what I mean. It'll do an excellent job of that salmon." David laughed. "And it beats the crap out of that little charcoal hibachi you used to use in Toronto.

Remember the time it set fire to your neighbour's picnic table? He was so pissed I thought he was going to cut your balls off!"

David went to fiddle with the stereo. A song started playing half way through, probably on satellite radio. Pearl Jam. Carlo sang along to "Tremor Christ" as he placed the fillets of salmon on the grill.

It was past midnight before Carlo and Laura started back along the Seawalk.

"Don't you think that she was a little cold?" Laura said.

"What?" Carlo resolved to feign stupidity for as long as he could.

"Farida. I mean, she became much friendlier over the course of the evening, especially after three, well (let's be honest) four bottles of wine, but at first, she looked like she would rather have the beggar down the street over for dinner. What's up with that?"

"I suppose you were wearing the same dress."

"Yes, I found that amusing. I'm about as white as you can get, but I have the same *couturier* as a brown girl. Who could have guessed that?" Laura stopped and held Carlo back. "All right. Enough bullshit. What's her problem?"

Carlo sighed, now resigned to the fact that Laura would pester him incessantly until he came up with a satisfactory answer. "She holds what happened with Lattanzio against you; past events, I don't know what to tell you. Persians are almost as bad about that sort of thing as Italians."

"Isn't that just fucking ridiculous? It's so long ago, and if you're ready to forgive me (I assume that you are at least considering it)," Carlo raised his hands in a gesture of surrender, "why is she the one to hold a grudge."

Carlo sighed. "I don't know; after all that has happened, she has started to be, well, let's say, protective of me. She hasn't said as much, but that's the way she behaves."

"So she sees herself as being in the role of your protector."

"I guess."

"Doesn't that bother you, at least a little?"

"I don't know. When I first picked up on it, I found it annoying, but I've started to find it a bit humorous. It is what it is."

"No, look," Laura turned to Carlo, grasping his shoulder. "Was this a mistake? *What* are we doing here? What the hell are we doing?"

Carlo stared back at her, startled by her sudden eruption. "Well, I thought, well, we're going to try to pick up where we, let's just say, 'left off', and that's what you want us to do, isn't it?"

"Well, I thought so, too. But we can't let every random, what's your word, *papessa*, dredge up the ancient history and sit in judgment of me without someone (that would be *you*) telling them to fuck off. I doubt if you will ever truly understand how horribly I'm still embarrassed by what I did!" Carlo was surprised to see tears forming in her eyes. "Pick up where we left off? I'd love to, but if we are, then you're going to have to stand up for me, tell people like her to fuck off!"

"I did just that, while you and David were out on the deck. We had words, and I'll put it this way: I don't think she's very happy with *me*, either."

Laura relaxed and took his hand as they started walking again. "And you know what else? It's bullshit! She's one to set herself up as Mother Superior. Has she forgotten that she fucked Dunstan when he was still living with Tina?"

"Probably not, but it wouldn't be a good idea to remind her."

"Oh, I won't, but it's still bullshit!" She clutched his arm. "I think I'd like to stay the night at your place again. Is that okay with you?"

....25

To: Carlo Buonsante
From: Catriona Lu

Re: You suck!

I found out from one of the Freaks that you were with a girl in Tulalip, one of their public relations minions. He thinks she's your wife!

So you're married!! You never fucking told me about any wife (or even some random girlfriend) that time you were in Seattle looking lost. I was seriously thinking of inviting you upstairs that night. Remember that? Would it have made it feel like a real player if you used me to cheat on your wife, or whatever she is? I thought you were a good guy but you're not.

You're an asshole.

C.

Catriona Lu
Associate
Guenter & Sadich, Attorneys
Suite 1800, 256 Fifth Avenue
Seattle, Washington 98300
Dir. (206) 631-2272

Carlo went to the washroom to splash cold water on his face before he came up with his reply.

To: Catriona Lu
From: Carlo Buonsante

Re: re: You suck!

The only reason that I'm replying to you at all is because we have to maintain some sort of collegial relationship. The Freak you were talking to was wrong and you're totally out of line. Her name is Laura, and we were together for almost nine years until we split up back in 1999. The first time we'd seen each other since a friend's funeral in Toronto about three years ago was at the Convocation, and yes, we got back together. That's a good thing, as they say, and so it's also a good thing that nothing ever came of that night in Seattle, because I would have felt bad getting back together with Laura but I would have done it anyway.

Carlo Buonsante
Barrister
GASKIN BARRISTERS
Fifteenth floor, Harbour Centre
555 West Hastings Street
Vancouver, B.C. V6B 4N4
Tel. 604 688 1777

Her reply came about ten minutes later.

To: Carlo Buonsante
From: Catriona Lu

Re: re: re: You suck!

Oh.

C.

Catriona Lu
Associate
Guenter & Sadich, Attorneys
Suite 1800, 256 Fifth Avenue
Seattle, Washington 98300
Dir. (206) 631-2272

Rue Mouffetard was quiet at mid-morning, save for the diesel-fuelled patter of a few delivery trucks allowed into the pedestrian shopping district. Basaraba walked back up the street toward his apartment, large by Parisian standards, on the fourth floor of a seventeenth-century building overlooking the square at the top of the rise. His two cloth shopping bags were filled to bursting with fish, wines, cheeses and especially proper bread he'd missed while he found himself in far-off British Columbia. He stopped in at L'Alsacienne, a bar with the classic deep red awning on the ground floor opposite his building, to indulge in a simple pleasure he'd learned to do without in Vancouver, and he'd be back soon enough. People there tended to regard you as depraved if you consumed even a drop of alcohol before the report of the twelve-o'clock horn at Canada Place on the inlet.

"Good morning, Jean-Pierre," Basaraba shouted as he entered the bar, which was empty except for two elderly ladies seated at the back, quietly conversing. The bartender was busy with a chisel, scraping the bottom of a table.

"There were a bunch of Australians in here the other night," Jean-Pierre grumbled. "They stuck their gum down here and no one noticed it until dried up." He rose from his crouch underneath the table. "And so, what would you like? I haven't seen you for a while."

"I think I'll get a Pernod and a coffee. No, I haven't been in Paris; I was in Canada for a few weeks. Thank God I'm back in France!" He laughed.

Jean-Pierre initiated the process to squeeze a demitasse out of the espresso machine behind him. "Yes, well, Canada is a beautiful place, too. Where were you, Montréal?"

"Yes, in Montréal for a week, and then in Vancouver, on the Pacific."

"Ah, the coast of the Pacific, and that ski resort," Jean-Pierre said, "I have never been out there. You knew that my son lives in Ottawa. He works for the Canadian government, so I have been to Montréal and Québec many times; my son and his girlfriend, they've been out to British Columbia, but not me."

"It's a bit, shall we say, *rustic.*"

"And maybe that's why I want to go there. My son's girlfriend, a very nice little blonde girl from *la Gaspésie*; you want to see rustic? Anyway, the last time I was there she told me that she thought that Montréal was a perfect little Paris on the Saint-Laurent! Can you imagine?"

"I suppose that Montréal is a very pleasant city."

"Yes, but Émile, Paris? It's not Paris."

"No," Basaraba said after the two of them laughed. "It's definitely not Paris."

After he finished his coffee, he crossed Place de la Contrescarpe and opened the large entrance door to his building. His apartment took up the entire upper floor at the top of the dark stairwell. As soon as he was inside, he heard a noise coming from the bathroom. "You can stop drinking out of the toilet, Mischa." A white and grey cat tiptoed out of the bathroom with a demeanour of innocence. "Mischa, Mischa, you are truly incorrigible," he laughed.

Mischa once belonged to his aunt, his mother's oldest sister whom he used to visit frequently in her townhouse in an old section of Kiev. After her death about a year earlier, the cat came to live with him. He was always careful to speak to it only in Ukrainian, never in French. Now the cat wanted to play. It ran off at the speed of a bee toward the kitchen; he chased after it and peeked around the corner into the dining room, finally catching up to it in the sitting room that overlooked the courtyard. "There you are!" He examined a chair that the cat had been trying to climb. "Mischa, if you insist on scratching the furniture, I'll tie a knot in your tail." He was distracted by the ringtone of one of his mobile phones in his office.

"Allô?" It was the one with the Paris area code.

"Is this Émile? It's Lewis. Lewis Barnard."

Lewis Barnard, the guy that he'd hired as the public face of Midland Shropshire in Vancouver; a competent, marmot-like man whom he'd recruited to exploit his close link with Terrence Goyter, someone whom Basaraba regarded as a hideous glutton but whose favour had to be cultivated because of his influence among the local notables.

"We got the power from B.C. Hydro." It was a Crown corporation and the provincial electrical monopoly. "At forty percent less than normal commercial rates."

Basaraba found Barnard's way of expressing himself unsettling. It was as if he wanted to finish speaking before he actually started.

"Well, Émile, now we've got it: what on Earth do you want me to do with it?"

Basaraba hadn't expected that his overtures to Goyter and a few of the other accidental Striationists would bear fruit so quickly. "Are those turbines - I'm talking about those four small hydroelectric projects on Vancouver Island - are they connected to the electricity network yet?"

Barnard gasped. "You mean the grid? Yes, I suppose, but they aren't producing so much as a watt of power. You told me that you didn't want..."

"Yes, yes, yes." Basaraba cut him off. "As long as they're connected to the network. All four of them."

"Yes, Émile. But so what? Nothing is coming out of them, not now, and it will be months before we can get them up and running."

"It doesn't matter," Basaraba sighed. *Up and running.* "Divert the power to them and release it back into the network."

"On to the grid? But why? What the hell for?"

"To sell it."

"Sell it? Who on Earth do you want to sell it to?"

Basaraba sighed. Most of the Reformed Striationists, or at least the two dozen or so that he'd met, tended to be remarkably obtuse. "To whatever you call it, B.C. Hydro, of course. Who else would you want to sell it to?"

Barnard started laughing after a brief silence. "Émile, Émile. You never cease to shock me. All right; I'll keep you posted."

He returned to the sitting room to resume chasing the cat. He peaked underneath a chair. "Where are you, you grey and white demon?"

....27

"Mind if I use your plug?"

Carlo looked up from his magazine to see a man who resembled a human axe brandishing a paper coffee cup in one hand and a laptop in the other. Carlo looked around Calista's. All of the other electrical outlets had been colonized by a herd of foreign students, Brazilians as far as Carlo could tell. "Sure." He motioned toward the chair nearest to the electric outlet. The man set down his coffee, darted like a weasel toward the socket and then set up his laptop. In an instant he started violently batting his mouse, occasionally clicking at his keyboard with rapid, terse bursts.

Marika was late, hardly unusual these days. Carlo's phone soon buzzed with a text message.

I'm at the dctrs office...running L8. See u at wk.

Once at his desk, Carlo spent most of the morning working on a preliminary opinion letter for the Striationists, this one regarding the summary disappearance of their bank accounts, a conundrum more self-consciously intricate than an exam question in second-year law. He went to their small library to find a text with some general principles of tort law. Declan was standing at the long table next to one of the bookcases, searching for something in an old volume of the *All England and Empire Digest*, flipping anxiously through successive volumes, replacing each one in turn. "I know it's in one of these. It must be somewhere!"

"What are you looking for?" Carlo asked.

"An article from the *Globe*; it was from back in the Seventies. They interviewed Lord Denning. He made some comments about the proper use of expert witnesses. Oh, I meant to ask you. Have you been over to interview the people at the Striationist complex on the Island, yet?"

"No, not yet."

Well, you should do it soon," Declan said. "It's up past Qualicum Beach, on the water. Marika can help you out with the address or phone number, if you need it. And when you get back, we'll have to meet and go over the file, to see how things are progressing. I don't want the file to stagnate; the Striationists can be quiet for months, then they suddenly get very demanding." Declan rummaged through another one of the aging volumes. "What are *you* looking for?"

"Fleming."

Every Canadian lawyer would have known precisely what he wanted. *Fleming on Torts*. "Over there, by the window."

Marika walked into the library carrying stacks of black three-ring binders. "Hey, guys!" Her long cotton dress was too narrow to comfortably accommodate the additional padding she'd acquired since Carlo had last taken notice. "Here you go, Declan." She deposited the binders at the end of the long table. "These are the productions you were waiting for from Gowlings."

"Gowlings?" Carlo asked. It was a large national law firm he rarely crossed paths with.

"They're on for Black & Decker. You know; the lady whose toaster exploded?" Marika said. "Can I just leave them on the table here?"

Declan bristled with a curt nod. "Thanks."

"Hey, no problem!" She turned and walked back toward her desk, her dress pulled tight by her swelling hips.

Declan watched as Marika left the room and then went back to searching through a Digest. "You know, it's a real shame. Marika's so young, just a short time ago she was such a beauty. It's really too bad that she's letting herself get so fat. She should really try to show a little more restraint."

Laura showed up at the office just after six. Carlo first heard her approach across the expanse of hardwood floor and then looked up to see her, dressed in a sweater and short grey skirt.

The click of feminine heels on the hardwood prompted Gaskin to come over for a closer look, and after Carlo rose to greet her, he corralled both of them back into Carlo's office and closed the door. "Ms. Thompson." Gaskin addressed her with exaggerated formality. "This is a rare treat. I don't think that you have ever been to my office. To what do we owe the honour?"

"Oh, hello Declan! I've come to rescue Carlo from *karoshi*, you know 'death from overwork'?"

"Ah. You two know each other?"

"Know each other?" Laura laughed. "We practically *live* together. Don't you guys talk?"

Declan's head snapped back. He looked at the two of them with his mouth agape. "I...I hadn't heard. How long have you two been...ah...together?"

"Oh, what do you think, Carlo?" Laura said. "About nine years and what, almost two months, with a little more than an eight-year gap in between."

"I see." Gaskin developed new jowls.

"Come on, get a move on!" Laura slapped Carlo's behind. "Our reservations at the Steamworks are for seven o'clock. We're going to be late!"

"Well, have a good time," Declan said, massaging his temples. He walked back to his office and closed the door.

Carlo and Laura passed Marika's desk as they left. "We're off." Carlo waved to Marika. "Oh, by the way, Marika, meet my girlfriend, Laura. Marika is one of the paralegals."

"Hey, best of luck with this guy's handwriting!" Laura laughed as they shook hands.

On their way down toward Cordova Street, Carlo ranted about Gaskin's stinginess. That morning, he had refused to reimburse Carlo for transit fares, decreeing instead that he should have bought himself a bus pass, which, as it turned out, would also go unreimbursed. "I'm surprised the old cheapskate doesn't force me to steam the postmarks off stamps, so that he can use them again."

Carlo heard a voice from behind them. "Mr. Buonsante!"

"Oh, hello, Thomas," Carlo said. "I'd like you to meet the most erudite person at Gaskin Barristers. Thomas, Balfour, isn't it? This is my girlfriend, Laura Thompson."

"Yes, Balfour." Thomas shook hands with Laura. "I don't think that it's too much to ask, Carlo, that you remember my surname."

"It's a lost cause," Laura said with a giggle. "He can't even remember where he puts his keys."

Thomas adopted a sober expression. "And where are you two going?"

"Down to the Steamworks for dinner," Laura said.

"A fine establishment for a young professional couple to find a bite to eat. Those of us who are older and less exacting prefer something more comfortable, the sort of place that gives the impression that once, in a past halcyon epoch, one might have actually been allowed to smoke. I'm off to meet my significant other for dinner at Jedediah's."

"Nice meeting you, Thomas."

"Likewise, my dear."

"I can see what you mean by *erudite*," Laura said after Thomas continued on his way. "And he seems like a nice man."

A hostess ushered them into the covered patio at The Steamworks. Once they'd ordered drinks, Laura grinned at Carlo. "So that paralegal, what's her name?"

"Marika."

"Who does the hiring around there? Gaskin's wife?"

"Carlo exploded into violent laughter, momentarily unable to speak. "No, no," Laura said. "She has a pretty face and nice hair, but poor girl, she makes *me* look like Kate Moss! Okay. Just stop. What's so funny?"

"I'll put it this way: if Paula (I'm assuming you've met her) hired her, that would be the ultimate irony."

"Oh yes, we've met; never a pleasure. The last time I saw her, we were at a retreat in Lund, of all places. It rained (big shock) and she seemed to hold the staff responsible. And what do you mean, 'ultimate irony'?"

"Oh, believe me, it would be." Carlo looked around; the adjacent tables were both empty. "Look, this has to stay between us. You cannot repeat it to anyone, even Yvette." *Especially Yvette.* "Okay?"

"Yes, sure." Laura's smile faded. Her eyes locked on his. "What's going on?"

"Well," Carlo's voice faded to a whisper. "Marika was hardly what you would have described as a 'bone rack' even before, but most of the recent increase in her size has a lot to do with Declan. He knocked her up after a two, maybe even three-year fling."

"*Knocked her up*? With a lot of other people I'd say 'no fucking way', but he's lived up to his reputation. But, come on; after three years, it's not a 'fling' anymore."

"Then what is it?"

"I don't know; a *liaison*." She pronounced it in the French way. "Wow, so she's pregnant? I guess I didn't take a good enough look at her. But as for Declan? True to form! He was carrying on with some girl about her age; as I recall, she was either a journalist or a spokesthingy for one of the environmental groups at the last retreat about a year ago. One of the times he went without his wife. You know what his nickname around media types is? *Woodstock Romeo!* His wife must know something about it."

"Oh, I'm certain that Marika didn't; and I'm sure that that his wife has less complimentary pet names for him than that."

"Oh, she's a total bitch, no doubt about it. But he is *such* a dog. He tends to avoid the Orthodox crowd; let's face it, they're old, smelly and hairy. But between the Greenpeace and Sierra Club contingents (they sometimes tag along on these things) and all of the reporters and *academics* and shit who show up at Striationist extravaganzas, he's had at least six affairs by my count." Laura made a sly smile. "You didn't have a go at her, did you?"

"At whom?"

"Don't be obtuse. At, what's her name, Kruella? I mean, it seems obvious to me; you've been working there awhile, until you met back up with me you were a single man on the loose, and before Declan did his magic, she would have been your type. So?"

Carlo smiled back at her. *Indeed.* "No, I didn't."

"Oh, come on, I know that the baby obviously isn't yours; don't be silly. Even back when we first got together, we were *children* for Christ's sake, you were always *ridiculously* cautious. You never saw *me* swelling up; knock on wood. I was just curious. And you know what? I always wondered why Declan never put the moves on either me or Yvette. Okay, with me it's a no-brainer; his usual targets are skinny as rails (except for what's her name), but Yvette...okay, what are you laughing about now?"

He told her about that evening at Tulalip when he saw Yvette dressed only in a shirt, fetching ice outside Declan's room. "And that, I suppose, is why we didn't see either one of them after the plenary session on the first day. They didn't come up for air until Saturday morning."

Laura sat back in her chair. "That fucking bitch!" she shouted, loud enough to startle people at a table across the patio. "You know," she said in a quieter voice. "She knows better than that, it's a pretty despicable thing to do. It's surprising, though, especially since its Yvette we're talking about. Back in the day, she could be such a priss. Remember? Always going on about how it was '*so* tacky' or '*so* embarrassing' every time you and I disappeared for (God forbid) an entire night alone."

"Oh, yes, I remember. *La papessa.*"

"So you see what I mean? And now, an affair with a married man; not *happily* or anything like that, but married nonetheless. And *that's* not embarrassing? It's pretty bad, you know. And I thought that she was still pining for Philippe."

"Who's Philippe?"

"Oh, an on-again, off-again deal that's been going on for years. But Declan? A pregnant secretary! Paula's going to rip his dick off."

"She's not a 'secretary'; she's a paralegal".

"I'm sure that'll make all the difference to Paula. She must have told him by now, if you know about it. I mean, how is he reacting to it?"

"He's doing his best to ignore it. And this is something that I've been struggling with. The bastard told Marika that he wanted to leave his wife and live with *her,* if you can believe it."

"What the fuck?"

"Yes; as far as I can tell, as an inducement to get her back into bed (she says they had a brief break-up), and she fell for it. But he seems to be in denial." He told her about what Gaskin said in the library.

"No, he's not in denial. He's just every bit the asshole that I always thought he was."

"But here's my problem. Should I tell her?"

"Tell who what?"

"Ò! What do you think? Tell Marika about Yvette."

"Oh, fuck no! Are you kidding me? If this goes public, we could easily lose the Striationist account. For a bunch of freaks they tend to be very strait-laced about such things. They're more than half of our billings. I'll go bankrupt! Please, please let me handle it. Don't say anything to what's her name. I'll deal with Yvette. Woodstock fucking Romeo," she mocked in a squeaky tone. "What a piece of shit!" She tilted her head and delivered a thoughtful glance; an unerring signal that she wanted to change the subject. "You know, when I told Gaskin that we practically live together, well, it's true isn't it? Every night, I'm at your place, or you're at my place. Having two of them is just a waste of money."

"True enough. But you probably don't want to live at my place. It's got a nice view, but..."

"No, not *that* postage stamp. It would have to be my place. It's not just that it's bigger, but I own it. Well, the bank and I own it."

"Well, I suppose that I could give my notice at the end of the month."

"Soon would be nice, but not that soon. I still have to figure out where I'm going to put everything. It's not like you have a lot of furniture, but I've lived there on my own for six years. And that bed of yours has got to go! Oh, I know, I know," she said over Carlo's groans of protest. "It's bigger than mine. So we'll get a new one. That piece of shit of yours sags in the middle, big time. And it squeaks."

It sags in the middle. Carlo thought it over. If she ever found out how the bed came into his possession, she would never consent to lay her body on it ever again, clothed or naked, no matter how many clean sheets were on it.

"Where did you get it?"

"Where did I get what? Carlo said.

"Fuck, try to keep up. Your *bed*."

"I...ah...acquired it from Mario's cousin Enzo."

"Enzo," she pondered. "Enzo. Oh yes, now I remember him, Enzo. Glad to hear that he's given up selling hash oil and stealing car batteries. He has, hasn't he?"

Carlo shrugged. "As far as I know. Now, shall we order dinner?"

Declan warily surveyed the restaurant, scanning the people in adjacent tables for an unwelcome familiar face.

"Come on, Declan!" Yvette giggled. "You've wolfed down your dinner as if an army is in hot pursuit."

And you're eating yours as if you're trying to delay your own execution. Declan was in the initial stage of panic. Paula was at an estate auction somewhere on Vancouver Island for the next four days, Yellow Point or some such place, but Vancouver was not nearly as big a city as people thought. Their mutual friends could pop up anywhere. Well, almost anywhere; he was not so fearful at The Flayed Fox, the pub in the West End where he and Yvette usually met, mainly frequented by graduate students and people with repellent tastes in music. Elsewhere, he always worried; one could never tell when his wife's creative crowd might tire of *authentic!* Neapolitan pizza and tapas bars and decide to sample someplace more *edgy.* Tonight he would have been delighted to meet at the Fox. Instead, at Yvette's insistence, they were at Trattoria Sant'Angelo, an unfashionably conventional Italian restaurant in Yaletown that still even served veal, and people he did not want to see were sure to soon show up. A classic joint presentation of *I Pagliacci* and *Cavalleria Rusticana* at the Queen Elizabeth Theatre would be finished within minutes.

"Hey," Declan struggled to appear calm. "How about if we get another bottle of *Petit-Chablis* at that shop in Cambie Street Village?" He knew it was one of her favourite wines. "And, of course, go back to your place." He looked into her eyes with what he hoped was a seductive smile.

Yvette tossed her head back and laughed. "You know what I think? I think you're a dirty old man!"

Fair enough, Declan grumbled to himself. Normally, he would take umbrage at being characterised as an 'old man', but this was no time for such superfluities. "Well?"

"All right, just let me finish chewing. *Petit-Chablis* would be a welcome change from, well, whatever *this* is."

"Soave."

"Oh. But no taxi. We're catching the bus."

Declan sighed. Yvette viewed driving within the city core as iniquitous and always insisted that they either walked or took public transit. He'd long realized that this time, he should consider himself fortunate. Two, no, three girls that he had been involved with, each of them in Yvette's general age group and professional *milieu*, held a fanatical attachment to bicycling equal to the religious fervour of novitiate nuns. Many times in the past few years he'd found himself pedalling and sweating, trailing his fling of the day on one of Vancouver's many bike routes, somewhere in the West End, or worse, on the hills of Fairview Slopes.

In the tree-shaded streets of Mount Pleasant, it was already dark. Yvette's house, built before the First World War but more recently divided into a duplex, seemed terrifying, almost Gothic to Declan. He braced himself for supernatural howls and a parade of phantoms every time he crossed the threshold. Yvette had crafted its interior in a dimly-lit, but lively way, true to her *belle-époque* style. Even if it had only been about ten days since he had last been to Yvette's place, she'd added new decoration, an antique walnut or oak coat rack in the entranceway, with an old Italian poster on the wall behind it, advertising espresso machines. Later that night, Declan sourly acknowledged that one item of new décor portended the payment of a karmic debt. The mirror in the entrance hall had been replaced by yet another old poster, this one dominated by a nude, buxom girl who bore more than mere passing resemblance to Marika, laughing while astride a giant bottle of Möet et Chandon.

Declan went into the kitchen to open the wine they bought at the specialty shop. Yvette's cat, a wise looking Burmese named Oskar who quite obviously detested him, sat glowering at Declan from his vantage point on top of the refrigerator. Declan poured two glasses and brought them back into the sitting room. It always amazed him that Yvette, with her long, thin limbs, could curl up like a kitten on her oval divan.

"So," Declan said, still standing, after he took his first sip of wine, preening the sides of his head with his hands and making an odd repetitive grimacing expression, the customary advent of a declaration of some sort. This time, he'd practiced it in front of a mirror.

"Okay, what's up?"

"I'm very concerned about your business partner," he said in a funereal tone.

"Laura? What the..."

Declan knew that this foray would make her suspicious. True, he and Laura knew each other, having met ten, perhaps a dozen, times since DesRosiers & Thompson had won the Striationist account five years earlier, but something about her annoyed him; he rarely ever mentioned her name. "Yes, you have to do something. You have to have a serious discussion with her." He sighed. "It has come to my attention that she's taken up with my associate. They're practically *living* together. You have to talk some sense into her!"

"Why? I think it's wonderful, almost like a real-life fairy tale. What's your problem? Have Carlo's billings dropped or something?"

"No, no, nothing like that. Laura's a beautiful girl; she shouldn't waste what's left of her youth, with such a reedy little, well, let me say it, a less than impressive guy. She could do so much better for herself, believe me."

"I'm not getting you, Declan. Carlo's a good-looking man, and he's stable, trustworthy, unlike the all of the other ones she's taken up with during the past few years. He's the best thing..."

"Oh, come off it. He's not even six feet tall; he's substandard. And she looks like the classic Rhine goddess. She needs someone more broad-shouldered, more, well I'll say it: manly."

"She's not German, Declan." Yvette said with a playful giggle. "Half-Scottish; half Danish."

"It doesn't matter; she's still way out of his league."

"Declan, now you're scaring me. You're being ridiculous."

"Come on, Yvette!" Declan raised his voice. "And what if they had children? Can you imagine that? Their kids would look like little weasels! Just think about it!"

"Now you're just being silly." She folded her arms. "And I'm afraid that you're alone in making that assessment. You know, back in the day, all of the old married ladies around Comox, even Laura's English Twelve teacher, would accost them in the mall or somewhere and gush on and on about what *beautiful* babies they would have. It drove Laura wild."

"Sentimental nonsense," he glowered. "Just the sort of thing you'd expect from people who live in a place like that. I bet those women even drank *sherry*."

"What the hell?"

"There's no need for profanity."

"I *really* don't know what's gotten into you, Declan." She wasn't smiling any more. "But it doesn't matter. The fact that we're even having this discussion just shows that you don't know either of them very well. Really, Declan? Children? Laura? If you actually *knew* her, you'd also know that she's more likely to convert to Islam."

"Women change their minds about that sort of thing as they get older. I'm being quite serious. And as her friend, you should be worried, too. I think that you should speak to her about it," he finished in a stentorian voice. "And you should do it sooner rather than later. When I saw her in the office, earlier in the week when she came by to meet Carlo, I was shocked at how heavy she's getting. Her 'best before' date is quickly approaching."

"You know, Declan, sometimes you can be such an ass! *Best before date?* Is that some kind of joke? I'm surprised I have to tell *you* that she's one chick who's never lacked for male attention."

"Well, I think you're being..."

"No! Before you pontificate some more, listen: the three of us go back a long way. As far as I am concerned, the fact that those two are back together is about as good as things could be. They were together for nine years, *nine years* Declan! They met when we were all kids. You did know that, didn't you?"

"Childhood sweethearts," Declan snarled into his glass.

"No, not childhood. Don't be so flippant. Back in the day, they always seemed like best friends. She was never quite the same after the breakup. Now she's as happy as I've ever seen her. It's taken years off her, regardless of what you think; and anyway, it really isn't any of your business!"

Declan pouted next to a watercolour of Porte Saint-Martin, occasionally sipping his wine.

"So what do you have against him, anyway?" Yvette said. "I don't get it."

"Oh come on! You're just being wilfully obtuse. I shouldn't have to explain it to you."

"Well, *yes you do*: you're trying to enlist my assistance in breaking them up. Not that I would ever do it in the first place. It's like *vandalism*, so unbelievably stupid! So now, tell me, what, exactly is your problem with Carlo?"

"I don't know. It just seems to me that his life has been too easy; he's never really had to fight for anything. You know, he starts to establish himself in a career in Toronto, and then *boom*, he decides on a whim to go to Italy for three years, like some sort of spoiled adolescent aristocrat. I just don't have a great deal of respect for him."

"Declan, please," she shouted. "You don't have the first clue about what you're talking about. You want to hear about how 'easy' he's had it? His mother died of cancer when he was twelve. And do you know why he went back to Italy? It wasn't a fucking 'whim', as you seem to think!"

"Could you watch your language, please?"

"Oh, *whatever*! Just listen! He couldn't stand it here anymore, and it's easy to see why. His girlfriend, the woman he lived with for almost three years was raped and murdered a few steps from their front door!"

"Hmm...I suppose he doesn't have the gumption to do that sort of thing himself."

"What the fuck kind of thing is that to say? You're being an asshole!"

"Stop it. Swearing makes you sound so cheap. No, he's spineless; a weakling. Laura could still have her pick of resourceful young men who would do a much better job of providing for her."

"Did it ever occur to you that Carlo *is* her 'pick', as you describe it?"

"If that's true (and I really doubt that it is), then she's making a tragic mistake. I simply can't believe that you would be so lazy and selfish not to intervene and stop her from ruining the rest of her life. I mean, when I compare him to the way I was at his age, it's easy to see that he's not going to amount to much. He'll certainly never build what I have."

"Well, that remains to be seen, doesn't it? But he wouldn't screw around on Laura, either way."

Declan stepped toward her and folded his arms. "It takes two to tango."

"You know what? You're right. And I'm done 'tango-ing'. Get your ass out of here! *Now*, Declan! And you better get whatever stuff you've left strewn around and take it with you, because I won't be letting you back in! And just leave those two alone!"

Declan slammed the front door behind him in what he'd hoped would be received as a dramatic parting gesture. He ignored her invitation to gather up his belongings, not because he wanted an excuse to go back to visit her, but because he wanted to avoid the ignominy of riding the bus home with underwear and a razor in his pocket after being thrown out of his mistress's apartment. He got off the bus on a stretch of West Broadway with several pubs to search for a suitable place to get a pint of Guinness before he walked home. *Well. That relationship has come to its inevitable conclusion. What now?* He considered his options. He thought of maybe waiting a few days and issuing an abject apology fortified by flowers and champagne. No, she was turning into a bit of a bore and it was far from certain that she'd have him back.

For the time being, he remained entangled with Marika. They still saw each other one night a week, two at the most, much less frequently than before. He was trying to, well, *phase her out*. She was growing more disgusting by the day, burgeoning with new rolls and bulges that were starting to fill him with such revulsion that he doubted that he would be able to bear the sight of her naked, much less get it up, for much longer. So who else? There was that accountant, she appeared to be around thirty, who worked on the fourteenth floor, perky and lean in her grey or blue pinstripe suits. She always smiled at him when they encountered one another and chatted, either on the elevator, or, almost as frequently, at the Whole Foods on Cambie Street. But then he saw her in the Starbucks downstairs, surrounded by a few of her friends, each of whom were moaning and squealing while examining her outstretched hand, a sure sign that she had just gotten engaged. *He who hesitates is lost.* Well, someone would turn up. They always do.

He decided on an English-style pub a couple of blocks from where he got off the bus. The couple sitting on the covered patio at the front startled him at first, but after he had a chance to look at them more closely, he saw that despite striking similarity, they were not Carlo and Laura. An alluring but nonetheless well-fed girl with abundant blonde hair and milky skin paired with a sinewy young man, a little shorter than average, lightly tanned, with brownish hair and Latin, or perhaps Gallic features. It must be some sort of fad, one that he would never understand even if a younger person, even one of his sons, tried to explain it to him. After he paid for his pint, his attention tuned to the television screen suspended above the bar. It was a hockey game, Toronto and Boston. He took his first sip. Toronto was losing. *Good.*

....28

To: Carlo Buonsante
From: Catriona Lu
Cc: David Sadich
Re: Striationist Totality v. The Royal Bank of Canada et al

Hi Carlo,

We have a problem. Call me.

C.

Catriona Lu
Associate
Guenter & Sadich, Attorneys
Suite 1800, 256 Fifth Avenue
Seattle, Washington 98300
Dir. (206) 631-2272

Carlo first wanted to wait until mid-morning before calling her back, but he changed his mind and punched in her number. Carlo was surprised that she answered. He usually got her voicemail.

"Hey. What's up?"

"Have you tried to serve Duckabush Investments with, what do you guys call it again?"

"The Writ of Summons?" Carlo asked.

"Yes, that."

"As far as I know; I'll check with my paralegal."

"I'm telling you, something doesn't make any sense here. Duckabush is on the Canadian title documents of all of the, what can we call them, the *misplaced* properties. But I can't find any evidence that it actually exists."

"But it must be local; what about that guy, Jason Stildt? Isn't the Duckabush..."

"Yes, yes, I know; the Duckabush *is* a river in the Olympic Mountains, which led me to believe that it was a Washington company. But it's not. It's not registered as a corporation or limited partnership anywhere in the United States or Canada. It has no presence on the web. And according to the guy we sent over to Quilcene to serve him, our Mr. Stildt claims to know nothing about it."

"But you're right; the name appears all over the place, in any number of the sales agreements. Marika!" Carlo called out as she walked past his office. Her pregnancy had not yet advanced nearly far enough to need the capacious maternity dress she was wearing, which billowed in front of her. "Have we served Duckabush Investments in the Striationist action yet?"

"No, not yet. I meant to talk to you about that. I haven't been able to find a single trace of it."

"Well, it seems that we've run into the same problem," Carlo said into the phone. "Do you have all of the real estate documents?"

"I have what you sent me," Catriona said.

"None of this makes any sense." Carlo sighed. "How about if we both go over the title and purchase documents and then talk later, maybe see if we can figure out what's going on?"

"How long are you in today?"

"I don't know; about six, seven, I guess."

"Okay. Talk ta ya, bye."

Carlo pored over the sub-file of land registration documents, which, despite the fact that Marika had left them well-organized, expanded a brown accordion file to its limit. He analysed and reconsidered what seemed to be a bewildering entanglement of unrelated facts: dozens of Agreements of Purchase and Sale forms, covenants, mortgages, easements, municipal and utility rights of way, and builders' liens. Whatever their other sins might turn out to be, the Reformed bunch had a marked aversion to paying tradesmen. He worked through lunch, his curiosity building with each discordant encumbrance, until after about four hours, a pattern emerged. Duckabush was on title as owner on each of the properties three or four times after a series of multiple resales. Every Duckabush purchase was financed by a mortgage, in each case issued by the same lender, Corvair Intermediaries, a Toronto outfit. The Corvair mortgages were always immediately assigned to a more conventional institution, either a bank or a credit union, but never to the Royal Bank, the Striationists' banker.

The Agreements of Purchase and Sale showed that with each repurchase by Duckabush Investments, the price went up with a mortgage to match, sometimes almost doubling. The signature of the authorized representative on all of them was an illegible scrawl in each case, except for one. On one of the earlier agreements, Carlo could make out a name: Ian McHarg.

He was just about to pick up his telephone when it rang, and he saw Catriona's number in the call display. She did not wait for him to say 'hello'. "Have you finished looking over the title and sale documents?" She sounded shaken.

"Yes. The problem's worse than we thought."

"Are you going to tell Gaskin?"

Carlo saw Paula Gaskin pass by his window, speaking to Bal on her way to Gaskin's office. "If I can get an audience, yes."

"I'll try to talk to Sadich before I go home."

"We're going to have to amend our pleadings, you know."

"To say what?"

"Yes, you're right," Carlo said after a long silence. "Have a good night; we'll talk tomorrow."

A few minutes later, he saw Paula leave Gaskin's office and commence her usual stroll through the office, with the self-command of a Capet traversing the Hall of Mirrors. She momentarily paused outside his office to glare as if she would be delighted to kill him and eat him.

"Oh, hello, Mrs. Gaskin."

After she grunted and walked away, Carlo saw an opportunity to go into Gaskin's office to tell him about Duckabush and the title documents. Declan's eyes seemed to be out of focus.

"So," Carlo said after a long explanation, "this adds an element of fraud against third parties, *banks* no less, not exactly a welcome development."

"Hmm, well, ah, I see what you mean," Declan said, still distracted. "How about you put what you've found out in a memo and I'll raise it with Hamish next time he calls?"

Thomas and Carlo spent the rest of the afternoon in the boardroom collating the remainder of the documents that Carlo and Marika scanned in Port Rattray. Marika, who had been organizing the documents all morning, had to leave early to go to yet another of her increasingly frequent medical appointments. As Carlo cross-referenced each document in an index he was putting together on his laptop, Bal walked in cradling another stack, and let it drop on the boardroom table with a violent thud in front of Carlo. She snorted and stomped out of the room.

Thomas peered at Carlo over his reading glasses.

"I have no idea what her problem is." Carlo said.

"Who knows?"

"Anyway, I've had about enough of this for today. I've got court on Monday. Small Claims. Fuck."

Thomas went back to sorting the documents piled in front of him.

Just before he was about to leave for the day, Carlo's phone rang, the call display showing a Vancouver Island number. A cheerful voice shouted at him. "You should come over here for a visit!"

"What?" Carlo often endured these kinds of exhortations from his father, but the voice at the other end of the line carried a mocking Scottish burr. "Who is this?"

"How soon they forget!" He laughed. "I'm hurt! It's Laura's father, Jack. I'm sure that you must remember me!"

"Oh, of course, Mr. Thompson. I'm..."

"Don't be ridiculous. I'm Jack! Just like you nice Italian boys from the city to call me 'Mister'. How are you doing?"

"I'm, well, all right, I guess; how are you?

"Waiting patiently for an answer to my question. So I ask again: when are you coming over for a visit?"

"Just out of curiosity, how did you find me?"

"You're the only 'Buonsante' in the Vancouver legal directory. And, counsellor, I just asked you a fucking question."

"I'm not the one you should be pestering. Ask Laura. And I'll be over at her place tonight. I'm going over to Granville Island, to get some Dungeness crab for dinner."

"Crab? Not live crab?"

"That was the idea. Why?"

"Have you ever brought home live crab before?"

"No...back in the day we were too poor. We only had it..."

"Take the advice of someone who knows. If you bring them home live, they'll become cherished pets. She'll have named them before the water boils. Bring them home raw, cleaned. Otherwise, you'll be dining at a good Scottish restaurant."

"Really? Which one?"

"McDonald's."

Carlo had his own set of keys for Laura's condominium, which was on the third floor of an off-white building at the western fringes of Kitsilano, of a style no doubt intended to evoke an impression of the Greek island of Santorini. As was customary in Vancouver, it leaked. He let himself in and carried his bags from Granville Island up the stairs, including two crabs that he'd asked the clerk at the fish market to thoroughly clean. By the time Laura arrived, he was in the midst of chopping parsley for the *risotto di frutti di mare*.

"Hey!" Laura flung her purse down on the counter and gave him a kiss. "Hard at work, I see."

"It's a living."

Laura went into the sitting room to turn on the computer. Carlo heard the cacophonous beeps that accompanied the resurrection of Windows.

"Oh, yeah," she shouted, "I meant to ask you, do you know a guy called Nathan Brooke?"

"Nope. Should I?"

"I don't know, he's a lawyer, as far as I know."

Carlo made a hybrid of a laugh and a sigh. "I am *very* happy to say that I am not personally acquainted with every lawyer in the lower mainland."

"No, no, as I said, I meant to tell you about this before. About two weeks ago, this Nathan guy called me at the office, on my *cell* no less, and asked me out for dinner. Said that he saw me interviewed on Global News (it was about some stupid Striationist dustup; it's not important) and he wanted to ask me out, get to know me better; the usual. I told him no; told him that I was married. I don't think that he believed me, but it worked. He went away and he hasn't bothered me since. Anyway, don't you think that's really weird?"

"Well, as much as I don't like the idea of random guys asking you out, it's not weird; take it as a compliment."

"I guess, but it's still weird. The TV interviews (and I don't recall being on Global; CBC and CTV yes, but not Global) were a *year* ago, Carlo. You were still in Italy. And this Nathan guy is calling me *now?*"

"How do you know he's a lawyer?" Carlo asked.

"After he called, I Googled him. He works in Burnaby at a firm called Tilsit & Quack or something."

Carlo laughed. "Quackenbush, Twiller." It was a firm of about twenty lawyers located somewhere in the dreary forest of glass towers surrounding Metrotown. "I've heard of the firm, but I've never dealt with any of them."

Laura went back to clicking away at her keyboard. "Oh, I wonder if you remember her; I met my cousin Darla for a couple of glasses of wine after work."

"Darla, Darla," Carlo pondered. "Isn't she the one who looks like Pat Benatar?"

"That's the one," Laura sighed. "She asked how you were doing. Maybe we should have her over for dinner some time."

"Oh, yes; sure. Oh, speaking of Islanders I haven't seen in years, I heard from your dad today. He called me at the office after lunch. I think it might be time for a visit."

"I know, I know. He called you at work? Sorry; since that man retired, well, semi-retired, anyway, he has way too much time on his hands. Yes, we have to go over, but these days you have to take out a fucking mortgage just to catch the ferry."

Carlo browned a crushed clove of garlic. "Oh, we won't þe paying, Declan has a list of things he wants me to attend to on the Island. I'll expense it."

"No shit? Then we can make a few days of it; visit my parents, then go off to Tofino."

"As long as I don't have to deal with the Old Skunks. I had far more patience with people like that when I was seventeen; I doubt that I'll still be able to hold my tongue and actually be polite to those frightful women."

"The Old Skunks!" Laura walked into the kitchen and put her arms around him. "I guess I shouldn't be surprised you still remember them."

"Oh, you bet: even if I live to be a thousand, I'll still remember them."

He disliked them from the first time Laura brought him to Comox. Even at seventeen, they liberated the same blended emotion of disgust, pity and embarrassment he felt whenever he saw an indigent defecate in public. It was only about a month after the two of them met; Thanksgiving weekend, as he remembered. The whole clan assembled at Laura's parent's house for an unruly, alcohol-drenched evening.

After dinner, the four Old Skunks, leavened by two bottles of rye, followed Carlo into the living room, where Laura's father was fiddling around with the stereo. Laura's Auntie Violet seemed to be attempting to make conversation, but it was plain to Carlo that they were trying to elicit admissions from him in furtherance of some sort of investigation. One of them wondered why a young man would take university courses in 'home economics', another pointed at his "Public Enemy" t-shirt and questioned why he was wearing pictures of 'coloured people'. The four of them seemed shocked that both his clothing and his car lacked any reference to either Pennzoil or the Vancouver Canucks, which they seemed to regard as the only true talismans of masculinity. "At least the little Spic speaks English," he heard one of them say as they walked back into the kitchen.

"Well, don't worry," Laura said. "If you want to avoid them, just stay away from the liquor store. We don't see them very much since Auntie Deanna divorced Uncle Frank; I guess she'd finally had enough of his screwing around. Oh, well; ancient history. Anyway, we should make our way over, maybe for a few days, even. We could go to Tofino."

"I heard you the first time. And we should stop in on Mario and Laeticia, on the way."

"If they're speaking to me. Where do they live?"

"Parksville, right on the water, not too far from that campground where the bunch of us almost got arrested that summer."

"Rathtrevor Beach? Not bad! They must be doing all right. Hey, hey! You're always so messy. Look at that, you've already spilled fish stock on the counter. It's quartz, you know."

29

Gavin paced back and forth in the departure lounge at the seaplane terminal at Lake Union. An unruly fog bank delayed his flight to back to Victoria. He hadn't wanted to make the trip to Seattle, but his investment manager insisted that he make an appearance at a morning meeting at Citibank. When reminded that he had about five million invested in the project that would be the main topic of discussion, he decided that it would be best to come over.

He answered his jingling cell phone.

"Good morning, Gavin." The raspy voice on the other end could have been one of several men he knew whose vocal cords had been ravaged by decades of smoking.

"Who is this?" Gavin said.

"Oh, it's Lawrence...Lawrence Gollander."

"Oh, hello, Lawrence." Gavin was astonished. "What can I do for you?"

"Where are you?"

"Seattle. I had a business meeting. Where are you?"

"I was, ah, just calling to get an update on your efforts to get approval for your SeaMent fixed-link testing."

Gollander's effervescence left Gavin even more confused. "Well, let's not get ahead of ourselves, Lawrence. It's just for the material itself; any talk about an actual *fixed link*, well, that's a long way off."

"I know, I know; but have you had any luck in setting up a test site for, I don't know, what shall we call it, the first phase?"

"Well, it looks like I've made some progress, I suppose. I got Egbert to go along with a test site, but no date has been set, so far."

"Good, good; glad to hear it."

Gollander was relieved to hear that Gavin wasn't in Vancouver, and even if he had been, he wasn't about to tell him that he was on his way to a meeting at Aloysius Crawley's office at Chancery Trust. After the eruption at the last meeting, neither Gavin nor Roland Egbert had been invited to this one. The same young receptionist ushered him to the boardroom when he arrived, where Crawley and a man in a black turtleneck sweater whom Gollander did not immediately recognize were engaged in a lively conversation in French. He felt the rising panic of a man lost in the back streets of a foreign city.

The man in the turtleneck looked up at him. "*Est-ce qu'il ne parle pas français?*", he said in rapid French.

"*Non; il n'a pas de diplôme.*" Crawley switched to English. "Good morning, Lawrence. How was the trip over from the Island?" He greeted the man he had just branded as uneducated in an obsequious tone.

"Good, just fine, but I came over two days ago. I was visiting my sister and her husband in Surrey."

"Oh," Crawley smirked. "Lawrence, I trust that you know Émile Basaraba, Master of the Treasure of the Striationists."

Gollander peered at him. "You know, I think we met some months ago in an office by the Hyatt, in Vancouver. Downtown. Do you remember? That meeting, with...Mr. McHale. At the bank.

"Yes, yes," Basaraba said quickly. "With McHale."

Crawley cleared his throat. "We were wondering, Lawrence, whether or not you have been in touch with Gavin Skoff. His efforts to test the prototype for a possible bridge are most appreciated."

"Fixed link." Gollander corrected him. "Yes, I just spoke with him today. He says he has permission for a proposed testing site, but hasn't decided on a date."

"But who is it that gives permission?" Basaraba said.

"Roland Egbert." Crawley picked his nose.

"Egbert, Egbert," Basaraba said. "Oh yes, now I remember him. He was at that *débacle* in Bastion Square. If I'm not mistaken, he's the gentleman from somewhere on Vancouver Island, the one who looks like an anaemic walrus."

The three men guffawed; hearty masculine laughter. "Yes, that's the one," Gollander said.

"You know, I always wonder about people like him," Basaraba said. "He's not one of us; he refuses to join the religion, and he has been invited to do so many times. But he won't."

"I don't know if it's that surprising. He's High Anglican, those roots go pretty deep," Crawley said.

"I don't know," Basaraba said. "I was raised as a Catholic, and I suppose the art, the liturgy, the ceremony; it's all very impressive. And I know that it's part of our history, our heritage as Europeans. But our new religion, it's so clean, so spare, so in synchronization with the serenity of this coast. And as far as I know?" He started to laugh. "No one from the Striationist Domains ever fucked little boys up the ass!"

Basaraba chortled as Crawley and Gollander both cringed. "Hmm, well," he mumbled. "And as Master of the Treasure, I'm most glad to hear your news about the SeaMent testing, something that will eventually be invaluable to the success of the McKee McWatney lands as time goes on."

"But, wait, I mean, I certainly hope," Gollander said, his voice a wan tremolo. "That the project isn't dependent on the...the fixed link. Is it?" His eyes shifted as he spoke.

"Oh no, no, nothing like that." Basaraba said. "Favourable test results would make things easier for them, but it is not essential to the project's success. The biggest problem is the atmosphere of stealth that they have to maintain out of necessity. All of their sales efforts have to be done by, well, we'll call them traditional methods; no Internet *publicité* to speak of, or so I've been told. Sure, there are rumours floating around rural parts of the Island. I must say that some of them are surprisingly accurate," he laughed. "It makes me wonder about the much-vaunted secrecy the politicians are always crowing about."

"But doesn't that make the developers a little concerned?" Crawley asked.

"Oh, I've warned them, but nothing seems to faze any of them. And besides, no one believes the...the *trafiquants* of these rumours. As both of you know, for years more than just a few of these backwoodsmen on *Île de Vancouver* thought that the Disney outfit had secretly purchased the same set of properties and was all set to erect a New Jerusalem (well, a New Disneyland, anyway) in the middle of that patch of weeds. Do you see Disneyland North anywhere?" Crawley and Gollander stared at him as he laughed, squirming in their chairs.

"This isn't a laughing matter, Émile," Crawley said. "The environmental community may scoff at these 'backwoodsmen', as you call them, but many of the people who invest with us take this very seriously. They've started to spend money on improvements and services in anticipation of this large, and as yet, mysterious project. We don't need..."

"Look, Aloysius, I am well aware; well, let's just say that the religion's investment profile reflects my expectations about these, well, "under the radar" projects. I want to give the faithful reason to rejoice when I address them at the Convocation in the fall."

"It's not up to me," Crawley said. Gollander remained resolutely still.

"It's not up to me, either," Basaraba spat. "Look, find out what you can from 'the Amiable Plunderer' about his SeaMent testing endeavour, when it will be subject to a field test, that sort of thing. And you, *Laurent,* please let me know what is going on."

"I'll do what I can," Gollander said after a long pause. "Now, that lawsuit, the one brought by the Orthodox people. It's still out there. What's going on with that?"

"I've seen to it that the defence is well in hand," Basaraba smiled. "We, or rather, the religion has retained Bernard Mackay at Worthington Price to lead the defence team. The Royal Bank and a couple of individual people have also been named as defendants; I don't really understand it all."

"McKay? Bernie McKay?" Crawley asked. "He's a very entertaining guy, fun to go for a drink with, but he's no barrister. I doubt he's been in court in his entire career. He's a securities lawyer, not even a solicitor really. He's more of a salesman." Both Gollander and Basaraba were frowning. "Look, he's very well known, I understand that, and I consider him a personal friend, but..."

"Someone with skill in public relations, a salesman, as you dismiss him," Basaraba said, no longer smiling, "is exactly the sort of counsel that we need for this. Don't you agree, Minister?"

"Yes, I suppose that it makes a certain amount of sense," Gollander said. "Keep in mind, Aloysius, Worthington's has a litigation department with forty lawyers. Bernie will have all of the technical assistance he needs."

"Oh, I suppose." Crawley said. "I'll just leave it in your capable hands. Let's meet here in three weeks."

After he left Crawley's office, Basaraba went to a European-style bar attached to his hotel on Coal Harbour and ordered an espresso with a shot of Pernod. *Yes, that pompous little prick is right. Mackay couldn't cross-examine a cat without botching it and he's more likely to shove legal documents up his ass than file them in the proper court registry.* He took a sip of Pernod and chased it with a healthy gulp of espresso. *But he's just the sort of lawyer I need, this time.*

Even if he would have preferred to avoid it, Basaraba opted to pay Mackay a visit before he left Vancouver. Mackay's office occupied a corner of the eighteenth floor of the sumptuous Waterfront Centre, one of the city's most envied addresses. He leaned back in his leather chair behind a capacious but desolate desk (light Corsican chestnut with Koa inlay), bereft of a computer, pens or even a meagre scrap of paper. "So, what can I do for you,

Uhmeel?" The expanse of Coal Harbour and the Stanley Park promontory filled the view from the window behind him. "May I offer you a gin and tonic?"

Basaraba inspected Mackay's slack facial features and droopy red eyes. It was already six; he guessed that Mackay had started drinking at lunch. He probably would have enjoyed a gin and tonic but he expected that this lawyer would have used it as an excuse to have another. "No, no, I have to drive." Mackay squinted at him. "To Whistler, later this evening."

"I see. So what brings you here today?"

"Well, as you know, we have to deal with this lawsuit that the Orthodox group, we'll call it the remnant branch of the religion, has brought against us. We need experienced litigators. That's why I've hired you as our counsel."

"It won't be a problem, I can tell you; it's just a..." He waved in a gesture of dismissal.

"No, no, no," Basaraba spoke over him. "You misunderstand me. I want you to conduct your defence in as protracted a manner as possible."

"Got it!" Mackay banged his palm on the surface of the desk.

Basaraba doubted that he had. "No. Please understand me. This matter can never go to trial. You have to delay the process at every stage. Now," he lowered his voice. "The Orthodox people are represented in Canada by Declan Gaskin. I trust you know who he is."

Mackay leaned back in his chair. "Nobody that I can't handle. I hear that he is a lightweight!"

Basaraba repressed a momentary yearning to break Mackay's nose. "Well, from what I have been told, he is a very accomplished barrister, but of late, it seems, he appears to be shirking his professional duties. Rumour has it that he has re-embraced his past hobby of pursuing young female flesh, with all of its attendant complications — my sources tell me that in recent weeks, one of his lady friends is looking unmistakably maternal.

That sort of thing has a way of consuming most of a man's attentions. So?" He shrugged. "He has delegated just about everything to junior counsel, I don't know much about him. Licensed to practice in both Ontario and British Columbia, but he was working as an in-house solicitor with a bank in Italy, in Rome apparently, before he started working for Gaskin."

"Momma Mia!"

Basaraba winced at Mackay's unprofessional and mispronounced outburst, but Mackay didn't seem to notice. "Now, this young fellow is untested and Gaskin has thrown him to the wolves. So maybe you could try to intimidate him, make him feel outclassed, outgunned."

"Well," Mackay leaned back, resting his hands across his stomach. "I am a Queen's Counsel, after all."

"Yes, I am aware of that. So perhaps you can do whatever you lawyers do to one another, like rutting elk, for the elders to establish their dominance." Basaraba smiled. "I will leave that to you."

"Oh, don't worry; you've come to the right place, Uhmeel."

His smile vanished. "And if it doesn't work? Remember, this matter can never go to trial. Delay, delay, delay. You need to drag this out for as long as possible."

Mackay's expression, smug at first, now betrayed confusion. "Yes, but then what? Eventually, civil actions come to an end. If they don't settle, they go to trial. So I delay it for one, two years. Where will that get us?"

"Don't worry." Basaraba smiled again. "I will let you know."

30

Mario and Laeticia lived in what was, in short, a relic: a simple cottage, with a cedar shake roof and weathered fir siding, conspicuous among cathedral-like, split-level log houses and Cape Cod revival seaside villas, one with a front yard waterfall cascading down a sumptuous granite flume. Even so, the view was the same for everyone along the beachfront row, the quiet Strait of Georgia framed by the Sechelt Peninsula and Tantalus Range of the distant mainland coast; long, undulating Lasqueti Island in the foreground.

"That must be it," Carlo pointed to the cottage as Laura drove slowly along the narrow seaside road.

"Are you sure?" Laura asked. "I'm not going to go knocking on random doors."

Carlo reached into his pocket and unfolded the printed e-mail with their address. "Yes, this is the place."

Mario walked down the steps from the deck facing the water and came out to greet them. "Well, *uagliò,* it's about time you got your ass over here! And Laura! It's been quite a while." He reached over to touch her shoulder. "It's so nice to see you. You're looking good, but your taste in men, I don't know..."

"Mario," Laura said as she folded her arms and looked at him, laughing. "I'm glad to see that you haven't changed a bit." After a brief silence, they held each other in a clumsy embrace.

Carlo pulled a bottle out of a cooler in the trunk "*Prosecco,* Mario. I'd assumed that you guys have refrigeration out here."

"That's what people in Bari used to wonder about Sannazzaro. Three glasses?"

"Well, two, if you're going to drink it out of the bottle like you always do."

Mario brought some glasses out to the deck. "I'll be back in a second. Try not to drink it all." Not long after Carlo had poured three glasses of wine, heavy footfalls made the entire deck shake.

Two noisy, unshaven men appeared as unkempt apparitions. "This guy made two hundred dollars today for doing sweet fuck all!" Russell announced with a good-humoured bellow. "Oh, I'm sorry; I expected to find Mary-O here. You must be that buddy of his from Italy!"

"And who's the lovely young lady?" Canmore leaned forward in an awkward bow.

Mario had already warned Carlo that he'd invited two of his frankly odd local friends for dinner. "Hi. Carlo Buonsante. You must be his two neighbours from down the road." Both Canmore and Russell ignored him and stared at Laura, each wearing lecherous grins.

Mario came back outside clutching another bottle of *prosecco*. "Oh, I see that you guys are already here! Carlo, Laura; Canmore and Russell."

Canmore? "Pleased to meet you both," Carlo said.

"Greetings and all that, eh," Russell said.

"Okay." Mario laughed and poured more *prosecco* into his glass. "You guys want some of this? There's plenty more..."

"Naah, we've got a case of Bud in the truck," Canmore said. "But can we use your fridge?"

"Yeah, yeah." He leaned over the rail at the sound of a car door closing. "It looks like Laeticia's home."

Laeticia came up on to the deck. Carlo remembered most of his professors as drab and dishevelled; Laeticia looked more like one of her students than faculty, dressed in jeans and a "Fuck Bush" T-shirt.

"Laura," Laeticia said in a hushed voice. "It really has been such a long time, but you've barely changed in, what is it, almost nine years?"

"Neither have you!" Laura laughed as the two of them held each other in an extended hug.

"Now I'm getting really horny," Canmore said.

"These two take a bit of getting used to," Laeticia whispered in Laura's ear. She turned to Carlo and placed her hands on his shoulders. "Well, I must say that I never expected to see you come back. Welcome home!" She put her arms around his neck. "I am *so* glad to see that you finally landed on your feet," she whispered.

"It's nice to be back," Carlo stammered.

Russell went out to his truck and came back with a case of Budweiser missing a couple of bottles. "Anyway, just like I was saying, this guy got paid two hundred in cash today for doing jack shit!"

"Well, it's not like I didn't do anything," Canmore protested. "I posed for some pictures."

"Pictures?" Laeticia asked. It piqued everyone's curiosity: why would anyone pay two hundred dollars to take pictures of Canmore?

"Yeah," Canmore said. "Dave McMillan, you know, the landscaping guy I did some work for last spring, he called me up, eh, just out of the fuckin' blue and told me to meet him today at the Shady Rest."

"You guys know the one," Russell said. "That fuckin' fancy ass pub up in Qualicum."

"Yeah, yeah, whatever. Then we all (there was maybe twelve of us) piled into a crummie and went off to this place way out in the fuckin' boonies. There were tractors, backhoes, a shitload of equipment just sitting there, eh, with no one there to work it; not that I could see. Then they gave us all shovels, put us in this fuckin' deep trench and told us all to make like we were digging. Then this guy in a suit started taking pictures snapping away at his camera, a big black motherfucker the size of a cinder block. After about half an hour, they drove us back to the Shady, and paid us two hundred each, cash." He shook his head. "I'll take it; but it's a bit fuckin' weird, eh?"

"See, what did I tell you?" Russell said. "Sweet fuck all!"

Mario got up to tend to the barbeque after Laeticia carried out a tray from the kitchen. "Hey, what are you guys cooking?" Canmore asked.

"Italian sausage," Mario said.

"Cool!" Canmore bellowed. "Those fuckers are spicy, right?"

"Yeah, I guess — garlic, mainly." Mario laid a few sausages on the grill.

"Hey," Canmore said. "Give me another beer, Russ'. A few more of those and a couple of sausages, and I'll be able to belch out 'Smoke on the Water'!"

By the time Russell and Canmore left, they had finished the case of beer they'd brought with them, two bottles of wine, and between the two of them, ten sausages. Not only was Canmore able to belch melodically as promised, but he imitated the harmonica intro to "Thunder Road" by pinching the bridge of his nose and performed a facsimile of the Chicken Dance through judicious use of his left armpit. By the time they left, well after dark, nobody was unhappy to see them go.

Still, Laeticia worried. "Do you think that we should have let them drive?" She pulled back the curtain and peered out of one of the windows facing the road.

"How were we going to stop them?" Mario said. "And besides, they live just down by the edge of the park. Ever since the McMorran's subdivided their lot, there isn't even a ditch along the way for them to drive into, although some of the neighbours...oh yeah, that reminds me. Carlo! I meant to tell you. Gavin; this rich guy who lives down the street. He owns a chalet in Whistler and he's having a party next month, the weekend of the sixth. He told us to invite as many of our friends as we could. You guys busy?"

Carlo and Laura looked at each other; both shrugged. "Sure, I guess we can make it," Laura said.

"Great!" Mario said.

"We're not staying there, I mean, in his chalet." Laeticia said in a decisive tone.

"Why not?" Laura asked.

"Because after the party's done it will be Phi Beta Fuckhead. I don't know about you, but I don't want to be groped by a drunken stockbroker, or worse, two drunken stockbrokers, on my way to the bathroom."

"I think that's a bit unfair, it wouldn't be that bad," Mario said, but both women ignored him.

"Yvette has a timeshare at a condo in Creekside," Laura said to Laeticia. "I'll see if we can snag it. Now, can we open some more wine? I'm parched."

The next morning, Carlo and Laura didn't get started on their drive up-Island until almost noon. "Do you want to drive?" Laura, who seemed to regard the late morning sun as a punitive nuisance, tossed Carlo the keys.

Carlo tossed them back. "Are you kidding me?" Laura was such a relentless critic of his driving that when they were younger, Carlo would never agree to drive unless she was so drunk that it would be most unlikely she'd stay conscious for very long after the engine started.

"Please? Come on! I'm tired. Laeticia and I stayed up drinking wine until three-thirty."

"Oh, all right. But I'm giving them back if you're not fast asleep once we get past Qualicum."

The radio came to life when Carlo started the car. "Oh, no, no; we're not listening to this again!" Laura had left it tuned to a Vancouver AM station, dubbed 'Chick 95' by both Carlo and Mario, one that featured vapid dance music and dismal ballads that sounded like children making ghastly moans as they flushed the toilet. Carlo searched through some CDs in the console, chose an old Metallica album and waited for the opening chords of "Enter Sandman".

"No! I said that I wanted to sleep. How about Taylor Swift?"

Carlo chirped a syrupy stanza in a mocking falsetto.

"All right; you've made your point," After a brief debate, they agreed on a CAKE album Carlo hadn't heard since before he left for Italy. Laura was asleep before "Opera Singer" finished playing. Carlo decided to take the old highway most of the way to Comox, passing through a scenic expanse along the water that he hadn't seen in more than ten years. Despite frequent stops for slowed traffic and the occasional traffic light, Laura did not stir. He had to wake her to give him directions.

"Shit!" Laura said, rubbing her eyes as she looked at the clock on the stereo. "I slept for almost two hours. Turn here; no, first we need gas. Stop at the PetroCan across the street."

Carlo pulled up to a pump and started filling the tank as Laura cleaned the windshield. "Oh my fucking God! The asshole's still alive."

A man wearing a Canucks jersey, perhaps in his middle forties, walked across the parking lot, smiling, in a way that Carlo found creepy. He first presented as a good-looking man, with a thick, cropped thatch of brown hair, but as he got closer, he seemed asymmetrical, as if someone had annealed his face, placed it in a vice and bent both his nose and his chin slightly to the left.

"You're looking good, Laura!"

"Hello, Robbie," Laura said, without smiling or even looking up.

"Here to visit the folks?"

"Yup."

"Well, have a good one, eh!"

Laura waited until he was inside the store. "That guy is subhuman! So many of his crowd, better people than he is, ended up dead in motorcycle crashes and climbing accidents. And that fucking waste of space: he actually tried to burn some guy alive when he was asleep on a bench in Cliffe Park. Haven't I told you about him before?"

She had. Robbie Bellamy had been a prolific supplier of hydroponically grown marijuana to Laura's high school class, far more potent and reliable than the usual pot, grown in hastily cleared plots in the power line right-of way. Although he was several years older, his status as supplier made him welcome at all of their gatherings, until he attempted to rape one of Laura's friends at a beach party after slipping something in her beer, stopped only by her boyfriend, who thrashed Robbie with a piece of driftwood until his T-shirt was soaked in blood. Even if his behaviour often aroused the attention of the police, the only time he was ever sent to jail came after he tried to set fire to a Filipino, whom he had apparently mistaken for an East Indian.

"Oh, speaking of drugs," Laura said, "I brought some combustibles with me. Later on, we'll have to wander down to the Enchanted Forest." Carlo remembered it as a pleasant grove of fir and maple down a short trail that started across the road from her parents' house, a refuge people often used to share a joint or two in private.

"It still exists?"

"Of course it does. And you can't come to Comox without smoking up there at least once. It's the *law*."

Laura's parents still lived on their four-acre farm on a knoll overlooking Seal Bay. A light, distant mist over the Strait obscured the view of the mainland coast. Carlo would not have recognised the property. The hayfield that dominated it twelve years earlier was now a young orchard; the lawn now a vegetable garden. The horse that lived in the paddock beside the orchard, no doubt long dead by this time, had been replaced by a pair of alpacas. Carlo was glad to see that Bruiser was still alive, howling as she approached. Carlo bent down to scratch her ears.

Laura's mother and father came out to greet them as they gathered up with their luggage. Her mother assessed Carlo with the same steady northern European gaze he'd always found unnerving. "Well," she finally smiled. "It was time you came back to visit; and you still look like a teenager." She'd changed little since Carlo last saw her. Her hair was just as blonde, her Danish accent undiminished.

"So I've been told. They still ask me for my driver's license at the liquor store from time to time."

"No doubt," her father said with a guffaw. If Laura's mother had changed little, her father had not changed at all. He looked exactly the same as Carlo remembered him; the same short brown, greying hair and shaggy moustache.

Laura's mother said something to her in Danish and led her to the kitchen. "Well, Carlo," Jack said. "Once you unload, we'll be on our way. It's time for the men to go out and forage for supper. We'll take the truck. It's in the garage."

Jack shifted the aging Ford into second gear, making it lurch forward with disquieting violence. "I thought that we'd go get a salmon for dinner. A buddy of mine has a hold full of sockeye at the docks up in Campbell River. No need to rush around, though. I think that we need refreshments first."

"Sounds good to me."

"So, I hear that you and Laura found yourself representing, how did she put it; the same *client?*"

"Yes," Carlo laughed, "It's actually a little bit disturbing. We were reunited by an assembly of babbling lunatics."

"Well, however it happened, Birgitta and I were both very glad to hear that you were back in the picture." The truck jolted into third gear.

"So am I." Carlo wondered what Jack was going to say next.

"Well, I'll just say this: I don't know what happened between you two and I don't mean to pry, believe me. And, oh, I'd like to say that both Birgitta and I are very sorry about what happened to, I apologize, what was her name, we never met her."

"Tina."

"Yes. We were very sorry when we heard about it.

"Thank you."

"But that takes nothing away from the fact that we're happy to have you back. She'll probably never tell you anything about it (believe me, I know better than anybody how proud she is), but Laura's had a rough few years."

"So have I." Carlo had no desire to discuss Laura's failed romances, especially with her father.

"Sorry. I shouldn't have said anything. Some things are better off consigned to the past." He turned right on to a narrow road, little more than a paved path. "And how's your dad?"

"He's doing fine; still in London, still grumbling about the weather."

"I don't know how anyone can stand that city; it's a *dust hole*! I worked there for a few months when I was about eighteen. I simply hated it, although I suppose he might wonder how anyone could bear to live out here in the sticks. Next time you talk to him, tell him that I say hello."

"Sure; I'll be talking to him on Thursday."

Jack erupted in raucous laughter. "Well, you'll be delighted to know that you won't have to deal with the Rafferty clan any more when you come over. What did you call those frightful women, the four aunts?"

"The Old Skunks."

"Well, I take exception to the 'old' part: they're all around the same age I am. But you got the second part spot on. Anyway, we don't see them much anymore."

"Yes, so I've heard."

"It was time that my sister's luck changed. She divorced that randy layabout; now he's living with a girl half his age on a houseboat in Cowichan Bay. You know, I could never really figure it out. When Laura was a little girl, those four, they used to make such a fuss over her, you know, braiding her hair, dressing her up in frilly dresses, the sort of clothes that would have made her shudder with embarrassment a year or two later. But you know, after she reached her teens (and especially after you came along) they were always simply cruel to her. Well, I'm not telling you anything you didn't already know. Anyways," he laughed. "We're done with them, thank God."

"And your sister, Deanna, where is she now? She used to come over to visit all the time when we were at UBC."

"Yes, she and Laura have always been close. Now she's down in Victoria, working for the province, some ministry or another. Thank goodness! Now, when the time comes, she'll have a pension." The road they were on ran parallel to the coast, past farms and clusters of tourist cabins. "You haven't been away that long. Recognize the countryside?"

"Of course. We just passed the entrance to, oh, Saratoga Beach, I guess."

"Good memory." They crossed an old wooden bridge and pulled into the parking lot of the Beachcomber Pub. "I'm sure you haven't been *here* for a while!"

"No." Carlo was surprised that he found the sight of the old place so comforting. The Beachcomber, a rural pub of a brick and cedar style characteristic of this part of the Island, had seen scant renovation since the reign of George VI (a large painting of whom still dominated the atrium) and little update in its décor since the 1970s. It was, and apparently remained, one of Jack Thompson's daily haunts.

Carlo and Jack went in through the side door, which still bore a faded overhead sign identifying it as the "Indian Entrance". Just as Carlo remembered, a small wooden plaque on the pillar facing them was decorated with a caricature of a man of sly expression and wild hair, with an inscription beneath:

Why Be Disagreeable?
When,

With a little effort...
YOU COULD BE A REAL STINKER!

In mid-afternoon, the pub was almost deserted, except for a group of boisterous men in late middle age. "Hey, Jack!" one of them shouted.

"Hey, Chuckie!" A man that Carlo recognized as Blackie Simpson shouted across the pub. "You're back!" He was surprised that any of them remembered him.

Much raucous chortling followed as the five men at the table rose to greet him, some slapping him on the back, others shaking his hand. "It's been a while!" Charlie Farrell shouted at Carlo as he looked him over. "Not that you've changed much. City life seems to agree with you. What are you drinking?"

Carlo looked over at the array of taps at the bar, the same selection as a decade before. "I'll get a Stella."

"Still drinking that cat's piss, eh?" Blackie guffawed. "For five-fifty a pint, it would have to be seven percent before I'd drink it, at fuckin' least!"

"Kelly!" Charlie waved the waitress over, a girl who was twenty-one at the most and seemed to regard them with a mixture of amusement and unease. "Another round of Carling Pil, except for a Stella for Chuckie here!" He slapped Carlo on the back again.

"You guys are just in time to hear Phil tell us all how he kicked Tiger Woods' ass in the

Myrtle Beach Open." Blackie chuckled.

"Oh, yeah; right!" Jack said. "You just got back from North Carolina. At least you didn't get rained on for the past three weeks."

The waitress returned with a tray full of beer. "Ha!" Phil McFarlane's manner was quieter than the rest of them. "It fuckin' rained plenty. And I didn't kick anybody's ass; the golf course was like a giant swamp!" He took a sip of his draft. "One thing, though. With the shitty weather, they had more than enough time to force real estate on us. Sure, a free meal, half off on a helicopter ride. But to pay for it, you had to go to one of their fuckin' real estate fairs!"

"Hey, I knew it, eh!" Blackie laughed. "You got suckered into another time share down south."

"No, no! Fuck that, I didn't buy fuck all. And it wasn't down there. Most of what they were selling was around here."

Everyone stopped laughing and turned to listen. "Around here?" Jack asked.

"Yeah. I mean I was just speechless; didn't know about any of this. They had these drawings of this huge development, from Qualicum to Union Bay, they called it 'Britannia' or some fuckin' thing...eight golf courses, five, maybe six town centres, heritage style buildings, and even fuckin' railway and streetcar lines."

"Qualicum to Union Bay," Jack said quietly, as if to himself. "A swath of sixty kilometres; that would take up thousands of acres."

"Oh, yeah! So I told him I was from the Comox Valley; that didn't mean shit to him until I told him it less than an hour's drive from their subdivision."

"I bet he turned up the high-pressure salesmanship." Blackie chortled. "I fuckin' knew it. You bought another timeshare, didn't you?"

"No, I didn't! Why would I buy a fuckin' time share in *this* rain forest? Anyway, let me finish! When I told the guy that I *lived* in the area and I hadn't heard that anyone had gotten the okay for such a huge development, well, that was my get out of jail free card." He gulped his beer. "They scooted me out of the banquet room before the presentation started and Janine and I still got our fancy dinner."

"Want another one, Carlo?" Jack pointed to his depleted mug.

"Why not?"

The afternoon of their last day in Comox, Carlo drove by himself down to Qualicum Bay, a small hamlet beside a long pebble beach on the Strait of Georgia. The Striationist compound just down the highway out of town was an old seaside resort that apparently failed back in the late

Seventies and remained abandoned for almost a decade before the Striationists took it over. Still,

Carlo wondered why the Reformed bunch didn't steal this property as well. The land alone was worth a fortune.

He was greeted at the gate by a lively border collie who seemed more interested in playing with him than protecting the property. Carlo saw a building near the beach that appeared to be the office, or whatever these people called it. Carlo crossed the lawn as the dog ran in circles around him. The front door of the building, facing the water, had an oblong wooden sign over it.

ORTHODOX STRIATIONIST TOTALITY – VANCOUVER ISLAND REGION

Before he had the chance to knock on the door, a woman with long, straight brown hair opened it. Carlo guessed that she was his age or a little younger, with the slim, muscular physique of a cyclist, unusually attractive for an Orthodox Striationist.

"Good morning, or, afternoon I guess. Ivanhoe!" She shouted at the dog. "Lie down. So, what can I do for you? I hope that our intrepid guard dog wasn't too much of a nuisance."

"No, no. I'm Carlo Buonsante, I'm the lawyer who works with Gaskin Barristers."

"Oh, yes; from Vancouver, I saw your e-mail. Come in. I'm Ulela." They shook hands. "Hey, I remember you! You're the guy who gave that really boring seminar at the Convocation in Tulalip. I'm sorry, I can't remember what it was about."

"That's okay. Yes, that was me. Sorry; it wasn't my idea."

"Hey, no worries; I slept through most of it. So, I gather that you want to look at some of the financial records."

"Yes, the ones that Mr. McHarg kept before the schism. Did you know him?"

"Ian? Oh, sure; he lived over there for about two years." She pointed at a white clapboard cabin at the back of the property. "He was even acting Master of the Treasure for about a year, give or take maybe a month or two, after old Abercrombie died."

"Abercrombie, he was the financial administrator for how long, about fifteen years?" Carlo could not bring himself to utter the words 'Master of the Treasure'.

"Yup. He was one of the founding members of the religion."

"And now you hold that position, or so I've been told."

"Yes. Pretty pathetic, huh, now that there isn't much in the way of 'treasure'". Carlo detected a slight American accent. "Ian kept meticulous files. I've got to scan them all; my plan is for us to go paperless within the year. We'll see. Anyway, all of his records are in this filing cabinet. I'll be at my desk, let me know if you have any questions."

Carlo started pulling files out of the cabinet, all stuffed with slips of paper, mostly receipts or expense vouchers, submitted by the faithful for reimbursement. All bore McHarg's signature for approval. After he'd gone through hundreds of them, he came upon a sealed envelope from the Royal Bank in Vancouver in one of the files. "What's this; do you know?"

She walked over to see what he was talking about. "Oh, yes, that. It came in about a week after Ian left. I just put it in the cabinet. It was too small to be a bank statement."

"Can I open it?"

"Sure, no problem."

Carlo opened the envelope and pulled out a copy of an account application. Ian McHarg had opened a new current account for the religion, granting himself, someone that Carlo recognized as a politician and the mystical Émile Basaraba signing authority. But McHarg's signature on the application was starkly dissimilar to the signatures on the many vouchers. "I'm going to need a copy of this." Carlo read further down the page. '*Dated at Vancouver, this 12ᵗʰ day of September, 2007*'. "Do you remember if Mr. McHarg went over to Vancouver shortly before he left?"

"I don't know. He may have, but I really doubt it. He was too into his rivers."

"His rivers?"

"Yes, the Big Qualicum, the Stamp, the Kennedy. We even flew into the Megin last year, it's on the west coast. He's a *fanatical* fly fisherman. Not one for cities, or, at least, not North American cities. He spent most of his free time fishing. He used to go after work almost every day, up in the mountains around here, to the Tsable, the Pentlatch, not that anyone can go fishing there, these days!"

"Oh? Why not?" Carlo used to go hiking in the area from time to time, in the Beaufort Range, before he and Laura moved out to Toronto.

"Oh, it's so disgusting! The company, you know, M and W, they say that it's because of all the vandalism. The whole place is locked down, sentries posted at the gates of all of the logging roads we used to drive on to get in. And I'm not talking about the Commissionaires they used to hire, you know, the old Boer War veterans. These guys look like they're all on leave from Baghdad, or mercenaries for the IDF; big rude apes. Anyway, he liked it *here*. Vancouver held almost zero appeal to him."

"Why did he leave?"

"One day, he said something about a family matter in Scotland. I think one of his aunts took ill, so a couple of weeks later he went back to Aberdeen; I think that's where he's from. Okay." Ulela gave Carlo a stern glance. "Look, I've heard people talk a lot of nonsense about Ian, saying that he's a thief, an embezzler. Whatever happened to all that money, he had nothing to do with it. He was as honest as you can get. He would never steal from anyone."

"I suppose you were around him for quite a while."

She sighed and looked away. "Yes. We were seeing each other, until just before he left. Then he suddenly decided that he was too old for me. Pretty shitty excuse, what do you think?"

After he left the Striationist compound, Carlo stopped in at a coffee shop next to an art gallery along the old highway to type up his notes from his meeting with Ulela into a memorandum for Declan. After he finished it, he connected to the local wireless network, first to check his habitual news sites, but after browsing for a few minutes, something occurred to him. What was that guy's name again? He typed 'Nathan Brooke' into Google.

Laura was right; according to his website bio, he was a partner at Quakenbush & Twiller who practiced employment law with a smattering of solicitor's work, mostly wills and the like. His photograph was unsurprising. Short blonde hair, a face bearing homogenized Anglo-American features. Called to the Bar eight years earlier. A devout rugby player, he played for the Maple Ridge Muskoxen and held the position of treasurer in the B.C. Rugby Association. Carlo laughed out loud. Brooke also had an interest in falconry. Back in the Google search results, Carlo found an old link on the second search page to the Canada Law List, a nationwide legal directory that was by necessity often out of date, owing to the ephemeral nature of lawyers' connection with one another. This was unexpected: five years before, he was an associate at Gaskin Barristers. *He probably sat in my chair.* Carlo shut down his computer and made his way back to Comox.

On their way down-Island back to the ferry, Carlo told Laura about his visit to the Striationist compound in Qualicum Bay. "And I gleaned at least one other interesting bit of information."

"What, in Qualicum?"

"No, when I was with your dad, at the Beachcomber. What was his name, Phil MacFarlane, he's been down to southern States." Carlo repeated what he had heard at the pub, the North Carolina sales pitch, the vast development unfolding on the Island.

Laura shook with peals of laughter. "You're still so gullible; such a sucker. This is Phil MacFarlane: the guy that told us that the CIA, the Mafia and the United Nations (like they go hand in hand) built a secret military base in a honeycomb of tunnels underneath Comox Glacier. Up there!" She pointed to the distant snowfield looming above them. "That Phil MacFarlane? And he was always on about black helicopters rising from a portal they'd bored into the glacier, coming out to spread some psychotropic powder over us all. Remember that? *That* Phil MacFarlane?"

"Yes, I remember." MacFarlane once tried to dissuade them from hiking up to Century Sam Lake, a small tarn at the base of the glacier, citing the lurking dangers of an assortment of paratroopers, assassins and spies.

"And Dad told me that for a couple of years after September eleventh, every time he saw someone who looked vaguely Middle Eastern, even some poor Sikh in a turban, he'd call the RCMP," Laura said. "Look, he's a very nice man; I used to play grass hockey with his daughter, but he's not exactly a reliable source of information."

"But it's not just him. At Tulalip, all of the Striationists from the Island were talking about some big development, usually centred on Horne Lake or Buckley Bay, always..."

"Oh, my God! The Striationists? Are you insane? Look, I know that they're your clients, and they're mine, too, but let's face reality: those people are *fucked!* And if there really was a development of that size planned for this part of the Island, thousands of your tree-hugger buddies would be painting themselves blue and lying down in front of bulldozers."

"I don't know; I think there's something to it. Anyway, I meant to ask you before: did you talk to Yvette about Declan?"

"Yes, but I didn't have to get too far into it, fortunately," Laura said. "At least she admitted their…what's the word you used, *fling*, but she said she'd already ditched him. She didn't want to talk about it, so I didn't ask why."

A couple of hours further down the highway, they went down a steep hill towards a gas station. "Remember this little place, Nanoose? It hasn't changed," Laura said. "I've always liked it, even if I never knew why. I still don't."

"No Dairy Queen?"

"Hey, I *like* their ice cream. You know what, I wonder if that place in Lantzville we used to go to, remember? I think it was called the Winchelsea Pub or something. I wonder if it's still there."

"Yes, it was a bit run down; a nice place though."

"If it's still there, let's go there for lunch." Laura turned off the main highway and followed the shore of the Strait of Georgia into the small seaside town. "Oh, my God, there it is!" She pointed ahead of her, to an old house overlooking the water. "At least they've painted it since we were last here." They parked in the lot next to it. In the intervening years, a small shopping centre and a two-storey medical building had sprouted across the street.

Three men rushed out the door as the two of them went in. Laura smiled at the one who held the door open for her, even if the other ones almost collided with her as they passed. Inside, it had changed little. It remained a pub firmly cast in the English style, with dark, stained wooden tables and booths, paintings of horses, stately homes and royalty; the obligatory dartboard. A few men who looked to be in their seventies sat around a table in sedate conversation. A Keno board flashed on a broad television screen above the bar.

"I'll go up and get a couple of pints," Carlo said. But the bartender sparked an unexpected feeling of alarm. Something about her made him think that he should recognize her, a woman about the same age as the men at the table; rotund, but with an incongruously sharp, bony face, brown hair flecked with white restrained in a ponytail. Her eyes, as grey as a blustery November sky, fixed upon him.

"We're closed," she said.

"My God, it's you, Auntie Gladys." Laura said. "I haven't seen you in..."

"Didn't you hear me? We're closed."

"Auntie Gladys, don't you recognize me?" Laura said.

"Oh, I know who you are. And I said that we're closed. Don't you understand English? Or perhaps the pretty couple still thinks that the rules don't apply to them."

"Come on, Auntie Gladys, what are you..."

"Stop calling me 'Auntie Gladys'," she mimicked with a sickly squeak. "You didn't turn out any better than any of us expected; no better than my sweet baby daughter, that slut; wiggling her skinny little ass to every doctor in Vancouver, peddling her Kraut medicines, no more respectable than a streetwalker. And you, just the way you were when you were eighteen! You haven't changed, still the same chubby little tart! Still wearing tight jeans to show off your big ass, still fluffing your hair and shaking your fat tits at every man who looks your way. Still opening your legs for this piece of shit."

The men seated around the table fell silent and cautiously sipped their beer. One of them spoke up. "Come on, Gladys. Stop it; just serve them a drink."

"Shut up, Walt! Mind your own fuckin' business!" she screamed. "This is between us, and it's a long time coming. You know it, I know it! Your parents used to laugh at Trianna."

"Nobody ever laughed at Trianna," Laura said.

"Shut up! Sure she got knocked up in high school; so did Fiona and Maria, and more than a few of their friends, so did lots of good girls. That could have happened to high and mighty Darla pretty fuckin' easily; that *should* have happened to *you*! Don't think that all of us didn't know how *you* carried on, always luring *this* little shit to take you someplace to set you on your back and strip off your tight, slutty clothes every time you thought nobody was watching! As far as we could tell, you spent most weekends during your junior *and* senior year with your heels in the air, gettin' fucked till you squeezed him dry! But Trianna, at least *she* got a real education; at least she grew up. And your mother, fuckin' bohunk, she *laughed* at her. I want you out! Now!"

The men sitting at the table looked at one another in confusion.

"But...nobody...laughed at Trianna", Laura said.

"I'm in charge of this pub. It's closed. That's the way it is, no matter how glamourous and fuckin' special you think you and your little fuckin' Spic might be."

Carlo saw that Laura was shaking and took her hand. "I'm Italian. We're known as *wops*."

"Get the fuck out of here, both of you. The pair of you make me fucking sick!"

Carlo led Laura to the exit. To his surprise, once they were back at her car, she grasped Carlo's shoulder to steady herself. A few tears were streaking her makeup. "You're going to have to drive," she said quietly and handed him the keys.

Carlo started back toward the highway. "So who's Trianna?"

"Her eldest daughter; quite a bit older than us. You met her a couple of times, she's the one who lived in Surrey."

"Yes, now I remember her."

"She'd be fifty by now; she died of cancer, maybe nine years ago. Just before I moved back from Toronto." Laura pulled a mirror out of her purse and fixed her makeup. "You know, if that was closure, the whole concept is highly overrated."

"That was closure?"

"I think it was. Sure, she acted as if she was my fairy godmother until I was about halfway through grade nine, but since then she's been a hundred percent bitch. Never missed an opportunity to tell me that I was getting fat, *praying* that I'd have a kid on the way before I hit nineteen, as if that would somehow put me in my place. And then there was that time at my dad's birthday? You don't know how much I wished you'd been there."

"Oh, *that* time. Probably just as well that I wasn't."

"Well, so yes. This is closure. A nasty, sour-faced old witch who spreads misery wherever she goes, whose husband (I always felt *so* sorry for poor Uncle Pat) finally had enough of her and moved into a leaky old cabin at Saratoga Beach just to escape her, and now her sole source of power is to deny us a pint in a pub in Buttfuck, B.C. Pathetic!"

"But you know, it's obvious that she never asked me my opinion on the subject."

"What are you talking about?"

"Well, if she'd ever asked me what I thought, as far as I was concerned, your clothes might have been easy enough to remove, but they were never actually tight or slutty enough."

Laura let out a sharp, surprised laugh. "Just drive."

31

"All right, Lawrence." Patricia closed her laptop. "You've been lurking about for the past half hour, staring at me like a cat expecting food. What can I do for you?"

In late afternoon, they were waiting in the lounge at Kamloops airport for the flight that would whisk them back to Victoria, after Willingdon dispatched them to a Chamber of Commerce luncheon at a golf resort a few kilometres out of town.

"Well," he stammered, still standing.

"Oh, for the love of God, Lawrence. Sit down!"

He took the chair across from her. As far as Patricia could tell, he seemed to be holding his breath. Finally, he spoke. "I need you to make sure that I get expedited environmental approval for a number of matters." He sighed and interlocked his fingers, twisting them about.

"No problem, as long as these 'matters' are safe, and don't result in landslides or dead fish. Wait a minute." His twitchy demeanour invited suspicion. "What 'matters', exactly, are you talking about?"

"Well," he swallowed. "It has to do with a number of condominium developments on the Island, between Bowser and Cumberland. A bit inland. We didn't think that it would be a problem but, you know, these days almost all institutional investors balk at putting money into any project that doesn't have a Yak." The Environmental Approval Certificate, he explained, or 'EAC', called a 'Yak' by those who dealt with them regularly, had become the *sine qua non* of any investment by companies and pension funds whose corporate charters imposed any hint of ethical standards. "So I need a Yak."

"Well, come on, Lawrence." Patricia sighed. "We aren't sitting on the Students' Council at some high school or another. I can't just bestow favours on my friends. You know the drill. The developer has to apply for approval, not just to us, but to the Vancouver Island Regional District, then, as usual, bury us in paper and then my staff will take a look at it, and after that, I can decide whether to sign a Certificate." Patricia found the term 'Yak' loathsome and refused to utter it herself.

"But there's a problem. It's too late for that at this point."

"Look, you'd better tell me what you're talking about. You're not making any sense." She lowered her reading glasses further down the bridge of her nose and peered at him. "What's going on? Look, we have too much respect for one another to speak to each other in meaningless code. Just tell me. Remember, I'm on your side." She took a sip from her glass and sneered; her white wine had been served at tarmac temperature. "So, what sort of project is this? When does the developer plan to build it?"

"That would be the problem. It's already built. The whole thing was arranged...off the grid. And now, for resale, mortgages; things like that, we're going to need..."

"Hold on! What the hell do you mean, 'it's already built'? So what you're really asking me for isn't expedited approval. You want *retroactive* approval!"

"Bluntly, yes," he choked.

"What have you allowed yourself to get talked into, Lawrence? What has happened is not only illegal, but it could end both of our careers if things are made public under the wrong circumstances. And actually, I'm having a lot of trouble imagining what the *right* circumstances might be. And that land. It's all logging claim, private tree farm license, right?"

"I guess, for the most part."

"You guess. Land that has been specifically zoned for silviculture, and, if I'm not mistaken, requires an Act of the Legislature to rezone."

"I'm not a lawyer," Gollander said, picking at his knuckles. "But you might be right, I guess."

"And now it has been transformed, in secret, I might add, into a condo development. Just delightful." She folded her arms. "We'll be bringing up the topic, front and centre, at the next full cabinet meeting." They sat in silence facing one another, like a couple married for decades engaged in yet another reprise of a recurring argument, each having exhausted ammunition to launch at the other. An announcement broke the silence.

Attention passengers. WestJet Flight 732 to Victoria will be delayed for one hour and ten minutes due to mechanical issues. The estimated time of departure is now six forty-five this evening. We apologize for any inconvenience.

Patricia looked out the lounge window at its view of a furrowed ridge covered with dry, golden grass. "Well, the wine might be piss warm, but I need another glass. Do you know any card games, Lawrence?" She pulled a deck of cards adorned with the BC Ferries logo out of her purse.

"I just learned how to play this Chinese game called 'Big Two'."

Patricia remembered it as a cross between poker and gin rummy with some odd variations in the rules. "Wait a minute. You can't play Big Two with just two players. You need at least three, or else it doesn't make any sense."

"I suppose you're right. How about euchre?"

"Sure, why not." She removed the deck from its box and handed it to Gollander. "I'll let you deal; it has been a while since I played."

"I still need a Yak."

"Could you please just deal?"

Patricia decided that whatever Gollander had been on about, she'd best confront it sooner rather than later. The next morning, she arrived an hour early and made herself comfortable on his settee, hoping to surprise him and find out exactly what was going on. As expected, just after eight, Gollander opened the door to his office with a delicate twist of the handle and peeked in, only to leap back in shock. "What are you doing here?"

Patricia looked up from her iPhone. "What is with you, Lawrence? Do you always enter your own office as if you're sneaking into the ladies' room?"

"You scared the crap out of me," he said in a shaky voice, surveying the room. "And what are you doing here, sitting in the dark? It's...it's just weird."

"No, Lawrence, it's *not* weird." She put her phone back in her purse. "At least, not compared to some of the other nonsense that seems to be going on around here." Patricia rose and walked across the office to the seat behind Gollander's sprawling walnut desk.

"You're in my chair, Patricia," Gollander mumbled.

"I know." She folded her hands on the blotter in front of her. "Have a seat." She motioned to a leather stool, which Gollander took without further protest. "Now, this EAC business. I tried to get some information last night from Terrence, I mean, who *else* would spearhead a clandestine venture like this, but when I asked him? He played dumb; he told me that he had heard a few rumours (he gave me that), but then he assured me in his bumbling way that any project wouldn't happen until the application had crossed my desk for approval." Patricia fashioned a gun with her thumb and forefinger and held it up to the side of her head.

"That's what Terry said, eh?"

"Yes, Lawrence, that's what he said. Now, he knows it's bullshit, I know it's bullshit, and I'm sure that he at least strongly suspects that I know that it's bullshit. But we still play this childish charade!" Gollander, who had been gawking at her as if her every word was an unwelcome surprise, swallowed hard with her last declaration. "So, what might be the problem? Is it because I've shunned that stupid-ass religion, such that it is? I didn't learn the secret handshake?"

"Now, Patricia," Lawrence said quietly, "I can assure you that..."

"You can't assure me of fuck all!" Patricia shouted. She felt a twinge of shame when she saw him cower. "Look, this is bad, almost as bad as it gets. Once this comes to light, this huge development taking up thousands of hectares, every environmental group in western Canada and the Pacific Northwest will be out to lynch me! Maybe I should move out to the Okanagan: the trees out there are so short that they'd only *sprain* my neck."

Gollander muffled a laugh.

"It's not funny! *I* am not going to be the one taking responsibility for this! And I will find out what's going on, you'd best believe it! So how about if you enlighten me?"

"I...I was sworn to secrecy."

"By whom?"

"All right, fine; I'll show you. But you can't, and I mean *can't*, tell anyone how you found out about this. He opened the front drawer of his desk to fish around until he found a folded scrap of paper scribbled with a multi-digit numeric code, and then turned on his laptop to type it in. "Okay. This, *this* is the website that is being used to sell the project, and I must say, it is quite well put together and professional."

Patricia leaned forward and examined the screen. "*Professional?* Good God, Lawrence! It looks like a ten-year-old with a bad case of post-nasal drip whipped it together on his mother's laptop. Let me use that mouse for a second." She clicked her way through the website menu and started laughing. "Oxbridge? *Really*, Lawrence?" As she read the text more carefully, her smile faded.

"Oh, my God, Lawrence, what have you gotten yourself into?"

"What do you mean, '*gotten myself into*'? It is long overdue that someone with ambition, with vision, assembled a project like this. It is going to be a great success, something so big that it will finally put rural Vancouver Island on the map!"

"Oh? Whose map? Really, Lawrence, you remind me of someone who gasses up his car with a cigarette hanging out of his mouth. I'm going up to my office."

As soon as she exchanged polite greetings with her staff and settled into her chair, she dialled Willingdon's personal cell phone.

"Hello, Patricia, what's up?"

"Garth, we need to have a serious chat."

32

A deep line grew in front of the bar at Calista's. The cashier, a new hire Carlo had never seen before, was a talkative elder who looked at least ten years past the age at which people once customarily retired. His banter was pleasant enough but so slowed the line-up that ordering even an unadorned espresso seemed to take forever. "Well, young lady," he said to Carlo, "here is your *latte.*"

"It's mine," Marika quickly retrieved it, as if to ensure that it wouldn't come to any harm. "I saved us a table, the one by the window.

Carlo caught up to her once he got his double espresso. An older woman whom Carlo had seen there frequently momentarily fixed her gaze on Marika's stomach, and then looked at them both with a welcoming smile.

"So." Marika tore apart her croissant. "Is the Dhaliwal discovery still on this morning?"

"Settled," Carlo said between sips of espresso.

"Oh. I hadn't heard."

"We put it to bed at about six yesterday; it was after you left. I had instructions to take the one-twenty they were offering, but I decided to pick up the adjuster up by his ankles to shake him and see what fell out of his pockets."

"What did you get?"

"One twenty-three. But I still have a discovery," Carlo grumbled. "As soon as I told Declan that Dhaliwal settled, he dumped the Baliol Mews discovery on me."

"Isn't that the builder who got shafted for some fancy-ass wood?"

"That's the one." Their client, a Striationist contractor who did renovations on older homes in the wealthier districts on the west side of Vancouver, usually Shaughnessy or Point Grey, ordered about two hundred thousand worth of custom cut old-growth Douglas fir planks from a rustic mill somewhere on the Island, whose owner demanded payment in advance but never delivered the planks.

"Did you read his Statement of Defence?" Carlo said. "The stupid fuck pleaded *non est factum*." It was a contract law refuge signifying that he didn't understand that there was a deal, successfully maintained only by mental defectives or those unable to speak English. "And he's the one who got his fucking money. Anyway, no one expects him to show up. But who knows?"

"Well, good luck with that but...gotta go. I have to stop by that exercise clothing store downstairs by the food court 'cause I need some bigger leggings." She sighed. "I'm getting *huge*, Carlo. These ones are about to split at the seams. So see you when you get back."

Gaskin had booked the examination at Sinclair Reporting, a court reporters' office on a higher floor in their building, which, as Carlo recalled from an earlier visit, distinguished itself from its competitors by using scented air fresheners that smelled like urinal cakes, and offering coffee and arid muffins supplied by a rotating roster of convenience stores

As expected, the owner of the sawmill, who went by the name Chester Hilton, didn't show up to be examined. Carlo waited the obligatory half hour before the court reporter stamped a copy of the Appointment, the formal document requiring that Hilton come to the examination, to certify that he didn't. On his way out of the reporter's office, he almost bumped into Farida on her way out of one of the examination rooms, the strap of her briefcase over one shoulder.

"Farida! What are you doing here? Isn't this place a bit downscale for you? Declan loves it because it's cheap."

"Well, I always book here when I don't expect anybody to show. It was a fair bet: a family law matter I took on through the Society. Examination in aid of execution for spousal and child support; I have good information that he's moved back to Iran to evade payment. What can I say? My people are vile. What about you?”

“The defendant in a collection file didn’t show. Pathetic small-time crook from the Island who stole from a Striationist.”

“Is that illegal? I mean, stealing from a Striationist.”

Carlo laughed. “Got time for a coffee?”

“Yes, definitely.”

They found seats on the deck outside a coffeehouse on Cordova Street, each carrying a drip coffee that required a much shorter wait than an espresso. Farida avoided eye contact, sipping her coffee. “I’ve been meaning to call you. Sorry I was such a bitch to Laura.” She tried to smile. “You were right; a lot of time has passed. And you do seem to be *much* happier than when you got here.”

“Look, that’s fine, but, well, if I was happy to consign those miserable days to the past, you should have been, too.”

“Look, I know, and weren’t you listening? I said that I’m sorry. But I’m sure I really pissed her off. I seem to remember that she has a bit of a temper. I suppose I’ll have to suck up to her.”

“No, no, I’m sure she’s forgotten all about it.” Carlo knew it was bullshit but he said it anyway.

“That I doubt,” Farida laughed. “Oh yes, something else I’ve wanted to tell you. Paula, Gaskin’s wife. She’s been at the Society’s office quite a bit lately; I guess she must be bored. Anyway, what did you do? She speaks of you in, let’s just say, the most uncomplimentary terms.”

“Like what?”

“I’d rather not say. I’m *far* too lady-like and refined to use language like that.”

“That bad, eh?” Carlo laughed. “Come on; it’s not like I’m hurt, or anything. She has contempt for everybody.”

“I guess. But she’s got a major hate on for *you.* Did you know that?”

"No. That's bizarre." Carlo stopped in mid-sip. "Okay. You brought it up. What's she said?"

"Oh, nothing specific. But she refers to you as 'that little prick' or 'that little asshole who works for my husband'; that sort of thing. "A couple of days ago she said, 'I'd tell Declan to fire him, but that would only make things worse'. That's as specific as she got."

"No shit? Well, there's not much that I can do about it. And 'fire' me? What's up with that? It's not like I do any work for *her*."

"Well, you're right about one thing. She says nasty things about almost everyone when they're not listening; such a fucking bitch." Farida added sugar to her coffee. "Oh, yes, the last time I was at Cordova Reporting I stopped in at that Calista's place and I saw that redhead you work with, you know, the one with the headlights? She recognized me. But it took me a minute or two to recognize *her*. As you must have noticed yourself, well, let's just say that she's *grown*. She should really lay off the *biscotti*. And you'll laugh at me, but last year, when one of the secretaries at our office blew up in such a big hurry, it turned out that she was pregnant."

"She is," Carlo said in a hushed tone, looking behind him as he spoke.

Farida looked at Carlo and narrowed her eyes. "So," she grinned. "Are congratulations in order?"

"No," he laughed. "That would have been the last thing I needed. But she's definitely pregnant."

"You and me both, and now David's starting to pester me. But anyway, with her so young, I don't imagine that it was planned. Silly girl. Although you know, maybe she *did* plan it. When I saw you two that time at Calista's, she looked like she couldn't wait to lure you inside to make a deposit." Farida's phone echoed with a deep, male voice — a new, cinematic ring tone.

And I will execute great vengeance upon thee;
and they shall know that I am the Lord!

"Oh, hey," she spoke louder to overcome the din of the coffeehouse deck. "I'm just having coffee with Carlo; we're at this place in Gastown." Farida's lips tightened. "I don't know," she sighed. "Why don't you ask him yourself?" She passed the phone over to Carlo.

"Hey, buddy," David said as Carlo brought the phone to his ear. "How's it going? How's Laura? Anyway, as I was telling Farida, I'd really like some salmon, sometime soon. I'd cook it myself but I always burn it. So how about, say, Friday?"

"Sure; why not?"

"Cool, but don't make that pasta, 'itchy' or 'tichy' or whatever it was. I really like that rice you make with little bits of fish in it."

Carlo laughed. "You mean *risotto di frutti di mare?*"

"I guess. That stuff you used to make all the time in Toronto. And bring a good bottle of wine or two: Farida always gets cheap shit."

"Looks like we'll be over for dinner again on Friday," Carlo said as he handed the phone back to Farida.

"Yes, sorry about that, but you know what he's like." She put her phone back into her briefcase and slung its strap over one shoulder. "Just make sure that Laura doesn't show up wearing the same thing as me."

33

The long, many-paned window of the Skeena Room in the Legislative Buildings in Victoria afforded a handsome view of the Inner Harbour. A portrait dominated the wall opposite, an ample oil painting of the former William Alexander Smith, who changed his name to Amor de Cosmos after he decided that he loved the universe and became one of the first premiers of British Columbia. Soon after leaving politics, he lost his mind, and ended up in an asylum after he tried to erect a fence across Government Street, then and now one of the main thoroughfares in central Victoria.

The entire provincial Cabinet assembled around the long oak table for the first time in months. Perry Chatham, whose lengthy banishment started after ComuniCare became public, was finally again being apprised of scheduled Cabinet meetings. He looked around the table. There was a time when he believed that he was generally well-liked by his colleagues, but for the past year, none had gotten in touch with him and those he'd tried to contact didn't return his calls. Only Patricia Wilson, who was engaged in animated conversation with Fabién Lerche at the far end of the table, would actually speak to him if they met up by chance on the ferry or at an airport.

The two youngest among the ministers, Naomi Kindersley and Gurjit Basi, both acolytes of Lerche, both made up to seem like porcelain dolls, sat facing him wearing expressions of exaggerated feminine surprise. Next to Basi was Gollander, who (as usual) seemed to be in the throes of an episode of St. Vitus's dance. And there he was, Willingdon, pond scum, pontificating to the ungainly Goyter. Yes, this was a most fitting opportunity for his announcement.

Chatham had no intention of enduring unnecessary ceremony. He wanted to make his exit before Willingdon could make a few words of introduction, customarily followed by yet another one of Lerche's hypnotic soliloquies. When Willingdon appeared ready to speak, Chatham interrupted him. "Before we begin, I have something to announce to you all."

Goyter cleared his throat. "Maybe you could wait until just before the end of the meeting, Perry. I think that we've got almost a full..."

Chatham cut him off; Goyter's voice was already starting to degenerate into mucous-tinged mumbles, anyway. "No, this will just take a moment. I am resigning my seat in the Legislature, effective immediately. I have scheduled a press conference at the Coast Harbour Towers Inn in half an hour to make the announcement publicly."

"Perry," Willingdon said without looking at him. "We have already discussed this. This is not the way things are done in this government. You didn't submit, or should I say, resubmit, a letter of resignation to my attention before announcing your intentions to anyone else, especially the press." He folded his arms. "You'd best reconsider."

"I must take pains to tell you," Chatham replied, affecting a deliberately baronial tone. "I am *not* asking your permission. I *will* be teaching a graduate course in international trade theory at the London School of Economics next October. I *will not* be a cabinet minister in any jurisdiction, especially this one." He placed a hand on his hip. "Hateful to me as the gates of Hades is a man who hides one thing in his heart and speaks another."

Kindersley leaned over to Basi. "More of his British shit, I know I won't miss that."

"No, no." Gollander whispered. "I know that it's a little before your time, but it's one of the things that Ernest Borgnine said to some Mexicans in *The Wild Bunch*."

Willingdon sat back in his chair without saying a word, with the bearing of a stray cat who'd just received a rich blast of water from a garden hose. Chatham sensed that everyone at the Cabinet table knew the implicit truth: he'd succeeded in placing himself well beyond Willingdon's gravitational field, outside any milieu where he had even ceremonial influence. He was no longer of British Columbia, where, for the time being at least, Willingdon reigned more or less supreme. He was even leaving Canada, where anywhere outside Québec, Willingdon could have called in a few markers to make Perry's existence moderately unpleasant. No, instead, he was returning to make his way in the English academic world, where people regarded Willingdon's sparsely-populated patch of earth at the very edge of the north Pacific as raw and barely civilized, and, as for Willingdon himself? Even among those who were aware of his existence, he commanded a level of influence somewhere on the continuum between that of an operatic potentate of some tropical former colony and the Governor of South Dakota.

Fabién Lerche rose. "Mr. Chatham, I believe that your insolence is emblematic of parasites; especially those of the academic world."

Chatham raised his fist and released a theatrical laugh. "*Monsieur de Rastignac! C'est à nous, maintenant!*" he shouted in a loud, resonant baritone, still barking with laughter as he strode out of the Skeena Room.

* * *

Carlo and Laura arrived late at the Horseshoe Bay ferry terminal, the customary link between Nanaimo and Vancouver, just after the three o'clock boat had started to unload. Both of them watched in amazement as the seemingly endless parade of foot passengers passed through the terminal. Mario and Laeticia took a while to surface in the torrent of passengers, their presence perhaps obscured by three high school volleyball teams and an Asian tour group. Laura eventually spotted them but had to scream to get their attention. Laeticia was famously near-sighted and Mario's attention was consumed by a girl with bobbed brown hair, long-legged in cyclists' shorts.

The four of them walked together towards the car, parked along the waterfront promenade in Horseshoe Bay village. "So what time is this party? Whistler's not that far away," Laura said.

"Gavin said that as long as we're there by about eight, it's all good," Mario said.

"Is that so?" Laura said. "I was reading an ad in *The Province*. The Mountain Aire Outlet Warehouse in Squamish; it's on the way. They're having a shoe sale all weekend."

"Excellent!" Carlo said. "You were about to run out."

"Neither one of you needs more fucking shoes," Mario said. "If you feel the need to shop, why don't you just go here?" He pointed to a dollar store next door to an ice cream shop.

"We don't have to be there for three hours. You have a better way to kill time?" Laeticia said.

"Yeah." Mario pointed toward a pub with a sidewalk patio, in a squat wooden structure near the end of the block. "Let's go for a drink!"

The four of them found a table facing the water. "What are you guys getting?" Mario asked Laeticia and Laura. "Wine?"

"Nope," Laura browsed the menu and caught Laeticia's eye. "What's this over here, at the bottom of the martini menu? The 'Farewell to Legs'?"

Laeticia ran a finger down the menu. "Hmm, sounds interesting."

"We'll get two of those!" Laura said to the waitress.

Carlo found the martini section. It had a literary motif of sorts: 'the Lost Tycoon', 'the Withering Heights', 'Pear Goriot', and so on. 'A Farewell to Legs', at twenty-eight dollars was the most expensive. He glanced at the list of ingredients and started to panic as its probable alcohol content occurred to him. "Who's driving?"

"You are." Laura handed him the keys.

Carlo sighed. "Drink up!"

They'd been following a narrow, paved track on a wooded mountainside opposite Whistler Village for what seemed like an hour. "Where is this fucking place?" Carlo asked Mario. Laura and Laeticia were in the back seat, slowly regaining consciousness. They had both slept all the way from the pub to Function Junction, a spot just south of Whistler named for its aggregation of public utility facilities.

"His chalet is way in back; it takes forever to get there", Mario said. "Oh, there it is, that's his driveway."

A girl with an Australian accent ushered the four of them into the chalet, a cathedral-like structure in the west coast style built of thick cedar beams and glass. Mario waved toward Gavin. "That's Gavin, the guy who owns this place; Gavin Skoff. He lives just down the beach from us."

Carlo was vaguely aware of Skoff, a financial pundit of robust self-opinion whose aphorisms were often quoted by cable network libertarians. Skoff approached them, smiling.

"So, Mario, is this, I suppose, your brother?"

"Well, if I had a brother, this would be him. Gavin, this is Carlo Buonsante, a good friend of mine."

"Gavin Skoff." Carlo and Gavin shook hands. "Tiffany and I live a stone's throw from Mario and Laeticia's beach cottage."

Mario put his hand on Carlo's shoulder. "I'm being paged." He pointed to Laeticia, who was talking to a young woman wearing green cargo pants whose eyes were magnified by thick glasses. Carlo assumed she was another academic.

"So, Buonsante. You must be Italian, like Mario." Gavin said.

"Yes, I am."

"Have you ever been over?"

"Oh sure, many times. In fact, I lived there for three years. I just got back to Canada a few months ago."

"Three years." Gavin pursed his lips in appraisal. "Were you anywhere near the village where they make my favourite wine?"

"Where would that be?"

"Montalcino, it's in southern Tuscany."

"No, I was in Rome most of the time, but I concur with your choice of wine."

"You're familiar with Brunello di Montalcino?"

"Yes, sure, of course." Carlo was surprised he would ask.

Gavin's attention shifted to the outside deck. "It appears that Tiffany (she's my significant other) is being introduced to shooters." He pointed to a tall, slender girl guzzling a brown liquid out of a shot glass, standing at the outdoor bar. Carlo saw Laura next to her, vigorously issuing instructions to the bartender. He noted the stark age difference between Gavin and Tiffany.

"Would you like a glass of Brunello?" Gavin asked.

"Please. Yes, of course."

"Come with me." Carlo followed him downstairs, to a small office overlooking the shaded ravine behind the house. Gavin pulled a bottle of wine out of a cupboard above his desk, uncorked it and poured two glasses. "This one is a seventy-six, I brought it back with me on my last trip to Milan."

A nineteen seventy-six, Carlo marvelled. "This is excellent," he said after taking a shallow sip.

"How do you earn your money? Are you another techie like Mario?"

"No, I'm a lawyer."

"Oh," Gavin stepped back. "I didn't expect that. Where do you practice?"

"At a, well, I suppose you could call it a boutique litigation firm called Gaskin Barristers."

"Wow, that takes me back a few years. Declan Gaskin. He did a lot of the litigation work for my ex-wife's group; they call it a religion. I suppose you're familiar with the Striationists?"

"Very."

"No doubt." He laughed as if pondering a private joke. "So, how's my old buddy Declan doing these days?"

Well, let's see. He's somewhere in his sixties; his most lucrative single client is a flock of loons, one of his mistresses isn't speaking to him and the other one is due in March, and if his wife finds out about either one of them, she'll have his testicles as an *amuse-bouche.* "I guess he's doing all right," Carlo said. "These days we're doing a lot of work for the Orthodox Striationists."

"Hmm, yes. I would have expected that he still does their legal work. Declan and I used to meet up at their retreats, usually on Savary Island, sometimes at this place on Melbourne Inlet. We (the two infidels) spent a great deal of time together, playing backgammon; arguing about politics. He's much further to the left than I am, as you can imagine." Gavin reached for the bottle. "Would you like some more of this?"

"No, I couldn't do..."

"Please; the pleasure's all mine. When you're the author of an international bestseller, you can afford a gazillion of these things." He poured Carlo another glass. "So, you're pretty lucky, it seems to me."

"What? Why?"

"Well, that hot young blonde who was ordering shooters for Tiffany, she's your girlfriend, right?"

"Yes, Laura."

"I saw you two talking as you were coming in. I can usually tell who is a couple. And it seems to me that you're lucky in yet another way. Declan's getting older; he has a *very* large practice and he's eventually going to pass it on to a younger lawyer. His sons aren't interested, they're both in the sciences."

This startled Carlo. "Sons? Declan has sons?"

"Yes, two, from his first marriage. They'd be about your age, maybe a little older, and they both live out of town. I think that the oldest one was living in Seattle, the last I heard; and if I'm not mistaken, the younger one lived in Europe somewhere, Geneva, maybe? The place with that particle gizmo. So you could end up taking over his practice when he retires."

"About my profession," Carlo gesticulated. "About my profession...I have learned only two truths since I graduated from law school. First, keep your mouth shut and speak only when necessary; and second, lawyers never retire."

Gavin laughed and poured each of them a little more wine. "Do you have your card with you?"

Carlo found Laura chatting with Mario on the upstairs deck. "And that girl," Laura said. "Nice enough, but has she *ever* led a sheltered life. I mean, someone who's *already* twenty-two, with a boyfriend who's as rich as a rock star, you'd think that she might know her shooters. But can you imagine? That chick had never heard of a Rocky Mountain Bearfuck!" It was a potent shooter that both Carlo and Mario considered a variant of nail polish remover.

"Hmm, no shit?" Mario mumbled.

"Oh, hey, Carlo! There you are," Laura said. "We were just enjoying the view." As evening descended into night, the lights of the Blackcomb ski lift became more distinct. You had a long chat with what's his name."

"Gavin," Mario said.

"Yes," Carlo said. "Nice guy, excellent taste in wine."

Two girls came up to Mario, both dressed in earthen-coloured outdoor wear liberally embossed with the Wilderness Co-operative's new 'WC' logo. "Hey, you guys out here to escape the Chamber of Commerce?"

Mario turned to face them and took a deep swallow of his beer. "Oh, hi, Morgan. Morgan and Tannie, meet Carlo and Laura, two friends of ours from way back. These guys are grad students, friends of Laeticia."

Both of them ignored Laura and set their attention on Carlo. "So, are you at UBC too?" Morgan asked.

"Nope," Laura said. "He's a lawyer, ladies."

They both seemed to have heard what Laura said but nonetheless pretended that she didn't exist. "A lawyer?" Tannie asked.

"You shouldn't have told them that," Carlo laughed. "How am I supposed to make a good impression, now?"

"What sort of law do you practice?" Tannie said.

"Civil litigation," Carlo answered warily.

"Oh, fuck," Morgan snarled, "Don't tell me that you sue people."

"Only if someone tells me to."

"You know what, that's just so disgusting," Tannie said. "Shit happens! All those people suing and getting ridiculous sums of money for some piss ass little injury. Like the McDonald's coffee case!"

Oh, here we go again.

"And what about the guy in the Winnebago?" Morgan laughed. "Put it on autopilot in New Mexico, went off the road, and sued. Got himself a free, brand-new Winnebago. It's such bullshit!"

The Winnebago anecdote had been circulating on the Internet for almost fifteen years. Misfortune befell the hapless Gazinski's when one day, either the husband or the wife (the story varies in the retelling) put the Winnebago on cruise control and went to the back of the vehicle for, depending on the preferences of the narrator, a cup of coffee, some tea or a beer, whereupon the Winnebago veered into a ditch (or a swamp, or a farmer's field) somewhere in Nebraska (or Iowa. or Illinois, and now, New Mexico). The Gazinski's sued, winning some money (the average came to about $1.7 million) and a new Winnebago.

"Oh, that's true enough," Carlo said.

"You've heard of it?" Tannie asked. "I saw it on *thelawisanass.com.*"

"Oh, I've heard of it. It's all bullshit; just an outrageous tall tale that somebody made up."

"Typical lawyer," Morgan said. Mario gazed toward the ski hill and continued smoking his cigarette, calmly waiting for this unexpected ordeal to come to its inevitable conclusion. "There's a website, *thelawisanass.com*. They look for examples of disgusting lawsuits and bad behaviour by people like you and they have a team of researchers to verify them!" She stood closer to Carlo, poking at his chest. "It's a public service! Pretty soon the gravy train will be over for you guys and you'll actually have to work for a living!"

Laura made a caustic grin at Morgan. "Oh, what do you do that's so noble?"

Morgan still pretended that Laura didn't exist but Tannie glared at her. "Who the fuck asked you?"

"No," Carlo said. "They probably don't do any research at all. Where is the official record of the lawsuit? If it existed, you could find it online." He pointed to a desktop computer in the sitting room. "It would take just a few seconds. Which law firm represented them? There wasn't one. That's because it never happened."

"I've heard about enough of this!" Tannie said.

"In fact," Carlo said. "I bet you could get, what's that website called again, to repost anything, no matter how ridiculous."

"Forget it, Tannie," Morgan said. "He's just an asshole. See you later, Mario."

"Wow," Laura said after Morgan and Tannie went back inside, laughing. "It's been a few years since I've seen an exchange like that; just like old times!" She punched Carlo lightly on the shoulder. "What faculty are they in?"

Mario pondered for a moment. "Social Work, if I'm not mistaken".

"I thought as much."

Carlo composed most of it in his head the next day, on the drive back from Whistler. Then he had to decide where he was going to post it: which website would yield the best results? Wikipedia would delete it as soon as a moderator noticed, and this time, he would probably be banned for good. His final warning came the last time after he concocted an entry about the landlocked Duchy of Dismocrania, an ostensible Presbyterian enclave in the eastern Alps, which, much to his surprise, remained posted for more than a week. He settled on another American site that wasn't so fussy. As soon as he was certain that Laura had gone to sleep, he started typing.

....34

Laeticia felt her mobile phone vibrate inside her purse with an incoming text message. It was Patricia.

Still in town?

She'd been in her new office since just after sunrise, an improvised, windowless closet ceded by the sociologists. At least a hundred first-year mid-term exams remained to be marked; Laeticia didn't expect to get back up to Parksville until the following afternoon.

Yup.

Her phone growled again.

Good. PGs at 7?

A glass of wine would be a welcome end to a stultifying day.

See u thr

She shut off her phone and pulled another stack of yellow exam booklets towards her, opening the one on top and repositioning her reading glasses.

Patricia finished what was left of her cappuccino and crunched the last bite of brioche at Gran Caffè Victoria, the narrow brick nook just off Bastion Square where she had her breakfast most mornings when she found herself in the capital. She left in search of a newspaper, walking with a quickening gait along Government

309

Street to the Inner Harbour, unrecognized, through the crowd on the waterfront. It was true that many of the people around her were tourists, mostly Americans and Chinese, but she was sure that not everyone wandering the causeway was foreign. Even if she'd been environment minister for almost three years, she was anonymous. Perhaps that was as it ought to be.

The Empress Hotel, a broad, château-style monument, loomed above the Inner Harbour. They'd have a newspaper in the gift shop, if only the local *Times-Colonist.*

"Hey, Joe..." She walked into the lobby, singing along with the background music. It returned her to an epoch a lifetime ago, just as she was about to enter her Master's program. Where was she, San Francisco, when she first heard it, in the apartment of a long-forgotten boyfriend, a black vinyl disc spinning on a device that these days seemed like an artifact from the Bronze Age. Jimi Hendrix! Back then, she would have assessed the chance that she would have been hearing "Hey Joe" in the Empress Hotel as roughly equal to her one day owning a castle.

She bought a newspaper but was already back outside before she glanced at the headline. By the time she had finished scanning the article beneath, her ears were hot to the touch, a life-long symptom of rage. *The coward! That spineless lummox! He didn't even have the guts to tell me to my face! I'm going to go over there right now and kick him square in his balls, but then again, he probably doesn't have any!*

Once inside the Parliament Buildings, Patricia passed through the main entrance hall to the Cabinet offices, at first searching one of the windowless rooms given to the press gallery. Most mornings when the Legislature was sitting, Willingdon started the day there, trading hoary, pornographic humour with some of the reporters. She eventually found him just outside his office, in quiet chatter with one of his young executive assistants.

"You gutless prick!" she shouted. His assistant vanished. "You demoted me! You didn't even have the balls to tell me yourself!" Even if he was several inches taller and substantially heavier than she was, he toppled almost off balance as she pushed him toward his office door. "Get into your fucking office!" Once they were inside, she slammed the door.

"Patricia, you know very well that this sort of thing goes on all the time." His tone carried an unmistakable pleading quality.

"Minister of Women's Issues!" she hissed. "What the hell does that even mean?"

"It's a perfectly worthy posting, Patricia. We're taking things in a new direction and I thought that you, with your connections in both the business and academic world, would be a perfect..."

"No!" She shouted over him. "You've exchanged me with an environment minister who doesn't really want to protect the environment. It's as if you suddenly remembered my background. Marine biology professors rarely support water pollution, or, let's say, stand idly by while salmon habitat is about to be trashed by a massive development, some collection of silly, make-believe European villages, for the amusement of thugs and brigands with too much stolen money." She thrust out her jaw. "*Sirmione*, Garth? Really? Which among those so-called 'Reformed' yokels could even find the real Sirmione on a map?"

"You weren't supposed to hear about that. Lawrence should have been more discrete."

"You see what I mean? Why shouldn't someone in the position of, let us say, a Minister of the Environment have full knowledge of that sort of project? What about applications, public hearings, environmental impact assessments? What about all of that? What year, no; forget about that. What *country* do you think this is?"

"Patricia, you're blowing this out of proportion, just calm down."

"Calm down? I quit! I'm out of here, Garth! Gone!"

"If you quit now, without my express permission." Willingdon leaned back on the edge of his massive desk. "You will find yourself at the furthest recesses of the back benches, so far back that the legislative pages won't even refill your water glass."

"You don't get it, do you, Garth. Do you know what 'gone' means? It means that I'm resigning my seat, not just my post in Cabinet. Women's Issues," she repeated in a mocking tone. "Back to academia for me. You, you lured me away from my research chair when I was doing some very interesting work. I'm going back to the university, which I should never have left in the first place."

"You still need my blessing, otherwise, there might be (we'll put it this way), *repercussions*."

"No Garth." She jabbed her finger into his chest. "No 'repercussions', regardless of your delusions. I'm a *full professor*, I have *tenure*. I am not beholden to you like some real estate agent, like poor Gurjit."

"You're being silly, Patricia. There are ways..."

"No, there are *not*. The tenure contract exists for the express purpose of protecting people like me from people like you. For me to lose tenure? I'd have to get caught giving a blow job to a goat outside the Student Union Building on Remembrance Day. See you in hell, Garth!"

Patricia rushed through the building, even ignoring a few greetings as she passed. She had already descended the stone steps at the entrance and walked along the cobblestoned lane almost as far as Queen Victoria's statue before she noticed it was raining.

* * *

The door to Declan's office was closed when Carlo got in. He could see Marika through the glass in an animated discussion with Declan, waving her arms in wide, rapid arcs that made the folds of the long, oversize dress draped over her exploding physique to flap like banners. Declan remained seated at his desk, regarding Marika with a patent gaze Carlo had come to identify as 'Studied Disinterest'.

"Hey, good morning," Carlo smiled as he passed Bal's desk. She grunted with a weak scowl and then looked back down at whatever she had been working on. Samantha and Terri, both on their phones, didn't even look up to acknowledge him.

While Carlo scanned his e-mail, Marika left Declan's office and waddled towards his. Bal, Jacquie, Samantha and Terri, who each appeared to be engrossed in mesmerizing tasks as Marika passed, each rose from their seats and leaned forward to conspicuously peer into his office.

Marika shut his door behind her. "Hey." She slumped into a chair. "I have to ask you for a favour."

"Sure, what is it?"

"I need someone to drive me up to the clinic for an ultrasound this afternoon."

"Well, I'm clear this afternoon. Why, does Declan have a discovery or something?"

Marika sighed. "No. It really doesn't sound like he's got much of anything, but he said that he would be busy all day, didn't say with what. He suggested that maybe *you* could take me instead."

Carlo examined her face for any hint of emotion. "Sure, no problem."

"Thanks. Sorry to be a pest. It's at two-thirty, just up by 12th and Cambie, in one of the pavilions at VGH."

He spent the rest of the morning trying to make sense of some banking records he'd requested from the Royal Bank. Once he made note of what looked like an obvious pattern, he called Catriona's direct line and left a message. About twenty minutes later, she called him back.

"Hey, what's wrong?" Carlo asked. The voice on the other end of the line was uncharacteristically wan and raspy. "You have a cold or something?"

"No, no," she croaked. "My sister just got dumped by her fiancé so we stayed up until four drinking wine. I had a one fuck of a time of it dragging myself in here. Anyway, what's up?"

"Well, I've been looking through the stack of bank records that the Royal sent over, and then cross-referencing them with the Kitsap Bank records that you sent me."

"Poor you; sounds boring."

"Oh it is. But it looks like that guy in Quilcene, Kaczynski. It looks like he was telling the truth to your investigator."

"Yeah, *and?*"

"You didn't believe him, remember? Anyway, the pattern of deposits is consistent with him merely collecting the Wellspring in cash from rustics on the Peninsula and the west slope of the Cascades who don't have bank accounts or credit cards."

"And then where does it go? Sorry, I'm not firing on all cylinders just yet."

"No, no, and that's the interesting part. Before the split, all of the money was transferred from the Kitsap Bank into the religion's general account in Parksville, and then most of that into their main account in Vancouver, probably by their financial administrator. But afterward, it was funnelled through another account with the Royal, one set up by Émile Basaraba, and then transferred to Corvair Intermediaries."

"Basaraba," she groaned. "I run across his name all the time, but it seems to me that there is no such person."

"Oh, somebody who is operating under that name exists. He gave an EU, well, more properly, a French passport issued in Paris two years ago as secondary ID to open the Royal account. Fifty-eight years old, born in Algiers. That would have made him a young child during the colonial war."

"Well, that's all very interesting, but..."

"Sorry. Anyway, in recent months some of the money collected by Kaczynski and transferred *to* Corvair is transferred back into the Parkville account *by* Corvair. It is by no means all of it, but it has been a steady pattern."

"Really? That's weird. How much?"

"About fifty thousand a month. All of which is promptly withdrawn in cash."

"Hmmm. I've got a couple of things that Sadich wants me to look into this morning. I'll call you back, say, later this afternoon? You around?"

"Yes, call me after about five. I have to drive one of the staff to a medical appointment."

Carlo looked up to find Declan looming over him. "I just got off the phone with Hamish. It seems that the Reformed bunch is having their own Convocation next month."

"Oh? Where?"

"At the Bayshore; I mean, where else? Anyway, I trust you can afford the five-hundred-dollar, what do they call it, enrolment fee? It's due on Friday. We should have a look see to find out what they're up to."

"*Five hundred?* Yes, I guess I can, but...you want me to pay for mine myself?"

"Well, who else is going to pay for it? Me?"

"How about our clients? Charge it back as a disbursement. I'm going for *them*, not for my own spiritual enlightenment."

"Oh, I suppose."

"So I imagine you'll be coming as well."

"Nope, life is too short," Declan laughed. "Just you. Such is the lot of junior counsel, and hey; better you than me!" No mention of Marika's appointment.

Carlo continued sifting through more of the Royal Bank's documents after lunch, fighting torpor as he sorted them into discrete piles. Just before three, his phone rang. Carlo answered it before he saw the call display. Unknown Number.

"Hello, Carlo Buonsante."

"Carlo, I'm not sure if you will remember me. This is Gavin Skoff."

"Yes, yes, of course; you had a party up in Whistler a few weeks ago."

"That's right. And you might recall that you left me with one of your business cards. There's a matter, a legal matter, one that I'd like to discuss with you, when you have some time."

"Sure, just give me a second to grab a notepad."

"No, no. This is a...a delicate personal matter. I would prefer to meet in person, face to face."

"I'm sorry; I don't practice family law."

"No." Carlo could hear Gavin chuckle. "It's nothing like that. Let's just say it's a commercial matter that I'm starting to find very, very embarrassing. Look, if Declan is too cheap to send you over, I can pay your travel expenses."

"No, no, we're about due for a trip over. My girlfriend's parents live up in the Comox Valley; they've been pestering us for a visit. We could probably do next weekend. Will that be soon enough?"

"Next weekend would be splendid."

Splendid? "Good. I'll call you back to confirm when and where you would like to meet."

Not long after Carlo hung up the phone, Marika opened his office door and shuffled up to his desk. "We'd better get going."

They stopped at the reception desk. "I've got an appointment," Marika said quickly to Bal. "And Carlo is driving me. We'll be back soon." Bal exchanged glances with Jacquie, the new bookkeeper. Samantha and Terri both looked away.

The drive to the clinic was dismal. Marika sat wrapped in a light overcoat, responding to his attempts to start a conversation with one-word replies. It wasn't until they were almost there that she finally said something. "It's just up here, to the right. I don't expect that you would want to come in with me."

"I can, if you want."

"No, it doesn't...well no."

He dropped her at the front doorstep of her clinic and then found a parking space. After strolling along the stately, tree-lined backstreets surrounding the Vancouver General Hospital complex for about half an hour, he met her inside the waiting room.

"Thanks," she said quietly, almost in tears. "Where are we parked?"

"Just out here."

He helped her up into the passenger seat. "So, is everything all right?" he asked.

"Oh, the nurse gave me a stern lecture about all the weight I've gained, big surprise, but other than that, yes, everything's just fine. Declan and I are going to have a little girl." Carlo could see Marika form a forced smile as she rubbed the front of her overcoat. "Maybe now he'll be a little more excited. He already has two sons."

"Are you going to tell him now?"

"No, not yet. Look, I know; it's way past time for us to have a serious chat, alone, just the two of us, but he keeps putting me off, trying to pretend none of this is happening."

Carlo glanced at the arc swelling in front of her. "Still?"

"Yup. You know, I should feel bad for thinking this, but I don't. Sometimes he can be such a colossal dick."

* * *

Laeticia arrived early at Pinot Grigio's, and was coveting a table near the window when she saw Patricia sitting at a table next to it, nursing a glass of wine and gazing out over the Inner Harbour.

"You're here already?" Laeticia said. "But...when the 'Ledge' is in session, I'm usually waiting for you?"

"I quit."

Laeticia's eyes narrowed to mere slits. "You *what?*"

"I'm done. Didn't you see this morning's *Times-Colonist?*"

"No, I almost never read that rag. Why? What happened?"

"We'll just say that I was demoted. From a respectable Minister of the Environment to 'Ministerette'."

"Ministerette?"

"Yes. It's bullshit! I've been a full professor of marine biology, with tenure no less, since when, since before Willingdon's first stint in rehab back in the Eighties, and he takes me out of Environment for what? The ultimate thankless, useless task: Minister of Women's Issues! And my replacement? A recycled Mulroney hack from rural Québec. Oh, I really shouldn't be so mean. Felix is a nice enough man, but as unsuited for the posting as they come. He probably thinks that 'photosynthesis' is the way they get centrefolds to take up more than two pages. Anyway." She sipped her wine. "I shouldn't be pissed off at him when it's really Garth Willingdon and the Smuglets who were behind it!"

Patricia stopped talking long enough to survey the room for unwelcome pairs of ears. "And in order to appease that bunch of crooks, he really had to shuffle the Cabinet, to shake things up substantially. Your suitor, Fabién, has been plucked out of Transportation and deposited in Economic Development, not exactly a promotion. And the oddest thing (don't get me wrong, he's a good friend of mine): Lawrence, Lawrence Gollander. Now he's the Minister of Finance. The Smuglets will choke on that one!"

"Gollander, Gollander." Laeticia pondered. "Isn't he that jumpy little guy that you introduced me to back at the VisualEyes meeting that time in Bastion Square?"

"That's him. And everyone knows why Garth did it, or rather, why the Smuglets made him do it. It's not like I'm suited to lead a 'Women's Issues' ministry, which, incidentally, did not even exist until today. I detest pseudo-intellectual princesses. Holy Mother of God! The first time some young miss who stirs up her hair with a stick, has a spike poked through her nose, shrapnel in her ears and a Death's Head tattooed on her neck started whining about how badly done by she was, I'd strangle her!"

"Patricia!" Laeticia gasped.

"I'm sorry," she laughed. "I am royally pissed off, and political correctness does not come naturally to people of my generation."

"Well, it *was* a little harsh," Laeticia bowed her head, extinguishing a smile. "But you're right, it is bullshit. So what are you going to do?"

"Back to academic life, my dear. Just like you. Maybe we'll collaborate on some research someday."

"Wow," Laeticia raised her eyebrows. "I never thought you'd leave politics so soon, but good on you."

"It was a stupid idea in the first place, getting talked into being a *politician*, for Christ's sake. My mother is *still* disgusted with me. Oh well, we all make mistakes."

"So back to being a scientist. Sounds good to me. Who knows, maybe we can do some research on Atlantic salmon farms once I'm done with this sea grasses project." Laeticia drained the dregs from her glass. "What are you drinking?"

"Yellowtail. Want a glass?"

"No," Laeticia waved at the waiter. "I'm ordering a bottle."

35

Mario's flat-screen television, as big as the patio door, displayed a soccer game unfolding on the other side of the planet: one team English, the other Spanish. Laura and Laeticia were both at the kitchen table, Laura playing solitaire with real playing cards, another odd inconvenience created by sudden paralysis of her notebook computer; Laeticia engrossed in a sheaf of handwritten notes, periodically typing on her laptop. They were sharing a bottle of wine.

Canmore sat staring at the television screen. "I guess the rules must be sort of like hockey," he declared to no one in particular.

"So, Mary-O." Russell took a long pull from his beer. He and Canmore arrived uninvited shortly after dinner, and now, less than an hour later, seemed to have both taken root in their chairs in the kitchen as they drank an apparently inexhaustible supply of Budweiser. "I thought of you kids when I was watching this thing on the CBC last night. I think it could make you rich!"

Mario was the only one who saw any need to respond. "Yeah, how so?"

"Oh, just listen to this! The government, eh, well, the Hydro, anyway; those guys are paying big money for people to generate electricity. You know, water wheels, windmills. Old Man Gunderson up the street was talking about investing in solar power."

"Just like that fuckin' black strip at the top of your old calculator that doesn't work anymore!" Canmore said.

"Anyway, they call it 'Power Partnership' or some fuckin' thing. A pile of cash to be made!" Russell said. "I wish I was ten years younger. You generate the power whatever way you like, eh, and the Hydro'll buy it from you at three times the going rate."

Carlo emerged from the guest room, zipping up his jacket. "Really?" he asked Russell. "Three times the going rate?"

Canmore and Russell both turned to him in stunned surprise. It entertained Carlo to watch their reactions whenever he demonstrated an ability to speak English.

"Oh, yeah!" Russell said after a long pause. "It was on the CBC, eh."

"Where are you off to?" Laura asked Carlo, finally looking up from her cards.

"To meet up with Gavin Skoff."

"I thought that was tomorrow morning."

"No, he flagged me down just down there by the mailboxes when I was out for a run, and asked me to drop by later on. He and Tiffany have to be somewhere tomorrow morning. Whatever. At this hour, I'm expecting a good glass of wine." He turned to Mario. "Their place is this way, isn't it?"

"Yeah, four or five houses down; I never really counted. It's bigger than the other houses."

"Of course it is."

"Anyway," Russell continued after Carlo closed the sliding glass door. "So there it is: generate it any way you want. Turbines on a river, windmills, solar, whatever the fuck, and the Hydro will buy it from you at fuckin' twice the going rate."

"I thought it was three times," Laura said, still engrossed in solitaire.

"Yeah, whatever. So there you go, eh, Power Partnerships or something. Smart young people like you, you could get rich."

"Oh, and how would we do that?" Laura asked.

"Well," Canmore said. "Instead of doing those light kind of exercises that you two girls do on the deck - what do you call them? It's like a dessert."

Laeticia looked up at Laura and caught her eye. Canmore had just unwittingly admitted that he had been watching them that afternoon as they were doing yoga-inspired exercises out back. Mario scrolled through his phone messages, smiling, shaking his head.

"Yoga," Laeticia said.

"Yeah, well, you two could do something more energetic, like ride on exercise bikes, with those turbine things attached. Generate electricity, you know...and then the Hydro will pay you for it."

"I don't know, guys. A suspicious girl might think that you were trying to tell us that we're in need of, what did you call it?" Laura said in a pedantic tone. "Something more energetic?"

Canmore, who had been wearing a benign, beer-nourished smile, now bore the frenzied expression of a man who just flushed his car keys down the toilet. "No, no," he pleaded in a high-pitched whine. "Both of you are very fit, Laeticia's so slender, and you're a bit huskier, I guess, but fit...come on, I wasn't saying that you ladies..."

"Saying what, Canmore?" Laeticia asked, unsuccessfully attempting to suppress a smile.

"What do you mean 'huskier'?" Laura asked.

"Stronger," Russell interrupted. "He means stronger." He clasped Canmore's shoulder. "Don't pay this guy no attention. Sometimes he has a bit of trouble expressing himself." For the next few minutes, Canmore uttered only a few obsequious observations about the rapidly fading sunset while Russell gazed with disinterest at the soccer game as he guzzled his beer.

"Say goodnight, boys," Laeticia broke an uncomfortably long period of silence. "These guys have a bit of a drive ahead of them in the morning and we both have to work."

"Sure, have a good one, eh." Russell quickly left his chair. "Hey, Mary-O! Do you mind if we leave a couple of Buds in your fridge until the next time we're over?"

"Sure." Mario avoided looking at either of the girls. "No problem."

As soon as they were gone, Mario opened the basement door. "I'm going downstairs to do a bit of work."

"Just keep your music low," Laeticia said. "We don't want to hear it."

It was a warm, still evening. The report of crickets added to the peaceable charm of the moment as Carlo walked along the beach to Gavin's house. Vancouver's lights in the distance lent the eastern sky a ghostly white glow. Gavin was sitting on his deck, nodding to the sound of waves as they gently touched the pebble beach in front of his house. "Carlo!" Gavin called out to him as he walked past. "Over here."

Gavin extended his hand to greet him. "Thank you for coming over. Let's go over to my office." The office looked like it had been built by the former owners as a guest suite, separated from the main house by a short breezeway. He had refashioned what had probably once been a bedroom overlooking the beach into a small boardroom. "Have a seat. I'll be back in a second. I have a Barbera d'Asti I'd like you to try."

Tiffany momentarily appeared in the breezeway, as if leaping. "Oh, hi...hi, Carlo, isn't it? Gav', I'm just heading out. I'll pick up coffee on the way home. And Carlo, you and your girlfriend should let us know when you're coming over next time. You should come over for dinner! Gavin could grill up some halibut."

"Oh, sounds great. Barbequed halibut; I didn't get too much of it in Italy."

"Good! It's so rare that we have people over for dinner." She rolled up a yoga mat. "Sorry, I've got to run. I have to teach an evening yoga class in Nanaimo."

Gavin poured two generous glasses of wine displaying a deep, satisfying purple colour. They both took a sip. "So, what do you think?"

"This is excellent!" It was several gradations above the cheap French table wine Carlo and Laura shared over dinner every night. 'Chateau Kootenay Loop', they called it, named after a bleak transit interchange in East Vancouver. "Where did you get it?"

"My post office box in Bellingham. I joined a wine club that I found in an ad in *Harpers*."

"Hmmm...I'm surprised that you would do anything with *Harpers* except burn it!" Gavin shook with raucous, masculine laughter. To Carlo's unease, his laughter died much sooner than expected.

Gavin turned to look out at the waves. The moon had started to rise over the Ballenas Islands. "You know, I guess, well, despite my reputation, I'm old school. I know that things are not done in the conventional way around here. I mean, this area, where we are now, was supposedly developed by this crazy Frenchman whose views were, well, unorthodox, let's say. He sold waterfront property a good bit lower than market value, back in the Sixties. Free water." Gavin shook his head. "But (from what I've been told), he was generous, active in Shrine charities, not like..." Gavin fell silent. "Anyway, look at this; tell me if you know what it is." He handed Carlo a cardboard Molson Canadian coaster. Carlo flipped it over to see what was written on the back.

79.120.86.255

"That's an IP, sorry, Internet Protocol, a Russian one by the look of it."

"Russian?"

"Yes. I learned to spot IPs from Russian sites when I worked at the bank. It's a 'tell' that someone is, let's just say, not exactly who they say they are. It's especially amusing when you receive a proposal from someone who claims to be Belgian or something but it has a Russian IP."

"Russian. It's come to this. Anyway, look, just as I was saying, I'm old school. Someone, it's not important who it was at this point, just wrote this down from memory on a *beer coaster* for

Christ's sake (and shitty beer at that, he could have at least found a Grolsch one or something). Investment vehicles are supposed to be supported by a detailed prospectus, public disclosure statements, proper documentation, not all this cloak and dagger bullshit."

"I'm sorry, you're going to have to be a lot more specific about your stake in all of this," Carlo said.

"Okay. I've already invested about a million, okay, let's be honest, closer to two, all of it, I don't know, let's just describe it as being under the trusteeship of the guy who handed me that coaster."

"What kind of an investment is it?" Carlo pulled a notepad and pen out of his briefcase.

"No, no," Gavin said. "Please, no notes. It's a piece of a real estate venture, and a big one at that. It takes up a healthy chunk of the central Island."

"I've heard a few rumours about something like that."

"Really? The people behind it think that they've kept it all very 'hush-hush'. That was his excuse for giving me this silly coaster when I asked for a bit more information about the project I'd already sunk a fortune in."

"Are you concerned that you've been swindled; some sort of Ponzi scheme?"

"Swindled? The thought has occurred to me. But it's not a Ponzi scheme: I have yet to see so much as a shiny penny in dividends, or *any* return, for that matter. But yes, I am concerned about the safety of my investment. I'm also concerned, about, well, let's just say the nature of the "project" itself." He rummaged through the drawer in front of him until he found a chequebook. "I would like to retain you."

"Retain me? But why? For what?"

"For the same reason that anyone ever hires you guys. Find out what the hell is going on and clean up the mess. And as for the solicitor who usually handles this sort of thing for me? We'll just say that he...he lacks objectivity when it comes to this venture. Ten thousand should be a good start on the retainer, I expect. And I know how this works. The old buzzard bills you out at what, three hundred and fifty dollars an hour?"

"Four hundred."

Gavin grimaced and filled out a cheque. "How long will it take you to figure it out?"

"I don't know. I'm not going to sugar-coat it; it might take a while."

"What does that mean?

"A while."

He detached a cheque and handed it to Carlo. "Anyway, we'll see how far that gets us."

Carlo could have found his way to the Russian IP address easily enough, but not without being detected. Mario, on the other hand, had no problem navigating the web with anonymity. Once he was back at the beach cottage, he found Laeticia and Laura on the deck. Laura was sitting against the railing and painting her toenails underneath the patio light. "Where were you? It's been almost two hours. We were getting worried."

"Stop it. It's not as if Gavin Skoff is a serial killer." He heard Laeticia snort. "I see that your two suitors are gone."

"We had to evict them," Laura said.

"Good. Where's Mario?"

"He's working on something down in his dungeon, listening to some of his disgusting music," Laeticia said.

Carlo descended into the basement. Mario had fashioned it as a workspace, a broad plywood table surrounded by an array of computer screens and light-emitting black boxes. A pair of speakers suspended from the rafters throbbed with Gallbladder Sludge, an alternative band from Victoria, playing a tune that Carlo remembered as one of the most ridiculous songs ever written.

Mario reached over to a computer mouse to kill the volume when he saw Carlo come in. "So what did Gavin want?"

"Such poetry. Anyway, believe it or not, he retained me."

"Seriously? Wait a minute. Did he get rear-ended or something? He's a really shitty driver."

"No, no; and that's why I'm here. I need your help. Computer stuff, that sort of..." A Skype session erupted on one of the screens. A guy with a shaved head, a teenager by the look of him, had a question for Mario. Their unfolding dialogue in computerese was as unintelligible to Carlo as if it were in Mandarin.

Once the boy's face abruptly disappeared from the screen, Mario turned to Carlo. "Now, what were you on about?"

"On about." Carlo waved his arms in exasperation. "I have a Russian IP address that I need anonymous access to."

Mario shot him a bemused grin. "Hiding a porn addiction from Laura?"

"Fuck off. I already told you. It's work-related."

"Hmm. Let me see it." Carlo handed him his scribbling of what was on the back of Gavin's beer coaster. "You're right," Mario said. "It *is* Russian. So, do you know what this is all about?"

"Real estate. So now you're bound by solicitor-client privilege; you're my consulting expert. And our client has about two million riding on this."

"No shit? Okay, well, we'll put this through a server that will assign us an American IP address. Illinois good enough?"

"How about Alabama?"

"Sure. Why not? Alabama."

After a few seconds, a screen appeared dominated by four large icons. It lacked the visual appeal of most contemporary websites; it was so spare and artless that it reminded Carlo, dredging the depths of his memory, of film strips shown in one classroom or another in elementary school.

"What's this all about?" Mario asked.

"A supposed real estate development covering a good chunk of the eastern Island between here and Courtenay."

"First I've heard of it." Mario opened the module indicated by the 'Showcase – Completed Communities' icon. It brought them to a black screen with six crudely displayed place names in yellow lettering, each one a link to another web page.

Fiorenza	**Salzburg**
Sirmione	**Aix-les-Bains**
Dinant	**Oxbridge**

"Holy shit!" Mario cried out in surprise. "They've actually finished some of this?" He clicked on 'Sirmione'.

Four pictures appeared in the top half of the screen, each displaying different aspects of a compact town along the shores of a small lake, a collection of white, pink and orange stone buildings and sprawling lakeside villas. A brief written description took up the bottom third of the page.

> *The 'Sirmione' portion of the project was inspired by the Lake Garda region of northern Italy, which has enchanted visitors and residents alike since the days of ancient Rome. It is linked to the 'Dinant' subsection of the project by both a picturesque mountain road and a short*

funicular railway. Please ensure that all invitees to sales presentations are made to understand that all units in this subsection are fully subscribed.

Carlo looked over each of the four photographs. It was as if someone had removed an entire village along one of the Italian lakes and transplanted it on the shore of a tarn in the Island mountains. The lake was a natural wonder in itself, its waters a deep turquoise. He wished that he had visited it, perhaps to spend a couple of crisp nights in a tent on its shores, before it became part of a freakish theme park for the upper crust.

Carlo tapped on the screen. "Click on 'Dinant'."

It took a few seconds for the page to load. Again, a series of four pictures filled the upper portion of the screen, one of them a location map reminiscent of a Michelin tourist guide. The remaining three depicted a pleasant riverside town at the base of a tall rock face.

Dinant is located along a swift flowing river filled with native species of trout. It is inspired by its namesake in the Ardennes Forest, a sylvan region of wooded hills straddling north-western France and southern Belgium. The site forms a rural hub and is readily accessible from the regional centre of Fiorenza and the education and library district of Oxbridge by light rail or two-lane highway. Please ensure that all invitees to sales presentations are made to understand that all units in this subsection are fully subscribed.

"'*Fiorenza*'?" Mario laughed. "Are they trying to say 'Firenze'?"

"Somebody in their ranks must be a student of Italian history. That's what they called it six or seven hundred years ago."

"You know, it's amazing. They've created this monstrosity covering a big part of the central Island, and nobody seems to know about it. It's all been put together under everyone's noses."

Carlo was still stunned, staring at the computer screen without blinking. "It sure seems that way." He pointed to the Michelin-style map. "Hey, can you print that out?"

"Yes; I can read into a .pdf and even print it out in colour."

"Cool. What's this icon, the one with all of the gears?"

The fourth item, bearing the title "The Work In Process" led to a page with an array of sixteen thumbnail photographs, each showing men and machines in the course of some sort of construction project in a forest, men operating bulldozers or wielding various implements; chainsaws, picks, acetylene torches, shovels.

Mario leaned over and peered at one of the thumbnails. "What the...let's look at this one. I'll make it a bit bigger." A man in coveralls standing in a deep trench, brandishing a shovel, soon filled the screen, his body visible only from the chest up.

"What the fuck?" Mario shouted. "That's Canmore!"

36

The First Annual Congress of the Reformed Striationist Community opened at noon in the Hollyburn Room of the Bayshore Hotel, a long-established luxury complex on Vancouver's Coal Harbour waterfront. The dimpled young hostess at the registration kiosk outside the ballroom issued Carlo a name tag and an attendees' kit, a portfolio stuffed with brochures. Once inside, he browsed exhibit to exhibit. The public address system piped a taunting verse of Doug and the Slugs' "Too Bad" into the ballroom at a low, tasteful volume.

The room was filled almost to capacity, the crowd indistinguishable from the Canadian Bar Association conventions he remembered from back in Toronto. Everyone was dressed in sumptuous wool suits. If there was a notable absence of synthetic fibres, there was a concomitant dearth of hand-woven hemp. As Carlo looked over an expansive wall map of the Salish Sea, the coast of southern British Columbia and Puget Sound, displayed for no obvious purpose, another young hostess approached him with a tray full of champagne flutes.

"Sparkling Norman apple juice, sir?"

"Why not?"

Carlo sipped the effervescent liquid on his way past another row of booths, displays of hand-hewn runes, aromatherapy potions and vials of sundry herbal extracts, useless items otherwise easily found at farmers' markets. Nothing Carlo had encountered so far seemed to be uniquely Striationist, nothing symbolising of the awesome power of the Earth, no icons of reverence for inelegant gouges in granite. But something else surprised him. Where the originalist branch of the religion, at their Convocation, made frequent, disparaging reference to the offshoot, here, it was as if the Orthodox faction didn't exist.

The plenary session, where a few Reformed luminaries were scheduled to speak, took place over a buffet luncheon held in the ballroom next door. Carlo was seated at a table near the back with four women whose nametags identified them as journalists, and a Catholic priest who was eyeing Carlo's nametag.

"I'm going to go out on a limb here, young man, and assume that you're Catholic," the priest said.

"Yes, Father."

"Where do you attend Mass?"

"Actually, Father," Carlo said. "I haven't been to Mass since I was twelve."

After that, everyone at the table did their best to ignore one another while they waited for their invitation to join the buffet line. Carlo was amazed by the absence of any local food, in an epoch where local celebrities unctuously vowed never to eat anything that was not grown, caught or slaughtered more than a hundred kilometres distant from their front doorstep. Marlin. Swordfish. Branzino. Grouper. Chilean sea bass. No salmon among the fish selections; the meat dishes included farmed wild boar from some place in the Abruzzi region, and Breton lamb.

The overhead lights dimmed and a speaker appeared at the podium. Carlo strained to see who it was. *Son of a bitch, it's Fabién Lerche!* Carlo, of course, had seen him many times on the local television news, one of the youngest members of the provincial cabinet, but Fabién, just two or three years older, had walked the same halls at UBC when Carlo was a student there. They didn't actually know one another, but Carlo remembered him as a resolute but unsuccessful student politician, someone whose odd political views, a blend of libertarian economics and strident sexism, immunised him from electoral victory.

Fabién apparently felt no need to introduce himself. "Good afternoon, ladies and gentlemen, you followers of Reformed Striationism. In the past twelve months..." (A time period which, Carlo noted, accorded roughly with the schism) "...our religion has prospered and attracted many new adherents. It will not be long before Reformed Striationism becomes the religion of choice for those who have selected this blessed piece of real estate, British Columbia, as their home, and for those who aspire to do so. We who enter this faith do so because we are elect, the ones who carry this society in its entirety, *carpe diem*!" He continued for about forty minutes, heedless that most people in the audience started consulting their phones. And then, quiet of voice, he turned to the audience and gesticulated as if he were the conductor of a symphony. "And so, we must always remember *to keep our currency strong*." With that, Fabién brought his lecture to an end. "Our Administrator of the Treasure, Émile Basaraba, would now like to address you about our success, spiritual and financial. "Upward and to the right!"

"Upward and to the right," the crowd chanted.

Carlo had been mystified about both Basaraba's role and his existence. His name appeared throughout the file, usually in the form of his signature, but this was the first time that Carlo had been able to confirm that he was indeed an actual human being. The room fell silent as he started to speak. Closely-cropped black hair, an ample admixture of grey.

"Many of you know me; I see many familiar faces." English was obviously a language he learned in adulthood, his accent a deep, resonant, wine-advertisement French. "In the months since last October, our religion has done exceptionally well financially." Just like the rest of them, he did not utter even a hint that the Orthodox bunch existed. A screen mounted behind him illuminated with the title 'Treasure (Net Assets)'. "Our Treasure has more than doubled in just a year!" He pointed to the next image, a montage of a long glacial striation artfully fashioned into an ascending line graph. "Our religion has been blessed by the life force of the Earth and its geology; its magnetic and spiritual field, with the accumulation of almost one billion dollars!" He raised his fist. "Upward and to the right!"

"Upward and to the right!" the audience repeated, this time with enthusiasm.

Carlo hastily finished his lunch, washing it down with water rather than paying a ten-dollar surcharge for a glass of red wine, two dollars less for Effervescent Elderberry. As he endured part of the afternoon plenary, something to do with the 'synergy' created by intense positive thinking (and the ostensible lessons of a proprietary podcast) when marketing bottled water from coastal streams, Carlo's attention started to wane. He started to rummage through the portfolio the hostess had issued to him. There were few references to the religion or any of the assumed tenets of their creed. Instead, it was filled with brochures, most of them advertising resorts and secluded cabin rentals on inlets and sloughs near scoured rock slopes. A logging outfit from Campbell River included an exhortation to allow less restrictive logging techniques to promote erosion, which, the pamphlet promised, would expose impressive striations.

Carlo decided to finish the afternoon with the aromatherapy workshop. He had expected it to be more informative, perhaps a discussion of some of curative benefits of the many herbs and succulents that grew in nearby forests, but it turned out to be a tawdry live commercial performed by a woman from Madeira Park who bottled ostrich ferns after she did little more than put them through a blender. "And remember," the supposed herbalist told the crowd in a high-pitched, saccharine whine. "You gentlemen who occasionally have your embarrassing *issues.*" She clasped her hands together. "If you spread FeistyFern on your morning toast every day, you'll see an incredible upness of your organism!" Carlo felt relief when his cell phone started to vibrate. He crept quietly out of the small banquet room to answer it.

It was Thomas. "*Signore!*"

He passed through the main foyer, where hotel staff were filling tables with glasses and uncorked bottles of Effervescent Elderberry, in anticipation of the gala dinner which would have entailed a seven-hundred-dollar surcharge. "Oh, hi, Thomas. Thanks for rescuing me," Carlo gathered some additional pamphlets and stuffed them into his briefcase.

"Well, did you learn anything today, young man?"

"There have been days when I've learned less."

Thomas laughed. "Well, after the truth sets you free, you might want to meet up with me at the Duke of York. I'm on my way there."

"That's the best news I've heard all day."

He thought it over during the walk to the pub. Why the schism? More established religions had remained unified for decades even if the faithful found themselves at odds over birth control and homosexuality. It seemed silly for a religion to split because of a difference of opinion about how to best assimilate the power of a glacial striation. No, the Reformed bunch, none of them truly in search of spiritual succour, identified an opportunity, a mother lode, but the religion as it was when they found it had proven impervious to a hostile takeover. And a religion it remained: such institutions, even those who divided themselves in two, collected their income without the inconvenience of having to pay taxes.

When Carlo arrived at the Duke of York, most of the tables were filled despite the fact that it was just after five o'clock. It took him a while to find Thomas, who was sitting at a table in a nook towards the back, reading *The Economist.*

"Good God, you're here already. You must walk at a frightful pace," Thomas said. "Normally, I don't leave the office for the refuge of the pub until at least five-thirty, usually six, but today the office was unbearable."

"Was it?" Carlo placed his pint glass on the table. "I mean, more than it usually is these days?"

"Well, yes." Thomas rubbed his reading glasses with a cloth before he put them back in their case. "Marika, we'll just say that hormones and God knows what else have started to assert themselves. She was in tears most of the morning. And the other women in the office? Always huddled in clandestine conferences, separating only to direct knowing glances at one another." He held Carlo in a steady stare. "The tension is building. Something is definitely coming to a head."

"Yes. It's true; I can shut my office door and ignore it, but the atmosphere of the office keeps getting more and more unpleasant."

"And I think you'll agree with me. It's the change in Marika, her *situation* (let's call it that) is quite plainly the source of all this disharmony." Thomas took a sip from his pint. "You know, until a little more than a month ago, I was satisfied that I was simply observing yet another depressing instance of a young beauty in the midst of casually eating herself round, uncommon enough, it's true, in these fitness-obsessed parts, but I still see it all too frequently. But now it's plainly obvious that there is a more accurate explanation for her newly domestic physique."

"You might say that it's obvious."

"And the office is getting worse, for some reason. You know, it's bad enough when you're out, but it's even more painful to watch when you're actually there. Bal seems to be profoundly displeased with you. You were once such friends! And the new bookkeeper, what's her name?"

"Jacquie."

"Yes, Jacquie. Otherwise a pleasant, cheerful girl. She seems to *hate* you. So does the South African girl these days, for that matter. Did you forget to bring coffee up for them one day, or something?"

Carlo opted to steer the conversation to where Thomas seemed determined to take it. "Well, as far as I can tell, they've all drawn the conclusion that Marika's baby is mine, and I don't know, maybe you have as well. That seems to be..."

"Oh, don't be preposterous, Carlo!" Thomas interrupted him in a sharp, scolding tone. "I am *not* one of those silly young girls. I've always known very well that you did not play any role in creating her current condition."

"That's very euphemistic of you."

"Well, I'm English. And I can tell from the way you speak to one another that you have never been intimately involved, and (I must admit) it was not until I met — I'm sorry, I can't recall her name. Oh, yes. It's Laura, isn't it?"

"Yes."

"Laura. Yes, it was not until I bumped into you two in Cordova Street that I finally understood your forbearance in that regard. Perhaps not in recent months, of course, but most certainly in the days after you were first hired; back then Marika was a most striking girl. But you two certainly seem to be close friends."

"We are."

"It *is* a little strange, I must say. She never speaks of any boyfriend, and certainly nobody matching that description has ever come round the office (which is probably why those young ladies jumped to the conclusion that they have). But they haven't been around as long as I have." He leaned forward toward Carlo with a conspiratorial leer. "I expect you know the identity of the overjoyed father-to-be."

"Thomas, I really don't..."

"I know; I'm sorry, I really don't expect you to betray a confidence. I assume that you've been sworn to secrecy."

"Come on, Thomas."

"Well, in that case, allow a venerable (I am not about to call myself 'old') gentleman to make a perhaps irrelevant observation on the human condition. All too often, people are drawn sexually to people who are not only unsuitable, but are actually toxic and dangerous to them. And despite making a clean break of it once, and on occasion, multiple times, the relationship always eventually reforms. These patterns, I have seen them replay over a period of years, even decades." He stared again at Carlo. "Have you ever heard of such behaviour?"

"Yes, I've seen it happen from time to time."

"Now I hope for her sake that Marika didn't fall into that sort of trap, taking up with an *old*, discarded beau." He enunciated the word 'old' in a dramatic baritone. "Only to have the reunion produce a child."

Carlo folded his arms. "I'm sorry, Thomas, but I am not going to continue this conversation."

Thomas held Carlo in an analytical stare and then looked away. "I was afraid of that," he whispered.

Both of them sat in silence. "Would you like another? Look," Thomas said quietly, "I can assure you that this topic of conversation has been exhausted."

"Sure, why not?" Carlo waved to the waiter. After a short discussion about the chance that the Azzurri, the Italian national soccer team, would repeat their success in the 2006 World Cup the next time around, Carlo remembered that he wanted to ask Thomas about something that had piqued his curiosity. "Oh, I was wondering, was there a guy named Nathan Brooke who worked for Declan?"

"Yes. He left about three, maybe four years ago. A rather insufferable fellow. But he and Declan remain good pals, as far as I know. The rugby connection. Why do you ask?

"The Canada Law List still includes him as a member of the firm."

"Good God, no." Thomas shuddered. "Those days are long since over."

....37

One unusually wet Monday morning in September, a grey panel van bearing the logo 'Mid-Island Construction' rumbled off the Gabriola Island ferry and continued down the road to the marina at the far end of the island, provoking the curiosity of onlookers as it passed. Once the van arrived at a parcel of waterfront land which (as everyone on the island knew) had just been purchased by some untrustworthy numbered company from Vancouver, its four occupants got out and erected a large sign, with brown letters in a playful, modish font against an olive background.

Coming Soon!
The Eyrie at Baneberry Ridge
Luxury condominium towers with superb ocean views
Reserve today at 604.683.2376
www.hirisegabriola.com

Later the same week, two other contingents arrived at the site. The first, an electrical crew, swiftly installed a large transformer on a flat area overlooking the water. Next, an excavation company showed up, and started digging two narrow trenches linking the adjacent hydro right of way with the transformer. Curious residents, who normally left the forgotten locale off their daily itinerary, made frequent detours in order to keep an eye on what was going on. Within days, the inevitable proliferation of handwritten public notices, advertising meetings of community activists who were organising in opposition to the project, appeared on telephone poles and neighbourhood bulletin boards. Gavin was actually surprised how little time it took them to link the project to him. A telltale headline appeared in the next edition of *Island Tides,* one of the newspapers that circulated throughout the Gulf Islands.

Vile ideologue behind Gabriola scheme

Gavin was even more surprised by how soon the opposition to the development boiled over from the island itself to the world at large, prompting admonishing remarks from people as far away as Kowloon and Zagreb. A painter who had achieved global renown since he left the Gulf Islands and moved to Berlin identified the Baneberry Ridge development as yet another example of the gleefully destructive spirit being brought to bear on the Edenic northwest coast of North America by a cabal of professional vandals who could not pass from this earth soon enough. Other commentary was more prosaic. The Islands Trust, the provincial government agency that regulated development on the dispersed Gulf Islands archipelago, expressed suitably muted outrage that the prospective developer had advertised sales without even having the courtesy to apply for a building permit.

Gavin hired contactors known to be reliably tight-lipped, with instructions to look as if they were keeping themselves busy with site preparation, when they were instead laying the conduits needed to supply power to the underwater electrodes that Davidson would eventually install. As the acrimony intensified, work on the electrical connections continued apace. Gavin paid almost quadruple the going rate so that the people on site would work in the middle of the night, to thwart those who might have been otherwise motivated to lie down in front of the equipment. The locally based opposition group, which had named itself 'Garry Oak Brigade' in honour of the tree species that dominated the property, had threatened to seek an injunction. Donations from all over North America swelled the Brigade's bank account, permitting them to produce television commercials that depicted the project as the utmost in hideous excess. Their signature advertisement featured a steam roller crushing a meadow filled with eager little squirrels and robins' eggs.

With some reluctance, Gavin admitted to himself that he would have to attend the public meeting scheduled for the following Friday night, to be held in what passed for a ballroom at a local resort. He briefly considered enlisting Tiffany's assistance, but, thinking it over, it occurred to him that she would have been very likely to side with the protesters, an unnecessary irritant to domestic harmony. He didn't want to involve Carlo, either. As much as the presence of a Vancouver lawyer would give his scheme more credibility, he expected that Carlo would decline the retainer once he explained what he was up to. Besides, Gaskin hired him out at a ruinous hourly rate.

So he went to the meeting by himself. Two people, one a man in a cardigan, probably a Nanaimo professional, and the other, a woman with long, untamed hair and unbleached cotton clothing more characteristic of the islands, convened the gathering of more than a hundred. Gavin, who was seated at the very back of the hall, was in equal measure both proud and aghast that they each spat out his name as if he were a war criminal or child molester. After their harangue, a duet that lasted about fifteen minutes, they relinquished the microphone to the audience at large.

The first presenter was a woman in her sixties with long, blondish hair and bright eyes, who spoke in luxuriant, emotive tones.

"The ridge, it is a supernatural place. I have a personal relationship with the stonecrop, the camas, the trees." She fell silent, raising her hands. Her eyes grew improbably wide. "There is a grove of old growth Douglas Fir, near the water. They sing to me! They sing a delightful, joyous song!" She lapsed into a high-pitched caterwauling of oscillating volume. Most of the audience clapped in rhythm.

A couple draped in discordant, brightly coloured clothing next approached the microphone. The man spoke first.

"We are members of the Striationist faith."

Oh great. More of these fucking people. Gavin shuddered.

"The true Striationist faith," the woman continued in a strident voice. "Not the bandits who call themselves 'Striationists'!"

The man started gesticulating with forceful thrusts, in contrast to his calm tone. "The striations on Baneberry Ridge..."

"...or Camas Plateau, as it used to be known," his partner interrupted.

"...are among the most powerful and spiritually replenishing on the south coast. It would be deeply sinful to befoul them with a condominium infestation."

The woman took over. "Our religion does not have a well-developed concept of sin, or of evil personified, a demonic figure like Satan. Now that we're being forced to persevere through this dire struggle, I believe that the Striationist faith has found its Beast: Gavin Skoff!" The crowd erupted in a wave of cheering and applause.

Gavin decided that he'd arrived at the most opportune moment for him to rise and address the audience. He made his way to the podium and smiled as the crowd grew silent. Despite his relative fame and his frequent appearances on American cable television news, nobody seemed to recognize him.

"It isn't very often that a guy gets an intro like that. Please allow me to introduce myself. I'm Gavin Skoff."

To his astonishment, the crowd did not immediately hiss and keen in revulsion. "The Baneberry Ridge project," Gavin spoke in an anodyne, viscous voice. "Will be environmentally friendly and include cutting-edge technology and state-of-the-art development techniques. I propose to preserve as much as eight percent of the property as parkland. And there will be immediate economic benefit to the island. My economic consultants estimate that the project will create as many as three full-time jobs."

The audience quickly abandoned its Canadian reserve. "Oh, bullshit!" an elderly lady in the front row shouted at him.

"We don't need plunderers around here, especially amiable ones," bellowed a shaggy man near the back of the room. Everyone started shouting uncomplimentary remarks at him. The tree singer rose to prompt a spirited communal chant.

"Save the ridge! Save the ridge!"

Gavin escaped from the meeting and drove back to a bed and breakfast on the other side of the island where Tiffany was waiting for him. The following week, after receiving assurances from his contractor that all of the electrical conduits were installed and secure, Gavin placed a simple, spare black and white advertisement in *Island Tides*, *The Nanaimo Daily Free Press*, and about a half-dozen other local papers.

The developers of the proposed Baneberry Ridge project have considered the very eloquent and moving public sentiment against the proposal. Under the circumstances we will be putting the condominium proposal on hold, pending further consultation. We thank the people of Gabriola Island for their participation.

GAVIN SKOFF

38

Carlo soon lived to regret answering his phone. A male elder, whose voice was of a timbre that sounded gravelly and whiny at the same time, taunted him from the other end of the line. "I am assuming that I'm talking to Boonstart — Carlos Boonstart. What are you, Filipino or something?"

"Who is this?"

"Bernard Mackay. In case you've forgotten, I represent the Reformed Striationists."

"I know who you are, Mr. Mackay."

"Well, then you also probably know that I'm one of the senior members of the Vancouver Bar. And someone like you, still quite wet behind the ears, but with no lack of eagerness, should pay attention to a Queen's Counsel. This action of yours against the Reformed Striationists, it's nonsense based on absolutely nothing. We'll accept a discontinuance now, but if you wait too long, my people might lose their sense of humour and demand their costs. You're familiar with the concept of costs, aren't you, Mr. Boondocks?" He wheezed musically into the phone.

"Buonsante. Indeed I am. And I might be inclined to seek those instructions. I seriously doubt that I might ever make that recommendation, but if I do, it won't be until after the examinations for discovery are complete."

"Well? When the hell is *that* going to be?"

Carlo paused, unsure of what to make of Bernard Mackay. "Mr. McHarg and a representative of the Royal Bank will be examined next week. Our respective clients won't be examined until sometime in March. I trust that you will be producing your treasurer, Mr. Basaraba, as the Reformed representative?"

"Look," Mackay shouted. "Don't you try to dictate who we produce!"

"That's fine, Mr. McKay," Carlo replied in a gelid tone. "If you produce someone else to give evidence, we will simply add Mr. Basaraba as a party. Good afternoon."

Carlo walked over to Declan's office, where he found him surrounded by unruly stacks of black three-ring binders filled with medical records. "I was just on the phone with this guy named Bernard Mackay, he's on for the Reformed bunch. He sounded like he was drunk."

Declan looked up at Carlo, startled, his eyes magnified by formidable reading glasses. "Bernie Mackay? He's always sounded like that. Although..." Declan looked at his watch. "At this hour, maybe he was. What did he want?"

"He wanted to talk us out of our action, and, get this: he threatened to seek *costs!*"

"*Oh no!*" Declan affected a terrified squeal. "Not *costs!*" Both of them erupted in fits of laughter. "How's that all going, anyway? Discoveries? Trial dates?"

Carlo rested his hands on the back of one of Declan's chairs. "The discoveries are split up. Two are next week, the two branches of the Striationists are in March, and you'll have to show up to those. Trial's in two years; it took us a while to find a twenty-day block of time in

Vancouver."

"No doubt. The discoveries next week - which reporter's office?"

"Bourassa."

"Oh, good. Classy place: they never have stale jelly beans."

The examination for discovery, or simply "discovery", is a necessary step in most civil actions. Sometimes fractious, but more often tedious, it allows parties to the lawsuit to grill one another under oath before trial, an effective way to avoid unpleasant surprises. In the Striationist file, as in almost every other, the examinations were to be held in a private office, staffed by a team of court reporters who deftly transcribed the parties' evidence.

Bourassa Reporting, a collection of boardrooms that occupied almost an entire floor of the HSBC Building in central Vancouver, was more elegant than most. Their boardroom tables were either chestnut or polished oak. Black and ochre reproductions, vintage maps of Paris, Madrid and Rome, hung on the corridor walls above urns of (organic) coffee custom roasted on Saltspring Island. Platters offering artisanal cookies and pastries were flanked by giant glass cylinders filled with almonds and cashews. There was even a balsamic vinegar dispenser. Carlo didn't see any jelly beans.

He arrived a few minutes early, while the court reporter was in the midst of setting up. The examination room, decorated with Impressionist prints, would have easily accommodated four times the number of people expected. A long table dominated the room. A young, pale woman with limp red hair was sitting at the far end by the window.

"Good morning," he said loud enough for her to hear him.

She flinched, startled. "Oh, good morning. I'm from Mr. Mackay's office, his student. Teresa Connolly." She walked across the room and extended her hand.

"Carlo Buonsante. I'm here from Gaskin Barristers."

He left to fetch a cup of coffee after piling some binders from his litigation bag on the table. On his way back, he almost collided with someone who appeared to be about his age, with gelled short brown hair and a ruddy, bloated face that Carlo found unsettling. He looked like he had been rudely scrubbed with a coarse brush and then steamed.

"Are you Declan Gaskin?" he asked Carlo.

"No, I'm his associate, Carlo Buonsante."

"Jon Angus," he said as they shook hands. "I'm on for the Royal."

Ian McHarg was the only witness scheduled to be examined that morning, but it was already a couple of minutes past the appointed time. Carlo browsed his notes but Angus tried to make conversation. "So, where did you go to law school?"

"UBC," Carlo said, looking up from his notes.

Oh, I'd just assumed you were from Ontario. I went to Dalhousie. UBC, eh?" He inhaled through his teeth. "You wouldn't happen to know a guy named David Brenner, would you?"

Carlo laughed. "Not only do I know him; he's one of my best friends."

Angus fell silent and stared at his knuckles. After a few minutes he came back to life. "He's almost fifteen minutes late."

"Excuse me?" Carlo asked.

"McHarg. He's almost fifteen minutes late. In *Port Neville Fisheries v. Warkentin Financial,* Judge Stone held that in this age of cell phones, the standard half-hour rule was obsolete, that the other party doesn't have..."

"He's unrepresented, Jon, and as far as I can tell, he's coming here all the way from Scotland. I think that even Judge Stone might cut McHarg a bit of slack. What do you think?"

"I guess you might have a point." Jon mumbled and sunk into his chair.

Ian McHarg arrived ten minutes later, with two or three day's beard growth on his face, his shirt half-tucked into his jeans. He was a tall, bulky man in his late forties, with longish dark brown hair. "Sorry I'm late," he bellowed. "I'm staying on the Island. As always, the ferries are a total pain in the ass!"

Carlo rose to shake hands with him. "Carlo Buonsante." Angus and the articling student at the end of the table both introduced themselves.

"Well, Mr. Angus!" McHarg bellowed. "It's a good thing that there's at least one other Scot in the room!"

"Are you sure that you want to continue without a lawyer?" Carlo said.

"Yes. I consulted with a solicitor a couple of days ago, a lady down in Victoria. I don't think that I need anyone to represent me. You will probably agree once you hear what I have to say."

"Okay. In that case, let's get started. Do you want to swear on the Bible or affirm your evidence?"

"I'll swear on the Bible."

Odd. He'd never seen any of the other people connected with the Orthodox bunch fail to take offence when asked to swear on the Bible. The reporter finished administering the oath and adjusted his recording equipment.

Jon broke the silence. "You do realize that you are now under oath?"

"Yes," Ian replied, as if to a child.

The reporter nodded at Carlo, prompting him to begin. "Could you state your full name for the record?"

"Ian James McHarg."

"Your current address?"

"Until about three weeks ago, Upper Apartment, 23 Balmoral Road, Aberdeen, Scotland. But now I'm, well *we're*, temporarily at 2715 Island Highway, Qualicum Bay. I live there with my girlfriend, Ulela Shriver. I understand you two have met."

"What is your occupation?"

"Chartered accountant."

"It is my understanding that you were once connected with the Striationist religion?"

"Yes, that's correct. My cousin, Ruairi Davidson, was, well, I suppose *is*, one of the Council of Elders. He introduced me to the religion when he was over visiting us in Scotland, a few years ago." McHarg turned away and sighed. "There was a time when I found it all, well, magical and fascinating."

"I take it that you are no longer one of the faithful?"

"No, and I am most ashamed to say that it took five years before it finally dawned on me that it was all a bunch of rubbish."

"You were the Master of the Treasure?"

McHarg shook with a resonant, masculine guffaw. "Yes, I know, it all sounds really quite stupid. After old Abercrombie died, I took over the position. Ruairi thought that with my experience in accounting; well, what could I say to him? I didn't think that I could refuse."

Carlo questioned him for about half an hour about the financial structure of the religion, the customary flow of funds, who made financial decisions and other details about how the religion handled its money. "Who had signing authority over the religion's accounts?"

"Well, that was a little complicated. I did, for all petty cash amounts under five thousand. For anything larger it required my signature and those of two Elders or a designate."

"What do you mean by 'a designate'?"

"Well, that would be one of the faithful who was so trusted by the Council of Elders that they invited him, or her, I suppose, to participate in whatever deliberations they were involved in." He laughed again. "I was never so honoured by the Elders."

"Who was, to use your words, so honoured?"

He met Carlo's gaze and then looked away. "There was a guy named Émile Basaraba, a Frenchman. He was more of a...a business agent. And then there was that jittery little bastard, oh, I'm sorry; do excuse me. A politician: Golliwog or something?"

"Lawrence Roswell Gollander?"

"Yes, that's the fellow."

"All right," Carlo looked directly at McHarg in a way that he hoped would be interpreted as threatening. "Did you attend a meeting at the Royal Bank in Vancouver on the twelfth of July 2007 to transfer funds to a brokerage in Toronto?" He placed a copy of the account application in front of him.

"No."

"So you that is not your signature on this document?"

"No, it is not. And this is the first time that I've been in Vancouver since 2002. Look, I'm not trying to be obnoxious, but I hate this fucking place." He shrugged at the court reporter. "I'm sorry; I did it again."

"Are you familiar with a Toronto firm called Corvair Intermediaries?"

"I believe that I'd heard of them, back when I was Master of the Treasure, yes."

"Did you ever transfer any of the religion's funds to it?

"No."

Carlo put the account application in front of him again. "And back to this document. You did not transfer last year's Wellspring to Corvair Intermediaries from this account in its entirety?"

"No, no...I didn't do anything with the...no," McHarg stammered. "Is that what this is all about?"

"Did you sign any documents to transfer real estate, any land holdings of the religion during your time as Master of the Treasure?"

"Well, no. Never."

Carlo placed the fourteen agreements of purchase and sale in front of him. In sequence, he denied signing each of them. "Were you aware that anyone within the religion as a whole wanted to transfer these properties?"

"No. No one ever said anything to me about it."

Carlo put his notes to one side. "Ruairi Davidson mentioned that you left British Columbia without a word to anyone and failed to show up to a family wedding in London a couple of months later." Carlo tried to hold McHarg's gaze. "Why was that?"

McHarg slumped back in his chair. "Well, I was facing a few, well, let's just call them *personal* problems. And Ruairi was already supremely pissed off at me. I quite bluntly told him what I thought of the religion about a month before I left."

"Just one last question, Mr. McHarg. Did you ever meet Émile Basaraba?"

"Yes I did. A couple of years back, at a Striationist do at Crown Isle golf course; you know, that resort up by Comox. Typical Frenchman, as I recall. He said little to me about either glacial striations or finances. He was most interested in fly fishing. He (let's just say) *interrogated* me for about half an hour about where I went, how I got there, what I caught, that sort of thing."

"Thank you, Mr. McHarg. Those are my questions." Carlo looked toward Angus and Connolly. "Counsel?"

"No, no questions," both of them replied, almost as a chorus.

"Have you decided who you're going to produce on behalf of the bank tomorrow morning?" Carlo asked Angus after McHarg left the examination room. "Declan has been asking you guys about it for months."

"Well, we're not producing one of the vice-presidents, if that's what you're asking." He leaned forward with an aggressive posture. "And, if you continue to demand that we do, the *Crédit-Suisse* case says that we would be entitled to increased costs!"

Carlo decided that the only way to effectively suffer Angus was to treat him with politeness bordering on pedantry. "No, no; there is no need for a vice-president. I just need somebody from the branch who knows the details of the Striationists' accounts before and after the split."

"My people are currently working on it. I will advise you as to all you need to know on the topic once I receive instructions."

* * *

Gavin, Dr. Davidson and Lawrence Gollander sat assembled in Roland Egbert's office, its unrelenting gloom extinguishing whatever elation the occasion might have inspired.

"Well," Egbert clasped his hands together. "This would appear to be cause for celebration. I'll go fetch a bottle of Tio Pepe." Egbert returned and distributed four small sherry glasses and filled each of them to just shy of the brim. "Now, Professor, you were saying?"

"Yes, the equipment, the algorithms, and, as Gavin said, the physical site are all ready and prepared." He winced after Gollander guzzled his sherry in a single gulp. "There is, however, one problem. We may not have access to enough electricity."

"Yes," Egbert said. "That is a problem."

"Now, Gavin and I tried to set up a few temporary run of river projects employing used turbines." Davidson continued. "But we ran into...let's call them bureaucratic difficulties."

"Yes," Gavin said. "I tried to get permission for the temporary generating stations, but the regulatory process would have led to far too much outside scrutiny, and..."

"Oh," Egbert interrupted, "I am so glad, Gavin, that we are finally on the same page on that issue."

"And," Gavin said, speaking louder. "B.C. Hydro would apparently force us to sell the power to them, so that they could sell it back to us. Just plain silly."

"Yes, indeed." Egbert nodded vigorously.

"It might indeed be 'silly', but we still need more electricity," Davidson said. "Can Hydro sell us some surplus power, just for the day of the test?"

"Nope," Gollander said. "No way."

"Why not?" Gavin asked.

"It's that Midland Shropshire project that the Reformed Striationists are so heavily invested in," Egbert explained. "Their point man on the project, the Master of the Treasure, what's his name, Pierre, Auguste..."

"Émile," Gollander grunted.

"Yes, yes, Émile. Émile Basaraba. He managed to negotiate quite a deal with Hydro, a substantial amount of power at twenty percent off the usual commercial rate."

"And he's drawing on it?" Gavin asked. "Already?" *That Basaraba guy again.* He'd been hearing his name mentioned more frequently.

"Oh, yes." Egbert nodded. "Almost to the limit of his permit. The Hydro commissioner for the Island (don't mention to anybody that she told me this) assured me that it was a good thing that his three run of river projects just by Mount Washington there were actually operational, otherwise they might have had a supply crisis. I suppose that it's not surprising; they're finishing work on about fifteen thousand units. I'm told that some offshore buyers have already taken possession and are in the midst of moving in."

"Hmm." Gavin mumbled. "Well, we still need power."

"We most certainly do!" Davidson said.

Gavin finished his sherry. "I have an idea: how about if we try to convince a few of the pulp mills, you know, Crofton, Harmac, Elk Falls. If they cut back on their power use, just that day, that would put us over the top, and we wouldn't need any permits for that."

"If you can convince them to do it, you have my blessing," Egbert said.

Gollander, who had been slouching in his seat like a discarded sandwich wrapper, snapped upright. "Oh, I think I can arrange that. I'll have to find some way to secure the funds for it, but I don't expect that it will be a problem. That is, if Mr. Skoff can get some of those people to give us the time of day."

Gavin smirked. "Don't worry."

"Splendid." Egbert said, clasping his hands together. "Now, assuming that you can secure the electricity, when will the test occur?"

"In late fall, November, I expect." Davidson said. "I will let you know the exact date in the next week or two."

"Please do."

"And I will spend the next few days on the phone with management types at all the pulp mills I can think of," Gavin said. "More than a few of whom owe me a favour for, for, let's say investment advice, and, well, related *arrangements*."

Egbert slowly raised his eyebrows. "I bet."

* * *

Angus was fifteen minutes late the next morning. Carlo and the court reporter, a freckled blonde girl who spoke with a spirited Newfoundland lilt, discussed the relative merits of a few of the nearby pubs while they waited. A tall woman with short dark hair, ascetic in her affect, followed Angus into the boardroom.

"Well *hello*, Carlo! It's been a few years."

Carlo recognized her as soon as she spoke but had to pause briefly to recall her name. "Leola. Yes, you're right. It's been what, eleven, maybe twelve years?"

"At least."

"You two know each other?" Carlo heard panic in Angus's voice. For the first time, he realized his irritating counterpart was at least five years his junior. "This is highly, highly irregular. I think that it is incumbent on you, Mr. Buonsante, to..."

Leola grimaced. "Oh, stop it, Jon. I'll be fine. Carlo and I were university students together way back in the twentieth century."

Carlo laughed politely. Leola Fortin, working at a *bank*! They first crossed paths on opposite sides of a fractious public debate in the Student Union Building, about whether a Catholic bishop from somewhere in South America should be allowed to show his face at a campus symposium: Carlo *pro*, Leola *contra*. Leola belonged to an anti-globalist, vaguely communist organization, '*Liberación!* or something. Now a pretty, expensively-dressed, but not conventionally elegant woman, in her undergraduate days she indulged in recreational hideousness. Back then, she sported abundant spikes and chains, her hair haphazardly self-shorn, dyed neon blue, always dressed in loose army fatigues. As far as Carlo could tell, she owned only three T-shirts, emblazoned respectively with images of Che Guevara, Daniel Ortega and Prince Peter Kropotkin.

Despite her stark contrast to Carlo, a friendship of sorts developed. They'd meet for coffee between classes. Carlo and Laura went to a few of her parties, where everyone was welcome except jocks and frat house boys. The last time Carlo saw Leola, at a gathering in a squat in East Vancouver, Leola's boyfriend, then in the advanced stages of drunkenness, sprayed spittle all over Carlo's face during an incomprehensible rant. Three weeks later, he heard she'd been summarily thrown in jail after a few members of her group threatened to burn down a Safeway in Shaughnessy in honour of the Squamish Five, a bunch of anarchists who had blown up a local factory about a decade earlier.

"My examination should take one or two hours, depending upon what your client has to say," Carlo said.

Angus bristled. "You'd better not speak so fast that my client can't make proper responses to your questions. In the *Davenport* case...."

Leola cut him off, rolling her eyes. "For God's sake, Jon, I go to *auctions.*"

Carlo asked his customary introductory questions. Leola, who at one time he would have described as a disciple of Leon Trotsky, had a degree in finance from McGill, a Master's degree from the Sorbonne, and recently qualified as a chartered accountant.

"What is your role at the bank?"

"I manage the operating accounts for non-commercial organizations, mainly religions, charities and other groups governed by the *Societies Act.*"

"What do you mean by operating accounts?"

"Well, the money that the society needs in order to pay for its day-to-day operations; salaries, normal expenses, rent. When the amount deposited appears to be in excess of short-term needs, I refer it to our investments and securities department."

"How many accounts did you manage for the Striationists?"

"Until a few months ago, just one. Some of the regional groupings, 'Domains' I think they call them, had their own in other branches, but I managed only one here."

"And how much money did that account typically contain?"

"Usually, between three hundred and three hundred and fifty thousand dollars, but when they collected the Wellspring (it's like a tithe), which was paid into that account, the balance would increase to as much as seven or eight hundred million."

"Most of which you would turn over to your investment bankers."

"Correct."

"What were their total holdings with the bank?"

"Before the split, approximately nine hundred million."

Carlo decided to change his focus. "Do you know a man named Ian McHarg?"

"Yes, he was the Striationists' comptroller; as I recall, he ran one of their administrative offices on the Island, Qualicum, I think."

"Could you describe him?"

"Medium height, slender; thin sandy blonde hair, greying a bit." Carlo noted that Angus merely scribbled notes and did not even react to his client's evidence.

"Did he speak with any particular accent?"

"No, basic Vancouver, Toronto at the most exotic."

"Just to be clear, he did not speak with a Scottish accent."

"No, no." She shook her head. "Definitely not Scottish."

Carlo pulled a thick cerloxed binder toward him and opened it. "Please go to Tab 12 of the bank's Book of Documents." Leola found it and put on her reading glasses. "It is identified as a bank statement from July of 2007 regarding the Striationist account, the last one before the split. It appears that eight hundred million dollars was withdrawn from the account on the eighteenth. Were you aware of that at the time?"

"Yes, but it wasn't a withdrawal, strictly speaking; it was a transfer between accounts." Leola explained that McHarg and two other men had opened another Striationist account a few months earlier, over which they both had signing authority. "The funds were paid into the new account. Mr. McHarg called me one morning and asked me to make the transfer. It was a transfer between accounts held by the religion; I didn't think that anything was amiss."

Carlo questioned her for another hour. She met with McHarg frequently, when he came to see her in her office in Vancouver, usually once per month over the course of the year before the schism. She never went over to meet with him on the Island, and spoke with him only once on the telephone, when he requested the transfer of funds. "Who came with Mr. McHarg to open the other account?"

Leola started flipping through the binder of documents in front of her. "I think that's right here." She examined what appeared to be a copy of a web page. "No," she said, surprised. "I have that information here, though." She pulled a very similar document out of her briefcase. "Yes, I remember the meeting. Three guys showed up, McHarg, this Basaraba guy (I'd never met him before)," she placed the page in front of Carlo, "and an older gentleman I later found out was a cabinet minister. Lawrence Roswell Gollander, Minister of Economic Development." Carlo examined the document. It was identical to the one he had found in Qualicum Bay: Gollander, Basaraba and the man claiming to be Ian McHarg had set up a commercial current account, each of the three of them having signing authority.

"Did they say why they were opening this second account?"

"Yes. They said that they were starting a campaign to solicit charitable donations from non-members. The donations (assuming that they got any) were supposed to go into that account."

"Were the funds transferred into the new account eventually referred to your investment banking department?" Carlo waited for her answer, the ultimate talisman as to whether her evidence could be trusted.

She tilted her head and looked directly at Carlo. "No, and you know, that is the part that always surprised me. I'd always believed that they were pleased with the results we got for them. The funds were sent by wire transfer, all but about one hundred and eighty thousand dollars, to some brokerage in Toronto, Corvair Intermediaries. Never heard of them."

"Did you speak with Gollander?"

"No, other than, well, just *polite* introductions."

"What about Basaraba?"

"We didn't say much to one another about...about *business*. We had a short conversation in French. The only thing that I really remember about it is that he spoke with a pronounced Algerian accent."

After the discovery ended, Carlo and Jon repacked their brief cases. "Carlo," Leola said. "Let's go for lunch at Imari Sushi, just down on Hornby Street. I love that place. We can catch up!"

"I'm coming," Jon said in a glacial tone.

Carlo suppressed a fit of giggles. "I wouldn't have it any other way, Jon."

The three of them walked down Hornby Street past the Art Gallery. "Jon, you look like you're being marched off to the gallows!" Leola burst into musical laughter.

Jon pouted, shuffling his feet. "Do we have to go for sushi?"

"Yes!" Carlo and Leola said.

Once seated at a booth near the window, Jon squinted at the menu. "Is there anything cooked on here?" he asked the waitress. She was pouring them a round of green tea.

"Yes, it's in the Bento box section, sir, on the final page."

"So, Carlo." Leola said. "Here we are, all mature and bourgeois."

"Speak for yourself," Carlo said, prompting Leola to laugh melodically again.

"So you were with a blonde girl, Tara or something?" "Laura."

"I don't imagine you're still together."

"Yes, in fact we are, believe it or not." Carlo did not want to give more detail than necessary. "We're living in a place not too far from Jericho Beach."

"Oh, my God. That's so, so (you'll hate me for this) inspiring."

"What about you and (if I'm not mistaken), Steven. That was his name, wasn't it? As I remember, he was very, let's say, *intense*."

"That's right; very good! No, that's really why we split up. After the charges were dropped, I decided that my anti-social, leftist insurgent days were over. I switched my major from political science to commerce; my dad was so proud (shocked is more like it) that he paid every cent for my *magistère* in finance from the Sorbonne. But Steven, well, he stuck with it, shaking his fist at anyone who looked like they may have more than two pennies to rub together. Didn't he start ranting at you one night? I think it was at a party at my place."

"He did, and I'll never forget it, that's for sure. I could never figure it out; he and his buddies (I guess that would be what you'd call them) all seemed to think that I was a pious Catholic or something. It used to make my friend Mario laugh until he pissed his pants."

"Oh, yes, Mario; for some reason I thought he was your *cousin* or something. He's the one who had a white-hot, rip-the-clothes-off affair with my friend Catherine, remember, the cute little blonde, the only one of our little circle who looked even minimally presentable back in the day. Anyway, yes, after our debate at the SUB that afternoon, our crowd branded you as some sort of devout parishioner. Most of them called you 'the Cardinal' because they couldn't pronounce your name. And whether you knew it or not, every time you opened your mouth, you were presumed to be speaking on behalf of the entire Catholic Church."

"No shit? So that explains it. At the party that night, Steven - he was quite agitated, out of control. Told me that I was a Jansenist. I think that was the last time that I saw you."

"Oh, so that was what it was all about. I wasn't really paying attention. *Stoned,*" she whispered. Jon was ignoring them, his attention consumed by a *Maclean's* magazine that he must have pulled out of his briefcase. "Hmm. Jansenist. That was during his Stendhal phase. It had an odd effect on him; he was always comparing himself to Lucién Sorel. Ridiculous. So what happened to that friend of yours, tall, kind of clueless. He was with...I think her name was Laeticia. I always liked her."

"You mean David. Married a Muslim."

"Now you're shitting me."

"No, no, he did! She's not very devout, we'll just say; she drinks as much wine as I do, and I've actually seen her eat *prosciutto*, but she's Islamic nonetheless, Persian. And Mario and Laeticia have been together for nine, ten years. It's funny how things work out."

"Really?" Leola raised an eyebrow. "He shouldn't have dumped Catherine. He'd be living the life. She's a successful actress; has a recurring role as a psychiatrist on one of the *Law and Order* shows. Anyway, you and Laura, still together. That's quite something. You know, all of the girls in my crowd, well, except for Catherine - all of us were vegetarians, skinny as twigs. Remember Heather?"

"Yes," Carlo sighed, "I remember her." Heather, a girl with straight red hair and a perpetual glower. She brought to mind an emaciated woodpecker.

"I suppose that I shouldn't be telling you this, but the bunch of them, especially Heather, they used to make horrible comments about Laura, you know, it was really over the top. I'm not going to tell you what they said, but we'll just say that they thought that she was a just little bit too, what's the word I'm looking for, I don't know, too *zaftig* for their aesthetic sensibilities. I don't know if she knew."

Carlo doubted that she did; he would have remembered the ensuing apoplectic rage.

"But you know what? All of us, down to the last girl, secretly would have given everything we owned (which wasn't a fuck of a lot back then, I have to admit) to have a body like that. But just for a week."

"Why just a week?" Carlo asked. Curiosity dulled his usual instincts.

"Because after a week, we would get sick of all of our pain in the ass friends going on about how fat we were!"

Jon seemed annoyed by Carlo's laughter and crisply closed his magazine. "It's getting on for two; we should get the cheque."

"*L'addition*," Leola said.

"*Il conto*," Carlo followed.

"Okay, you guys, all I was saying is that we have to pay." He started rummaging around in a little grey Armani pouch.

When the waitress came back with the bill, Leola scanned it. "Well, we all had bento boxes and split the *edamame*; why don't we just divide it equally three ways?"

Jon took the bill and put on his reading glasses. "Oh! The *edamame* was almost ten bucks." He counted the pods remaining on his plate and cast an investigative gaze at the dishes in front of the other two. "It looks to me like we got about sixty of them with the order; I ate seven, and it looks like you guys had the rest. Leola four more than Carlo. So at approximately fifteen cents each, that's a dollar five for me and..."

Carlo reached into his wallet and threw his Visa down on the tray. "How about if I just pick up lunch?"

"Oh, you don't have to do that, Carlo." Leola glared at Jon.

"This file has a long life ahead of it. One of you can get the next one."

"Sounds good to me." Jon put his wallet back in the pouch. "Sorry, I've got to run to a two o'clock meeting. Leola, be *very* careful what you say to this man."

"Sure thing."

Leola and Carlo walked together along Hornby Street.

"So it's odd; how is it that I haven't seen you before today?" Leola asked. "I've been back in town for, what, about four years now? I don't see people from those days all the time, but on the street? I see some of the old crowd from time to time."

"Oh, well, we were in Toronto for a while..." Carlo's voice trailed off. He wanted to remain as vague as he could.

"Oh yuck! I get sent there by the bank, two, maybe three times a year. Toronto sucks!" Leola voiced an opinion held almost unanimously in Vancouver. "I'd really love to see you guys, it's been so long. You know where a lot of people from our old crowd go? It's this place called the Basement, a bar on the Granville strip, this side of Davie. Nineties Thursdays; recorded music. They play mostly grunge, although they play some stuff from a little before, you know, Green River, Fresh Young Fellows, Mother Love Bone."

They exchanged business cards. "Yeah," Leola said, "I'd really like to get together with you and, what's her name, Laura? So remember: Thursdays at the Basement."

"Sounds good to me."

Carlo slid her card into the pocket of his suit jacket. *Mother Love Bone,* an old Seattle band that he hadn't thought about in years. What was the name of the vocalist, the guy who died, Andrew Wood or something? A long-forgotten stanza from "This is Shangri-La" welled up in his head, a tune he hadn't even thought of for at least fifteen years. Andrew was right. Most men do look bad in shorts.

39

Fabién Lerche had an intense distaste for the natural world. Hiking might have been a pastime that most people around him at least dabbled in, but it still struck him as a sign of derangement. As far as he was concerned, to suggest that he visit a green space, whether a distant wilderness park or an urban garden, was tantamount to proposing that he go to the moon. He preferred sterile Japanese noodles to potatoes, avoided fruit and considered vegetarians unspeakable, even worse than people who insisted on eating tripe or testicles. Some vegetables repelled him more than others; he once shrank from asking an otherwise alluring girl on a second date simply because she ordered fiddleheads. Fabién's sentiments were so different from everybody else in Victoria that people who knew him well told him he'd be happier in Calgary.

So he was aghast when Willingdon dispatched him to accompany Felix Gervais, Wilson's replacement as environment minister, to a meeting with an assortment of Earth scientists, environmentalists and other people he considered rabble. The premier insisted on his presence at the meeting of the Georgia Basin Environmental Studies Steering Committee ostensibly due to his familiarity with the University of Victoria campus, but Fabién knew better. Patricia Wilson's resignation left a significant gap in Cabinet. She had been one of five, including Lerche, who had completed a post-graduate degree and the only one, after Chatham's exit, to have achieved a doctorate. Willingdon hinted that if he and Gervais, both francophones, were heard publicly conversing in French, people might be less inclined to view his government as a bunch of hicks.

It amused him that Willingdon assumed he and Gervais were of the same ethnicity, akin to equating a Londoner with a Texan simply because they both spoke English. Gervais, Québecois with some Mohawk in his background, grew up in Sept-Îles, a port town hundreds of kilometres distant from Montreal. His political career started in the Eighties when he was elected as a Conservative Member of Parliament in an Ottawa-area riding and ended with his sepulchral defeat in the 1993 election, prompting him to move west in search of a job. Fabién's parents, on the other hand, were both French, his father an investment banker, his mother an actress, who met and married in Paris but parted soon after his birth. Fabién could not remember ever having seen them together in the same room. His mother soon took up with an environmental activist from Vancouver and consigned Fabién to a childhood and adolescence in Canada. Still, he and Gervais were good friends who shared a mutual hatred of the Vancouver Canucks, and often met at a sports bar near the Inner Harbour to watch hockey whenever Montreal was playing.

Fabién and Gervais walked down the paved pathway to the entrance of the Faculty Club, a squat but otherwise pleasant wooden structure at the periphery of the UVic campus. "At least this time they gave us space in the Faculty Club," Fabién said. "The last time that Willingdon made me go to one of these things, we ended up in a smelly seminar room in a cinder block and stucco hell-hole that looks like public housing in one of the *banlieus.*"

"I've never had the pleasure," Gervais grunted. "But I'm not surprised. From what I've been told, the entire original campus was built in about a day and a half."

"Well, anyway, let's get this over with. And keep your voice down. More people speak French around here than you might expect."

A young man with a shaved head escorted them to the meeting room, which overlooked the parking lot. He spotted Laeticia, sitting with her back to them. A shaggy fellow in a rain poncho whom Fabién did not recognize sat in a chair at the far end of the room, hunched over for some reason. "Hello,

Laeticia," Fabién oozed. "Laeticia Bradbury, this is Felix Gervais, the new Minister of the Environment."

Laeticia rose and extended her hand. "Pleased to meet you."

Fabién and Felix approached the man at the back, who, while not actually sitting upright, had straightened up enough to show that he appeared to be massaging his calf muscles while picking something or another from the hair on his legs. "Oh!" He pulled the rolled cuff back over his sock. "Thor Sandvisk," Gervais, the more seasoned politician, shook his hand in a firm, vigorous clasp; Fabién gingerly offered his hand as if picking a crushed rodent out of a mousetrap.

Laeticia was amused by the uncommonly rich attendance. Gervais was an unknown, a variable whose value had yet to be calculated. She had no idea what Fabién was doing there.

Gervais brought the meeting to an uneasy start. "For those of you who don't know me, I'm Felix Gervais, the new Minister of the Environment. This is my first meeting with the Georgia Basin Steering Group. And I would like to introduce my colleague Fabién Lerche, Minister of Economic Development. Our ministries are co-operating in a number of *joint initiatives*." He warily surveyed the room.

"Good afternoon." Fabién bore an immutable smile.

"All right," Gervais said. "I suppose that I'm the one who has to call this meeting to order. Who wants to give the first report?" Dr. Sandvisk raised his hand. "Very well, professor, you can begin."

Sandvisk described an experiment, not yet complete, where his team was developing a mathematical model to predict elk migration routes in alpine passes based on forage and lichen loads. Gervais first listened with a polite smile but finally retreated to the refuge of his phone to type a text message. "So far," Sandvisk flapped with excited gesticulations. "It is the data from the Ucona River area of Strathcona Park that has shown the most encouraging results!"

Gervais seemed surprised that Sandvisk finished his report so quickly. "Thank you, Professor. Who would like to be next?"

A woman with long white hair wearing a khaki-coloured blouse spoke up next. "Eileen Saunders, Sierra Club of British Columbia." As she started speaking, Gervais listened for a few seconds before he returned to his phone. Within a couple of minutes Fabién felt his phone vibrate. He glanced at the screen.

what a bunch of freaks!

More than an hour passed before Laeticia had a chance to speak. "Laeticia Bradbury, University of Victoria Faculty of Biology." She gave a brief synopsis of the progress of her research. "And, as my project concerns salmonid populations in the creeks and smaller rivers of the mid-coast of central Vancouver Island, I have been focusing my efforts on Baynes Sound, Minister Gervais. Your predecessor offered to make available some historical aerial photographs of the district to help me track the extent of sea grasses in the area over time," Laeticia stated in a friendly but formal tone. "Before her, her, ah, departure from the government. This information, which I believe is still stored on microfiche, would be invaluable to my research."

Gervais assessed the young woman across the table from him. True, she seemed pleasant enough, undoubtedly sincere, but it would not have been the first time in his political career that an academic, however innocently, happened on delicate information and stirred up trouble. And Baynes Sound: Gervais was vaguely aware of some sort of project in the district, something quite secret that seemed to be of overriding importance to people like Goyter and the Premier. Quite opposite to his own expectation, his renewed political career seemed to be ascendant. He didn't want to risk being held responsible for causing an embarrassing spectacle.

"I don't know. You see, *mademoiselle*," he said, activating Gallic charm that would have prompted his cronies in Sept-Îles to laugh at him until Labatt's 50 spewed out of their nostrils. "I have not held this portfolio for very long and I am not yet, let us say, as familiar with it as Patricia Wilson most certainly was. So I must insist that you follow the usual Freedom of Information application protocol. I am so very sorry."

She sucked in a breath. "Thank you, Minister Gervais." This would delay the completion of her research by several months, and perhaps even more than a year.

The meeting came to an end after Gervais made some encouraging remarks to a girl, younger than Laeticia, who represented a consortium of salmon fishing guides. Gervais and Fabién retreated to the far corner of the room, where they both started whispering into their phones.

Laeticia looked up to see Fabién looming over her as she stuffed her notes into her briefcase. "Ms. Bradbury."

"Oh, hi, Fabién." She had come to regard him as a benign nuisance. His unceasing text messages and weekly delivery of flowers at her office, as unwelcome as they were, did not strike her as menacing. As much as they annoyed her, their presence was as quotidian as the tides.

"Look," he said quietly, glancing around the room behind him. "I'll work on Felix; there's no reason why we shouldn't just release the historic data you want without a ridiculous freedom of information fracas." He seemed mildly embarrassed. "He's a little nervous: it's the first time he's been at the Cabinet table since Mulroney was in office. Doesn't want to make any mistakes."

Laeticia was surprised. Although Fabién's unbalanced public ravings had yet to touch on matters environmental, she would never have imagined that he might ever take even passing interest in her research. "Thanks! Much appreciated; it would really help me at this point."

"No problem. Do you need a lift back to your hotel?"

"No, no. I've checked out. I have to head over to UBC tonight, to give a paper at a graduate seminar tomorrow. From here, I'll just, I don't know, catch the bus or something out to the ferry."

"Oh, I can run you out there," Fabién said. "I'm meeting some friends for dinner out at the Otter Cove Chalet."

Laeticia knew the place, a seafood restaurant at the far end of the Saanich Peninsula, little more than walking distance from the ferry terminal. Mario had taken her there for her twenty-seventh birthday four years earlier, when they were still living in Victoria. She remembered that the bill almost matched their rent.

"I think that I'll be okay." She shrugged. "But thanks for the offer."

"Hey, it would be no problem at all. It's practically on the way."

Laeticia didn't want to be rude, and besides, he was a Cabinet minister, one who just offered to help her with her research. "Okay, thanks, as long as it isn't too far out of your way."

"Oh, no; not at all. I'll just say goodbye to Felix."

The passenger drop-off lane in the parking lot at the Swartz Bay ferry terminal was almost deserted between sailings. Two teen-aged girls smoking outside the foot passenger gate giggled as they examined the screens of each other's phones.

Laeticia had regretted accepting a ride from him almost as soon as she agreed. Fabién had remained uncommunicative for the entire trip after they left campus, shooting her occasional lascivious glances followed by long intervals of silence. Laeticia tried to make conversation as they pulled into the parking lot. "The ferry is late," she said. "It should have been coming around Piers Island about ten minutes ago."

He drove his Lexus into a parking stall next to a motor home. "No surprise. These overpriced rust buckets are always late. If it were up to me?" He raised his voice to orchestral timbre. "We would privatize them!"

"Ah."

"You know," Lerche said, more animated than he had been since they left the university. "I have my own, well call it an audacious way of looking at things."

This is not going to end well. "Oh, yes, how is that?"

"*Carpe diem*, as they say; go for what you want. When I see something that I want, I just go out and I take it!" He pivoted to seize Laeticia's thigh with his right hand and then grabbed one of her breasts with his left.

Laeticia had already surmised that he was right-handed, so she took hold of his left hand with her right, and sharply bent back his fingers until she heard a sickening but unmistakable crack.

"Ow!" he howled. "What the fuck was that for?" Laeticia felt fleeting shame at her glee upon seeing tears in his eyes. He bent forward toward the console and moaned. "You didn't have to break my fucking fingers."

She could no longer consider him an annoying but otherwise remarkably successful novice politician, an ambitious *wunderkind* with a self-imbued Napoleonic aura. Instead, he was just another whiny young man, engaged in the squalid behaviour of his kind. "Oh, yes I did! Maybe a couple of weeks in a cast will convince you to keep your hands to yourself from now on." Laeticia's reaction to men who casually groped her was usually more incendiary. This time, she sensed a rare opportunity.

"I could have you charged with assault," he squeaked as he massaged his hand. "They'd never let you cross the border to go shopping again!"

Laeticia folded her arms and gave him a look of disbelief. "Seriously? *You're* going to report *me*?

Panic tinged his pained grimace. "You're not going to tell anybody about this little..."

"Stupid ass, dickheaded, adolescent stunt?"

"I was going to call it an 'indiscretion'," he whispered as he cringed in agony.

"You're an asshole, but I'm not going to tell anybody. Not even my husband."

"You're not married."

"Listen to you! Yes, as far as the law is concerned, we are. Okay. I'm not going to say anything to anybody, but in return? That means no more flowers at the office; no more text messages. It means *no contact at all!* Now fuck off!" She slammed the car door and briskly walked towards the foot passenger terminal.

40

"Carlo!"

"What's up?" Carlo was in the kitchen, ripping large leaves of chard into pieces. Laura was at her computer again, shrieking with laughter.

"You asshole!" She laughed. "Come here, you fucking asshole! This has got to be you. I know it is!"

"What are you talking about?"

"Oh, I bet you know. And you've hit the big time. It's on Nikki's Party." Now Carlo was even more confused. *Nikkisparty.ca* was a sprawling blog that featured news, politics, gossip, and cultural detritus that defied classification. Its founder, Nikki LaPierre, once a MuchMusic hostess before she was jettisoned for being too old after she turned thirty-two, was now the wealthiest young woman in Canada. Laura read it for about half an hour every night after work, usually when Carlo was cooking dinner.

"Oh, yes; the *Huffington Post* for people who drink too much Malibu."

"*What-ever*! Okay. Are you going to deny that this is your handiwork?" Laura pointed at the screen.

Nikki's Party

The Gambler's New Teeth – More Adventures in Legal Idiocy

Jacques Schitte of Trois-Rivières, Québec was awarded $375,000 by a jury in Federal District court in Jackson, Mississippi after sustaining multiple injuries to his jaw. Mr. Schitte, a Québec resident, stayed at the Belvedere Casino Resort in Biloxi and lost all of his money after a drunken weekend of gambling. Remembering that one could sell one's blood to blood banks in the United States, Mr. Schitte concluded that he could also raise funds by selling his teeth, so he extracted all them while seated at a slot machine, then *attempted to exchange them at the casino cashier. The resort, having just been told by Mr. Schitte that he'd run out of money (and noting that he was spurting an unsightly amount of blood) promptly tossed him out in the parking lot. Upon his return to Canada, Mr. Schitte purchased a used set of false teeth from St. Vincent de Paul. One evening, in a fit of rage, he started gnawing on a lamppost and severely injured his temporomandibular joint, which aggravated latent osteoarthritis. His legal team sued both the resort and the manufacturer of the false teeth. The resort, despite its formidable surveillance apparatus, failed to stop him from removing all of his teeth. This shortcoming obliged the resort to buy them, to give him an opportunity to win enough money to afford something better than used dentures. The denture manufacturer was found liable for failing to warn Mr. Schitte that it was unwise to use their product to gnaw on lampposts.*

(reblogged from *thelawisanass.com*)

"Nope." Carlo peered at the screen, unable to suppress a smile. "Don't know anything about it."

"Oh, bullshit! This has *you* written all over it. And just look at you. Are you seriously still going to deny it?"

"No," he finally laughed. "I'm not. And I bet that pair we met in Whistler swallowed it whole and then whipped themselves into a righteous rage."

"Well, I'm glad that you're proud of yourself. But I'll get a good laugh when you can't keep a straight face the next time you're accosted by those two granolas."

"Looking forward to it."

"I'm sure you are. Anyway, I was thinking; I'd like to go out for dinner tomorrow night, maybe the new seafood place on Fourth. Do you think that Farida and David would like to join us?"

"Oh, probably. And it's Thursday; maybe we could stop by the Basement for an hour or two and listen to some music.

"The Basement? What's there?

"Leola Fortin, remember her? We had lunch after a discovery; well, *her* discovery. She told me that Thursdays are Nineties night."

"Leola, Leola - oh, wait a minute. Yes; Leola. She was one of *those* people, those friends of yours who looked like a bunch of dumpster divers."

"She's changed," Carlo sighed.

"Sure, why not. I never thought that I'd ever hear myself saying this, but at this late date, a little Soundgarden may be good for the soul."

Marika padded up to the counter in Calista's, self-conscious of her own bulk. Carlo wasn't there to meet her; she remembered that he was on his way to a mediation or something in New Westminster.

"Medium organic rosehip, please."

"A *what?*"

"Third one down on the chalkboard."

"Ah. That will be two seventy-five." He handed her a tall steaming cup. "Don't worry, dear," he said. "We're never as enthusiastic about the whole thing as you ladies are. But in a month or so, when he holds the little darling in his arms, he'll be just as happy as you are."

Marika took her tea and lumbered to work. The guy at the counter was the same half-blind old man who had mistaken Carlo for her about a month earlier. If he could tell that she was about to give birth, everyone else in Vancouver would have figured it out weeks ago. It was time to have a proper conversation with Declan.

Declan was in his office, his desk piled high with accordion files. He was reviewing a thick binder, probably a set of hospital records. His computer, as it did more often than not, displayed the Blue Screen of Death.

"Hey," Marika said.

Declan looked up from his binder. "Marika." His tone betrayed that he was not unambiguously pleased to see her. "Good morning."

"Good morning indeed. I was trying to call you last night. Paula's still away, isn't she?"

"Yes, yes. I fell asleep on the couch during *Three and a Half Men.* You never left a message." His affect was disconcertingly serene.

"No, I didn't." She sat down. "Look, things are obviously progressing." She caressed her belly. "Did I tell you? We're going to have a little girl. And I'm going to need your help...unlike you, I've never done this before. And tell me, have you even told your wife?"

"Told her what?"

"Are you kidding me?"

"Whatever are you on about?"

"I can't believe it! You haven't even told her that I'm pregnant (well, I'm sure that she's figured *that* part out), but what about the part about where it's *your* baby? You haven't, have you?"

Declan put his reading spectacles back in their case and re-arranged the pens in the crystal cylinder on his desk. "Look, just calm down," he eventually spoke. "There's really nothing to spark such...such panic. Everything will work out just fine, you'll see." He smiled.

"Are you insane? What the fuck am I supposed to think? You've as good as just admitted that you haven't even told your wife yet!"

"Look," Declan said. "There's no need to swear. And what did you expect?" His tone changed to the one she recognized as 'staged exasperation'. "Do you think that it is easy, abruptly ending a marriage; a life together, by telling your wife that another, much younger woman is about to have your baby?"

"And do you think that it's *easy,* to use your asshole way of expressing yourself, *easy* to get huge and bloat up to the size of a walrus? *Easy,* to have to get around with a belly that is rapidly getting as... as big, I don't know, as big as an exercise ball, with some guy's kid in it, without the slightest idea how I'm going to survive, two, three, four months down the road? Fuck you!"

"Please stop swearing. And come on, I'm not just some guy."

"Look, Declan! I'm running out of patience. Do I have to see someone about enforcing my numerous legal rights?"

"Marika." Declan maintained a quiet voice. "I'm on it. These things are much more complicated for someone my age compared to someone of yours. There are accountants and family lawyers to be consulted, property to be divided up. Believe me, I'm working on it."

"Okay. I'm sorry. I'm just a bit on edge these days."

"That's okay," he said, rising to embrace her for the first time in almost a month. *Walrus,* he thought as his arms spanned her circumference. *More like a whale.* He kissed her on the forehead. "We'd better get to work before Thomas and Bal get in."

Marika smiled and made her way to her desk. As he watched her waddle across the office, Declan knew that it was time to quit procrastinating. His opportunity was about to disappear.

41

By the first days of November, a spate of court applications and examinations for discovery allowed Carlo frequent escape from the office torpor; Marika sitting numb at her desk performing repetitive tasks, her cheeks often damp with a stray tear or two; the awkward, sullen silence as Bal and Jacquie stared at him with mounting contempt. Gaskin had been pensive and ill-tempered all week, pacing around the office with no apparent destination, usually rumbling with a coarse growl. He uttered scarcely a word to Carlo until Friday, summoning him into his office after Marika called in sick.

"Sit down." He motioned to one of the chairs in front of his desk. "Have you not become a little concerned about Marika's... ah...let's call it her *condition?*

"Condition? I suppose that's one way of putting it." These days, even the most obtuse observer could tell that Marika was about to have a baby. Whenever she and Carlo went to their customary lunch spots and coffee houses, the serving staff would adopt knowing smirks when the two of them walked in, sometimes even offering congratulations.

"You *suppose?*" Gaskin tossed his pen down on his desk. "For the love of Christ, Carlo, can't you take responsibility for anything? I think that it's time for you to publicly acknowledge what everyone already knows: that in a very short time, Marika is going to give birth to your child!"

Carlo marvelled at Gaskin's strategic use of language. "Oh? What makes you think that I'm the father?"

"Don't try to be coy!" Declan shouted. "At minimum (in addition to whatever else you two might have been up to), you were out of town with her for a few nights at Port Rattray Lodge. Back then, Marika was an extraordinarily beautiful, sexy girl. I find it impossible to believe that you didn't sleep together on that trip.

In fact, I bet you had her out of her clothes at the first opportunity!"

"No, I...I didn't," Carlo stammered in disbelief, starting to catch on. "We never...no, it never happened."

"Oh, bullshit!"

"If you don't believe me, why don't you ask her yourself?"

"I'm not going to fucking ask her! I don't have to!" Declan shouted. "When you consider how *far along* she looks, the Port Rattray trip fits the time frame perfectly. And you should know that you were seen going into her cabin, but not always leaving, every night you were there." Gaskin leaned back in his chair and folded his arms. "And there were no condoms in the waste-paper basket."

"You had people watching us?"

"Look," Declan said, his voice softening, "I can understand your reluctance, especially when you consider how Marika has...ah...transformed. But I would have been more understanding if you were some young lad, maybe twenty at the most. But you're a grown man; surely you have enough experience to know the way things are. Girls with bodies like she used to have, they're fun to play with, aren't they? But you have to be *very* careful, or else *boom*! Before you know what hit you, they're carrying your child. Then they're like ripening fruit; they start rounding out, and in a blink of an eye they get so fat and heavy that they fall off the tree."

Carlo sat looking at him, too stupefied to respond.

"This should not have come as a surprise to you." Declan's tone was uncharacteristically shrill. "And it is certainly no excuse to evade your responsibilities!

"Okay," Declan leaned back in his chair and nudged his head down, creating jowls. "I don't expect you to marry her, although that *would* be the honourable thing to do, under the circumstances. I can easily understand why you would rather keep house with that gorgeous blonde from the public relations agency. But come clean, acknowledge your responsibility, and move on!"

"This is nonsense!" Carlo shook his head.

"And know this, Carlo! If you don't live up to your responsibilities, it may call into question your continued employment."

"Are you serious?" Carlo strained to avoid losing his temper. "I think that it's time to put this all to rest."

Gaskin broke into a broad smile. "Good, I thought you might eventually come to your senses!"

"All right. You're convinced (for some reason) that Marika and I had sex in Port Rattray, that's clear."

"As well as countless other times, I'm sure."

"Well, you are completely off base. We never had sex, not in Port Rattray or anywhere else. Even if I was single back then, she wasn't. It seems that she's in love with her boyfriend, and Marika's not the kind of person who cheats."

"*Boyfriend.*" Gaskin said with exaggerated disbelief. "Who's this *boyfriend* you're on about? I've never seen one around. She's never spoken of one, not within my hearing, and you're the only *boy* I've ever seen her with. I'd say this mystery man you've invented out of thin air will turn out to be *you!*"

"No, Declan. It won't. Her boyfriend, well, he's been very careful to, let's just say, stay in the *background* so far, but he won't be able to do it for too much longer. And who knows, maybe we're being unfair to him. If not, I'm told that DNA testing these days is mercilessly accurate."

"DNA testing? You're not so selfish that you'd let it come to that, are you?"

"I have no role in this at all, Declan, but if it does come to that, it will be at Marika's insistence, not mine. And it's not going to be me she'll be pointing to, I can promise you that."

Gaskin seemed to physically shrink, even if his tone remained belligerent. "So you mean to tell me that you could not possibly be the father of Marika's baby?"

"That is exactly what I'm telling you."

Gaskin contemplated the blotter on his desk. "Well," he mumbled, "you have to understand, that's how I've explained it to my wife."

Carlo's hands were still shaking an hour later. He was too enraged to do anything productive. After sitting at his desk angrily surfing from one website to the next, he reached for his cell phone and sent a text message to Marika.

> Time for tea-Im paying- meet at plc with stone chmny by ur bldg in 45

Even if her pregnancy was entering its final stage, Marika had yet to seem even the least bit maternal. Instead, by her gestures, the way she sat in her chair, even by the timbre of her voice, she seemed more like a reluctantly sober high school party girl, swelling with the result of an ill-considered back seat tumble. Her mounting rage accentuated the effect, rendering her devoid of any hint of domesticity.

"What a fucking prick!"

Everyone in the coffee house tried to seem disinterested, but Carlo could easily sense that they were straining their ears, eager to hear their conversation. "Just try to keep calm. I thought that I should tell you." Carlo did his best to sound soothing.

"So that's what the stupid old bastard said! He tried to blame *you* for *this*!" She waved her hand over her belly. An older woman at the table across from them looked up from her laptop with a puzzled expression.

"Yes. I must admit that it is the first time in a while that anyone has succeeded in shocking me."

"The stupid fucking piece of shit! The fucking asshole!" Marika's eyes moved back and forth quickly and unsteadily. "I've been a complete fool, taken in by that fucking cunt!" Carlo knew that her language signalled the crossing of a momentous emotional divide.

"I'm not coming into work tomorrow," she shouted. "Oh, fuck, what a ridiculous thing to say. I just don't know what to do!" Her face quivered as if sobbing, but her eyes stayed dry.

"You do have rights, you know. He is, well, rich; he will owe substantial child support to you in a very short time. If you need some help, Farida, a good friend of mine (you've met her), another lawyer…"

"I thought of all that," she interrupted. "But until right now, I basically believed him, the total loser that I am. No, no," she said over Carlo's gestures of protest. "I *am* a total loser. I should have known. I've been around him *far* too long to not have had his number. It should have dawned on me a long time ago, certainly before this happened." She gently rubbed her front.

"Well, now you know that you can't trust him; you have to get someone to help you. You can't deal with him on your own."

"Oh, you've got that right." Marika picked up her mug with both hands and took a gulp of her tea. "I don't know. So Farida, is it?"

"Yes, I'll text you her office number," Carlo said as he searched for his phone.

Marika shuddered with startling violence. "No! I am not going down that path. No fucking way. And I'm not staying here. I have to get far away from him. You're one of the few people who would understand what I'm talking about. He's a manipulative prick! I don't want his fucking money. Everyone thinks that he's so generous, thoughtful, concerned; but the truth is, he just knows exactly how to tell you what you want to hear, and finds a way to make you believe it."

"Not staying here? But where else would you go? Montreal?"

"To my mother? No, I'm in no mood for the sermon. Definitely not Montreal, not now." Marika drew a deep breath. "I don't know, one of my cousins (she's about your age) lives down in Portland, but then again, I have an aunt (*much* cooler than my mother); she lives in Toronto with this German guy. I think that's probably my best bet, just now."

"You can stay with us, you know that."

"Yes, and Petra has offered me the same thing. She's *much* less trusting than I am. She thought that I'd hooked up with an asshole from day one. No, I think that it's much better that I get the fuck out of here."

"Look, that's a bit drastic, don't you think? We would help you. Farida would help you. He's not invincible."

"He's pretty fucking close! The fact that he got me to believe him that he would leave his wife and be with me is pretty supernatural. Look, he's been telling judges and juries that black is white and up is down since before either one of us was born. Let's say I did go after him for child support. How would that work out? There are people who used to work there who he's been in litigation with for *ten years*! And then, after what you've told me about what he said today, who knows what he'd do with *you*, how you would figure into it. What's her name, Lexie, would probably leave you."

"Laura. No," Carlo said. "She wouldn't."

Marika rubbed her face and pulled back her hair. "No, there's no way! Carlo, he's the fucking devil. You of all people know that. I've got to get fuck out of here." Both of them fell silent, Marika sipping what was left of her tea.

"Do you need some money?" Carlo said.

"I didn't want to ask, but yes."

"There's a branch of the TD by the bus stop. Let's go."

Once they were outside, Marika leaned to clutch him around the waist, buried her face into his shoulder and shook with paroxysmal sobs. Carlo felt the moisture of her tears, soaking through his suit jacket.

The office had an eerie ambience in the days that followed. Ill-concealed hostility towards Carlo faded into a morose acquiescence, even if none of staff except Thomas seemed to notice Marika's absence. Declan didn't even appear distracted, not even a hint that anything serious might be amiss. Instead, he tried to strike up light-hearted chats with Carlo, usually about his files, and when that fell flat, tedious celebrity gossip. It was not until the following week that he even asked after Marika's whereabouts. Carlo overheard him ask Bal to try to find her, but he never discussed anything related to Marika with him, not even obliquely.

Carlo did his best to ignore Declan after their bizarre confrontation. The Striationists so consumed his attention that he didn't have much time to think about it. As long as his paycheque didn't bounce, he didn't really care.

One morning about two weeks after Marika left, his phone started ringing minutes after he got in.

"Good morning, Carlo. This is Paula Gaskin." Carlo drew a shallow breath as he suppressed incipient gloom. "I am Declan's wife. You may recall that we met at my gallery on Granville Island last spring. I've been around the office a few times since then."

"Of course, yes."

"I'm just finishing a meeting with one of my artists in Gastown. I wonder if you have time to meet with me at Kensington Teahouse on Cordova Street in about half an hour. It's just a little more than two blocks away from you."

Carlo looked at his daytimer; no appointments that morning. "Yes. I can meet you there."

"Good. I'm looking forward to it."

Carlo felt both a premonition of an unpleasant epiphany and overwhelming curiosity. Although he'd never heard of the teahouse, he had no difficulty finding it.

Paula was waiting at a table next to the window facing Abbott Street. "Thank you for meeting me, Carlo." She smiled with an aristocratic countenance that he found infuriating. "Amanda." She waved to the approaching waitress. "Please give Carlo a menu. I would suggest something on the 'Assam' list."

He glanced over the menu. "I'll have one of the ones from Darjeeling. The second one."

"Darjeeling." She pursed her lips with approval. "You surprise me. I never would have identified you as a connoisseur of teas."

"Well, one of my aunts, she's quite a tea lover. When I lived in Rome, she would always ask me to bring back various types of tea from this little *drogheria* by, well it doesn't matter, whenever I went down to Sannazzaro for a visit."

"Oh, yes, now I remember. You were living in Rome. I've been there; a few times with Declan, but he finds it boring. He says that he likes Paris better. Whatever. What part of town did you live in?"

"Trastevere."

"Oh." She pondered. "I don't know that area. Tell me, did you ever see Mr. Berlusconi when you lived there?"

"Yes, often enough. For the few months that I was working with Winterstone's (it's a London solicitors' firm)."

"I know who they are."

That Carlo doubted, unless she had somehow become familiar with obscure international transactions between banks which required custom drafted letters of credit. "Anyway, I walked to work past Montecitorio (that's the parliament); the office was not too far from Piazza di Spagna."

"Oh, yes, the Spanish Steps. So he lurks around there, does he?"

It defied simple explanation, the prurient fascination with Berlusconi that seemed to occupy the attention of people in London, and apparently in Canada, too. Most of Carlo's friends in Rome regarded him as an embarrassment to be hidden from the rest of the world, like a wayward uncle who masturbates at the beach. Here he was, a disgrace, a renowned lecher and cheat, yet he held the Anglosphere in thrall. "Yes. I would see him from time to time, being escorted through Piazza Colonna."

"So, what can you say about him? Does he have horns and a tail?"

"No. But he's much shorter than most people think."

"I see." Paula tilted her head back. "I didn't ask you here to discuss Roman landmarks. My concern is one of your co-workers; Marika."

"Oh, yes." There were a number of directions that this conversation could have been going, all of them fraught with hazard as far as Carlo was concerned.

"I will be blunt." She held him in her gaze; her eyes conveyed festering contempt. "As I'm sure you are aware, I am one of the directors of the Fraser Region Women's Legal Resources Foundation."

"I am. A friend of mine, Farida Hamizadeh, is one of your volunteers."

She regarded him as if he were a pallet of rotting cabbage. "Is she? Perhaps you could ask Farida next time you see her to explain to you what the Foundation would do with a young man, hypothetically, *hypothetically*, who casually impregnated a co-worker with whom he had a relationship for several months, and then, once she starts to show the classic signs, unceremoniously ditches her for a younger and, thanks to him, by then a *much* skinnier blonde bimbo, and then refuses to acknowledge his responsibility for her condition, leaving her feeling abandoned and scared. Ask her what *she* would do to such a skunk!"

"What are you asking me?"

"Don't be so juvenile, although I suppose that it is your stock in trade. You know very well what I am talking about. And if you don't show right away that you are going to take some responsibility for what you have done, don't think that I will hesitate to assign her one of our volunteer counsel; maybe even your friend Ms. Hamizadeh!"

Carlo restrained an escape of laughter. "I don't expect you have actually spoken to Marika, your, we'll call her your prospective client."

"No, I haven't," she responded in a tone of controlled anger that reminded Carlo of an idling chain saw. "Look, would you grow up? Everyone knows that her baby is yours!" Carlo was more annoyed than embarrassed when he noticed that other people in the tea room were starting to eavesdrop.

"This is ridiculous. We have never been romantically involved." Carlo instantly regretted his choice of words. "We are, however, very close friends."

"Romantically involved. Who do you think you're talking to?" She started to raise her voice for the first time. "Do you think I'm some kind of naive old matron? Even the night you two met, at my show (as you might recall), you looked like you were about to rip each other's clothes off!"

"I have had about enough of this. We were never together, that night or any other night."

"*Together*! Would you just stop this annoying *nice Italian boy* act? Her kid is yours, and now you're going to have to help pay for it!"

Now he was enraged. "All right, have it your way. I never *fucked* her, and you can bet that I regretted my lack of trying, I can tell you, before I met up again with Laura. She's the 'bimbo', you were just talking about (a despicable misuse of a perfectly good Italian word, I might add)."

"Someone you met in a bar, I suppose."

"Nope. A casino. We actually *reunited*; the circumstances are, of course, none of your business. And she's eight years *older* than Marika."

"Kindly lower your voice."

"Kindly lower yours. And maybe you should have talked to your husband before you hauled me up for this...this...childish attempt at a bourgeois public shaming." It was the first time Carlo used the word 'bourgeois' since second-year university. He returned Paula's gelid, unfriendly gaze. "As I told him, she's had, well, we'll call him a 'boyfriend', for years. Chances are, the baby's his. And if there's any question? It's 2008. DNA testing will remove any doubt!"

"You talked to Declan about this?" Paula took a deep breath. "Well, so what? What would that prove?" she said, without meeting his gaze. "Those tests are wrong, sometimes."

"Sometimes? How about *never*?"

Even as she maintained a scornful, defiant mask, Paula realized that her original assessment, given ample encouragement from Declan, couldn't be correct. Subconscious fears and insecure thoughts had smouldered for a long time, ignited when her husband hired a young paralegal with superlative flowing red hair and improbable curves. She'd caught him with — what was she — that young journalist who looked much the same as Paula had, twenty-five years before, and, after that unpleasant episode concluded, she convinced herself that Marika was plainly too hefty for Declan's tastes. Her few remaining doubts seemed to have been extinguished when she sensed fierce electricity between Carlo and Marika at her gallery, confirmed later that night when they openly snuggled in the back seat of her car as she drove half the office home. For weeks afterward, Declan would come home grumbling that he saw his two employees too frequently in each other's company. When Marika, of buxom but unchanged physique for three years, suddenly began to fatten like a bored housewife, Paula drew what then seemed to her to be the only reasonable conclusion. Still, the ugly contempt for Carlo which she had nurtured over the past few months did not quickly dissipate.

"So, if you are such *good friends,* you must know where she is. Declan says that she hasn't been in to work for almost three weeks."

"Look, I'm really not comfortable discussing this with you."

Paula laboured to concentrate; her mind was too occupied with considering events of the past year or two she'd since dismissed, correlating them with comments and excuses that struck her as odd to her when Declan made them, but did not seem very important at the time. New interpolations and scattered thoughts were guiding her to an entirely different conclusion. Now she wondered what was lacking in her powers of observation, and the intelligence she'd taken such pride in for most of her life.

When she was younger, she always wondered why they didn't figure it out sooner. Paula, whose slender form, thick black hair and blue eyes had rendered her much in demand when she was Marika's age, never succumbed to the temptation of a married man. Several of her close friends were governed by less exacting ethics; three decades before, some of them spent their twenties as little more than the nocturnal playthings of moneyed, much older men. Even though their barely concealed trysts seemed conspicuous to Paula, the wives never figured it out until someone's mistake brought it all unsparingly before them. Paula, at twenty-five, never thought that she would ever be such a dunce.

Anxious for information, Paula changed her demeanour. "And Declan told me that Bal tried to find her; and she's cancelled her phone number, moved out of her apartment and her cell phone is not in service. Doesn't this concern you?"

"I said that I don't want to discuss it with you."

"I would think (although, thank God, I have never been in that situation) that a young, apparently single woman who was about to give birth may have some interest in letting the father of her child know what was going on. Maybe she's with him."

"Let's not..."

"Look, I get it. You don't want to talk about it. But if you do know who the young man is (seeing how you insist that it is not you), maybe that would help Bal find her."

Carlo found the introduction of a note of warmth in her tone annoying. "Okay. We're not having this conversation. Anything she said to me is...

"So she told you the identity of the child's father."

"Mrs. Gaskin, I really don't think that I want to discuss this any further."

Paula paused and locked him in an intense, investigative stare for more than a minute, long enough to bring Carlo's feelings of unease to the frontiers of panic. Finally, she took a deep breath. "Tell me: is it Declan's?"

Carlo looked down at his napkin, trying his best to lose himself in the maze of its paisley design. He bit his lip but said nothing.

"I see." Paula's tone lacked identifiable emotion. "I would like to thank you for your candour. Now, if you don't mind, I would like a few moments to myself."

"Of course." Carlo rose and paid for their tea on his way out. Fifteen dollars with tip. For tea! Bullshit.

He walked deep into the Downtown Eastside, through a thicket of people, all of them crazed and greasy, flailing and staggering about on the sidewalk, but oblivious to his presence. Then he caught one of the False Creek ferries, bobbing in the sheltered tidal inlet that tourists quite understandably often mistook for a river. Eventually, he found himself in a pub on Granville Island, sipping slowly on a beer he hated, a *frambozen* he never would have ordered if he hadn't been so distracted. He reached for his phone and called Laura's cell.

"Hey, what's up?"

"I'm not going back to work this afternoon: I've had it with that prick. He's the devil, he's..."

"What the fuck is going on? You sound like shit! Where are you?"

"La Liègiose," Carlo said. "On Granville Island – the Belgian place – it's off by Emily Carr."

"I know where it is. Wait there. I'll be there in fifteen."

When Carlo saw her walking across the patio, Laura's usually straight hair was stirred into a mutinous cloud. "All right; it's time for you to tell me what the fuck is going on. You haven't been yourself for the past month."

Carlo sighed. "He represents your biggest client. I didn't want to get into this...this...soap opera crap with you if I didn't have to, but, well, here we are." He gave her a terse summary of his recent past, his encounters with Declan, Marika, and most recently, Paula.

Laura sat back in her chair, her eyes wide but not blinking. Carlo noted with petty amusement that for the first time in the two decades he'd known her, he had left her speechless. "Well," she finally spoke. "Looks like this might actually be the end of a match made in hell: Woodstock Romeo and the Wicked Witch of the West."

"Oh, I expect that they're already done. But I feel sorry for her, having to deal with *him*, knowing what she knows."

"She knows? Did you actually tell her?"

"In a manner of speaking, yes."

"Really? Holy shit! And where is she now, I mean, what's her name?"

"Marika. She's on her way to her aunt in Toronto. And I lent her some money before she left."

"How much?"

"A thousand."

"Wow." Laura whistled. "She's not going to be able to pay us back anytime soon."

"I don't care."

Laura didn't say anything, unusually quiescent when it came to the subject of money. And Carlo knew why.

"So what now? I guess you'll have to bring your résumé up to date."

"No; not yet, anyway," Carlo said. "I'm going to...what's the expression? Wait for the other shoe to drop."

"Are you kidding me? You're not going to stay there working for that asshole, are you?"

"That depends entirely on what he has to say. If I restricted myself to law firms that don't happen to be run by assholes, I'd be doomed to lifelong unemployment."

"All right, that's it! Let's get out of here. Now. Finish your beer. Let's go somewhere far away."

"I don't need to finish it. It sucks. And can you just blow off the afternoon like that?"

"The afternoon? No, we're going to 'blow off' two or three *days*, and that's all there is to it. Come on, get a move on and we'll make the next ferry. You owe that fucking prick precisely fuck all. As for me, I own half the company. Who's going to complain? The owner of the other half? It's only thanks to modern pharmaceuticals that Woodstock Romeo didn't knock her up, too!"

42

The late autumn sky was a deep blue; a light mist obscured Protection Island, just across the harbour. Joggers and cyclists on the Nanaimo seafront promenade dodged people sedately walking their dogs. The morning of the first field demonstration of the SeaMent electrolysis experiment had finally arrived.

Professor Davidson spent weeks testing the platinum alloy cylindrical net, and now it spanned Gabriola Passage underwater, held in place by tactically-placed floats and sub-surface stays. He hoped that it would be the first phase of a demonstration, a prototype: an underwater tunnel from Gabriola Island, the broad, oblong mass across Nanaimo Harbour, to Valdez Island, wooded and almost uninhabited, extending far to the south. Davidson and about twelve of his staff, most of them post-doctoral research assistants and graduate students, had set up a remote command centre in an upper-floor suite in the Coast Bastion Hotel where a battery of web cameras afforded ready inspection of the experiment site twelve kilometres distant. Gavin, who'd insisted that he was entitled to a spot in the control room, looked on helplessly as Davidson and his assistants monitored a variety of computers and mysterious devices as the experiment quickly moved towards its commencement.

Davidson, usually a properly dishevelled academic who appeared to lack an iron, wore a crisp business suit, fearing ridicule if anyone saw him wearing a white lab coat for the occasion. Even Gavin, who rarely travelled to Nanaimo dressed in anything more formal than his favourite leather jacket, was wearing a suit. Despite his wealth, Gavin disliked being taken for a hayseed. Both expected that the first test would demonstrate at least ambiguous success, enough so that they could fish for praise when Willingdon, the federal Industry minister and a bevy of senior federal and provincial bureaucrats turned up later that afternoon when the experiment would be entering its concluding stage. As far as they knew, a handful of the premier's staff were watching events unfold in Victoria, on closed circuit television.

"There's more than enough power to get this phase done," Davidson said as he peered into a laptop screen which served as the monitor for electric current. "The extra juice from the pulp mills put us over the top." Gavin smiled, unable to deny himself a flush of self-satisfaction.

By Gavin's count, ten monitors displayed images from underwater cameras, showing the environs of the test site from a variety of perspectives. A few others showed conditions on the surface, the surrounding forested coastline, and the rocky shore opposite. Young assistants scurried from workstation to workstation, typing in the required codes and commands. Gavin had no idea what they were doing. The control centre seemed inoffensive, commonplace; not much different from the security room in a shopping mall or a medium-sized resort.

Davidson surveyed the room. All of his assistants seemed to be sucking in their breath.

"All right, ladies and gentlemen, we're about to go live." He turned to Gavin. "This is the central control module." He pointed at a large flat screen monitor attached to a series of two or three plastic rectangles. "And this is the main timer." A smaller flat screen.

0:00:00:00

"Okay, everyone, hold on to your hats," Davidson said as he selected menu item on the central control monitor, that opened a busy window conveying a bewildering jumble of information. Then he moved the cursor over with his mouse and clicked it. Gavin was disappointed: in his mind's eye, he had expected that the whole thing would start up as Davidson cackled maniacally and then flipped over a chunky knife switch, preferably adorned with a spooky black handle. "We're on."

At first, Davidson focused on the screens showing the progress of the process itself. "Oh, look at this." Gavin moved over to look at the screen where Davidson was pointing. A thin coating that looked like eggshell accumulated on portions of the round wire cage. "Good, it appears..." One of his assistants interrupted him. "Professor, come here."

"This is unexpected," Davidson said in an apprehensive tone as he peered into the screen. "The cage assembly is drawing substantially more power than we thought it would."

"Isn't there some way of turning it down?" Gavin asked.

"It doesn't work like that, Gavin," Davidson said, distracted by the data scrolling past on the screen. "And if you remember, we were more worried about not having enough power rather than too much."

"Dr. Davidson, we have a problem," a young woman shouted in a shaky voice.

Davidson ran across the room to another screen. "Damn it; it's killing more fish than we'd projected." From his monitor, Gavin could see some rockfish and what looked to him like little trout floating upward to the surface. Davidson returned to the main monitor. "Right," he said with relief. "Accumulation continues apace, at a slightly faster rate than predicted."

Gavin peered in horror at the monitor. At first there were just a few more fish, belly up, but in an instant, from shore to the horizon, the sea was filling with seemingly endless reinforcements of dead fish floating to the surface. "Christian; I'm telling you, we've got a situation!" He was surprised by the trill of panic in his voice. Davidson's reply was cut short by the beep of his cell phone.

"Yes?" Davidson's face turned ashen; his body abruptly fell limp. "Stop the experiment," he shouted. "Cut power now!" Two of the assistants rushed between a series of monitors and keypads, typing in codes, clicking switches.

"What's going on?" Gavin asked.

Davidson sat down on a stool and dangled his hands about his knees, hunched over like a vanquished boxer. "It's the ferry, the Queen of Coquitlam." He named one of the ferries in the provincial fleet that made a frequent voyage between West Vancouver and Nanaimo. "The electronic sounding and navigation system apparently started delivering nonsensical data. Then it ran into a submerged rock just off Snake Island. It all happened very quickly." Davidson held his breath. "It sunk."

Everyone in the room acquired a funereal mien. "All right, everyone," Davidson said. "It would be best if we didn't stay here any longer than necessary. Start dismantling the command station as soon as you can. Use the freight elevator and do not, whatever you do, *do not* discuss this with anyone. Balbir?" He turned to one of his students. "Help me park the vans by the rear fire exit. We'll pack up there."

"And where are we taking it?" A graduate student asked, one who to Gavin looked like a twelve-year-old girl. "Back to Sedgwick?"

"No, Donna, I don't want to take the equipment back to the mainland right away," Davidson said. "I don't know. I think that an early return to campus would provoke too many unwelcome questions." He looked at Gavin for some sort of solution.

"I own a strip mall off the highway in Chase River," Gavin said, but Donna looked back at him with an uncomprehending expression. "It's on the old highway, just south of town. There's a storefront, an old Subway franchise that went bust. It's been empty for months. I'll get the key from the manager of the drugstore next door; he's looking after it for me until I find a tenant. You can store the equipment there until I rent it out again."

"Thank you, Gavin," Davidson sighed.

"What about the platform? The electrodes?" another graduate student mumbled as he disconnected cables and gathered computer mice.

Davidson shot a glance at Gavin, as if the issue had not yet occurred to him. "There is nothing we can do about that, certainly not now," Gavin said. "We can only hope that nobody notices. All I can suggest, Christian, is that I keep on paying the security guards; they'll keep inquisitive people off the access road. Even if that's not going to block any wayward kayakers, well, who's going to figure it out?" He could see rivulets of sweat descending Davidson's face.

"Jessica," Davidson spoke to another faculty member, whom Gavin recognised as the girl who was dressed like a Goth when he and Gollander visited Davidson on campus. "I don't want everyone going back to the mainland *en masse* so soon. Take the crew to Tofino for a few days, but instead of submitting the expenses to the department for reimbursement, submit them to me." He smiled for the first time since the experiment 'went live'. "And I don't want to see any more than one group dinner at Wick' Inn," (A renowned dining room attached to a luxury resort.) "The rest of the time, you can eat at a pub. You're young."

Gavin remembered something a childhood friend once told him, someone who had always been fascinated by all things nautical and eventually became a supertanker captain: even large ships (assuming a confluence of unfavourable circumstances) could sink in less than two minutes. He always dismissed such talk as alarmist, the storied *worst-case scenario*. "How did this happen, Christian? How could the project cause a ferry to sink? And so quickly" he asked Davidson.

Davidson responded slowly, as if addressing someone who was mentally defective. "I don't know, Gavin. I must admit to having a certain curiosity myself, but the last thing that I want to end up doing is testifying before the inevitable committee of inquiry, or worse, in a courtroom. My principal concern is treating the wound before it becomes infected."

"Sorry."

Davidson leaned over to Gavin, and said in stage whisper, "Just like the old song: we'd best clean up this mess, or else we'll both end up in jail." As he helped one the students lift a heavy flat-screen monitor, Gavin looked at the screen showing elapsed time, frozen at the time of the phone call.

0:12:52:10

A small convoy of UBC minivans crossed downtown Nanaimo without anyone taking any apparent note of their existence, all of them eventually congregating in the parking lot of a suburban strip mall. Once Gavin had opened the door to the empty storefront, they quickly emptied the vans of their many cases and boxes. Davidson's phone started to beep after they were in the midst of loading the last of the equipment into the empty storefront unit.

"Yes? Oh, hello." He adopted the frightened scowl of a dog fearing a vigorous beating. "Yes, yes. He's right here. Yes, that's fine, we'll be there, see you then."

"What was that all about?" Gavin asked.

"Willingdon. Not a happy man. He wants to see us in Fabién Lerche's office in Victoria, first thing tomorrow morning. I gather that he interprets that as being about seven-thirty."

As the students got into the empty vans and started their journey to the west side of the Island, Gavin and Davidson walked across the parking lot. "That early, eh?" Gavin asked. "What do you suppose they want?"

"Look, I wouldn't be all that surprised if they had us both executed by firing squad and buried in shallow graves in North Saanich. That was a joke. No." He looked down at Gavin. "I think they want to make sure that we're on board with ensuring that this episode never sees the light of day."

"Well, I suppose that we'd best make our way down Island; we might as well take my car. I just have to call Tiffany to let her know." He paused in mid-dial. "Christian, do you drink Scotch?"

"I most certainly do."

"Glad to hear it. I know this place on Government Street that has the best selection of single malts this side of Edinburgh."

"Good, let's not waste any time. If I didn't drink whisky already, this would be a most opportune time to start."

....43

Nikki's Party
Nikki's Best Gossip – This Week

This week Nikki is way out in the wilds of British Columbia. Could it be that our Casanova of the rainforest is losing his touch? My old friend, Fabién Lerche, our favourite Victoria politico, he of the sleek dark hair and seductive smile, who has lured many an actress and one or two student activists of tender years into passionate (but, Nikki notes, rarely lengthy) affairs, showed up at a Vancouver Board of Trade bun toss last weekend with his left hand in a cast. A Times-Colonist reporter who happened to be in the emergency room at Victoria's Royal Jubilee Hospital in (let's just say) the recent past, saw Fabién massaging his injured paw, complaining that his wounds were the work of some young lady or another (he didn't use those words). None of the hospital staff are talking, and Victoria politicos are keeping mum about it, especially young Gurjit Basi, the Cabinet colleague who reportedly rushed to Fabién's bedside and helped him lick his wounds. So who finally resisted the reputedly overbearing advances of our soggy west coast Lothario? Among the candidates are Traci McSween, lead vocalist in The Fenceposts (whom Fabién was seen to be pursuing with embarrassing ardour until quite recently) and Caribbean beauty Laeticia Bradbury, assistant professor of marine biology at the University of Victoria and frequent wine bar companion of the former Minister of the Environment. Whoever it was, good on her. It was long overdue that someone finally taught Monsieur Lerche that simply because an alluring female was close at hand did not entitle him to treat the occasion as if he were a four-year-old in the stuffed animal section of Toys 'R Us.

43

QUEEN OF COQUITLAM TRAGEDY
Thirteen dead, more than two hundred cars destroyed
Numerous pets perish

Sipping his morning espresso at Calista's, Carlo felt mounting horror as he read the front page of the *Vancouver Sun*. He and Laura had been on one of the ferries that day, although on a different route. Ferries just don't just sink in calm seas for no reason. Although he was tempted to order a second espresso and linger for another twenty minutes, he decided that he'd better get to work after being away for the better part of a week.

Nobody was sitting at the reception desk. Bal and Jacquie looked down as he came in, theatrically engrossed in their files. Carlo greeted them on his way to his office; both offered tentative smiles. Thomas appeared in his doorway as his computer sparkled to life.

"I'm glad to see you back, Carlo."

"Oh hi, Thomas. I don't suppose you know what's been going on."

"Not only do *I* know what happened, but so does everyone else on this floor, if not the floors above and below. Oh, don't look so puzzled! Paula came here the day you disappeared, and shouted quite a list of transgressions at the top of her lungs. It's amazing how such a slender woman can have as powerful a voice as Maria Callas. Anyway, I gather that Declan would like to have a chat with you." His smirk faded. "How *is* Marika?"

"I haven't heard from her for almost three weeks. She was on her way to Toronto the last I saw her; she has an aunt there."

"Toronto? Did Declan give her any money?"

"No, I did."

"Oh."

The display on Carlo's office phone warned that he had forty-three voice mail messages; he never had the opportunity to record an extended absence greeting before he and Laura decided to take off. An equally daunting number of e-mails inevitably awaited him. Before he could check any of them, Declan came into his office and shut the door behind him.

"I think that it would be best if we had a frank discussion sooner rather than later." Declan sat down in one of the chairs facing his desk. "As I am sure you've heard, I have a number of ...of...of...personal issues to deal with right now."

"That really isn't any concern of mine."

"I suppose it's not." Declan sighed, his face a cadaverous shade of grey. "I am not asking for sympathy. Look, I realize that I have behaved in a despicable, cowardly way and I do not expect your forgiveness, after the way that I treated you."

Carlo folded his arms and looked over at Declan. "Then what do you want?"

"I want to talk about your continued presence here, as an associate. I am hoping that you will stay on. You have done an excellent job on the Striationist files, as well as the other ones I have assigned you; and you even managed to bring in a high-profile client."

"Gavin, you mean."

"Yes."

"Well, I guess I have to ask myself, can I still work with you? I don't know. I mean, what you did was despicable. You had an affair for years with Marika, and when you finally slipped up and, how did you put it, she 'got fat and fell off the tree', you faced getting caught so you tried to dump the 'evidence' on me."

Declan, listening with a rapt and unblinking gaze, interrupted and held up his hand. "I know what I did. And I am sorry."

Carlo examined the figure sitting in front of him, who displayed the irritating ability to appear at once both haughty and abject. He doubted that Declan was genuinely contrite. This time, however, it was not mere artifice. His apology was clumsy, in striking contrast to any of his past attempts to convey an apt mood, a tactically timely gesture, which were always so callow and emotive that it was obvious he was simply replicating a technique he had learned at some seminar or another. Still, any suggestion that Declan's demeanour betrayed an essential humanity seemed preposterous. In the months that Carlo had worked for him, Declan had never shown the capacity to feel either shame or even token concern for anyone else.

Carlo considered his situation. Before, he found Declan's incessant posturing and manipulation to be tiresome distractions that demanded too much concentration. He would be better able to work with Declan now that there remained no question that he was thoroughly untrustworthy. Besides, Carlo sensed an opportunity to gain some sort of advantage, however temporary.

"All right." Carlo said. "I think that we can do business. But these are my terms." For the first time that morning, Declan appeared to be actually engaged in the exchange in a way one would expect from a lawyer who had been in practice for four decades. "First," Carlo tallied with his fingers, "Laura and I have to go over to visit my father (he lives in London) and inevitably, he will want us to go with him on a trip to visit the family in Italy when we're there. I would like an additional two weeks of vacation."

Declan flapped his arms in an extravagant wave. "As long as the work gets done, you can take all of the time off you want."

"Good." Carlo added his next demand out of spite. Although it was not strictly necessary to keep him there, it involved the expenditure of money and was almost certain to drive Declan to the brink of apoplexy. "And second, since I have been back in Vancouver, I have been able to get a better idea of the local market." He savoured the disquiet evident in the set of Declan's jaw. "Now, before I had to leave Toronto I had been practicing for almost seven years. But I know, realistically, I was completely out of the game for three years. But even a two-year call these days makes ninety thousand dollars in this city." Carlo used the common legal argot referring to someone who'd been in practice two years after being called to the Bar. "I realize that this is a very small firm, so I am asking for eighty."

Declan leaned back in his chair and exhaled theatrically. "Look, I need you here. I won't be able to get through this project without you. If you say that the going rate is ninety, I'll pay you ninety. Do we have a deal?"

"Yes."

"I am very glad to hear it." As he rose and reached for the door handle, Declan turned back to face Carlo. "Look, I know that after all that has happened, we will never actually be *friends*. But I expect that we will be able to work together."

"Yes, I expect that we will."

"Good. Sometime later this week, you will have to give me a full briefing on the Striationist file. My mind has been on ...ah...other things. It is time for us to develop a strategy, moving forward."

"I agree," Carlo said. "But we will have to wait to do it until next Monday. I have to go over to the Island this weekend to do one last little bit of research."

"Oh? Anything that I can help you with?"

"No, not really. There's just one last detail I have to firm up before I can give you a full report, we'll just say."

Declan bit his lip and looked back at Carlo. "Oh, yes; there was something else I want you to do. Under the circumstances...I suppose, ah, well, you know the file better than I do, I think you should be the public face of this firm when dealing with the religion, particularly." His tone deepened. "With respect to any interaction with that public relations outfit. You have, after all, a less, well, I suppose I mean to say, a *better* personal connection."

That evening before dinner, Laura found Carlo in the spare room, gathering up his backpacking equipment. "What, did the asshole piss you off again? Did you quit?"

"No, no," he laughed. "It's about that big real estate development up by Buckley Bay, you know, the one in the Pentlatch valley. There are a couple of things that I want to check out for myself, on site, we'll just say."

"You don't really believe that bullshit, do you?"

"I don't know…it looks like the Reformed bunch has actually started selling, and there is too much evidence I can't just ignore to show that it might really exist." He told her about the website. "So something's up. It isn't just a lot of gossip. I think I've found a way to tiptoe in and have a look see."

"Really? How?"

"There's no way to get in on Pentlatch Forest Service Road; the security perimeter is insane." Some of the reports that Carlo found on hiking websites amply verified Ulela's observations. The main access, a dusty two-lane gravel road that McKee McWatney acquired during the Nineties, was under constant guard by a diligent security detail. The ostensible purpose of all this vigilance was to protect company property from vandalism, but now, Carlo wondered. "But remember the Mount Joseph trail?"

"The one where we got lost that time?"

"That's the one."

"Look, I still think it's all a steaming heap of bullshit, but there might actually be something to all this. I'll come with you. How about that?"

"*What?* After that time you told me you never wanted to go backpacking again."

"Oh, I've tried it again a couple of times since then; my stuff's down in storage. And at this late date, it sounds like fun. It's sort of work related, and it beats the crap out of sitting around here reading *Nikki's Party.*"

"Hey," Carlo laughed. "Why not?"

"So are we staying a night with my parents, or…?"

"No, I really don't want to involve more people in this than I have to. I've booked at Mud Bay Cottages tomorrow night. I was going to head up the trail the next morning."

"Wow. Mud Bay Cottages; just like old times. Not exactly deluxe accommodations, if memory serves, but they beat the fuck out of the back seat of your Datsun. As long as we don't bring home bedbugs."

They spent part of the following afternoon in an outdoor equipment shop in Nanaimo where they found topographic maps of that part of the mid-Island. Once at Mud Bay, Carlo spread them out on the small dining table in their cabin. "Here's the Michelin- style tourist map that Mario printed off for me."

"Mario? How is he in this?"

"As a consultant. He knows how to hack into hidden websites without anybody knowing."

"Hmm, I guess his porn addiction eventually paid off. So here's the real map." Laura pulled the government contour map towards her. Although the physical features and watercourses shown on the website map did not accord precisely with the local topography, the Dinant and Fiorenza developments appeared to be located in the broad upper valley of the Pentlatch River; the Sirmione project, rested on the shores of Bilberry Lake, a long, narrow tarn in a hanging valley above it in the Beaufort Mountains. "So how did you want to get in?"

"This way, up the road on the other side of the mountain to the trailhead; all of the hiking websites say there's no security around there; no problem getting to the old trailhead." The trail scaled Mount Joseph, the peak that rose just to the south of Bilberry Lake. "Then we leave the trail and bushwhack through here to the lake." He ran his finger along a flat ridge shown on the map.

"Oh, I see what you mean. Hey, wait a minute: once we're at the lake, we can scoot over here."

"If there isn't some bogus mountain village in the way."

"Oh, there won't be. We can camp at the lake and walk over here; see? The contours show an abrupt end to the ridge. It'll give us a panoramic view of the whole development, if there is one."

The next morning, they made their way through an old logging road network. After two hours of driving his Jeep along turbulent, often overgrown backroads, they finally found the trail.

"Are we lost again?" Laura said.

"No. There it is." Carlo pointed to a path that joined the road just ahead of them, marked by ribbons of orange flagging tape, entering a thick second growth forest. They both slid on their backpacks, brightly-coloured, expensive nylon pouches, and made their way up the rustic path.

The trail was much as he remembered; a steep, rocky track, lately rendered indistinct in spots by patches of helicopter logging slash. They left the trail as it crossed the narrow benchland shown on the government map, east of the lake, which connected to the broad plateau to the west of it, covered by a pleasant, open subalpine forest.

After they'd walked for about an hour, Laura pointed to an azure expanse visible below through the trees. "Look! There's our lake!"

They found a meadow along the shores of the lake and dropped their backpacks, thankful for the absence of snow. Carlo took out his camera to snap a few pictures. *Sirmione.* He pondered the narrow, brushy peninsula on the other side of the lake. *Sirmione indeed.* Bilberry Lake, its wooded shores and glacial, opaque turquoise water — the only hint of a recent human presence was a rock ring with the charred remnants of a few logs of firewood.

"Told ya!" Laura said.

The sky was clear; the autumn air was dry and chilled him when the two of them stopped to rest. Carlo expected that it would almost certainly fall below freezing that night. After they set up their tent, they both drew a cup of water out of the lake.

"Let's head over and check out the view," Laura said

They whacked their way through thickets of mountain blueberries and trudged toward the viewpoint at the edge of the Pentlatch valley, just to the west, according to the map. It indeed afforded as broad a panorama as Laura had predicted, but instead of a vista of a constellation of European-style towns, they saw an expanse of nothing but spindly second-growth trees, with the odd patch of logging slash here and there. The alders and broadleaf maples that lined the valley floor were almost bereft of leaves.

"Just as I said it'd be," Laura said. "Jack shit!"

"Let's make sure. If there's any work going on at all around here, it will be down closer to the river."

They continued down to the valley bottom. Once within sound of the rush of the current, they followed an old logging grade and eventually found a broad gravel bar just downstream from the conspicuous bluff that marked the site of the supposed Dinant development. But instead of a maze of cobblestone streets and austere, stone Walloon buildings, all they saw were river rocks, driftwood and the sun-bleached skeleton of an elk. No need to continue to see if the Fiorenza and Oxbridge developments existed. The forest on the bank opposite was a nettle-choked jungle. Nobody had been doing anything in this valley for a decade at least, and the forces of economic development were unlikely to return until the trees grew back.

"Well, it's not exactly Belgium, but I like it," Carlo said. "It's a nice place."

"Oh, I'd like to come back here sometime, but for the time being, let's get the fuck back to the campsite before someone sees us," Laura said. "And besides, it's going to get dark around here sooner rather than later.

Once they climbed back up to the lake, Carlo lit his camp stove, to heat up some *cicoria e fave* he'd brought in two plastic Nalgene jars.

"Is that what I think it is?" Laura said.

"Hey; it's nutritious, and I had some left over in the freezer."

"It's also one of the things I missed about you the least. Oh well, doesn't matter. I'm so hungry I could eat *anything* just about now. You brought wine, didn't you?"

"Of course I did; you know me better than that. But we're supposed to be in Sirmione." Carlo laughed. "With all of its five-star hotels, *trattorie*, bars. Lakeside patios. So first, an *aperitivo*. "*Ò! Uagliò!*" he shouted at an imaginary waiter. "*Mi porta due birre!*" The trill of Laura's laughter echoed from the bluff on the opposite shore.

44

Premier Willingdon decided that it was time to gather the inner Cabinet, his trusted five. He and Terrence Goyter, joined by Lawrence Gollander, Fabién Lerche and Gurjit Basi, sat facing one another on randomly scattered barstools, assembled in a dank room in the basement of the Empress Hotel. No windows, no table.

"All right," Goyter announced with his well-known phlegmatic growl. "Nobody knows that we're here. So far, I've been fully briefed by both Skoff and Professor Davidson. Skoff assures me that no one, least of all anyone on Gabriola Island, has any idea what was going on. Both of them were able to identify only ten other people, all academic staff, who were aware of the project at all; and it's only the six assistants, the ones who were actually there in the Coast Bastion, who know what really happened to the ferry. And Skoff (who has more common sense than I ever gave him credit for) ensured that none of the contactors or third-party suppliers had a clue about what the electrical connections and power conduits were being used for. Of course." He grimaced. "They were outrageously well paid."

"And there's *us*, of course," Gollander said.

Basi was the first to show any curiosity. "Well, how did it happen? I mean, what interfered with the ferry's navigation equipment?"

"It was really the inevitable result of the combined effect of strict secrecy and narrow specialization," Goyter said.

Basi wrinkled her forehead in confusion.

"Well, Davidson, thank God, made sure that nobody at the university knew what he was up to, holed up in that old building on the fringes of the Endowment Lands, other than the fact that it had something to do with SeaMent. And as brilliant as he is in the field of marine sciences, he didn't have the opportunity to consult with someone equally brilliant, in, let's say, electromagnetics, so that maybe he could determine the effects of the project on navigation equipment. He says that it never even occurred to him."

"But Skoff had been beaking off, telling whoever would listen that...", Fabién said as Gurjit nodded in agreement.

"Yes, he had been." Goyter didn't let him finish his sentence. "But fortunately, there really isn't enough information out there to even tweak some crazy-ass blogger to put two and two together. Now, I've already met with the six young academics to impress upon them the need for the utmost discretion regarding anything that involves the SeaMent project, and especially the Gabriola test. They seem to get it." He nodded to himself, as if assessing a valuable figurine. "And so that they know how much we expect it, we have arranged to provide each of them with suitable promotions in exchange for their...let's say their 'forbearance'. But no tenure; not yet. We want the ability to run them out of town if they ever show signs of wanting to go public. And besides." He released a light belch. "Not one of them is even thirty, yet."

Willingdon sat forward to exert control over the meeting. "From now on, no one is to speak of this. If you become aware of *anyone*, and I mean anyone at all, mentioning even a hint of this on any medium, you be sure to *immediately* bring it to the attention of Jasmine Smollitt in my communications department. She's very competent; I've put her in charge of the clean-up crew."

Gurjit typed something into her phone. "What effect do you think that this might have on the McKee-McWatney lands; that project that Midlands Shropshire is building; what is it called, Europa or something?"

"Nothing, as far as we can tell. All of us Striationists," Goyter smirked. "We're well acquainted with Émile Basaraba; he's one of us, after all. He's also Midland's point man on the project and he assures me that the project will be finished by next June and sales continue apace. I don't know what to tell you; it's almost fully subscribed."

"But now we know that there isn't going to be a bridge anytime soon." Gurjit said.

"Bridge, fixed link." Willingdon said. "Call it what you like. It wasn't going to be built next week anyway, and now it remains what it has been for the past hundred years: a mere future consideration, a bit of swamp gas that the editors of *The Province* and the usual suspects in the real estate industry dredge up from time to time whenever they want to stir up trouble."

"And," Willingdon spoke up. "If you look at that aftermarket for the partnership units that Basaraba has been selling, what's it called, that place in Toronto?"

"Corvair Intermediaries," Gollander said.

"Yes, Corvair," Willingdon said. "Anyway, the aftermarket, it's quite active. People who missed buying early on have flocked to the online exchange. The price per unit has almost *doubled* on resale. It's *insane*; it's just insane."

Once back in his office, Gollander pulled up the Corvair website. *Only it's not insane.* Several months earlier, he bought up two thousand partnership units on his own account, at well below the initial subscription price. He watched with unbridled delight as their price steadily climbed, probably, he suspected, through the manipulations of a secretive collection of dictators, gangsters and tax cheats who used them as a parking spot for illicit cash.

Gollander never expected to be in Cabinet in the first place, despite his lifelong friendship with Willingdon. But Minister of Finance? He had shown them, *those people,* and the party had more than its share of them: either west side patricians with pert, upturned noses and perfect skin, or the impatient children of immigrants from fetid locales. Either way, all of them looked at him as if he didn't bathe. It was different for people like Willingdon. His addictions, gambling during the seventies and cocaine during the Eighties, blighted the trajectory of his career despite his Cambridge education, but people of that ilk always land on their feet unless they turn out to be pedophiles. It was his own story that ought to have inspired at least some respect, the son of a defrocked priest who eked out a pittance delivering vegetables; an east side boy who grew up admiring hubcap thieves.

Gollander summoned his executive assistant to his office. Guy Tsang had worked with him for almost ten years, first as an intern during the year after he was elected to the Legislature.

"Good afternoon, Guy." Gollander looked up when he saw him come in.

"Good afternoon," Guy said with his usual hushed calm. He sat in the stool facing Gollander's desk.

"Are you familiar with the Midland Shropshire partnership units?" Gollander smiled. "They're the ones traded by Corvair Intermediaries."

"No. Midland *who*? And I've definitely *never* heard of Corsair."

"Corvair. Anyway, how much is in the first and second quarter contingency fund?"

Guy consulted his iPhone. "I would estimate that it would be around fifty-two million."

"Good. I want you to use it to buy partnership units. The way they have been going up in price, we may be able to return, conservatively, twenty or twenty-five million extra to general revenue." He laughed. "We'll look like a pair of financial geniuses!"

A look of horror passed over Guy's face. "We can't — well, it's against the guidelines for us to invest the contingency fund in anything more speculative than T-Bills. And *that* sort of investment, it has to be vetted and approved by the Treasury Board."

Gollander sat back in his chair. "I'm sorry, I'm new at this. Is the Treasury Board the Minister of Finance?"

"Well, no. You are, of course."

"Right you are!" Gollander slapped his desk. "Please, Guy, please trust me on this. It's what I used to do for a living. We won't be leaving the money there for long, but just long enough to earn us a bit of praise."

Guy rose from his chair. "All right, it will take me a bit of time to prepare the special warrants. I trust you'll be signing all of them, and the deputy minister; I don't suppose that he'll be countersigning?"

"Oh yes, this is solely on my authority," Gollander answered him in a hushed voice. "So I would hope that you do not discuss this with anyone."

"Oh, no; of course not. What was it called again, Corvair Intermediaries?"

45

As soon as they awoke the following morning, Carlo and Laura packed up their equipment and hiked back to the Jeep, allowing themselves only enough time to gulp down a pot of coffee. By noon, they were already at the ferry terminal, waiting for the boat back to Vancouver. Carlo knew that he had to call Gavin immediately. It was not likely to be very long before his partnership units, to the extent that they ever really existed, would be reduced to electronic phantoms haunting cyberspace, worthless strings of binary code. It would have presented far too much of a risk to warn him by calling him on his mobile phone. The office landline would be the most secure way to tell him, other than meeting him face to face.

By the time Carlo arrived at the office, it was already mid-afternoon. Declan sat slumped forward, all elbows and fists, cloistered in his office with the door closed in the midst of a telephone conversation. Carlo had little doubt that the call was somehow occasioned by Paula, who, according to the gossip prevailing in the office (and, more raucously, amongst the fractious Vancouver bar), wanted to be rid of Declan at the first opportunity. He went into his office to dial Gavin's home number. No answer; he left a message on their answering machine, Tiffany's perky voice extending the greeting. Carlo busied himself answering a few e-mails before Gavin called him back.

"What's up?" Gavin sounded out of breath.

Carlo dispensed with the customary exchange of pleasantries. "There's no delicate way to put this. You have to sell *all* of your investments in Midland Shropshire, or anything to do with that bogus development, now. Immediately."

"What do you mean, *bogus*?" Gavin said with a tone of annoyance that changed to one of bewilderment once Carlo explained what he'd found in the Pentlatch Valley. "So there aren't any condos? No golf courses? No...no..." Gavin searched for words. "Little Belgian villages?"

"It's all bullshit, Gavin. Just trees, trees and more trees. You have to get rid of those partnership units *now*. They won't even qualify as junk bonds once this becomes common knowledge."

"But how, I don't know..." Gavin's voice trailed off.

Carlo could easily understand why the prospective loss of almost two million might leave Gavin dissonant. "Look, I think that we can do it by the end of the week; we'll have to put the whole thing through our trust account. I'll try to make it look like I'm acting for five or six investors. But we'll have to meet in person. I'll need your signature on several documents. And bring the, the, what are they called?

"Partnership certificates."

"Yes, those," Carlo said. "Bring them over with you."

"I'll be there on the morning seaplane from Nanaimo," Gavin sighed.

Carlo walked across the office and knocked on Declan's door. No audible reply; Carlo opened the door a sliver to peer in. Declan was sitting at his desk, his swivel chair turned to face the window. He appeared to be staring at Mount Seymour. "Never get married, Carlo," he muttered.

Carlo suppressed the reply that immediately came to mind. "We have to go over the Striationist file, to bring you up to date. I'll spread the file out at the library table." After about twenty minutes, Declan emerged from his office and sat down in the library. Carlo spoke rapidly, trying to explain what he knew without choking his description with too much detail.

"So," Declan said as he wiped the lenses of his reading glasses. "I want to make sure that I actually understand this. This year's entire Wellspring was basically hijacked by that weird little Gollander fellow, Basaraba (who I still have trouble believing actually exists), and the former Master of the Treasure, Ian McHarg." He looked over the disorderly jumble of documents spread out over the long table in the library. "You know, I never met McHarg, I knew old Dave Abercrombie; he held that position for years, but McHarg hasn't been around very long."

"Yes, only it wasn't really McHarg," Carlo handed Declan a photocopy that displayed McHarg's actual signature, taken from the files Ulela showed him in Qualicum Bay, and the one on the bank documents used to open the new account and effect the transfer.

Declan peered at the two forms Carlo showed him. "Yes, they are quite different."

"And Leola Fortin, the account manager who met with the three of them, described him as a short, skinny man with thinning reddish hair and a Canadian accent. The actual McHarg speaks with an incomprehensible Scottish accent; and he's *big*, over six feet tall, with a full head of long, dark brown hair."

"Hmm, forgery." Declan looked over some of the documents in front of him and shook his head. "But didn't the woman at the bank think to ask him for ID?"

"Yes, where is it?" Carlo said as he rummaged through the productions binder. "Here it is, the B.C. driver's license that she copied when they opened the account."

Declan put his glasses back on. "Doesn't even *look* like a Scot. All right." He rubbed his eyes. "The land. What happened to all of the property that was transferred out from underneath the Orthodox bunch?"

"That's where it all gets very confusing, and fortunately, only a small part of it is actually our problem."

"Excuse me?"

"The properties have each been sold and resold to and from a variety of numbered companies, few of which actually exist. At each stage, the purchase was financed by a mortgage issued by Corvair Intermediaries in Toronto, which in turn was immediately assigned to a Canadian or Asian bank (but never the Royal) if the land was located in Canada or one of many American and European (usually French) banks if it was in the U.S."

"So, how do we know that the Reformed people were behind the whole thing?"

Carlo pulled a legal-size form out of the pile. "Because each of the initial Agreements of Purchase and Sale were signed by Ian McHarg."

Declan looked over the form Carlo put in front of him. "Hmm, the same signature as the one at the bank." He sat back in his chair again and gazed out the library window. "So what you're telling me is that the Reformed bunch defrauded the banks?"

"Well, somebody did, and they did it many, many times. Either the Reformed Striationists were behind it, or perhaps someone else did it with their...forbearance, let's say. Not to mention the fact that they were at least tangentially involved in defrauding people who thought that they were investing in a condominium development, which, as it turns out, doesn't exist."

"Doesn't...exist?"

"The Orthodox bunch, remember how they were on about some real estate development supposedly planned by the Reformed people on central Vancouver Island? Well, it wasn't just their usual delusions. Someone pretended to build it, and then proceeded to sell it off for real by peddling 'partnership units', all orchestrated by the same Corvair Intermediaries that issued the fake mortgages. Only there is no real estate development."

"How do you know about this, these...these partnership units, whatever they are?"

"Because Gavin Skoff bought about two million dollars' worth."

Declan rubbed his temples and closed his eyes. "I'm sorry; I must be getting old. You're giving me a headache. Explain it to me again, but this time, slowly." Carlo commenced a methodical explanation, a chronological synthesis of what Gavin had told him, the contents of the Russian website, and the primeval scene that he and Laura found on the ground when they went to the sites of the ostensible Sirmione and Dinant developments.

"And you're saying there is nothing there?"

"Not so much as an old outhouse."

"My God," Declan sighed. "Does Sadich know about all of this?"

"I assume that he does. I've been in regular telephone and e-mail contact with his associate."

"Oh, yes, the Chinese girl. I guess I'd better get on the phone with Sadich."

"I suppose that we will have to contact the police; the RCMP Fraud Squad or something," Carlo said.

Declan leaned back in his seat and looked at him, a bemused grin spreading across his face. "You know, it's times like these that you make it brutally plain to me that I'm not dealing with seasoned counsel, a lawyer of twenty-five, thirty years of experience. *Of course* we're not contacting the police. The power structure, the élite of the province and the Reformed Striationists are one and the same. Going to the authorities, such that they are, would only allow the perpetrators enough warning to destroy evidence and give their public relations people enough time to come up with innocent-sounding explanations for all that's been going on."

"I guess that you're probably right," Carlo mumbled, not entirely convinced.

"*Probably?*" Declan laughed. "You are so lucky that you have me, the sage, experienced voice of reason to keep you out of trouble. If you went to the police, we'd end up being sued by our clients and your legal career would be in ruins." Declan fell silent, deep in thought. "But be that as it may, you have to find a way to bring this to a head, and sooner rather than later. Some way to make the people behind this scheme to either show their hand or turn on one another, once they find out that an outsider is on to them."

Carlo's eyes narrowed. "Such as?"

"You tell me. You know the details, the ins and outs of this whole escapade much better than I do. I'll leave it to you to come up with something that will fit the bill. But you have to make sure that it is done with absolute anonymity. *Nothing* can be traceable not back to our client, not to you, not to the firm."

Carlo was scribbling on a yellow pad as Declan spoke, looking up after he finished. "I have an idea."

"I have no doubt that you do." Declan grinned again. "And as I was saying, this whole charade, which is what it appears to be, has been going on long enough. The longer it continues, the less likely that the Orthodox bunch will be able to get any of their money back out of it."

"I think that..." Carlo started gesticulating. "That the best way to..."

Declan held up his hand. "Not a word. I don't want to know anything about it."

It took Carlo a few minutes to find the Circolo Santo Spirito, an Italian men's club on a side street off Commercial Drive. On his way toward the bar to ask where Mario was, he passed by a table where three men were in the midst of a game of *scopa,* an Italian card game played with *carte napoletane,* Neapolitan playing cards, which resembled tarot cards more than they did the ubiquitous French ones. One of the men shouted as he triumphantly slapped a card down on the ones lying face up in the middle to claim the coveted *settebello.* Most of the other men in the room glumly watched the soccer game displayed on various big screen televisions, where Napoli, the team favoured by most of the members, was being brutally schooled by the ascendant Juventus.

"*Ò! Uagliò!*" Carlo heard someone shouting from a table squarely facing the most spacious of the televisions, surrounded by a group of seven or eight men who seemed to be in the midst of a lively debate. "Carlo!" After he focused his eyes in the dimly-lit room, he saw Mario's father waving like a deranged traffic cop.

"Ó, Zio Peppino!" Since childhood, both Carlo and Mario had been expected to call the other's parents 'uncle' and 'aunt', although Mario quite understandably shrank from referring to Linda as 'Auntie Linda'. "I'm looking for Mario; Zia Rosa said that he's here."

"Yes. He's in the back, playing with computers." He stood up and grabbed both of Carlo's shoulders. "You haven't been over for a while! And I hear that you're back with Laura. *Bene*! You should come over for dinner; well, what about this Sunday? Zia Rosa is making *bracciòl*; it's still the best on the west coast."

"We'll see." Carlo reached into his pocket and brandished his cell phone. "I'll let you know; I have to check with the lady in charge."

Peppino repeated a ribald aphorism in *barese* dialect that Carlo did not fully understand, something about the wiles that women used to ensure that they maintained the upper hand, which caused everyone else at the table to chortle uproariously. "Ò!" he pointed to Carlo. "See, all grown up; *ú figg' d' Vito Buonsante.*" He identified Carlo as the son of a former member of their circle who had long since disappeared, back across the waters. They all murmured and smiled as Carlo shook hands with them in sequence. "Anyway, go see what my son is up to, playing with his computers. And let me know about dinner."

Carlo went into the small, disordered office behind the far end of the bar. He heard Mario before he saw him.

"Motherfucker!" Mario grunted, twisted in an awkward position. "You fucking cunt!"

Carlo found him crouched underneath a table holding the end of one sort of cable or another. "What are you doing?"

"Oh," Mario grumbled, "Somebody's son's girlfriend mentioned to one of the members that you can get Italian television, with *all* of the soccer games, for free over the Internet, so Pop volunteered my services to set it up."

"That doesn't sound like such a big deal..."

"Motherfucker! That hurts!" Mario shouted. "No, but it *is* when they expect me to make it work with these pieces of shit. I feel like Indiana fucking Jones in the Museum of Ancient Technologies. Typical, cheap old *baresi.* This fucking thing is probably older than *we* are!" He motioned toward a conspicuously antiquated computer tower and its beast-like monitor. "It's barely suitable for Pac Man."

Carlo watched him click away at three separate keyboards for about half an hour. "Okay," he said. "I've linked them into *la RAI* and all of Berlusconi's stations. Oh, shit, wait a minute." The sound of vigorous catcalls rose from the main sitting room. Mario had inadvertently switched the image on the big screens from the game to the news item playing on RAI 24, the twenty-four-hour news channel, something about a nurses' strike in Brescia. The noise subsided after he found the game again and put it back on. "There! My work here is done. So, what's up?"

"Remember that phantom website with the Russian IP you helped me get into? The one I got from Gavin?"

"Yeah, sure. It was kind of weird, but..."

"Well, it was all bullshit. The Pentlatch hasn't changed a hair; nothing going on there, a few heli-logging operations and maybe a mine or two, but not much else."

"No condos?"

"No condos."

"But that doesn't make any sense."

"Oh, it might; which is why I came down here to find you. Is there any way that you can edit the web page at that IP?"

Mario snorted and sat back in his chair. "Let me get this straight: you want me to hack that Russian website?"

"If you want to put it that way."

"I guess those assholes do it to us all the time. What do you want me to do?"

Carlo reached into his pocket and handed him a post-it note and a flash drive. "Here's the IP again, and here is the stuff I want you to plant on the site."

Mario plugged the flash drive into his laptop and brought it up on the screen. "Who did this for you?"

"I did it myself; I bought this book at Chapters called *HTML for Dummies* and..."

"Well, *that* description fits anyway." He scrolled through one of the modules. "But this isn't half-bad." As Mario read further down the page, he started to shake with low, guttural laughter. "You don't expect that anyone will actually believe this, do you?"

"Well, I do. Never underestimate the gullibility that accompanies human greed. But it's not really necessary that anyone actually buys it."

Mario shuddered. "You know, I'm not even going to ask what you're up to. It'll take me about forty-five minutes, maybe an hour to do this. Go out to the bar, get us a couple of pints of Moretti, and it's all good."

....46

Premier Willingdon stood at the front of a long table in one of the Hotel Vancouver conference rooms, waiting as a group of about twenty people wandered in, each carrying coffee and paper plates stacked with fruit and muffins. Gurjit, sitting with Fabién at the far end of the table, looked over the religion's new banner, completed just in time for this hastily arranged assembly of the Reformed Striationist upper echelon.

THE REFORMED STRIATIONIST TOTALITY
Splendor Sine Occasu

Shining without sunset. At first, Gurjit felt a twinge of shame that the Reformed offshoot blithely appropriated British Columbia's Latin motto to serve its own purposes, which was presumptuous enough in its historic spot on the provincial coat of arms, flanked by an elk and a mountain sheep. She reminded herself that the only other slogan that enjoyed any support with other Reformed notables was "Established in 2007", which merely underscored the precariousness of the entire gambit. A high-definition image of a glacial striation, flanked by moss and stonecrop, filled the television screen beneath the banner.

The room fell silent as Willingdon turned and raised his arms in a messianic pose. "This is such bullshit," Gurjit whispered in Fabién's ear.

"I would like to welcome all of you to the second annual meeting of the Reformed Central Committee. Soon, the religion's coffers will be full to the brim! The Europa project, where we put almost all of our liquid assets, is fully subscribed. And the value of each partnership unit just keeps on climbing!"

The guy from TriMar, Peter Scranton, she remembered, shook his head extravagantly.

423

Gurjit examined Scranton with a ferocity that would have surely made him nervous had he noticed. She hadn't seen him since that debacle in Parksville, when Gavin Skoff shit the bed with his frightful slide show. Then, Scranton oozed smugness and glowed with a patina of well-being borne of inexhaustible cash flow. The man she saw sitting at the table to her left fidgeted with an occasional twitch, his face a florid hue suggestive of alcoholism or circulatory ills.

Willingdon tilted his chin to effect a dramatic pause, but Scranton interrupted him. "Look, Garth, this is all very...well, I'll just say, confusing. I'm glad to hear that the Europa project is doing so well. But us, I mean TriMar, we're still on the hook for millions in infrastructure upgrade costs, most of them in the Gateway module, in Parksville. We're being bled dry. And we have yet to see a dime in dividends from Midland Shropshire."

"Well, all that I can tell you is that the project is complete and almost ready for occupancy; within weeks, I've been told. I'm sure that things will soon start to fall into place."

Willingdon attempted to flash a warm, charismatic smile. *Fuck.* Gurjit cringed. *He shouldn't do that; it makes him look like a child molester.*

"I don't know, Garth." Gurjit turned to her right to have a look at the woman who had just spoken up. *Oh my God! It's Joanne Trapp!* When she last saw Trapp at the TriMar presentation, she looked like a madwoman. Now, almost a year later, her austere hairdo of hideous bristle had transformed into a modishly styled, shoulder-length mane of dark brown hair and her ungainly west coast collection of mismatched rags had been replaced with a tailored suit; a vision of mature feminine beauty worthy of a perfume ad in one of those European fashion magazines that cost more than a decent bottle of wine. "I've been a real estate agent for more years than I care to count. I've tried to get clearance for a viewing of some of the project. You can't even get a peek! If you go off the highway, those apes Midland or whoever has hired as security quickly shoo you off. Now." She raised her voice. "The Dinant and Sirmione sections have supposedly been complete for several weeks but they still won't let me in to see them. I'm beginning to..."

Goyter, still seated, cleared his throat to cut her short. "I spoke a couple of days ago with Émile Basaraba. He's not only Master of the Treasure but he's Midland's point man here on the coast last week. He said that they will have a full open house for the entire project with their grand opening in about a month."

Scranton groaned. "Grand opening! And are you kidding me? That 'Basaraba' guy again? I might as well start believing in the Tooth Fairy."

"There is no justification for outbursts like that!" Willingdon slid his glasses further down his nose. "Basaraba is out of the province on some other business; he's much in demand, that fellow, and we're lucky that he's one of us. You're simply going to have to be patient for a little longer." He folded his arms.

"And the bridge, or fixed link, or whatever it is." A woman that Gurjit didn't recognize raised her voice. "We've heard nothing on that front for months." She turned to catch Fabién's eye.

"There have been a couple of technical delays on the project, scientific matters that I do not profess to understand." Willingdon grimaced. "But I will keep you posted as soon as I hear anything."

"Garth," Fabién almost had to shout to make himself heard from the far end of the table. "I have a question. Is..."

Goyter rose to approach the lectern as Willingdon sat down, "I just have a few things to share with you," he growled, as if Fabién hadn't said anything. "Now, most of you are known to the usual suspects in the Vancouver and Victoria media. If anyone, and I mean *anyone*, reaches out to you to ask you anything about the religion, the Europa development *or* the fixed link, please make sure that you direct them through the new Reformed Public Affairs Agency. It's being headed by Jessica Smollitt, she's..."

Fabién seemed determined to let his curiosity get the better of him, once again. "But she's with the Premier's office. She's, well, let me ask you this. Is she being paid by...?"

"Don't you worry, lad." Goyter waved in his direction without looking at him. "She gets a healthy stipend from the religion for her efforts, I mean her efforts solely on the religion's behalf. So, if anyone wants any information about us, about the Island Gateway, about Europa, direct them to Public Affairs. We'll have a phone number and e-mail address out to all of you by tomorrow morning."

Willingdon rose from his seat. "We would like to thank you all for your time."

Fabién and Gurjit left the boardroom ahead of the rest of the group. They rode the elevator together without exchanging a word and walked through the lobby, a polite cacophony of European and Asian languages. Once they were clear of the swarm of bellhops and tour guides, they crossed the *porte-cochère* behind the hotel. Gurjit lit up a cigarette as soon as she could, the first time she'd smoked since the night of the election, three years earlier.

"Gurj', you're not yourself. What's up?"

She didn't answer him until she took a couple more drags from her cigarette, blowing the smoke in the direction of a large utility fan. "This is all just too weird. What do you think is going on, Fab?"

Fabién bit his lip. "Fucked if I know."

Basaraba was back in Paris. He had just spent two weeks in Moscow, an experience which, as usual, left him quite fatigued. He found Russians exhausting. Where other Europeans might have looked on with a degree of bewilderment whenever they encountered it, he intuitively grasped the prevailing Canadian reaction to Americans. Now he was home after manipulating a series of interlocking bribes in anticipation of the successful bid by Sochi for the winter Olympics, to the benefit of a group of Koreans whom only the most naïve would describe as 'his clients', and, of course, himself. He sat for a while on his balcony, sipping Calvados and reading *Le Canard Enchaîné*, and then returned to his computer. It was time to do some revisions on that clandestine website for that business in British Columbia.

It continued to perturb him. He'd divulged the Internet protocol to at least twenty people, maybe one or two more, to slake their curiosity, or (more to the point) to assuage the quite justifiable handwringing and paranoia that usually accompanies an investment that appealed to avarice rather than intelligence. Gullible but unreliable, these '*sophisticated investors*'. They accepted the IP address, carefully maintained as impervious to even the most thorough of search engines in exchange for their assurances that they would not share it with anyone else, a solemn promise that none of them honoured for very long. And he knew that as its readership slowly expanded, the website would need a few changes to remain an effective palliative tool.

Once he loaded the website, he noticed that it had acquired two odd additions.

Fiorenza	**Shropshire**	**Città del Vaticano**
Sirmione	**Aix-les-Bains**	**Roma**
Dinant	**Oxbridge**	

Vaticano? Roma? One of his agents must have been fiddling around with it, without any sort of authorization. But who would have done it? All of them were very well compensated, it was true, each selected for their skill in acting or in sales. But Basaraba couldn't think of even one of them who exhibited anything more than average technical ability and none of them had ever altered the website before. A wave of concern consumed him.

He moved the cursor over and clicked on 'Città del Vaticano'. The screen filled with a classic image of St. Peter's basilica; the photograph manipulated to make it appear as if located at the edge of an expanse of evergreen forest on the shores of a river slough. The Photoshop effort, though not as masterly as his own work, was stolid and more than adequate to dazzle those *sophisticated investors*. He would have otherwise burst out laughing, but this unexpected entry was significantly off-script.

Appartamenti S. Pietro, the most cherished of all of the residences in the several Europa communities, features a three-quarter size scale replica of the classic Vatican landmark, constructed entirely of Tuscan marble by skilled Italian masons and their students and apprentices, all drawn from the more reliable ethnicities of eastern Europe. Discerning purchasers and investors will appreciate the delicate homage to one of the most sacred locales in Christendom. The ground floor is a grand lobby with several thousand square feet of commercial space; apartments in the four upper floors will be popular with foreign and local buyers alike. Suites in the cupola will be priced at thirty percent extra.

Something was seriously amiss. He moved to the 'Roma' link. The image was not nearly as convincing as its companion; an ungainly depiction of the Pantheon, the revered *Rotonda* in the historic centre of Rome. It remained one of the best-preserved Roman structures in existence, but as displayed on the monitor in front of him, it seemed humiliating, the architectural equivalent of an elderly vice-regent forced to dress up like a sidewalk clown. A crisp image of the stately Pantheon had been artlessly superimposed to appear as if sinking in the middle of a swamp, with a ridiculous bamboo walkway leading through the reeds and cattails to the front entrance. However unsettling the visual might have been, the explanatory notes were decisively worse:

Eternity. That is what preoccupied the philosophers, the poets, the senators and emperors of ancient Rome, whether statesmen or scoundrels. The Pantheon, once a place of worship honouring all of the Roman gods, has been more recently transformed into the tomb of beloved popes and Italian kings. It remains the most conspicuous exemplar of the very concept of Eternity in Western Civilisation and has been faithfully replicated in a peaceful bog not far from the Fiorenza node. The opportunity to be interred in such an august structure is now available to individuals who personally invest more than three million in U.S. funds (€1,75 million). The burial site identical to the tomb of the second monarch of a united Italy, King Umberto I (who was savagely assassinated by an anarchist), will be bestowed upon the first individual to invest $US 10 million (€7 million) in the Europa project. This offer is not open to corporations or joint ventures.

Someone had figured it out, and now, whoever that might be made a pointed effort to ensure that he knew it. Basaraba examined the logs recording the Internet protocols of people who had gained access to the site over the past several days. He could identify four of them, three of them his sales operatives in the southeastern United States. The other was his own, when he entered the site to post more information, his preferred method of communication with people in the field like Padraig, due to its negligible risk of detection (or so he'd believed up until now).

What was this? There were subtle fingerprints, anomalies in the HTML script. Whoever it was, they'd been altering the site, about five days earlier, but they had carefully erased any indication of their IP before leaving. Basaraba's passing wave of concern was quickly turning into panic.

"Hello, Mischa." The cat had jumped on his lap while his eyes were transfixed on the computer screen. "I expect that you're hungry, aren't you?"

Basaraba made a mental tally of the relevant figures; by now he was sufficiently adept at this sort of analysis that he didn't have to write it down. Almost a billion euros in cash from the Striationists, another three or four hundred million derived from the public sale of 'partnership units' (he would have to thank Padraig for coming up with that one), and well, one could call it the *subscription* of that barely literate 'finance minister'. Another two hundred million or so from the proceeds of sale of all that land, and that much again from the manipulation of the commercial paper. And minor issues, the electricity resale, the 'seminar' fees. Of course there were *expenses*; fifty million or so flung into the wind to bankroll the testing of the SeaMent tunnel, the preposterous sideshow that so bedazzled the Reformed offshoot, and then there had been the enormous cost of ensuring the forbearance of those guys, the supposed logging outfit whose corporate name sounded like a pub in Disneyland, if they had such things. He estimated his haul, after everyone had been paid enough to ensure their silence, as a little more than a half billion euros, enough to allow him to retire, at least until the next time he got bored. Besides, it was important not to get too greedy. Avarice had cost many men their freedom, some who were far more cunning than he was.

The cat leapt from his lap into the sitting room and wanted to play. It was a game they'd agreed upon months earlier. Mischa brought over a small foam ball in his mouth; Basaraba would retrieve it, toss it toward the opposite wall, then the cat would chase it, grab in its mouth and run it back to him. "Mischa, Mischa, you're distracting me," he laughed as he threw the ball. "I'm working."

He couldn't stay in Paris. Even if the apartment was in the name of a non-profit medical research foundation he had set up years earlier, one which was loosely affiliated with an order of nuns in Carcassonne, Paris was still too much of an international crossroads. Someone might see him, and start asking questions.

Basaraba quickly dismantled the website and rendered its Internet protocol inaccessible. He reached into his desk drawer and retrieved one of his cell phones, the flip-phone with the Manhattan area code. It was time to cash out, to bring this arrangement, this *scheme*, to a premature conclusion. He opened the phone and started punching in a multi-digit code, the first of half a dozen phone calls.

But where would he go? Not his apartment in old Québec; no matter what those people tried to tell him, it was still Canada. Too many people in Algiers knew who he was. He had an idea: Sardinia. There was his place on the east coast of the island, far to the south of the more fashionable and crowded Costa Smeralda; essentially an old shepherd's hut he had spent the better part of a half million refurbishing, even building a stone stairway down to the pebble beach below. Maybe he would call that television weathergirl from Livorno, what was her name, that one with the red hair? Annalisa? Maybe she would come over from the mainland for a couple of days. But not too much more: after a few days, Basaraba started to find her irritating.

"Well, Mischa." He threw the ball again. "Your cousin has to go to clean up his house in Sardinia; you can't come, the wild dogs would eat you. But I'll be back." After a few more repetitions of their game, he went into the kitchen and placed some minced *langoustine* in the cat's feeding dish before he went to pack a small satchel for himself. *This damned cat eats better than I do.*

Basaraba was careful to lock his apartment and the large entrance door on the narrow street off Place de la Contrescarpe, then he went to *L'Alsacienne*. Jean-Pierre was at the bar, which remained almost deserted in the early afternoon. He was leaning against the bar, watching an old movie.

"Émile." Jean-Pierre smiled. "What can I do for you? A Kronenbourg?"

"Sure, but just a small one. I have to go on a trip." Basaraba paid him almost thirty thousand euros a year to look after his apartment and keep him apprised of any unusual activity in the neighbourhood. "To my place in Algiers. And please, feed the cat while I'm away. I shouldn't be too long, but this time, maybe a little longer than usual. There's food in the refrigerator. If you need more, it's in the freezer, with labels on the boxes."

"Of course, Émile, sure." He drew a glass of beer from one of the taps.

"And..." He looked behind him to ensure that no one was listening. "The cat, Mischa, he likes to play this game with a little foam ball, you throw it towards the wall and he runs to get it, and then grabs it in his teeth. He brings it back, in the manner of a dog."

"*Ah bon?*" the bartender asked with a bemused expression.

"*Mais oui!*" Basaraba laughed. "Anyway, can you do it, maybe a couple of times a week?" He pulled his wallet out of his pocket and retrieved two five-hundred euro notes. Jean-Pierre shrugged and accepted the money.

....48

From: Catriona Lu
Re: Striationist Totality v. The Royal Bank of Canada et al

Hi Carlo,

Call me.
The minute you see this.

C.

Catriona Lu
Associate
Guenter & Sadich, Attorneys
Suite 1800, 256 Fifth Avenue
Seattle, Washington 98300
Dir. (360) 501-2222

Carlo was about to dial Catriona's direct line before Declan bounded into his office with an unusually vibrant stride, brandishing a newspaper. "Calling someone?"

"Yes, Catriona in Seattle."

"Oh; the Chinese girl."

"That's her." Carlo put the handset down. "Her boss is actually quite confused about the whole McHarg and Basaraba thing, how it all could have been allowed to happen. He's got dozens of questions, never calls me himself but gets Catriona to ask me instead. She's getting just as impatient with him as I am. What's up?"

"I don't suppose that you've read the front section of today's *Vancouver Sun*?" Declan placed it in front of Carlo, open to one of the inside pages. "I'm sure that you had nothing, absolutely *nothing*, to do with this."

"No, I haven't had the chance." He scanned the open page that Declan had placed in front of him, all of which was taken up by a McKee McWatney advertisement. Half the page was dominated by a picture of a forest of massive old Douglas fir trees, obviously located somewhere far away from the company's operations. In the left quadrant beneath there was a group photograph of men and women of varying ages, each wearing a hard hat bearing the corporate symbol, and beaming warmly at the reader. The lower right quadrant featured a terse declaration.

The Board of Directors of McKee McWatney Limited would like to dispel a rumour that many in British Columbia and elsewhere appear to have accepted as true. It concerns a supposed change in the use of the Beaufort woodlands on central Vancouver Island, which comprises our Pentlatch, Tsable and Comox Valley forestry divisions.

We would like to make it clear that we have neither sold nor commissioned a real estate development on those lands. Any assertion to the contrary is completely incorrect. They remain part of the working forest. It is the express intention of McKee McWatney Limited to continue managing the Beaufort woodlands in accordance with our world-class silvicultural methods as we have done for the past seventy-five years.

We sincerely regret any public confusion created by these rumours.

Euston Burwell,
CEO, McKee McWatney Limited

"What was it that Shakespeare said about protesting too much?" Declan whistled. "Whatever you did, it caught somebody's eye."

"Odd," Carlo mumbled as he re-read the advertisement. "But when I tell Catriona about this, Sadich is going to shit icicles."

"I think that's a little disrespectful." Declan walked out of his office while Carlo punched Catriona's direct line into his phone.

It took another four days. CBC Radio One blared in the background; Miles Davis provided the musical interlude on the Sunday Edition after a segment about an organization from someplace in suburban Toronto that opposed vaccination with zeal that probed distant regions of mania. Carlo waited for the eleven o'clock news, even if it was a Sunday, and he didn't expect to hear anything of any consequence.

Carlo rushed in from the balcony to turn off the gas under his *caffettiera* after the hissing started. Laura had left earlier that morning to meet Farida somewhere downtown, something to do with a manicure, a pedicure, then a facial followed by shopping of one sort or another. As expensive as it all sounded, Carlo was merely relieved that they were finally getting along. The first two news items, leading with a report about a teachers' strike in Nova Scotia, the next about a grocer in Owen Sound who was fined for selling frozen lobster after its best before date, did not veer from expectation. The next item, on the other hand, piqued Carlo's interest.

The Liberal government of British Columbia, plagued by chronic scandal in the recent past, received a bitter blow today. Lawrence Gollander, a long-time political ally of the Premier who was recently appointed Minister of Finance after a Cabinet shuffle, was yesterday revealed to have misappropriated more than fifty million dollars to invest in a speculative real estate venture after having invested almost three hundred thousand dollars on his own

*account. We join CBC legislative bureau chief Christian Li in
Victoria for more on this developing story. Christian?*

Carlo turned up the volume to hear what Christian Li had to
say, taking notes as he listened. Gollander had been arrested the
night before, millions in government assets had been frozen and
government property sequestered, awaiting investigations by a
flock of federal agencies. The CBC research, however hasty, had
already managed to link the venture to the McKee McWatney
lands.

> *The venture involved a supposed real estate development scheme,
> dubbed 'Europa', which involved the construction of a number of
> European-style village centres connected by railways and mountain
> roads in a ten-thousand hectare swath of central Vancouver Island.
> CBCs investigation of the matter remains ongoing. We were able to
> confirm with McKee McWatney earlier today that it has neither
> sold any of the property nor approved the erection of any
> permanent structures.*

For a few brief seconds, Carlo felt the warm comfort of self-
satisfaction but his mood shifted to panic when he heard Christian
Li's closing words.

> *Sources reported in this morning's edition of the* Globe and Mail
> *indicated that the Reformed Striationist religious organization, of
> which much of British Columbia's political and financial élite are
> members, was heavily invested in the project. No one from the
> religion could be reached for comment. Many questions have been
> raised about the source of those funds in light of the schism in the
> religion about one year ago. CBC News is currently attempting to
> reach Declan Gaskin, the Vancouver lawyer representing the
> originalist Orthodox Striationist religion in its lawsuit against the
> Reformed offshoot, for his comments regarding these
> developments.*

Carlo searched his cell phone for Declan's home number. After six rings, Declan finally answered. "Hello?"

"Declan, this is Carlo. We've got, well, we've got a *situation*, let's say. Lawrence Gollander, he's been arrested, and they've connected the dots between the schism and that real estate project on the Island, and all the money, they've...and they're looking for you, for a comment."

"Carlo, Carlo, calm down," Declan said with a soothing voice. "You're hyperventilating, you're not making any sense. Slow down!" As Carlo explained himself in a slower and more sedate tone, he heard what first sounded like the rustling of bedsheets, followed by the opening and closing of a sliding glass door. "This was on CBC?" Declan finally replied, without any discernible emotion.

"Yes."

"Not the best way to start a Sunday, but at least something is, well, *transpiring*. Okay, well, I'd better get in touch with Ruairi Davidson. Have you called up anyone in Sadich's office?"

"No, not yet."

"Well, do that, and while you're at it, let your girlfriend know. Is she at home?"

"No, she's downtown with..."

"Well, you'd better let her and...her partner know what is going on, and sooner rather than later. And whatever you do, do *not* go anywhere near the office."

Carlo started dialling Catriona's number as soon as he hung up.

"What?" she answered, annoyed.

Carlo could hear what sounded like a windmill and the creaking and clicking of metallic objects striking one another. "It's me. Where are you?"

"I'm at the gym. What's up?"

"One of our politicians just ended up in jail." Carlo explained again what he had just heard on the news. He went over to the computer and pulled up the *Globe and Mail* website. "Oh, and it looks like now, the entire world knows that the Europa development is a steaming heap of bullshit."

"Just let me walk over to a quieter spot." Carlo waited as the rhythmic, metallic racket started to fade. "Jesus fucking Christ! Has anybody heard from the Freaks?"

"Declan is calling Ruairi Davidson. But you'd better let Sadich know what is going on."

"Oh, I will. And leave your phone on."

Carlo had almost forgotten about his coffee. He emptied the *caffettiera* into a large mug and went back out on to the balcony. Before he could enjoy the first sip, Declan called him back.

He sounded subdued. "Well, they're some pissed off at us. They seem to think that there was something that we could have done to forestall this or something. I think I probably convinced him that there was no way. But they still want to meet with us at this place up on the Sunshine Coast, as soon as we can arrange it. Both of us. I'll get Bal to set it up and let you know."

"Not at Port Rattray, I hope."

"No such luck. Sechelt. And the place is called 'Hall of Cauliflower' or something."

* * *

Patricia walked with a brisk pace. Her heels clicked in military rhythm as she approached the main police station in Victoria, on a side street off Centennial Square. On Sunday, in late afternoon, the front desk was staffed with a commissionaire rather than a regular police officer. "I heard that you were holding Mr. Gollander here, in the pre-trial lockup," she said to the officer, a woman who appeared to be in her late seventies. "May I visit with him?"

"Are you his lawyer?" she croaked with an accent that Patricia placed as Welsh.

"No. I'm an old friend."

"Please have a seat." She pointed to a row of plastic chairs. Patricia removed her overcoat before she sat down. Although it was just above freezing outside, with a brisk wind, not unusual in mid- February, the temperature inside the police station matched that of a convalescent home. After about twenty minutes, the commissionaire returned. "Place your cell phone and your purse in one of those lockers and come with me."

Patricia followed her through a windowless hallway, and then past a metal security door with a loud electronic lock. She led Patricia into a room with a series of glass windows divided by short wooden walls with drain-like wickets. "All right. You have fifteen minutes."

"Thank you." Within a few seconds, a male office brought Gollander to a seat in front of one of the windows.

"Well, Lawrence." She folded her arms and regarded him before she sat down. He looked like, well, what he was: a Germanic man in late middle age, slightly diminished since the last time she saw him, the slimming effect of overwhelming stress, the pallor of a man in the throes of a debilitating hangover.

He averted her gaze. "I bet you think I'm a complete idiot," he whispered.

"No, Lawrence, that's where you're wrong. I *know* you're a complete idiot. What on earth were you thinking?" Before he could speak, Patricia held up her palm. "No, no, don't say anything, not in here. Do you have a lawyer yet?"

"Yes, I've got...well, Garth retained Bernie Mackay for me."

"No, I mean a real lawyer. That's the best those two could do for you? I bet they're plotting as we speak, dreaming up the best way to hang you out to dry!"

"Well, no; from what I can gather, Terrence and Garth have their own problems to sort out. I just overheard two of the officers talking. One of them said that both of them are now in police custody, Garth in Vancouver, Terrence in Surrey."

"Hmm, both of them. I hadn't heard that; somehow it escaped the notice of the press. And Surrey, how *apropos*." Patricia ran a finger over the screen of her phone. "Well, anyway, we need to find you a suitable lawyer and get you bailed out of here. Leave it with me, Lawrence. We'll have you out by tomorrow."

"Thank you, Patricia." His head bobbed as if it was too heavy for his neck.

"Well, it's the least I can do. Even if you are a complete idiot."

Laura looked up from her magazine to survey the baroque disorder of Carlo's office. "What a disaster area! How can you work in this mess?"

Carlo stopped highlighting a medical report in mid-swipe. "I know exactly where everything is. And it keeps the riff-raff out."

"*And what the fuck is that?*" she gasped, pointing to a plastic medical model on top of the metal filing cabinet behind her.

"Oh, that's an eye." The plastic orb, a remarkably lurid facsimile of a human eye, unblinking, displaying every blood vessel, terraced to show visceral detail as if layers of tissue had been stripped away.

"No shit?"

"Well, not a real eye, of course. It's something that Declan got from a medical supply place somewhere in California. I think he used it as demonstrative evidence at a medical malpractice trial a few years back."

"So why is it here?"

"He told me that junior counsel need this kind of thing to impress prospective clients."

Laura turned it so that the iris faced the wall. "He's a lunatic, Carlo. And it's high time that we get out of here."

"Hey, I told you — I have to finish this. It'll take me just a couple more minutes."

"No, no; I meant that I (I mean *we*) need a vacation. It's time we went over to see your dad. And see this?" She turned her magazine to face him. "It says here that we can get flights to London for less than eight hundred dollars, British Airways and everything. I'm booking. Tomorrow."

"Oh, fine," Carlo said, highlighting a few more lines. He heard Laura's phone whistle, announcing the arrival of a text message. Laura turned her phone around to face him. "Fuck, look at this! Yvette is terminally punctual. They're already at the restaurant."

"I guess I'd better get a move on," Carlo initiated the ritual required to shut down his computer. An antiquated image filled the screen.

"Windows 98?" Laura said. "Really? That man should really make an effort to enter the twenty-first century."

"We're lucky he sprung for computers at all. So what did you say Yvette's new boyfriend's name was?"

"Oh, that's right, you two have never met. Philippe. He's not new, he's sort of recycled. It's one of those on again, off again things. And try not to look shocked. He might be younger than Declan, but not by much. Still, I'm glad they're back together. The breakup was pretty ugly, about a year ago, and knowing what I do now, I'm quite certain that Declan had something to do with it." Laura stuffed her phone back in her purse. "Anyway, let's go."

Laura was standing on one foot, refitting one of her shoes as Carlo shut off the lights to the office. Feminine giggling filtered in from the other side of the office entranceway. The door burst open. Declan and a much younger woman tumbled into the office, the girl still laughing, her arms entwined around him. Carlo placed her in an instant: spare, with wavy, shoulder length brown hair and unseasonably tanned skin. *Susan Wiltshire.* Boyfriend troubles indeed.

"Oh, you're still here!" Declan stood up straight. "Susan, I'd like you to meet my associate, Carlo Buonsante, and his girlfriend, Laura Thompson," he said in the sort of tone he might use to point out easily overlooked paintings in a gloomy alcove.

"Hello," Susan said quietly. She looked in Carlo's direction without meeting his eye, her smile condescending, as if visiting him in a penitentiary. She did not audibly acknowledge Laura's presence but instead eyed her up and down with an expression of genteel disgust. "Well." She turned to Declan. "We'd best be off!"

"Well, you two have a good time," Declan said. "And remember, Carlo, on Tuesday we have to meet the Directorate in Sechelt. Maybe you could do up some sort of briefing memorandum." Susan took his hand with a proprietorial grasp as they walked into his office and shut the door behind them.

"I'm not surprised that *she* didn't waste any time," Laura said as soon as the elevator door closed.

"You two have met?"

"Well, we'll just say that we've crossed paths, and she's a piece of work. She used to be a reporter with, I don't know, one of those tree hugger rags, was it the *Salish Sea*? And for about three years she was at all of the Striationist meetings. A while back, long before the Striationists split, Declan came without Paula to a couple of the meetings at the Savary Island place, and it was obvious (to me, anyway) that those two were an item. As I recall, it was just over a year ago that she dropped out of sight, didn't see her at any of the Striationist functions anymore. And wouldn't you know it, now that Paula's taken herself out of the picture, she appears in a puff of smoke."

"It *is* odd that she's here all of a sudden. She was in charge of hospitality at Port Rattray when we were sent up there."

"Hmm, I'm surprised she didn't try to fuck you. Never did like her; sneaky, two-faced little bitch. And you know what? That friend of yours, the paralegal; she got knocked up by accident, I'm guessing."

"Well, yes. As far as I know, anyway."

"With Susan? I give it a few months at the most before she arranges to get that way by design. Oh, and what was this about Sechelt? Do you have an audience with the Freaks or something?"

"Yeah, Declan mentioned that we have to meet with the bunch of them now that the Reformed faction has imploded, you know, in light of current events. They apparently want to see the whites of their lawyers' eyes. An opinion letter isn't going to cut it."

"So where are you going to meet them? Don't tell me: is it at a place called Hale Kai?"

"Yes; I had to look it up on line after Declan gave me his version of the name. How did you know?"

"Been there. Hope you liked the Seventies 'cause you're going back." Laura pointed to a row of taxis parked in front of the atrium. "Maybe we should catch one of those. I'm in heels. And they're already there."

"Why, where is this place?"

"It's in Yaletown, just by the Roundhouse." It'd be a twenty-minute walk. Laura's purse started to emit a piercing oscillating beep. "Fuck, Yvette, take a chill pill. Just a second," she said as she answered her phone. "Oh! Darla! Hi, what's up?" A look of deepening surprise appeared on her face as she listened. "My God, Darla, that's terrible. I'm so sorry. Are you all right?" Laura swiped her forehead with her free hand as she listened. "Okay, well you take care. Let us know if there's anything at all that we can do. I'll be over as soon as I can." She was shaking as she put her phone back into her purse. "Darla's at Nanaimo Hospital. It's Auntie Gladys. She was at work, at the pub, and had a heart attack. They managed to revive her and take her away by ambulance, but she died about half an hour ago."

"I'm sorry, Laura." Carlo put an arm around her shoulders. "Do you still want to go out for dinner?"

"Yes, look; I'm not going to lie and try to tell you that I'm...I'm in mourning. I just feel bad for Darla. And at one time, many years ago now, Auntie Gladys was actually nice to me." She looked down toward the sidewalk with a sagging, slack countenance. Despite what she said, Carlo could only interpret it as grief.

"Come on, get us a cab," Laura said. "Let's just go to Vesuvio's; after I tell Yvette, we'll all raise a glass of wine in Auntie Gladys's honour. I think that even *she* would appreciate that." She slumped, crying as Carlo held her.

....50

Satellite radio whined through the rear speakers in Declan's new car, a BMW sports model that reminded Carlo of a pizza wagon in a hallucinogen-inspired cartoon. He sat in the passenger seat, enduring interminable Iron Butterfly. Declan had to slow for left-turning traffic as they drove north toward Sechelt past clusters of waterfront cottages.

"Now, Carlo," Declan intoned. Carlo prepared himself for a numbing homily.

"This is crunch time for us," Declan continued. "We have to show some results for these people, they've paid us north of a hundred thousand in fees so far this year, okay?"

"Okay, but how are we going to handle it today?" Carlo said. "You'd have to agree with me, these people are a little, well, more than a little eccentric."

"Yes, they are. But I've dealt with them for years. You have to do a bit of an orchestrated performance: part carnival huckster, part professor, part judge, part imam. Just the way it is. Anyway, follow my lead, and nod and smile appropriately." Declan slowed to avoid a bounding deer. "So this place, do you know anything about it?"

"Hale Kai? Laura told me that it's a bit of a Seventies throwback."

"Oh, is that what it's called? I suppose it could be worse. The pubs around here are disgusting. Thank God most of these people don't drink. Now," Declan's jowls made their customary reappearance. "As I was saying, follow my lead. They look up to me as their long-time legal counsel; I hate to say it, their *éminence grise*. So I will give them the big picture, that's my job."

"Okay."

"You'll probably end up in my spot, some day." Declan's tone deepened, as if to impart academic wisdom. "Watch

445

carefully: many of these people are retired and semi-retired professional people themselves. You have to set out the details quite precisely, with a painstaking exposition of a mathematical proof. Oh, maybe you don't know what that is."

"My major in undergrad was economics."

The furrows in Declan's jowls tightened. "Oh; I didn't know that. Anyway, I'm looking for you to be the detail man. If I ask you in an aside about some trivia that one of them gets fixated on, just answer it quickly, so that I can just get on with my presentation. The sooner we're done, the sooner we're back on the ferry."

The highway emerged from a patch of gloomy forest to follow the beachfront. "I think we're here," Declan said. He pulled into the Hale Kai parking lot and chose the stall closest to the covered entrance. Dozens of large plastic cups were strewn about. Carlo walked more carefully after he tripped on an empty bottle of Bacardi and fell backwards against the car. A banner festooned with hearts of various sizes hung by a single string from the rafters underneath the entranceway roof. Carlo tilted his head sideways to read it.

Congratulations Siobhan & Derek !

Once they entered the lobby, they were swiftly enveloped by a dreadful triumvirate; the combined odours of vomit, cigarette smoke and stale beer. A man in a cardigan, swishing a mop to smear a pool of viscous grey liquid over the linoleum lobby floor, looked up at them. "May I help you gentlemen?"

"Yes," Declan said with a forced smile. "We're here to meet the Striationist Directorate."

"Oh, yes, sorry; please excuse the mayhem." The man with the mop chirped with a nervous giggle. "There was a wedding reception here last night. People in these parts like a good party. Anyway, you guys are in the banquet hall at the top of the stairs.

There are a few people there already. Help yourself to coffee, it's in the urn on the landing."

Carlo and Declan walked through the open door of the banquet room facing the assembled eight elders of the Directorate. Margaret Davidson, draped in a Haida cloak. Her husband, Ruairi, in a hemp shirt and a floppy beret. The man with the shaved head whom he'd met in Port Rattray, in bicycle tights and gum boots. There were a few he didn't recognize. One of them looked like a retired judge; floppy concrete-grey moustache, dark brown tweed jacket.

Ruairi Davidson presided with a serene smile. "Good morning, gentlemen. I hope that the ferry ride was pleasant."

"At least it didn't sink!" Declan winked theatrically.

Except for Ruairi, each of the elders sat arch-backed and hummed.

Ruairi squinted at something on the table. "Let's try to keep that kind of quip to a minimum," he said, still not looking at Declan. "There has been a bit of a theological debate in some quarters about whether the Queen of Coquitlam sank due to a disturbance, well, we'll say *disruption*, of terrestrial energy that resulted from that new condominium development in the hills overlooking Hammond Bay."

Declan frowned. "Oh?"

"Yes!" Margaret barked. "They blasted six very powerful striations into oblivion in order to accommodate that abomination. And your old backgammon buddy, Gavin Skoff, has money in it!"

"It's all right, Margaret; it's not his fault," Davidson said, a half-hearted attempt to sound soothing. "Now, Declan, what do you have for us?" Something in Davidson's tone convinced Carlo not to pass around copies of the memorandum he'd put together the day before.

"Well." Declan leaned back in his chair. "We have to return to *first principles* here." He positioned his two index fingers erect, parallel to each other. "We have two distinct issues here. First, the disappearance of last year's Wellspring from the Royal Bank, and second the repeated transfer of the numerous parcels of real property out of the possession and legal ownership of the religion without consent." His index fingers danced together in a distracting 'W' pattern.

He cleared his throat. "Now, the disappearance of the funds clearly raises the application of the doctrine of *respondeat superior*, while the transfer of the land, well the transfer at first instance clearly invites an inquiry into the issue of ostensible authority." Carlo saw one of the ones he didn't recognize, a man with shaggy, beaded grey hair, shake his head and curl his lip. Declan seemed to be oblivious to the reactions of other people in the room, "And the subsequent transfer of the lands raises the legal principle of *nemo dat quod non habet*." The man with the floppy moustache embedded his face in his palm.

"Look," Ruairi said, pointing at Declan. "Don't try to play us. We've already paid you guys a fortune. Now, are we going to get our land and our funds back?" He sat back in his chair and folded his arms.

Declan first appeared stunned but then regained his bearing. "Well, Carlo, whom most of you have met; he's been working on most of the fine details of that sort of thing. So I'll turn the floor over to him."

Well, you detestable old buzzard. I'd like to reach across the table, snap your neck, impale you with a spike and roast you slowly on a spit. "Yes." Carlo turned to Davidson. "With respect to the land, the short answer is 'yes'. But there is a - well, there will be a few interim steps."

"What sort of steps?"

"All of the land will have to be placed in a trust with the religion as sole beneficiary until, I imagine, we can satisfy the court that there are no valid charges against it."

"I don't get it." Margaret said. "If the land is ours, why do we have to be, what did you call it, a 'beneficiary'?"

"This was not the simple theft of your lands." Margaret and a few of the other elders leaned back, nodding on hearing the word 'theft'. "Since the split, most of the properties were transferred more than twenty times, some as many as fifty times." The elders rumbled with a low hum. "And during the course of each transaction, the purchaser granted a mortgage to one of several lenders, who in turn quickly assigned the mortgage to someone else; Scotiabank, Crédit Agricole, to name two. The court will want to make sure that none of the transfers, and none of the mortgages, are actually valid before clear title is returned to the religion."

"What a nightmare!" Margaret whimpered.

"All I can say," Carlo said. "Is that it could be worse. I will be able to tell you more after the hearing of my application in chambers in just over a month. I'll be asking a judge to vest title to all of the properties in the trustee and..."

The man with the shaved head interrupted him. "And who is going to be 'the trustee'?"

"Ashburnam & Willits in Victoria." The proposed trustee was a solicitors' firm in Victoria which took up two floors of a brick edifice in the old town, well known for administering large estates. Carlo noted with relief that the Elders didn't seem to have any opinion one way or the other.

"What about the American lands?" Margaret folded her arms. "Is Mister, well, that fellow in Seattle. Sadich is it? Is he aware of what you are doing?"

"Yes," Carlo said, watching Declan's reaction. "That was my next point. I have been working closely with the solicitor handling the file in the United States, Catriona Lu. There will be a parallel application in Federal District Court in Seattle for the same day."

"And when is that?" Ruairi asked, intermittently clicking his pen.

"Tuesday, the tenth of March."

"I'm David Lindley." The man with the droopy moustache spoke with a correct, clipped London accent. "I don't believe that we've met. Is this going to end up being an action for declarative relief, for priority, I imagine?"

Carlo, thankful that one of them seemed to have a good bit of legal knowledge, turned to him and smiled. "I certainly hope not. That would truly be a nightmare. For now, it appears that none of the mortgages are actually valid. When I go to court next week, I will ask the judge for directions, basically to set the ground rules for restoring clear title to the Convocation."

"But I *still* don't understand," Lindley said. "Not valid? How could that be?"

"What happened here is that the people behind this, probably a very small group, orchestrated a series of sequential sales of the properties meant to create an illusion of rising prices, and indeed, with each transaction, the price went up. The purchaser granted a mortgage over the property at every stage, which was quickly assigned for value to a bank. In almost every case, neither the purchaser nor the mortgage actually existed. The bank bought worthless paper."

"But, that's preposterous!" Lindley sputtered. "How could a *bank* be so careless?"

Declan tilted his chin upward. "That," he growled, "is just yet another example of the sorry state of our modern society!" Each of the eight Elders turned to stare at him, and then looked away.

"In any event," Carlo continued. "I will deliver a full report after the hearing next week."

"Wait a minute," Margaret said. "That might deal with the land, but what about the money? The Wellspring?"

Carlo looked down at the table. "That, I am sorry to say, is much more problematic. We might not be able to get the money back."

"What?" Ruairi shouted, showing genuine anger for the first time. "Do you mean to tell us that someone can steal seven, eight hundred million dollars and there is not a thing we can do to get it back?"

"What I mean to tell you," Carlo said as softly as he could. "Is that the people behind this are extraordinarily adept, well, *crooks*. They have walked off with almost three *billion*, and we still aren't certain who they are. Now, as far as getting your money back? With the implosion of the partnership unit scheme, which was based on a development project that did not actually exist, the money has disappeared into thin air. The Royal Bank might have transferred it without proper instructions, but successfully suing them? It will be extremely difficult. That's our best avenue of attack, but we can offer no guarantees."

Davidson massaged his eyes. "Tell me." He sighed. "Did my cousin have anything to do with this?"

"No," Carlo said. "He did not."

"Good. I'm relieved."

"All right." Declan clasped his hands together. "I think that we have gone as far today as we can. Does anybody else have any questions?"

Margaret Davidson jolted forward and appeared poised to say something, but she shook her head and leaned back in her chair.

"Thank you, Declan," Ruairi said as he rose and extended his hand. "Thank you for driving all the way up here. And thank *you*, Carlo, for all of your hard work. Be sure to let us know how the hearing goes."

"Of course."

Carlo maintained a rigid pose in the passenger seat during the ride back to the ferry, gazing toward the sea. The sky was starting to clear over the Strait of Georgia. His attention drifted over the water, often fixing upon the many reefs and islets that flanked the mainland coast. As they passed by the assortment of bungalows and machine shops that marked the outer fringes of Gibsons, Declan, who'd maintained an imperious pout since they left Sechelt, unexpectedly snorted. About five minutes later, he did it again.

It wasn't until they were descending the long slope toward the ferry terminal that Declan finally said anything. "Just one thing, Carlo."

"What? Sorry?"

"When you do your reporting letter after the application next week, I want to review it before it goes out. And it will go out over *my* signature."

Jack Thompson adjusted the knot in the tie he was plainly unaccustomed to wearing. "I have a very deep suspicion of these sorts of events."

"Funerals, you mean?" Carlo asked. The two of them were walking together behind Laura, her mother and her Auntie Deanna, on the serpentine, brick covered walkway toward the entrance to the United Fellowship of Christ Bible Church. Only the cross on the atrium roof identified it as a place of worship. Otherwise, it resembled many other structures, warehouses, car dealerships and offices, in the geometric glass and cinder block landscape of north Nanaimo.

"No, no," he laughed. "Although as far as I'm concerned, only old ladies are actually comfortable at funerals. But I've been told that it isn't really even a memorial service. It's a 'Celebration of Life'. That's what they call it, not that there was really much of a life to celebrate."

Carlo looked back at him with a curved, bemused smile. "I'm sorry," Jack said. "I guess that I'm just not a very good Christian. I just can't muster any charitable thoughts. Do you think I'm wrong?"

"I think..." Carlo focused on the path in front of him, "I think that it brings bad luck to speak ill of the dead."

Jack's initial expression of shock soon gave way to laughter. Birgitta turned to look back at him with a reproachful glance. "Oh, I'd better keep it down," he said in a tone just louder than a whisper. "This *is* supposed to be a sombre affair."

An usher, someone Carlo recognized as one of the Rafferty cousins, handed each of them an Order of Celebration as he met them at the front door and escorted them to seats just behind the area cordoned for close family. Laura ended up with the aisle seat;

Carlo sat between her and her father. A spiritual played at low volume over the public address system.

> *Joshua fit the battle of Jericho*
> *Jericho, Jericho, Jericho*
> *Joshua fit the battle of Jericho*
> *And the walls came a-tumblin' down*

Carlo turned to look behind him and then leaned toward Laura's ear. "Is that Patrick?" The ushers guided a man with red hair flecked with grey, accompanied by a tanned, slender woman with long blonde hair, into the family section ahead.

"Yup, that's him: 'poor bugger Uncle Pat', as we all used to call him," Laura sighed. "If anything, he looks younger than he did the last time I saw him."

"After the way she treated him," Jack mumbled, "I'm surprised he's here at all."

Twenty minutes elapsed before the chapel filled, a hundred people or more, Carlo estimated. Many he recognized, members of the Rafferty clan, and their sundry friends and workmates, people whom Carlo had met so many years in the past that it seemed like a lifetime ago.

"Ooh," Deanna said with an indulgent, condescending smile. "There's my ex." He was much slimmer than Carlo remembered him, with a little more grey hair, entering the chapel with a woman with straight dark hair and blended European and Asian features, perhaps forty, forty-five at the most. As the crowd grew, the languorous opening guitar solo of "Wooden Ships" played in the background; something less religious and more peaceful.

A few minutes after the appointed hour, two in the afternoon, the lights dimmed. The pastor, clad in a white gown trimmed with purple, approached the podium on the raised altar, flanked by a collage of photographs of Gladys and some of her possessions, each commemorating an epoch or significant passage in her life.

He was unusually tall, at least a head taller than anyone else in the chapel.

"Good afternoon. I would like to welcome you all here. I am Pastor William Robinson of the Fellowship of Christ. We are here to celebrate the life of Gladys Rafferty," he announced in a soporific voice. "Wife, sister, mother and grandmother, and friend to many who more recently grew fond of her in her new, adopted home of Nanoose, just next door to where she worked as a pub manager, in Lantzville. Gladys was born in England but spent all but the first three years of her life here on Vancouver Island. She is survived by her daughter, Darla, her ex-husband, Patrick, and three grandchildren, children of her eldest daughter, Trianna, who predeceased her almost ten years ago." With the mention of Trianna's name, Deanna bowed her head and shut her eyes. The pastor commenced a reading from Ecclesiastes.

> *To every thing there is a season,*
> *and a time to every purpose under the heaven:*
> *A time to be born, and a time to die;*
> *a time to plant, and a time to pluck up that which is planted*

At the end the passage, he looked up to address the group. "I have asked Gladys's youngest daughter, Darla, to say a few words in her mother's memory."

Darla rose from her chair in the front row and walked up to the podium. She briefly surveyed the room, and then looked down at some notes before she started to speak. It startled Laura that her cousin, always the brash and unforgiving scourge of lecherous men and bellicose women, stood trembling at the podium.

"My mother was born in Bristol, England, the youngest of three daughters." Darla commenced a detailed biography, describing the family's emigration from post-war Europe, first to Victoria, and then to the Comox Valley, her school years and her brief stint as a waitress at an A&W drive-in. "Some of you remember my mother as she was when she was young, an eager skier and fisher, the high school grass-hockey player. But I am sure that my sister, if she could be with us today would agree: when she was older, she had to contend with us, and what I can only describe as *hordes* of cousins." Many in the chapel laughed politely.

"So she became a stern disciplinarian. But regardless of some of the words we may have had between us all those years ago, we always, all of us," Darla swallowed, "always felt loved." She spoke of her mother's life in recent years, a few brief anecdotes about the times she and her mother had together when she had been over to visit her in Nanoose.

"Now." Darla continued. "For those of you who were not already well aware of this, I can assure you all of one thing: my mother was not one for poetry. She had very little use for it at all. But I think that it is customary at a memorial, or (excuse me) a Celebration of Life, that one should select a fitting, suitable poem in memory of Mother. It was not an easy task." Darla looked down at her notes. "I am thankful to my father and, of course, my cousins Laura, Brendan Jr. and Fiona for their insights. We've been talking about this for the past few days, and I believe that we all agreed that Percy Bysshe Shelley said it best and most appropriately." Carlo turned to Laura in surprise as Darla recited the first stanza of the passage, closing his eyes in anticipation of its conclusion.

> *And on the pedestal these words appear:*
> *'My name is Ozymandias, king of kings:*
> *Look on my works, ye Mighty, and despair!'*
> *Nothing beside remains. Round the decay*
> *Of that colossal wreck, boundless and bare*
> *The lone and level sands stretch far away*

The pastor looked like a man blinded by the beam of a policeman's flashlight as he returned to the podium. "Thank you, Darla." He looked around the chapel. "Now, everyone, please join me in the Lord's Prayer." Pastor Robinson bowed his head and started the prayer; a modest proportion of the group followed him and mumbled the words that few of them had recited since grade school. "Forever and ever, amen," he finished in the same quiet, hypnotic tone.

"Now, Darla and her father asked me to invite family and friends to come up to the microphone and share with us their recollections of Gladys." He pulled his arms toward him to beckon everyone to the podium. "Please, please, feel free to come up to the front. No need to be shy."

Gentle murmurs could be heard here and there throughout the room. A man of about eighty; tall, erect, betraying a military background, walked in a slow, deliberate pace and stood in front of the microphone. "I haven't known Gladys for very long, maybe two years," he spoke with a Maritime accent, Nova Scotia, Carlo guessed. "I got to know her at the Winchelsea, a few steps from my front door. Sure, she could be a little gruff, but she was a breath of fresh air. She always poured full pints and never tried to short-change me. And she didn't act all put out if I didn't leave a tip." He limped slowly back to his seat.

Another man, the one Carlo recognized as the older gentleman who had been at the pub, shuffled carefully to the microphone. "I'm Walter, and it would not surprise me if none of you except for this young lady." He pointed to Darla and tried to smile. "Have any idea who I am. I lived with Gladys for the past year and a half. We met at the Winchelsea. I am not going to lie to you people, she never spoke of anyone from her former life up-Island. I did my best; she could be a very difficult woman and I have nothing but praise for her daughter. Darla and I, we did our best to make sure that she was well looked after." He looked down at the lectern. "But she was..." His voice grew louder. "In her own way, in her heart, a very kind, gentle person. I will miss her terribly."

A few more people, most of them from the pub, came up to the microphone and delivered benign but brief remembrances. Finally, a woman who appeared to be about seventy who was sitting near the back rose and walked to the front. "Hello." She spoke with forced cheer. "I'm sure only a few of you remember me. I'm Janet Wilkinson. I went to high school with Gladys and her ex-husband, Patrick. I doubt that many of you know this, but I was Patrick's girlfriend through senior year, right up until just before graduation." She squeaked with a nervous laugh.

"Everyone, me included, expected that we would get married that summer, but Gladys and Patrick met at a dance. I wasn't there, of course, I was visiting my grandmother in Vancouver. After the dance, they (I mean Gladys and Patrick) had a whirlwind affair." Another nervous squeak. "So we didn't get married, but Gladys and Patrick sure did. Back in that innocent time we used to call it a 'shotgun wedding'."

The audience, many of whom had coughed and shuffled their feet through some of the earlier testimonials, now stared at her, motionless. "Really seems so quaint now!" She giggled. Darla cringed and sank in her seat. "You won, Gladys!" she shouted with more forced cheer as she shook her fist above her head and looked skyward. "It wasn't at all fair, but you won. And you!" She pointed at Patrick, her face an enraged rictus. "You, you're no better a man than you were back then, abandoning her to take up with this, this *Australian* tramp!" She stammered a few words of thanks and then walked quickly out of the chapel.

A fraught stillness filled the room. Darla left the safe haven of her seat and walked back up to the podium with a stiff gait. She looked down at the empty lectern; when she finally looked up to confront the audience, her eyes opened unnaturally wide, her face contorted and waxen, she opened and closed her mouth twice without uttering a sound. Eventually she was able to speak. "Pastor

Robinson asked me, well, we'll just say," she said, finally smiling. "Implored me, to play a song, a piece of music that was my mother's favourite, or one that she enjoyed, as we close this afternoon's service before everyone leaves the chapel."

"If it was true that my mother wasn't one for poetry, it was just as true that she was not much of a music fan, as a rule. But in the past day or two I asked my father, and a few of my older cousins, and we all put our heads together. There was one song that we all knew that she enjoyed, because she would sing along with it whenever they played it on the radio." Darla looked down at the podium and cleared her throat. "And after the service, you are all invited to come to a reception in Mother's honour, at the Winchelsea Pub in Lantzville."

The pastor then retook the podium as Darla returned to her seat. "Friends, I would like to thank all of you for coming here this afternoon to celebrate the life of Gladys Joyce Rafferty. Before we all leave the chapel, we would like to share with you what was apparently Gladys's favourite song. I hope that it might bring to mind pleasant memories for all of you, of enjoyable times that you spent with Gladys."

Carlo recognized the opening strains but could not immediately identify the song. With the repetitive rhythm of piano chords that followed, he figured out what it was. Then Randy Newman's voice belted out the stark opening lyrics of "Short People."

Deanna and Birgitta both sat upright, their arms folded tightly, as if grimly but decorously enduring scorched veal at a dinner party. Laura had tilted her head toward the ceiling, her lips formed into a tight 'o'. Her father chose to sit with his eyes closed, waiting for it all to end. Carlo looked down at the cover of the Order of Celebration, with a picture of Gladys at sixteen or seventeen, a pretty girl with dark brown hair, not dissimilar in appearance to her daughter, but exuding bland domesticity. Darla in the Age of Elvis. He glanced at the caption.

Gladys Joyce Rafferty
1942 - 2009

A frigid paroxysm, like the sudden breath of a winter squall, chilled the back of Carlo's neck. She was born the same year as his father.

After what seemed like half an hour, the song arrived at its final stanza. As the coda played out, most people started to get up to leave. Carlo, Deanna, Laura and her parents did not stir until the final note, when they rose to walk out of the chapel in single file and make their way down the bricked path. It wasn't until they were all back in Deanna's Ford Explorer that anyone uttered a word.

"The Winchelsea; I've no idea where it is," Deanna said, distracted, as she manoeuvred out of the chapel parking lot.

"We know where it is." Laura pointed ahead. "Just get back on the highway and take the Lantzville exit. Once we're in Lantzville, you won't be able to miss it."

"You know," Jack said, "When the time comes, please make sure that you give me a simple, quiet, what do they call it here, United Church; yeah, a United Church service."

"Well, Jacob," Deanna said. "That's the first thing that we've agreed on in years. Yes, me too, I couldn't agree more." Birgitta made a quiet declaration of some sort in Danish.

"Stop it!" Laura shouted. "That's enough out of the lot of you!"

....52

They did not linger at the reception in Lantzville. After expressing the appropriate condolences and drinking the requisite pint, Jack cited the long drive to Comox ahead of them. The five of them spoke little once they were on the highway; no fond remembrances, no sharing of endearing stories about Gladys. Carlo had been around long enough to know that there weren't any. Laura drove in silence, usually a sign of annoyance. It wasn't until they were almost home that she said anything,

"I invited Darla to stay with us tonight. I hope you don't mind."

"Good." Deanna said. "She never was one of them. Not really."

After dinner that night, Carlo joined Deanna and Jack on the back deck.

"As far as I'm concerned," Deanna said, cradling a large wine glass. "The reception was far too...too...we'll just say, altogether too *festive.*"

"Oh, come on, Deanna!" Jack laughed. "What did you expect? She wasn't exactly the Queen Mum."

"I know, I know." Deanna sighed. "But they all did everything but break out into a chorus of "Ding, Dong, the Witch is Dead"! And who knows, the way they were all pounding back the alcohol, they might very well be doing exactly *that* as we speak. I don't know, it just seems sad."

Jack sipped his beer. "Oh, it's sad, that's true enough."

"And those frightful women. What did you used to call them, Carlo?" Deanna asked.

"What? Call whom?"

"Sorry to wake you! Those four aunts (well, now, I suppose, there are only three left)."

"Oh, they would be the Old Skunks."

"Yes, yes, how could I forget, The Old Skunks," she laughed. "Good one! Vi in particular seemed crestfallen that I hadn't gone bald and lost all my teeth. And I wish that I'd taken a picture of the looks on their faces when they saw Laura walk in, such a beautiful girl. Vi even remarked how slim she looked. I'm sure they'd all been hoping to see a moon-faced matron who'd blown up into a hideous blimp. Good Lord! When you showed up, she was all of fifteen, and for the love of God, those four couldn't wait for her to fall pregnant and turn into an elephant" She laughed, touching Carlo's forearm. "But I suppose that this afternoon we all found out about one possible source of Gladys' bitterness."

"You mean that was the first that you'd heard of it?" Carlo asked.

"Oh God, yes," Deanna laughed, "there is no way that she would have ever shared that little tidbit with the likes of us; no way. But I must say that at a funeral, of all places, some things are best left unsaid."

"Yes, but I must say that it was a rather unsophisticated way for Patrick to break an engagement." Jack said. "What a bunch!"

Deanna fashioned a fierce look at Carlo. "And so, young man. Now that you two are back together, what are your intentions toward my niece? Are you finally going to marry her?" She held him steadily in her gaze.

"That's enough, Deanna!" Jack laughed. "Leave the poor lad alone. Maybe you should ask your niece the same question."

Deanna broke her gaze and started giggling. "I'm sorry, Carlo, I was just being silly. And it's not every day that I get to play the fierce, no-nonsense Scottish auntie. It's great fun, once in a while."

"Deanna..." Jack rolled his eyes.

"I know; I'm terrible," Deanna said. "When you consider all of the *wonderful* things that marriage did for me, it would be the height of cruelty for me to recommend it to anyone else. So where is Laura, anyway?"

"She and Darla went down the trail to the Enchanted Forest."

"Good. Darla needs it."

Darla exhaled a few wisps of blue smoke and passed the joint to Laura, who was sitting next to her on a log. The Enchanted Forest was an expanse of deeply furrowed Douglas fir interspersed with thick, misshapen maples. The creek, in full spate, was so noisy that it obscured Darla's words, her voice newly hoarse. "The first time we smoked a joint here, you were what, fourteen? I was vain enough to think I was leading you astray, until you turned out to be the one with the roach clip."

Laura took a deep toke. "Hey, at our high school? You'd be looked upon as a fuckin' geek if you didn't carry one around with you wherever you went." She started coughing. "What is this stuff? Some of the shit that Brendan Jr. used to grow up by the power lines?"

"No, no," Darla laughed. "And take it easy; it's from a grow-op out in Abbotsford. One toke too many will land you flat on your ass, even you."

"That wouldn't take much. I'm a little out of practice."

"You and me both." Darla accepted the joint from Laura and took another toke. "What a day," she said as she exhaled.

"It must have been very hard for you; I can't even imagine..."

"Apples and oranges, my dear. No, it wasn't as hard as you might think." Darla sighed. "The last time I saw her was about a month ago; I stopped by after meeting a client in Nanaimo. You know what the last thing she said to me was? First she told me that my skirt was so short that it made me look like a hooker (bullshit: just a basic business suit). So then she says, 'Is that part of the deal? What do you do, give all those doctors a quickie every time you make a sale?' What a bitch! Let me tell you, it's really hard to mourn someone like that. And I lied. I *never* felt loved, not by her."

"Well, it's not like you could have told the truth." Laura wheezed after a deep toke. "My last run-in with her was, well, interesting." She recounted what happened at the pub, months earlier.

"Wow, that's, well, I'm not going to say it. She actually called you a...a *tart*? It's funny that she never mentioned that she saw you guys. Oh, where the fuck is that roach clip when you need it?"

Laura reached into her purse and rummaged deep into the spacious sack.

Darla yelped in surprise. "No way! You still have it?"

"You bet!" She pulled the roach clip out of her purse. "Here you go."

Darla clamped the smouldering remnants in the jaws of the alligator clip and inhaled with rapid, shallow breaths. "Fuck, I'm still reeling. I have to say: the things that come out at funerals!"

"Don't tell me that you didn't know?"

"Nope. Not even a hint. I knew that she was very young when she had Trianna, but that's the way things were back then. It certainly explains why Trianna was her favourite, following in Mum's footsteps. But none of it excuses her behaviour, not towards me. And the way she treated you? I don't know, let's drop it; water under the bridge." Darla handed the clip back to Laura. "You know, we should hang out more often."

"Oh, we should. Hey," Laura said in a hoarse voice after sucking the last few wisps of smoke from the smouldering roach. "You know what? The old gang, all of us are getting together at Mario and Laeticia's place in Parksville the weekend after we get back."

"Oh, yes; so I've heard. Off to meet the family again. I love Italy; a few years back four of us rented a villa in Tuscany and, well, what can I say? Too much wine. So when are you back?"

"Beginning of May. So I know, you looked upon us as a bunch of little kids back in the day, but why don't you come? You'd have fun."

"Mario, Mario. Oh yes, I remember him. I always thought he was Carlo's *brother* or something. And what about that other friend of his; tall, good-looking but seemed kind of dumb?"

"David. He'll be there, too. He and his wife, she's another lawyer. Doesn't take any shit, you'd like her."

"I don't know, Laura, it might creep me right out. Those two: Mario, and what's his name again?"

"David."

"Yeah, David. I don't know, Laura. I have no doubt, no fucking doubt at all, the way that they looked me, back in the day. I'm sure those two used to think about me whenever they jacked off." Darla reached into her purse for a cigarette. "Sure, why not? Give me the address; I'll be there. Nobody's a kid any more, especially me."

* * *

Fabién wandered the corridors of offices and seminar rooms on the second floor of the maze-like Cornett Building at the University of Victoria, after consulting a directory that was even more confusing than the building itself. He'd heard an anecdote about some students who had bricked shut one of the hallways back in the seventies, and no one noticed for days. After searching for half an hour, and eventually resorting to asking someone for directions, he found Laeticia's office. He was relieved to see that she was at her desk. "Hello," he said, knocking on her open door, trying to smile. "Do you have a couple of minutes?"

Laeticia looked down at an old copy of *The Salish Sea* that was facing her, on her credenza. "What part of 'don't ever contact me again' did you have trouble remembering?"

"Look, I'm not here to...no, listen, I have some information that I think that you should know about, that someone in your field should be aware of."

"All right."

"It is important that you know about this. I found out about it just hours after it happened, but until now, after everything that has been going on, I kept my mouth shut."

"Then why are you telling me about it?"

"Because you're well respected as someone who is becoming prominent in marine biology around here, as an academic. So..." Fabien made a sweeping gesture with his arm.

"Save it, Fabién."

"No, no; look, I'm not hitting on you. I have a girlfriend now; another politico. She's the one who came to get me at the hospital after you broke my fingers, and then we finally got together after flirting for years. We're getting a place together in Cook Street Village. I suppose I should, I don't know, *thank* you." He relaxed when Laeticia smiled. "May I sit down?"

"Sure. Why not? Have a seat."

"This is important; I don't know what significance it has, I mean, scientifically, but I would appreciate it if you would keep it between us. The reason for this will be obvious. But..." Fabién looked away. "It important to me that somebody like you knows about it."

Laeticia abandoned her mocking smirk. "All right, Fabién. How about if you tell me what the fuck you're talking about?"

Fabién tilted his head back and rubbed the stubble on his chin. It occurred to Laeticia that he probably hadn't shaved for two or three days. He started to speak in an uncharacteristically wan voice. "Okay, do you remember that ferry that sank, the Queen of Coquitlam?"

"Yes, of course."

"It might have been an accident, but it was not some freak occurrence, some random marine mishap in the Straits. The SeaMent experiment, you know, the one that Gavin Skoff was pushing, not that the funding whores at VisualEyes weren't behind him one hundred percent. That's what caused it."

"How...I don't get it. How did some silly, I don't know, carnival trick, sink a ferry?"

"Look, I don't know what to tell you. *I* certainly don't know the science behind it. They were doing some kind of *experiment* that morning. The electrolysis, or whatever the process was, it was so powerful that it fucked with the ferry's navigation equipment. It hit a reef, which gouged a huge gash in the hull, and the boat sank in less than two minutes."

"Holy shit! People died."

"Yup." Fabién nodded. "We paid out generously for the lost property, and even settled all of the personal injury and wrongful death claims, and there were lots of them, so that we wouldn't have every lawyer in Vancouver nosing around asking embarrassing questions. So there you go. And why am I telling you this?"

"I'm a bit curious about that, I must admit."

"Not so that it will be made public. No one would believe you. Trust me on this: don't do it. But I have a feeling that there might just be a few longer-term effects of Skoff's silly pipe dream. Fish with three eyes, just like on *The Simpsons*. Split-level oysters, that sort of thing. I mean, who the fuck knows?"

"Does Gavin Skoff know about all of this; I mean, the ferry sinking?" Laeticia sighed, leaning back in her chair.

"He was in the control room when it happened," Fabién said in a hoarse whisper.

Both of them sat in silence for an uncomfortable couple of minutes. "Well, thanks, I guess, for letting me know." Laeticia allowed herself to laugh for the first time since Fabién walked into her office. "So, with things the way they are, politically, I mean. What are you going to do now?"

"I really don't know. Things are so fucked up right now. If we lose our seats in the next election, Gurjit (that's my girlfriend's name) wants to take a few months off to go travelling. But for now, I'm just clinging to the wreckage. Oh! And that brings me to my next point. You were friends with Patricia Wilson, I seem to remember."

"Still am. Why?"

"Well, maybe you could help us out. We're trying to drag her back out of academic life, you know, to lead the party, now that half the front bench on the government side could be facing prison time. We'd even take Chatham back, pompous old prick that he is."

"No thanks. I think that I'll stay out of it."

He stood up, and extended his hand. "Anyway, I'm sorry that I behaved like such an ass."

Laeticia shook his hand. "Well, I guess I'm a little sorry that I broke your fingers."

"Hey, don't worry about it. I sort of deserved it."

After Fabién left her office, Laeticia pulled her cell phone out of her purse and typed a text message to Patricia.

> Fabién Lerche was just in my office, apologising. Said that they want to get you back into politics, lead that party or something.
> True?

About three minutes later, a text whistled its arrival.

> Yes, indeed. And I'm going to do it. Bet your ass.

Laeticia read her text with disbelief.

> Seriously?

Patricia's response came within seconds.

Oh, yes! Once you get to be my age, you'll see that revenge and spite are the most rewarding of motives. So I'll be in Vic on Tuesday. Pinot's at six?

Laeticia grinned at the screen and started giggling.

Yup.

53

Carlo stuffed the cerloxed volumes for the application at the Vancouver courthouse that morning into his briefcase. From her desk across the hardwood expanse of the office, Bal look over at him with a weak, humble smile, a peace offering, perhaps; the other two, who were both single and more likely to be convalescing from romantic indignities of their own, still glowered at him and offered uncommunicative grunts whenever he looked in their direction. Perhaps he didn't turn out to have been the villain; it was the infamous Woodstock Romeo who was exposed in grandiose display as the real protagonist in the office scandal, but Gaskin signed their paycheques, and anyway, he was still male and *must* be guilty of *something*.

"Well, today's the defining operation to the grand campaign," Thomas said, looking up from a sheaf of mortgage documents; as usual, with large reading glasses perched at the end of his nose.

"Not to put any additional pressure on me, of course."

"Do you know where you are on the list?"

"No list, thank God. I have a special appointment." Otherwise, he'd be waiting in the daily queue of interlocutory applications, a conveyor belt of litigation glitches waiting to be summarily repaired by a Master, a subordinate judicial officer. Carlo was fortunate enough to have reserved a two-hour audience with a judge. "One of the last things Marika did before she left."

"She was a jewel, that one," Thomas sighed. He mumbled something else as Carlo wandered out of earshot.

His cell phone beeped. "Carlo!" It was Catriona. "Are you ready for this? This is it." She spoke with an anxious, breathless air that reminded him of Laura, back in university, just before she went to write an exam. "Where are you?"

"I'm still in the office. I'm..."

"Still in the *office?* Court starts in six and a half minutes! A bit relaxed, aren't we?"

"In Vancouver, court starts at ten."

"*Ten?* Wow, Club Med or what? When I grow up, I want to be a judge in Canada. Call me when you're done."

"Good luck."

Once inside the court house, a squat concrete wedge on the southern flank of sprawling Robson Square, he looked over the daily hearing list. Courtroom 57. Judge Finnegan, a name he didn't recognize. The lugubrious corridor was deserted as Carlo made his way to the barrister's lounge, where he found a table and reviewed his notes. An older lawyer in his barrister's vest and tabs sat across from him, quietly flipping through the tabloid pages of *The Province.* A few minutes before ten, he went through the sunlit Great Hall and up the leafy staircase to the fifth floor and Courtroom 57.

Judge Finnegan was hearing a brief application before Carlo's ten o'clock appointment. The lawyer at the podium, an incisive woman from one of the national firms, wanted him to lift a charging order against building materials somehow connected with an insolvent real estate development in the Okanagan. By the time she finished her submissions, the judge looked as if he was about to fall asleep. He quietly signed the draft order she handed up to him.

The clerk rose and announced Carlo's application. "My Lord, the matter of *The Striationist Convocation v. The Royal Bank of Canada et al.*"

Carlo approached the podium and set down his binder. "My Lord, my name is Buonsante, initial C." He spelled his name. "I appear on behalf of the Applicant. This matter was brought on notice to multiple parties; none has responded."

Judge Finnegan raised his palm and peered down at Carlo as if he were an unsightly rash. "Counsel, I have glanced at your materials. As far as I'm concerned, it speaks ill of the current state of the legal profession that a lawyer of any experience at all would actually believe that he could get away with this nonsense." His features invited the expectation that he might speak with a vestigial Irish lilt. Instead, he berated Carlo with the belligerent whine of men who call open-line talk radio.

"If I may begin, My Lord."

"No, counsel, it appears that what you are trying to do is have land re-conveyed to your client after they have lawfully disposed of it."

"That is not correct, My Lord. If I might..."

The judge interrupted him again. "Before we embark upon what is likely to be a waste of time, could you please indicate what authority you are relying on."

"My Lord, at this time I would like to file my Summary of Argument."

"You're evading me, counsel," he bellowed. "Now for the second time, please indicate what authority you are relying on! Then I'll decide if I am willing to hear this. I'm inclined to dismiss your application right now."

"My Lord, I am handing up the Applicant's Summary of Argument, with appended case and statutory authorities. If this court is not prepared to hear my submissions this morning, I would like to apply for leave to file supplemental written argument."

Judge Finnegan squinted and then sighed as he peered down at Carlo. "Proceed, counsel."

"Thank you, My Lord. This is an application brought by the Orthodox Striationist Convocation for an order placing fourteen separate real estate properties in a trust administered by the Victoria solicitors' firm Ashburnam & Willits."

"Again, counsel," the judge removed his glasses and rubbed his eyes. "What authority are you relying on?"

"The applicable authority is at tabs one and two of my brief. The first is *Sarawak Mercantile Company v. Immobiliers Daladier*, a 1902 decision of the Judicial Committee of the Privy Council." It took Carlo almost twelve hours of tedious research in the UBC law library to find that one. "It concerned a dispute over some lands in the Straits Settlement, then a British colony, which were the subject matter of an ill-fated real estate speculation scheme. The situation was analogous to the one at hand, as..."

Judge Finnegan raised his arms skyward. "Any *Canadian* authority, counsel?"

That decision is binding on you, you old prick! "Yes. This sort of situation was dealt with in the numerous *Hurontario Trust v. Great Erie Investments* cases. The *Sarawak Mercantile* case had been cited in one of those decisions, which concerned a similar series of real estate and mortgage transaction relating to properties in..." Judge Finnegan was interrupting him again.

"Counsel, I expect that I am much more familiar with the *Hurontario* situation than you are. What, if anything, is your point?"

"In the *Hurontario* situation, the various lands were ultimately placed in a multiplicity of trusts, requiring any number of applications to what was then the Ontario High Court. Instead of requesting a number of orders over a period of several months, on a piecemeal basis, I am proposing that this court apply *Sarawak Mercantile* to create a single trust arrangement."

"I don't know, counsel," Judge Finnegan flashed a toxic smirk. "I'm almost inclined to order that the listed properties be re-conveyed to the Reformed Striationist Convocation and have the various charges dealt with under *their* tutelage!"

"The Reformed Striationist Convocation never owned any of the properties," Carlo said in a louder voice than he'd intended.

"Excuse me?"

"I refer to Exhibits 'F' through 'T' of the affidavit of Marika Balodis, the paralegal who performed the land title searches,"

Carlo flipped through the pages of Marika's affidavit as he spoke. "When each of the properties were transferred away from the Striationist religion, they were transferred to one of about twenty numbered companies, some of which exist and others which do not."

Judge Finnegan thumbed through the binder containing Marika's affidavit, sighing anew as he turned each page. "All right, counsel. But your client still sold the land."

"No, it did not. The affidavit of Ruairi Davidson, First Elder of the Orthodox Striationist Council of Elders, is at tab two of Volume One of the applicant's materials."

"I'm reading it now, counsel," After what seemed like fifteen minutes, the judge took off his reading glasses and rubbed his eyes. "I trust that you have at least attempted to put all of these numbered companies on notice of this application."

"Those which actually exist."

"Yes, those which exist. And, I suppose, the assignees?"

"Yes, some of them. There are quite a few involved, most of them in Asia and in Europe. More than half of them are in Eastern Europe and a variety of Asian countries that were provinces of the former Soviet Union."

"The 'Stans." Judge Finnegan smiled for the first time.

Carlo laughed politely. "Yes, the 'Stans. And some are of a rather, let's just say 'shadowy' nature. The contact information for all but a handful of the Asian assignees is deficient."

"Well then, let's get this over with." He put on his reading glasses and read from one of the binders. "As I understand it, your client is seeking the return of fourteen parcels of fraudulently transferred land that comprise about..." He read down the page. "About four thousand hectares. You want an order placing these properties in trust pending a determination of the validity of more than a thousand mortgages that were granted under highly suspect circumstances, following which the properties will be handed back to your client. Have I got it? Is that essentially what you want?"

"Yes, My Lord; that is it precisely. We will also require directions from this court as to how the process of allowing the various mortgagees to prove whatever entitlement they might have."

"All right." The judge slid his glasses further up the bridge of his nose. "There's no reason to waste any more time here. I order that the lands listed in the schedule to the Notice of Motion be vested in the Ashburnham firm as trustee for a period not to exceed one year. Each of the mortgagees will be given thirty days' notice of a hearing to be held within six months to determine the validity of the mortgages and any other encumbrances on the properties. And, this includes the issue of legal and beneficial ownership."

"But My Lord, the uncontradicted evidence before the court is that the properties were fraudulently transferred. And none of the parties have responded. I'm the only one here."

"I'm well aware of that, counsel, but I'm not deciding the ownership issue this morning. And I am now seized of this matter. All further appearances and applications flowing from this one will be brought before me. Anything further, counsel?"

"No, My Lord."

"Very well, counsel," he said, straightening his glasses. "Leave a draft order at the Registry for entry, and I will sign it."

After he left the court house, Carlo dialled Catriona's cell phone as he crossed Smithe Street but got her voice mail. "Hey, it's me. I'm just leaving the court house. I got the order."

A light but relentless mist accompanied Carlo as he walked along Granville Street on his way to the office. Rather than rush straight back, he stopped in at Calista's. It was empty. The only person in the coffee house was the elderly barista, the guy with the thick glasses who, a couple of months before, had mistaken Carlo for Marika. "Double espresso, please," Carlo said as he dragged his litigation bag toward the counter.

"Sure." The barista started pulling levers and switches on the Nuova Simonelli machine. "That girl who used to come here with you, I haven't seen her in a while."

"She's off visiting her aunt," Carlo said. "In Toronto."

"Ah," he smiled. "Three seventy-five, please."

Carlo handed him a couple of toonies. "Thanks." He sat at the small table near the window, the one where he and Marika usually had their morning coffee, before work. He sipped the refreshing, bitter infusion.

Cordova Street at late morning exhibited a motley parade of the young and unkempt, all in need of a shower, all with ragged clothes but healthy skin and taut physiques, who had apparently chosen penury as a hobby. It had been weeks since he'd been in Calista's with Marika. He wasn't surprised that he missed her, someone exuding youthful, feminine energy who had yet to concern herself much with polite restraint. Poor Marika. In the month or two before she left, her native exuberance faded to gloom, a sad and swollen presence across the table, listless as she worked on the crossword puzzle in *The Province*.

The obnoxious beeps of his cell phone jolted him back to the present. It was Catriona. "What the fuck? You were done before me? How is that even possible?"

"We're efficient in this country. Well?"

"It was tough going, but I got basically what I wanted. 'Mission accomplished!' as a noted imbecile once said. The judge, she even appointed the Canadian firm, Ashburnham & Company, as trustee."

"Ashburnham & Willits."

"Whatever. They're appointed as trustee. But they'll need to get an address for service in Washington."

"It's an office in Port Townsend, I think, if memory serves."

"No surprise there."

"Why not?"

"Victoria and Port Townsend. They sort of look the same. I'll call you later. Sorry, gotta go."

Once Carlo was back in the office he found his mail slot stuffed to capacity. Bal rushed from the photocopying alcove onto the expanse of hardwood floors; another crooked smile. *Don't worry*, he wanted to say, *I don't hold it against you.*

She stopped as she brushed past. "I thought you should know." She spoke just louder than a whisper. "Patty and Jacquie have both quit. It happened this morning. They just got up and left. Oh." She handed him a binder. "This is yours. And I can't say that I blame them one tiny little bit. If my husband and I didn't need every last cent we can get our hands on for a down payment, I'd be gone, too."

"Really? Why? What's going on?"

"Oh, believe me, we'll talk later. To tell you now would spoil the surprise."

Declan appeared at Carlo's door just before lunch. "Well, well; our conquering hero has returned! How did it go?"

"Surprisingly well. I got the order we wanted."

"Who was sitting?"

"Finnegan."

"Ah!" He stood in a ceremonial pose, as if poised to bestow a set of Cross pens. Susan appeared behind him, expressionless, peeking past his shoulder. "You have a new paralegal, Carlo! Susan Wiltshire. I hired her over the weekend."

"Hello, Susan," Carlo said. Welcome aboard."

"Okay." Declan clasped his hands together with elation that the event did not demand. "I know that you're busy these days. I will leave it to you to assign Susan well, whatever you think would be appropriate." He backed out of Carlo's office.

"Have a seat." Carlo motioned to Susan.

Susan cast a sideward glance in Carlo's direction, hoping that her smile didn't seem too counterfeit. They still had to work together. She wondered where the attraction she felt at Port

Rattray came from, toward this bantamweight ass who ignored her and stayed in the orbit of that fat cow, and look how that turned out. *He got what he deserved.*

"For next three months," Carlo said, "I will need a lot of help on the Striationist file. I expect that Declan has told you about it."

"Well, no. Not really. But believe me, I'm no stranger to the Striationists."

"It's why I was in court this morning. I will have the order entered, but while I'm away, you will have to put about a thousand entities, mainly shady numbered companies and foreign financial institutions, on notice of another follow-up application to deal with the validity of the mortgages. I will draft up the motion materials, the ones to be sent out for service, before I go."

"While you're away?" She tilted her head. "Are you going somewhere?"

"Yes, after Thursday I will be gone for three weeks. Didn't Declan tell you?"

"No, no, he didn't; no real shock there." A tight smile. He really hadn't told her. "So where are you going?"

"We're going to Italy, well, first through London."

"Ooh, three weeks in Italy, eh? I'm jealous." *We? Looks like that fuckin' blonde bitch snagged herself a lawyer.* But as a corollary thought intervened, Susan felt pleasing, radiant warmth. *Serves the prick right! Three weeks in Italy is more than enough time for Public Relations Chickie to end up just like the one he knocked up at the lodge.* She glanced at the jumble of court documents strewn on Carlo's desk and started to shift impatiently in her seat. Even if she'd convinced herself not to confront him so soon, her curiosity prevailed. *I wonder how the asshole will try to explain it away.* "So, when you were up in Port Rattray, there was a girl with you; I assumed that she was someone who worked here."

"I was beginning to think that you didn't recognize me. Yes," Carlo looked away. "Marika. She was a paralegal here; in fact, you're her replacement."

Come again? Did you just hide the hippo in an attic somewhere while she hatches out your kid? "Oh? Did she find a new job somewhere or...?"

Carlo folded his arms and tried to smile. "Met a guy and...and moved away, Toronto, I think."

Hmm...must have had an abortion. She must be smarter than she looked. "Oh, good for her!" Susan said with forced cheer. "So, is there anything for me to do, today, I mean?"

"Funny you should ask. I'll put the file in the library. It takes up five accordion files and twelve binders." Carlo sighed. "Go through it and start preparing a list of the mortgage holders and their addresses, e-mail, that sort of thing. And if you need help deciphering real estate documents, just ask Thomas. You've met him, haven't you?"

"Oh, yes, yes...the old British guy."

"Yes," Carlo winced. "That's him. Anyway, thanks for your help."

"You bet."

Thomas knocked with an authoritative rap on the open door of Carlo's office the following afternoon. "Come on, *signore*! Consider this the factory whistle!"

"Sorry?" Carlo looked up at him in a daze.

"You're leaving tomorrow morning. I'm going to take you for a pint. Surely nothing that you have on your desk is so important that it trumps *that.*"

"Sure, why not?"

The Duke of York was already near capacity with its customarily earnest, murmuring after-work clientele. Carlo and Thomas found one of the last tables, in the corner and lacking a view of either television screen, one showing a German soccer match, and the other an NHL game between the Toronto Maple Leafs and the Mighty Ducks. Still, people still found reason to cheer.

"So, back to the Old Country," Thomas took a sip from his pint. "Off to Italy, my spiritual home. And London. Every time Declan does something to piss me off, my mind wanders back to my favourite reading spot, this bench beside The Serpentine in Hyde Park. I read *Lucky Jim* there many years ago, and in one sitting, too." He rubbed his eyes. "I'm sorry; I'm behaving like a silly, homesick old man. Anyway, on to more important matters: the precarious state of the office. Two very competent members of the team have found someplace better to work, and no doubt more remunerative, too."

"I'm only a little surprised at their reaction, quite honestly. But come on, they must have known that he's a lecherous old goat."

"That's only part of it, but no, I really doubt that they did. In days gone past he was very accomplished at keeping his private life just that, private. But this time? We'll just say, Carlo, that the evidence was savagely cast before everyone's eyes." Thomas leaned forward and continued in a hushed voice. "And I can assure you that this was far from being the first time that one of Declan's lady-loves found herself up the spout, including at least two others that I know of who were on his payroll, but Marika was the first of them who had the bad manners, or the pluck (take your pick) to carry his baby to term." Thomas took another gulp from his pint. "And what he tried to do to you was despicable. *I* considered quitting when I figured it out."

"I doubt that what he did, or tried to do with me had much to do with it," Carlo laughed. "As far as I could tell, both Jacquie and Pat had aspirations to be a paralegal, and then surprise, surprise, after Marika's gone, his latest, what did you just call them, 'lady-loves'? Then his new lady-love comes slinking in. My take on it? They might have coveted Marika's job but neither one of them wanted to fuck Declan to get it."

Thomas choked on his beer. "I have little doubt that those two found that particular prospect most unappetising. And no doubt either one of them would have been of more use to you than someone who, lacking any experience, strolls in on Declan's arm. Have you heard from Marika?"

"No. I expect that she wants to put this miserable chapter far behind her."

"As should you, young man." Thomas raised his pint. "To Italia!" They clinked glasses. "When you're in Rome, will you be breezing past Piazza Farnese?"

"Sure; I always used to walk through there on the way home from work. One of my favourite places. Why?"

"Are you familiar with the church of Santa Brigida? It's the one off to the side, facing the French Embassy."

"Yes, ah, sure."

"Could you – well, I would be very appreciative if you would take a picture of it and send it to me by e-mail."

"Okay. But why that church in particular? There are hundreds of them in Rome."

"I lived in Rome for a few months; I lectured for a semester at La Sapienza. I'd stop in there in the afternoon, when all of the shops were closed. It's a beautiful, lovely little chapel, I must say, inside and out."

"It is. I used to stop by once in a while, myself."

"Did you? I most enjoyed the priest. By the time I left to return to Florence, he thought that I was poised to convert. Little did he know that I ducked inside for the sole purpose of avoiding forty-degree weather." Thomas drained what was left in his pint glass. "Would you like another?"

"Why not?"

54

It was just before noon. The three women noisily plunged back into the apartment, each festooned with shopping bags from sundry boutiques on Oxford Street, together making a piercing racket. Alone, the only one of the three who anyone would describe as 'bubbly' was Elizabeth; Linda tended to be somewhat taciturn and Laura typically became effusive only after quite a bit of wine. Carlo, still suffering from jet lag, had slept in and was barely awake. He was lighting the gas burner under the *caffettiera*, having just made his way to the kitchen.

"Carlo!" Laura shrieked and pointed to a blue bag she'd dropped on a chair. "I got a new bikini at La Sirena. Wait 'til you see it on me!" she said with a seductive moan.

"Oh, you'll love it, I know!" Lizzie laughed. Carlo peered at the two of them, temporarily unable to speak.

"Did you just get up, you lazy boy?" Lizzie said. Carlo nodded and turned his attention back to the burner.

"Looks like someone isn't quite awake yet!" Laura laughed.

Carlo's father walked down the narrow stairway from the loft, massaging the knot in his tie. "Is the coffee ready yet?"

"No," Carlo said quietly, as if trying to create a vogue. "It should just take a couple of minutes."

"What are you three up to today?" Vito asked Linda.

"I'm taking these two young ladies to lunch at that place we went the other week in Notting Hill Road." Linda gave Vito a peck on the cheek. Carlo noted with relief that Laura and Elizabeth seemed to still enjoy each other's company, leaving him pleased with his decision not to tell Laura that he and Lizzie had once had a short-lived fling. "We'll be back by six," Linda said. "And we'll leave it up to you two to choose the restaurant for dinner."

After they left, Carlo and his father sipped their coffee in silence. "What happened to Nigel?" Carlo asked.

Vito seemed momentarily confused. "Nigel...Nigel; oh, yes, the boy who was ugly and stupid." Carlo admired his father's uncomplicated assessment. "Well, no surprise; *la signorinella* kicked him to the curb and took up with another accountant from her office. Much better looking, but still, just like the other one, dumb as a chicken. But if they're so inclined, they will have beautiful children," his father laughed. "Just like you and Laura."

Carlo dodged his father's remark. "If they do, strict justice demands that the kid comes out with a horn in the middle of his forehead." Both of them exploded in laughter.

"So, I have to go to a meeting at Barclay's Bank. What are you going to do for the rest of the afternoon? Just sit around here?"

"No, I'm going for a walk, maybe out to Kensington or something."

"Well, you heard Linda; be back here by six. And if those three show up drunk, it might be amusing to us, but we'll take them to a pizzeria I know of just off The Strand. Don't worry, the owner is from Lecce. We'll let the young couples who frequent Vecchia Romagna on Saturday nights enjoy a romantic dinner in peace." He glanced at his watch. "We'll leave the house at seven; both places are close by. So remember: be back here by six."

Carlo stuffed his laptop into his day pack. When he left, the mid-day was beset with the gloom of a low ceiling of cobblestone-coloured clouds and bountiful drizzle. He spent the afternoon wandering around Marylebone, but eventually strayed and decided to stop at a pub near Paddington Station. After scanning the array of taps at the bar, he settled on ordering a pint of cider.

"What'll you have, mate?" the bartender asked.

"A pint of Blackthorn's, please." He pointed toward the black and yellow handle.

"Where are you sitting?"

The pub was almost empty, except for a scattered audience engrossed in a soccer match playing on the television at the back. Carlo spotted a seat by the window with an electrical outlet. "Over there, by the window."

"Right, mate. I'll bring it over to you. Three pounds ten."

The bartender set down his pint before Carlo finally achieved union with the pub's wireless network. He took a sip of cider and then checked his e-mail. The list contained the usual cadre of spam and advertisements, a few political announcements, and one from someone he had not expected.

From:Marika Balodis <mbalodis@yahoo.ca>
To: Carlo Buonsante <buonsantecarlo@gmail.com>

Dearest Carlo,

I'm in Montreal. As I'm sure you have figured out, I had my baby (a girl, but I think that you already knew that). My aunt was wonderful to me, and so was her boyfriend, but I had to leave Toronto, put that phase of my life behind me, start again, and try not to fuck up so badly this time. I decided to give up the baby for adoption just after I left Vancouver, a couple of weeks before she was born. Who was I kidding? I probably couldn't even keep a cat alive. Remember that fern I bought when we were shopping in Yaletown that time? You probably don't, but anyway, it died. I am totally unfit for motherhood. A couple in Waterloo adopted her, I'm sure that she will have a much better life with them than I could have ever given her. And I would have had little choice but to chase the devil himself for child support. Can you imagine that? He's such a piece of shit that he would have tried every conceivable (I know, bad choice of words) legal trick to avoid paying me. I never want to have anything to do with the asshole ever again. What a conniving prick, trying to trick you into believing that it was yours. I still can't believe that even he would have tried something like that. And I'm so sorry that you had to put up with all of those poisonous glares from Paula, that sarcastic old praying mantis, whenever she was in the office. I always wondered what she thought you did to deserve that hate on she had for you. You know what, Carlo? I wish that my baby had been yours. Isn't that terrible of me? I really wish that we'd been able to make a go of it, but fate intervened. Declan intervened. And I'm sorry, I never got to know her, what is her name, Leona? I regret that, you were a so much happier person after you met up with her. And the fact that you were reunited after so much time, it was so (and you will hate me for this, it's a chick thing) romantic, and even, well, magical about it. You deserve to have a happy life, as for me, I'm not so sure, we'll see what happens. I'll try to send you the money I owe you as best I can, but I'm working part time as a cashier in a Provigo in Outremont and sharing a walk-up in Côtes-des-Neiges with three other girls. I hope we see each other again but these days a trip to Vancouver for me is as likely as a trip to the moon. If you guys are ever planning to come to Montreal, please send me an e-mail. Bye for now.

Love,
Marika

Marika, Marika, Carlo laughed to himself. *Paragraphs are your friend!* He took another sip of his cider. Her e-mail banished the sense of calm and equilibrium that developed within him after he and Laura left Vancouver. He tried to browse a few of his usual news sites, but found himself able to concentrate on only a couple of gossip-ridden articles in the Huffington Post.

He returned to his inbox and read Marika's e-mail again. It was disquieting enough for Carlo to reflect upon what it inevitably meant. *I wish my baby had been yours.* True enough, Gaskin's lavish deceit was detestable, just shy of fundamentally evil. But for the first time, it occurred to Carlo that it easily could have succeeded. A nimble conjurer, Gaskin must have sensed enough an attraction between them to allow him to suppose that his gambit was not as silly as it must have seemed on first impression.

And Laura sensed it too. In the now-distant past, whenever the hint of a potential rival showed itself, Laura's response was incendiary and merciless. But with Marika, she probably felt empathy, even kinship. Which would have been worse, Carlo wondered: getting knocked up by Lattanzio, an aging teenager pushing forty, or one who was old enough to retire? Like a drug, she said. Laura might have been momentarily weak enough to yield to her own conjurer but the spell dissipated in time. She'd been lucky, and she knew it.

By the time he finished his cider it was too late to walk back to Soho. Getting there on foot would make him at least forty minutes late, so unacceptably tardy that it was sure to enrage his father. Instead, a Central Line train whisked him to Tottenham Court Road, a leisurely stroll past the pubs and wine shops on Brewer Street to the apartment. He turned keys in the many locks at the entrance off the street, to the dark landing inside that radiated the classic, comforting scent of urban northern Europe, old stone leavened by centuries of periodic cool and dampness.

He could hear them before he even reached the top of the stairway. The three women were wailing with laughter, enjoying a joke that Carlo could not infer from the few phrases of conversation that passed between them. He tried to greet them on his way past the sitting room, but Laura interrupted him. "Where have you *been*?" she shouted, more concerned than annoyed. "We'd expected you would have been back here hours ago."

"It's what he does, my dear," Linda shrieked. "Whenever he's here for a visit. Wanders all over London. I've encountered him in some of the most extraordinary places. I'm sure that he knows every beggar in Baker Street."

"Carlo," Liz shouted at him, pointing at her empty wine glass. "Be a duck and open us another bottle of wine; white, please!"

His father was quietly loading the dishwasher as Carlo walked into the kitchen. "You're four minutes late!" He tapped the crystal on his watch. "You should really learn to wear one of these!" Carlo smirked. *Il tedesco.* "Oh," Carlo's father pointed behind him. "I put some of your fancy beer in the refrigerator. It should be cold by now."

"Thanks." He first opened a chilled bottle of wine, a Locorotondo, and carried it out to the sitting room.

"The apple doesn't fall far from the tree," Linda said between wails of uneven laughter. "That's your dad's favourite, too!"

"What do you think, Liz?" Laura laughed, her eyebrows arched in cartoonish deliberation. "Is this waiter better looking than the one who served us at lunch?"

Liz choked on a sip of wine and then cackled, but Carlo did not wait to hear the verdict. Once back in the kitchen, he opened a bottle of Orval, poured himself a glass and joined his father at the table, who was quietly sipping from his own glass of beer, his attention absorbed by the sports pages of *La Stampa.*

"Pizza?" Carlo asked as he sat down.

"Pizza."

55

Gavin and Bilbick dodged potholes as they walked down the broad dirt swath that was once envisioned as grand Princess Diana Boulevard.

"Look on the bright side, Irwin. You're still the mayor." Gavin said with strained levity.

"That's really looking on the bright side, Gavin." Bilbick sighed as they passed a partially excavated ditch, lined with orange plastic webbing. "I doubt that anyone will be running against me, anyway. Who would want to deal with all of this?"

"You're not going to try to finish the project?"

"No, I don't expect so; there's not...we don't have access to even a fraction of the money we'd need." They passed an untidy heap of paving stones. "And as it is, it's going to cost at least five million (probably closer to ten) to clean up this mess."

"Well, come on, the provincial government got you into this."

"So did you, Gavin, in no small measure. Are you going to pony up, I don't know, maybe a million toward the effort?"

They'd walked almost another block before Gavin said anything. "Wasn't this thoroughfare supposed to be lined with chestnut trees from France or something?"

"Quebec. No," Bilbick laughed. "And they were lindens. But the linden trees never came, and that was before we flat-out ran out of money, but we still couldn't pay for the trees. Gollander got arrested before we got the, well, what was supposed to be the biggest of the three grants."

"You know, it was all so stupid." Gavin shook his head. "Even if what I've heard is true, that he might do ten years, I can't say that I feel sorry for him."

"Nobody does." Bilbick said. "And look at that!" He pointed at a collection of abandoned construction equipment; the one closest, a backhoe with its shovel raised and slightly extended. "They just, they just *ran off.* I can't even begin to tell you how exasperated I feel. We're totally broke, not even close to finishing even the first phase. So the work crews fled as soon as they figured out that we wouldn't be able to pay them. Not that I can blame them, but my God, they didn't even...they didn't even finish the arches!"

"What do you mean?" Gavin regarded one of the entrance arches, looming ahead of them. "They look complete to me."

"No," Bilbick grumbled. "They didn't weld in all of the letters. We simply ran out of money, and the specialized welders that we hired to make the arches, the cost us a fortune, they were *ahtists.*" He touched the back of his wrist to his forehead. "And they spent weeks bending and shaping the rods and then weaving them into arches. It was actually fascinating to watch them forge the lettering. It was that part that they never finished, not that I would have expected otherwise. They're in demand all over the world, and we ran out of money. If I were one of them and I wasn't getting paid, I'd skedaddle too!"

Gavin looked up and peered at the arch. "I still say that it looks fine to me."

"No, Gavin." Bilbick shook his head. "As I told you before. It's supposed to say 'Welcome to Parksville'. As it is, we have many other things that we have to spend our money to fix. Huge ditches, full of rubbish; they all have to be properly cleaned out, filled in with dirt, and then the whole place has to be landscaped to meet umpteen regional, provincial and even *federal* safety codes. And what...well, do you have any suggestions? What do you think we should do with about a billion paving stones?" He pointed at an expanse of stones cut to size, packaged in mesh and neatly piled.

"Anyway." He tilted his chin toward the arch looming over them. "Since fixing it is so low on my financial priority list (maybe someone will find the money to get it done by 2095 or something), it will confuse tourists for decades to come. Maybe we can say that it's the civic motto in Latin; the opposite of '*Carpe diem*'; 'Just Relax' or something. Albertans and Californians wouldn't know the difference."

Gavin craned his neck to examine the upper edge of the arch again. "Doesn't it say 'Welcome to Parksville?"

"No, Gavin," Bilbick sighed. "It does *not*. Put on your glasses or something and read it more carefully."

Gavin squinted and started shaking with laughter. "I see what you mean."

"I'm glad that I was able to provide you with such amusement. *Schadenfreude* is a base emotion; you do know that, don't you?" Now both of them were looking up at the arch; even Bilbick couldn't quell the smile that played briefly on his lips. The words, which, it was true, would prove to be cryptic to the uninformed, stood bold in their crafted, metallic elegance:

ELCO   *PARKS*